I0668494

LEGACIES

By
Edward F. McKeown

AN IMPRINT OF COPPER DOG PUBLISHING, LLC

Moondream Press
An Imprint of Copper Dog Publishing LLC
537 Leader Circle
Louisville, CO 80027
www.copperdogpublishing.com

Ordering Information:
Special discounts are available on quantity purchases by corporations, associations, and others. For details, contact the publisher at the address above.
Printed in the United States of America

Credits:
Author: Edward F. McKeown
Managing Editor: Michael H. Hanson
Creative Director: Helen H. Harrison
Editor: Traci Loudin
Continuity: Schelly Keefer
Cover Art: Image by Stefan Keller from Pixabay

ISBN:
978-1-943690-32-9 (Paperback)
978-1-943690-xx (Kindle)

Fiction: Science Fiction

CONTENTS

DEDICATION

To Andre Norton who opened up a universe for my eyes.

CONFEDERATE MILITARY INTELLIGENCE ANNUAL SUMMARY- TOP SECRET ACCESS

FROM: HEAD OF SECTION:

SUBJECT: ARTIFICIAL INTELLIGENCE, MAAURO: AKA MAAURO TRIGARDT AKA AURELIA TOYAMA

I am closing the file on the android, Maauro. While she was of considerable service to my distant predecessor, decades ago, her whereabouts are now unknown, assuming she still exists.

For those members of the committee who may not know of this, Maauro was an ancient relic from an unknown alien species, discovered on an asteroid. The machine, the only known self-aware AI, adopted a female appearance and befriended a human named Wrik Trigardt. She and Trigardt were brought, albeit unwillingly, into military intelligence, by Director Candace Deveraux, but she lost control of the pair after several years. This was largely due to interference from Olympia's head of security, Shasti Rainhell, after Maauro and her then husband, Trigardt, immigrated to Olympia. We were able to confirm that Maauro's artificial intelligence was downloaded into a human body made for her by Olympian genetic engineers. She apparently existed for over fifty years as a living being, but was unable to simultaneously inhabit her android body while her human body lived.

Rumor has it that she and Trigardt fled to a remote world to live out their lives. Because of the rebellions and general degradation of transit and intelligence gathering in the Confederacy, further data is not available. It is assumed Trigardt has succumbed to natural causes after all this time, but as to what has happened with Maauro, whether she died as a human, or reoccupied her machine body, nothing is known. You will note that no images, or other files, are attached to this report. In an apparent parting gesture, Maauro scrubbed almost all data out of Confed databases with a worm that seeks out and destroys all information on, or images of her. The results of this, and our disinformation efforts regarding her, have led many to denounce her story as a hoax...

CHAPTER ONE

DUA-DENLENN HOMEWORLD INSIDE CONFEDERATE BOR-derspace, Thieves Guild Novice Quarters.

I awakened in darkness and lay very still. The instincts that had preserved me as a Guild trainee kept me frozen, yet alert. I turned over in the hard, narrow bed that bore my name, Dassa Falkayan, in marker, on an erasable board, so tentative was my hold on this place. What has awakened me, some additional test of my instructors?

I turned my head slowly, to look into the courtyard of my uncle and master's house. The plasta-glass panel showed me nothing but the yard, two aircars and the cages that his hunting beasts slept in. Beyond, stood my uncle's tower and the comfortable quarters, occupied by the favored of the family. Only one small, blue light added illumination to Arala's Lesser Lamp, the Major Lamp having long set in its eternal chase of the sun.

I sat up slowly, fearing to wake the other ten novices who would not thank me for disturbing their sleep without reason, and would use it as an excuse to add to their torments of me, granddaughter to an infamous traitor to the Guild. Yet, I feared failing some test of my instructors far more.

My eyes adapted slowly to the darkness and I found myself wishing for the night-sight of an Enshari. Nothing moved among the dim, gray shapes outside. Still, that was unusual in itself. Usually a guard paced in the courtyard, and there was an attendant for the hunt beasts. It came to me in a flash that the absence of the guard's regular and measured tread might have tickled my subconscious.

A shadow flitted across a rooftop, past the parked aircars and was gone. Could it be a nightwing on the hunt? Bed was no longer an option, but I still did not have enough to wake the others, especially Elshiva, my chief rival for my Uncle's chilly affections. I slid my feet into house-shoes and stood. I'd make my way to the bathroom. If the instructors did raid the novitiate's quarters, they would at least not catch me abed. If anyone found me out of my assigned place, I could plead an upset stomach. If needed, I could sleep sitting in a stall. I'd slept in less comfortable places.

Straining my ears brought nothing but the sound of blood running through my slender, spear-tipped ears. I walked slowly, heel and toe, to prevent the shoes from slapping and making any noise. Years' of sufferance here had made me a quiet as any woodland animal. Only Elshiva stirred momentarily, her eyes slitting open. I froze under their regard. Unlike most of us, whose eyes are blue, lid to lid, hers were a predatory, reflective yellow, but they dimmed as her eyelids dropped down.

CHAPTER ONE

Then I was out of the room, moving quicker and easier. No lairing instructors seized me as I made my way toward the bathrooms. Just before the bathrooms, under a murmuring heating unit, was a door to the courtyard. A few moments study assured me that the inner door was not booby-trapped or alarmed. I cracked it open and cool night air washed across my body. I wore only my underclothes, black briefs and a bra I barely needed on my gangly body. Like all good Guilders, I had a small pouch on me, with my valuables. Novices stole from each other as a matter of training and pride. A thin and flexible knife was built into the strap that carried the pouch, not much of a weapon, but all I was allowed indoors.

I drifted further from the doorway. Overhead, a spacecraft rumbled, heading for orbit. It had to be military; my uncle's connections did not allow civilian aircraft to overfly his compound in the hills.

Dared I go on? The dilemma remained. Was this a real danger, a drill, or the effect of constant and brutal training? I almost turned back, but decided to check on the hunt beasts. The animals knew me and would not fuss, and my own fondness for them was well enough known that my punishment would be light if I was caught. I turned toward the cages and gave the soft cooing sound I used with the six-legged beasts. But no lambent eyes opened on me.

I stood by Unambra's cage, my favorite and as close a thing as I had to a friend here. Her huge shape lay in the cage, resting on straw next to her water basin, oddly still for night time. Frightened now, I looked past her cage and saw a figure on the ground, booted feet splayed out. I drew in a deep and instant breath.

"Alarm!" I screamed as loud as I could and rolled backwards from the cage. Shots splattered the cage and thunked into the dead animal within. As I turned toward the door, an explosion rocked the compound. More blasts shattered buildings over my head, and I dropped to the ground, crawling toward the dead guard on elbows and knees quickly skinned and bleeding from the rough flooring.

The guard lay with one blue eye open, staring accusingly at the world. The other socket was a mere hole, where some silenced projectile had gone in. I rolled his body up to protect myself as shots and explosions sounded, and shrapnel and debris fell all around. The corpse would stop some of the flying metal and mask my heat signature. His pistol was still in its holster, and I grabbed the weapon out. Not much firepower, but better than my knife.

Two additional blasts, far larger than the first volley, struck the compound. The second blew over both me and the guard's corpse. I rolled to my feet in a world without sound. I could see more flashes, as some enemy worked the compound, and defending streams of tracers arcing out. Flashes signaled grenades or rockets, but I could hear nothing beyond a buzzing.

CHAPTER ONE

Above me a flyer flashed in and out of sight, too fast to give me a clue as to who was attacking. I shook my head to clear it, fighting off shock. Around me, all the buildings adjacent to the courtyard were in flames. I saw the other novices driven from their burning quarters, led by Elshiya. One second they stood about her, the next they lay in blood-stained heaps. An armored body rolled off the roof and fell into the courtyard. Its gray armor now tried to match the black stones on which it lay. I could not see a face, but it was bipedal and large, yet tailless. That eliminated several possibilities, but helped me in nowise. The corpse showed that the attackers were not having it all their own way, but there was no question that the compound was falling.

I looked in the direction of my uncle's tower, where only he, his women and my cousins could go. Flames shot out of every level. Some enemy of my uncle's had moved against him and in a very public and bloody way atypical for the Guild. The firestorm around me would surely bring both firefighters and the Patrol, or even government troops.

As I watched, the tower shuddered and began to fall on attacker and defender alike. Ah, no more of cousin's taunts and jeers. No more of my uncle's cool eyes, as he wondered how to spend me. I got to my feet, pistol held in both hands, and raced for the back of the animal quarters. Beside the gate, through which the animal cage waste was taken, hung a stained and malodorous coverall. I threw it on gratefully; its dark color would hide my pale, coppery skin and protect me in the brush beyond.

I risked two shots on the gate lock, then threw open the gate and raced for the cover of that brush, half-expecting to feel the shock of a bullet or beam, but no one tracked me. Where before the night had seemed too dark, now I wished for the Lesser Lamp to set too and leave the night sky to true darkness. The burning compound was a beacon, lighting up the surrounding countryside.

A stream cut through my uncle's land, peaty and dark, but fast moving. I stumbled down toward it, wondering how long my house shoes would last against the abuse. While upstream might have made for a better deception, it would take me back toward the Guildhouse. No, downstream as fast as I could go would be my only salvation.

I knew every twist and turn of this stream, but only the sureness of the death behind me gave me the courage to commit myself to its darkness. I hoped that the water would also mask my IR signature if someone was hunting for me with a nightscope. So, I slid into the stream's icy embrace with a gasp and began half-wading, half-swimming, hampered by the too large overall and the need to hold onto my weapon. I knew I would not have the stamina to endure the cold water long, so I made the best time I could. Downstream lay the spaceport and the city. If I could reach either, I would be a harder kill for the attackers than if I hid in the countryside. For all I knew, there could be spysats over the compound.

CHAPTER ONE

I continued on, never looking back, determined, fearful and alone.

CHAPTER TWO

MAURO'S HOME: CONFEDERATE SPACE, PLANET EVENFALL

HAVE POWERED MYSELF DOWN AS FAR AS I CAN. ONLY THROUGH ONE subroutine, do I keep any contact with the universe. Once, I passed 50,000 years this way, voyaging into a future that held pleasures and agonies I could not even conceive of when I was first activated. Perhaps this sleep will be permanent as I hide from the pain. Oh, I wish I could be free of this existence but... I promised Wrik.

I do not dream, but some tiny fluctuation in power has caused memory to well up. It happened just as the Ribisan Predictor foresaw, before I destroyed it. I stand over a medbed, looking down at Wrik, my partner for over 150 years. He is pale, his skin waxy, his hair is silver, but the eyes are still that warm brown for all that the shadows of old pain still lurk in them.

We are in our home and Wrik is dying.

His eyes focus and he smiles at me. "There you are, beautiful as ever."

"Are you comfortable?" I manage. My chest hurts, though I do not know how this can be, but grief is surging beyond this moment, waiting to claim me. Yet, I look back on memories of more than a century, memories that are so, so, I lack the words to say. "Precious," is inadequate. Every moment we have spent together is a treasure of infinite value, even the arguments, disappointments, the failures, large and small.

"I'm fine. Oh, Maauro, the only thing I regret is leaving you behind. I'm afraid for you."

"I will..." I start to say the word, manage, but it dies on my lips. I cannot manage, cannot survive what is coming, the final sundering of my network.

"Listen to me," he says, and I know he sees the fear in me. "Don't just turn yourself off after I am gone. There is a wonderful universe out there. Terrible too, but I traveled it with you. The things we saw, the things we did. There's still more to see and do and others—"

"No!" I say. "There will not... there can be no other you."

"I should hope not," he says. "But there may be reasons to carry on, friends yet to be made. Be open to the possibilities. Be open to hope. Always remember how I loved you. Remember how you rebuilt a shattered man into someone worth knowing. How much you gave me. I was the luckiest of men."

"Don't forget what you are to me," I whisper back. "You were always my first. You found me. You were my first friend, my first love. Through your belief in me I broke free of being a programmed weapon and became

myself. Always, always, you were there for me. I did no more for you, than you did for me."

Wrik smiles his sad and gentle smile for me, one last time. The eyes fix and stare somewhere that I cannot see and cannot follow. I place my face against his still chest and sorrow such as I did not dream existed, rushes in to envelop me.

A day passes and the courier delivers the package from the crematorium. That, which was once Wrik, is now only ash. This is something I could have done myself, but I could not bear it. Now, confronted with his clean dust I can do what I wish. I take the package down to the machinery I have built in the basement. I add the ash to the pressure tank, so very carefully. I set the pressure and temperature and wait, though for me time has little meaning. It has passed both too slowly and too quickly. The unit calls for my attention and I open the door inside, the ash is gone, replaced by the bright, blue stone I had hoped for.

This I take and with infinite care I gently carve into a heart shape. It had always puzzled me why the shape was so different from the actual human heart, but there is perfection in its simple symmetry that answers that. I wonder why I never saw it before.

I stare at the stone, reliving memories for...hours days, weeks? Does it matter? Then I press the blue heart to my own chest. It passes within, carefully moved until it reaches the innermost redoubt of my being, the last citadel of what I am. Only the memories of the life we lived are more precious than this artifact. The heart cannot now be destroyed but that I am destroyed first. I will never be parted from Wrik.

Wrik, I miss you. I am so alone. Grief attacks with a savagery no enemy has ever shown me.

I lower my power levels further and mercifully awareness fades.

CHAPTER THREE

THE MORNING SUN FOUND ME ON FOOT AT THE EDGE OF the spaceport, heading for the pawn shops run by Shajork, the Baron, a senior Guilder. The city and the spaceport were on alert, government troops and police very visible. The road to the Confed Embassy was barricaded by Marines. I stopped in a public transit station, staying clear of both security and the early work-shift, who stood about, murmuring and watching the video screens overhead which showed the burning compound of my uncle.

A smooth-faced commentator was expanding on the attack by unknown forces at the suspected Guild compound and the search for survivors. Fortunately, the transit station led to the spaceport itself. I dared not take the tubeway; it would be impossible to escape from a MagLev train with security on board, but there is a Traveler's Rest nearby, a shop catering to those temporarily on world. I strolled up to it, as casual as I could manage. I was in luck; the shop was manned by a Drisnian. The small, gray-skinned humanoid sat behind his counter, staring at his screen. He eyed me with disinterest as I came in.

I looked back at him. "I need a traveler's cloak and some other items. Do you have any used clothing?"

I expected him to ask why a Dua would need the gray cloak of a traveler, a garment so innocuous as to insulate any traveler from offenses against the local culture, but he didn't. He merely pointed to a rack in the back. I made my selections, used cash, and exited as quickly as I could.

Aware of my disheveled and disgusting state, I dropped into a restroom and bathed, making myself as presentable as I could manage. The shoes were foam-fitters and adjusted to my feet; they were cheap, but would last until I could find better. With relief, I changed into fresh clothes and threw the cloak over my shoulders, pulling its light, cloth-mask across my face. It was as much protection as I could obtain.

I left the malodorous coverall and the rest of my soiled clothes in a restroom trashcan and covered them with paper waste. Then I set out, using a few more of my scant credits to purchase a sandwich and a container of hot eideran. I consumed both while starting my long walk to the spaceport. Trucks and other vehicles passed me. None stopped to offer me a lift, nor did I expect it. Spontaneous generosity was not a feature of my species. Had I been walking as myself, I might have been solicited, offered a ride for sex or money, but the travelers cloak indicated an alien, or a nonconformist. Either was too risky for a casual encounter. So, I was left alone to make my way.

CHAPTER THREE

The Baron's pawn shop was outside of the spaceport itself. A deliberate choice that spared both it and its visitors the jurisdiction of the failing Confederacy and the planetary government, corrupt and venial as my people and the Guild had made both. The building had been cobbled together out of several older structures and rambled in all directions. I studied the shop for the better part of an hour, before I dared approach. Spacers of various species walked in and out. Fewer than I would have expected, either the early hour, or a fallout from the troubles beyond the city.

A rear door opened and Besa, a Guild gunner, leaned out. She wore a holstered laser and her narrow face was stony. The open display of the weapon was a warning, a potent one in the hands of an experienced Guild gunner.

Her eyes fastened on me, despite my position well back from the road, and they narrowed. I froze, even at this range; Besa would not miss if she drew. She stared for a few seconds, then gave a barely perceptible nod. The gunner disappeared back into the broad low building, but the door remained slightly ajar.

I glanced up and down the street. More traffic was building. Beyond the pawn shop, a transport began to rumble spaceward. I moved, quickly crossing the street, my cloak wrapped around me. I stared at the salvation of the doorway, my heart pounding, expecting a challenge or a shot. Then I was through the door, facing Besa and her leveled weapon.

"Strip," the older woman ordered.

I dropped the cloak, then both pants and shirt. She walked past me and leaned out, scanned the area then resealed the door. From behind me, she ran her hands over my small breasts and down into my underwear in a quick and professional search. Then she took the pistol from my dropped pants. I was somewhat surprised she didn't remove my thin knife.

"The Baron will see you in his office. He wants a full report."

"Has anyone else made it out?"

"Talk to the Baron. Pick up your clothes and move."

The interior of the pawn shop was full of armed Guild, guarding windows and doors. A few staff might be out front tending to customers, but that would be only to maintain the cover. The Baron had drawn in every gunner he could find. Doubtless other Guilders, with heavier weaponry and vehicles, waited in the nearby warehouses. Still, what could Guild criminals do against a full-scale military assault, such as had destroyed my uncle's compound? Guild power had always resided in bribery, blackmail, drugs, whores and politics, not firepower. Today though, the more public location, and its proximity to what passed for law and order on our world might be the better protection.

The Baron's inner office was four deep in guards, who ran cold eyes over me as I trailed Besa. Its doors, salvage from some old spacer, opened smoothly and admitted me. The Baron, his hair gray-gold with age, stood before a battery of screens and holos. I could see newsfeeds from various agencies and video of the area around the shop on some of them. His number two stood next to him, a middle-aged Dua with a scarred face. The Baron waved at the man to leave and with another motion, silenced the holos and screens, then turned to face me.

Yellow eyes, much like the unfortunate Elshiya's, regarded me. "Report, Guilder."

I relayed the night's events in a terse and professional manner that might have made grandfather proud. The Baron listened, then questioned me closely, going over the few details of our attackers I had seen. After he fell silent for a few minutes, I ventured a question of my own.

"Did anyone else escape?"

His eyes flicked to mine. "No. The slaughter was quite complete. Even the newsfeeds commented on how no one, high or low, was spared. It seemed they intended to kill you all. This makes no sense, why waste such efforts on staff or novices? A Guildmaster making such a play would offer realignment to the survivors, once the principals were taken out."

I nodded. My species were the ultimate in practicality, with the weak yielding to the strong. Once the leader was taken out, along with his lieutenants and blood kin, staff was up for grabs. Most would realign with no tears spent for their previous masters. This flexibility had earned us contempt from other species, but our wars were small affairs, perhaps constant, but without millions of deaths from collateral damage.

As for my uncle and his family, I too had no tears for those kin. Indeed, with their disappearance and this new disaster, there might be opportunities from me that had been beyond my reach. I gave some thought to a future where my grandfather's legacy would not lie so heavily on my shoulders, then shook free of my reverie as the Baron spoke again.

"I have talked to the other Guild leaders left alive. None have been offered realignment. Nor have any been approached about a change in leadership. But worse, D'agosta and his family were on their yacht, which is missing.

More bad news, I thought, *the second highest Guilder onworld, whose yacht was an old surface warship displacing 50,000 tons.*

"So this may be more broadly aimed," I murmured.

"It is," the Baron continued. "Many of our political connections have disappeared, along with our friends in the military. I do not believe these attackers are local military, but no one could bring in such a force of mercenaries unnoticed by our connections."

I did not know what to make of it. All morning, I had dreaded arriving at the pawnshop, only to find it realigned with the new power. Worse, as blood kin of a fallen house, even in whatever low regard I was held, I might be offered as blood price to the attackers. Schadenteer, the fear of entirely losing one's place in the pack had trembled within me. To be without a pack was to be food for anyone and anything.

But no offers of realignment had been made, and the Baron himself might be feeling schadenteer though no sign of it was on his stony features.

"There is concern that this is a move on the Guild itself," he said. "Such have occurred before, by some reformer or other, provoked by some excess. They amount to little, the Guild moves or goes further underground. This is different. We were struck out of the night by someone who has great power, managed complete secrecy and has detailed, almost total, knowledge of our operations. That has never happened before."

"That means insiders," I added.

He grunted at my recognition of the obvious, and I resolved to remain silent unless asked, but was surprised when he asked me a question.

"What do you know of Project Alchemy?"

I considered quickly, was there an advantage to pretending knowledge? No, a Guilder like the Baron would see through me in an instant. "Nothing, sir."

He sighed. "Sensible, a novitiate should see much, but speak little. It was too much to hope, even though you are blood kin. Project Alchemy is a Guild research project that your Uncle committed vast amounts of the Guild's wealth to. Even he only inherited Alchemy, which has run for more than a thousand years. Before yesterday, it would have been death for a Guilder of your rank to even know that name. I lost people to your Uncle's forces trying to find out. Even I know only the name, and that the tithe for supporting it was immense. Rumors, and there were few of those, said it was a project that would increase the Guild's power to where it need fear no government."

I considered. The Guild had outlasted species, but it had rarely contested governments. A clandestine organization of criminals could outwit and outmaneuver governments, but could never reach the levels of mass of governmental militaries and police forces, even using mercenaries. The few attempts made, were taught to novitiates as examples of hubris and disaster.

"You are a remarkable young person," he continued, which immediately put me on guard. "Your escape shows as much. Would you be of more use to your Guild and gain favor?"

"Order me," I replied, giving the only response my lack of power made sensible.

"Our communications have been cut, both on world and off. One suspects there have been strikes made against our shipping and bases out in the system and no help is immediately to hand. We may have survived due to our proximity to the Spaceport. Gods be praised that the planetary government ceded sovereignty over the spaceports to the Confederacy!

"So we must look further afield for help, and to spread the warning if this disaster is not confined to our own world. Who knows, even Mystic might be endangered."

Despite my promise to myself, I was startled into blurting out, "Mystic? I thought that was a myth."

The Baron actually grinned. "Mystic is real, Child. It was originally just a base for pirates, but the Guild has a long and friendly history with those, and pirates are a solitary lot. Organizing a secret base is well beyond their capabilities. One does not find Mystic, it reaches out and finds you, if you are worthy. Once its location is known to you, it is death to you and yours to reveal it.

"But as to your mission. My surviving personnel are too well known to the law and military to move about in the spaceport. You are not. If anyone even knows of you, they may believe you're dead in the wreck of your Uncle's compound. You must escape this world and journey to the House of Dame Vildeau, a human Guild boss on Rukia. She too, has shared my interest in Project Alchemy. You will inform her of the developments here: the attacks, the lack of realignment being offered. Advise her that this is an attempt to exterminate the Guild, at least in this system and my own suspicion is this act involves Alchemy."

He reached back to his desk and opened a small box, which revealed a green data crystal, the color showing that it was encrypted to the highest degree. With a casual toss, he sent it in my direction. I snapped it out of the air and quickly placed it in my personal pouch. "That contains all that is known of Alchemy and of what has happened. Give it to the Dame. Tell her that if she sends a ship promptly, we will realign to her with enough wealth to make it worth her while to rescue us. If you are in any danger of being captured, you must destroy it. Credits and passage will be arranged for you. I can spare no one to go with you. Frankly, I doubt you will make it, but you are all I can afford to lose just now."

I was silent, it being nothing that I did not expect.

"Get some food and rest. Besa will set you up with the necessaries and a room."

"I will need a crystal reader."

He gave me a look, as if suddenly reconsidering his choice to use me.

"I have a crystal of my own I wish to read. I'm quite aware the other is encrypted to the tenth degree."

"Ah. There's one for inventory next to the break room. You may use it."

I bowed and backed out of the room. Besa was waiting for me, whether she had been listening, or simply knew the Baron's mind, I did not know. She handed me a large suitcase. I followed her to a small room with a sink and a bunk in it. She quickly showed me the weapons, cash, and specie, hidden in compartments a basic scanner would not penetrate. There was body armor that would shape itself to my form. I felt like putting it on immediately, but restrained myself.

She looked at my pistol, taken from the dead guard. "Clean it. I'll bring you more ammunition. When you get to the ship, turn it in to the ship's purser. If anyone suspects that you're Guild, it will be as well to surrender a weapon. It might make them less diligent in looking for others. One can hope so, anyway."

I nodded as she left. I checked in the area around my cell and found the crystal reader. It was an older model and required two hands to lift, but I moved it into the room. Once inside, I locked the door, though that was no protection against snooping, electronic or otherwise. I reached into my pouch, fingering the scant credits therein and the two crystals. I drew out a colorless one and, with a deep breath, fed it into the reader. A holo image glowed above the reader.

"Hello, Grandchild," Dusko Falkayan said. "I am doubtless long dead by the time you read this. The fact that you have activated this before your majority means you are in desperate trouble, or a fool, so we will proceed to the message I left in that eventuality."

There was a barely perceptible flicker.

"So, you are in trouble I cannot predict. Despite my... reinstatement in the Guild, I am not loved, nor truly forgiven, merely allowed to exist. The effect on your father and mother's lives you doubtless know.

"I have made some provision for you. At the end of this message, you'll find code words to accounts and parties who may be of use to you in your struggle to survive. It is not a fortune, but enough to give you a chance to flee and maneuver.

"Beyond those things is a chancy connection, but one, in extremis, that may serve you. I served with the android Maauro, in the Lost Planet organization. She was a remarkable being, made before we wandered out of caves, by a species that disappeared, the first and only truly sentient AI to arise, as far as we know. For all the disinformation spread about, sometimes by Maauro herself, the truth was far more remarkable. If you ever meet her, you will understand what I mean.

"My service with her was more complete than many would suspect. You see, Dear Maauro often had the need for a persuasive liar, though she herself was not above using untruths when it served her, especially when it came to the clueless human she wrapped herself around. Yes, Wrik Trigardt might have been surprised to know how often Maauro entrusted the custody of her lies to me. Of course, she enforced her reliance on me with a literally iron fist.

"But I digress, Grandchild. If you are in desperate straits, and no other help will avail, then make your way to Evenfall in the Thera system, look for a home owned by the Travers. That is the name Wrik and Maauro used when they moved there. When you find her, mention the secret that

I kept longest and best for her. Mention the name, Lilith. She will know what is meant and what is owed. I pass her debt to me, to you, Child. I cannot guarantee she will acknowledge it, strange creature that she is, but it is a chance. Bargain well and don't disappoint my shade by dying prematurely."

The image snapped off.

I sat in something like shock. I knew of the existence of Maauro, and the Guild version of how my grandfather came into her service. But the exact details of what really happened were known only to a Morok with a grudge against Dusko, Maauro, and the members of Lost Planet. Of my grandfather's further service, we knew what was in the public arena, the discovery of the Lost Colony and such, though the full details of many of the adventures were classified, or had been obscured. But that he had an intimate connection with his original captor was new and amazing news.

Maauro had proved a deadly enemy to the Guild, costing the lives of thousands of operatives, several bases and ships and some VIPS. The eventual revelation of her existence, and the fact that she'd been granted citizenship and a commission in the Confederate military caused a brief public hysteria, but when no horde of ravening robots followed her, the reaction faded. Maauro had dropped out of sight late in my grandfather's life, her existence as a self-aware AI being of more interest to scientists, ethnicists and the religious than to the general public. But my grandfather had apparently known of her whereabouts twelve years ago.

I shook my head, as interesting as this was, and as welcome as the credits and connections were, I was a Guilder with a mission, and none of this was of use right now. I rested and ate. Besa returned with the promised ammunition. Her face was cut and her clothes smelled of smoke. She handed me a wallet with travel papers, credits, a speciecard, and some gems in case I needed untraceable funds.

"Get down to Lake Two Pad at 2300 hours. The vessel *Nightbreaker* leaves at 2500 hours. You're on your own from the minute you leave. Our power no longer extends beyond these doors."

I nodded, but it had occurred to me that, gunmen or not, I might well be safer beyond the walls of a known Guild location. So, I took my supplies and slipped out of the pawnshop and headed for the quiet and darker locations of the large and rambling spaceport. I reported to *Nightbreaker*'s boarding area as late as I dared, and checked my luggage, having donned the body armor. Retaining my handgun, I made myself scarce and ran down the clock in a broad dining hall, clutching my travel cloak and mask about me. No one molested me and I watched the newsfeed above my head as the announcer darkly reported more disaster to the Guild in the new "internecine war among the criminal classes."

A shuttle took me the rest of the way to the launchpad where *Nightbreaker* sat, a middle-sized freighter and passenger vessel. Her sides gleamed white and orange in the spaceport lights. Intake was brief and, though I disliked it intensely, I checked my pistol. To my surprise, I found I'd been booked into a single, albeit small, cabin. I locked the cabin door with relief, and waited for ship's impellers to assure me that I was going to escape my homeworld.

CHAPTER FOUR

I RODE OUT THE REEMERGENCE INTO THE UNIVERSE IN MY cabin, with the minimal drug therapy. The trip was a short one, with an easy emergence, and I didn't want to be woozy. While the ship had been a safe haven on the voyage, we were now back in the space-time. More than four months had passed in the period we'd opted out of the passage of time. The gods alone knew what had occurred back in the rapidly decaying Confederacy. Humans had an expression that doubled as a curse, "may you be born in interesting times." I was taken with the wisdom of it.

Nightbreaker emerged relatively close in Rukia system. It was well-mapped and the gravitational fluctuations were so well studied, that the exit from hyperspace was within the orbits of the two inner planets, at least when those were on the far side of their orbit. Three days on standard reaction drive would bring us to station orbit of Rukia.

Trouble did not wait for the third day. I was taking lunch in the main dining hall when the news broadcast caught my eye. I picked up an ear-bud and excused myself from the human woman who had made "understanding me" her pet project.

"The continuing war among the crime guilds has claimed a new and exalted victim, Evelad Villdearau, known as Dame Villdearau, a reputed Guild chieftain, died in an explosion of a precision guided munition with a military-level yield, which utterly destroyed her country mansion. Government officials deny involvement, despite the apparent use of shock troops and aircraft. However, prosecutors have followed up on the opportunity..."

Shock spread through me. The Dame, dead? The purge that had struck the Guild on my world had preceded me here. I quickly excused myself and returned to my cabin. There I logged on and cancelled the mail I was to broadcast just before making stationfall. No need to advertise that a new Guild target had arrived. Normally, I would never have considered myself worth the chase, but I was a Guild courier now and whatever else this purge was, it seemed thorough.

I needed protection. The law would not shield me. Even if it was not the source of the purge, which I doubted, it was clearly exploiting the holes blasted by others. The Guild, what was left of it on Rukia, would be on the run. If it could not defend VIPS, what would it bother trying to do so for me? My mouth drew into a grim line. Desperation could sometimes only be relieved by desperate gambles. It was time to reconsider my grandfather's advice. I would not land on the world ahead. On the station, I would find the first of the connections that would eventually bring me to Evenfall. Thank the Gods my grandfather had arranged accounts for me. With what the Guild had provided and working my way, I should find the means to reach Maauro's homeworld. Even if she was not to be found, or was sensibly unwilling to help, it was a world on the periphery of settled space. There I might find some means to survive. It was a mad plan, but all was madness now.

As soon as the ship docked, I fled into the hanger area, then found a seedy docker bar to hang out in for a few hours while I searched for a ship outward. Fortunately, several vessels were in a hurry to leave the area, their masters unsettled by the attacks. I set my mind to the long task ahead.

A year's travel, working as everything from a steward to a wiper on various ships, finally brought me to Evenfall. All of known space was abuzz over what was now called the Guild War. Ships and soldiers had struck from space on many worlds, undetected by Confederate defenses, but the enemy fell only on the Guild. Bodies had been recovered and this was the real shock, revealing a new race of humanoid aliens, slender, with bulging eyes and bald craniums. Those few who'd been taken, went into irreversible comas that ended in death. No trace of where they had come from had been detected in either their ships or bodies. As no one knew what they called themselves they were known as the Pale Ones though humans often called them simply, Baldies.

The Confederacy had reacted to this intrusion with counterattacks on a limited basis. There was no concern over Guild, at least none that did not originate in the Guild, or its rapidly diminishing supply of allies. There was no communication with the swift black ships that brought the raiders in, they vanished into deep space or died in battle. Despite Confederate patrols, the alien vessels, which were almost impossible to detect, continued to score on Confederate worlds, but only against Guild targets. The Confederacy and the other non-aligned worlds where the purge had struck, could not be sure it would stay that way. None appreciated the violation of their sovereignty and a new cat and mouse game had begun between the black ships and the other powers of known space. This was the new universe that I inherited, the interesting time I was born in.

These thoughts crowded in on me as I watched Evenfall grow in the screens of the tramp freighter, *Three Islands*. I'd booked passage on the vessel under my assumed identity, as I could find no open berth on her for crew. My funds were running low, but would see me to the planet.

Evenfall had only one small space station. There had been a Confederate destroyer squadron based there, but when we emerged, we found it had been withdrawn. All that remained was a single elderly cruiser and several local customs cutters from the Evenfall self-defense force.

CHAPTER FOUR

The planet still acknowledged the Confederacy, based on Star Central, but the attachment seemed nominal. Local laws on weapons were few, as usual on a colonial world. I received my weapon back for only a signature, after docking. The more potent weapons in my high-tech case remained undiscovered.

I passed through customs with only a cursory examination of my false identity. Once outside the crumbling spaceport lounge, I passed by a line of elderly cabs and walked over to a scenic overlook. I wanted some sense of the world that contained what was likely my only chance.

Evenfall was pleasant and green like my homeworld. Except for the hydrogen-breathing Ribisans, and, to a far lesser degree the Solari, the races of the Confederacy all liked similar real estate. Admittedly the Moroks would prefer the damp, tropical part of a world, while the Denlenn preferred cool mountain forests. We Dua-Denlenns, like humans, were more flexible in our land tastes.

I could see Oron City in the valley below, a river curved around it and small vessels, most of them barges, plied the water. Looking further, I could see the sparkle of the sea. Oron was the capitol, following the same pattern that almost every colony world did, with the spaceport marking the original landing site. Settlement had spread from there.

I'd never been off my homeworld before and was surprised by how similar it looked. Only when you focused on the details did you realize that trees were the wrong shape, decked with silver and white flowers. The color of the sky was different, shot through with clouds of a distinctly greenish cast. I scuffed some of the ground at my feet, stirring some pebbles. They shone in a way that appealed to me. Giving in to a childish impulse, I reached down and selected a shiny bit of quartz, shot through with veins of some darker stone, and put it in my pocket. I could use a good luck charm.

A wind kicked up and I clutched my traveler's cloak around me. Once I had some idea how common my kind was on this world, I might trade the cloak for an ordinary jacket. Past a point, the cloak could be a liability, marking me as an outsider, though right now my luggage uncomfortably marked me as such too.

The thought brought back bitterness. When had I not been an outsider? I'd been pushed to the corner of my family. Even in an organization of the outcasts, I'd found bare tolerance. Finally, when I was on the verge of making my novitiate, the Guild itself seemed likely to disappear. Whenever I neared a drawbridge, it was drawn up against me. How I longed for power, power over others, power to destroy my enemies and maybe power to build something lasting for myself.

My mouth drew tight. Maybe that power lay on this world, but even if I found it, how could I tame it to my command?

I shook myself. First things first, I needed to check in with the Guild on this world and provide them with warnings and information, though

I would keep the crystal the Baron had given me to myself. Whatever Project Alchemy was, it was fraught with power. I didn't want to contact the local Guild, but if they found me later, operating undeclared, they'd be entitled to regard me as an enemy.

So, I returned to the spaceport, rented a biosensor locker, and cached my crystal and the special case the Baron had given me, taking only some necessaries in a bag so disreputable I doubted anyone would consider boosting it. I found a bus into the city, far cheaper than the cabs lairing at the terminal, and made my way to the seedier side of the city by asking the driver what places a young female like me should avoid. In minutes, I had a pretty good map of Guild ops. The local crime lords were probably not actual Guild, but associates at best, or perhaps some actual, ranked Guilder might be hiding out in this hinterland.

Of course, there could be another reason. Maauro had been implacably hostile to Guild. True, the Guild had initiated the hostilities, but after we ceased to trouble her, indeed, orders came down from the highest to avoid her at all cost, she ceased to trouble us. If she'd made this world her home, it would be brave Guilders who'd dare operate near her. Perhaps her desire to be undisturbed and unknown in this quiet world had led to some de facto truce?

The bus pulled up to one of the budget hotels that sponsored it. I dismounted, remembering to thank the driver, as such was expected among humans, about his warnings. But I did not go into the simple, yet well-maintained structure. After the bus pulled out of sight, I shouldered my small bag and walked off toward the warned of places. As I moved, my eyes searched the streets. I watched for more of my own kind, but while I saw a Morok and an ursine Okaran, I saw neither Denlenn, nor Dua-Denlenn. It seemed the travel cloak would remain my best defense.

I entered the seedier, commercial part of town that always surrounded a spaceport. Wherever people, particularly males, are transitory, there is illicit traffic of many sorts. It was late afternoon and early for many of the businesses that served crime. Like any other business though, they often worked more hours than their doors were open for. I moved around, asked questions of some locals who looked like they might know something useful then, settled on a pawnshop similar to the Baron's and went around to the trade entrance. There, I chimed the com and waited an inordinate amount of time. An ill-favored, human male, balding and with slits for eyes, stared up at me as he opened the door.

"We ain't open," he mouthed in standard, with an accent that made him hard to understand.

I gave a Guild recognition hand sign that signaled I was a courier. The complicated pattern was not easily learned and was death for any but Guild to use.

"What are you waving your fingers at me for? Hey, you ain't putting some sort of curse on me?"

"If so, it would be for stupidity," I said, opting to seize the high ground. "Guild. Go fetch your master."

He looked for a second as if he might argue, then decided the wiser of it. "Stay here." He vanished into the building. In his place, a smaller and frightened-looking young man held the doorway. I ignored him, hoping my height, cloak, and mask were intimidating.

Squint-eye returned, trailed by an older woman. She had once been beautiful, but time had turned that beauty hard-edged and gaunt. "Who are you?" she demanded.

I made the Guild sign again. I could see from her darting eyes that she recognized it. Respect and fear followed.

"Enter, Guilder," she said, her tone softening. "Forgive Baldan, we so rarely see a courier that I've not taught him such signals. We're only associates here. I am Fren Dirrath, and hold the membership."

I nodded and stepped in. "So word in the street says." With the door safely shut behind me, I removed my mask and threw back the cloak's hood. I knew I appeared young, but likely they'd never seen a Dua-Denlenn in the flesh, and humans found our eyes frightening, especially in low-light, as they reflected like an animal's. I needed any dominance I could muster.

"Baldan," she ordered, "have food and drink brought to my office. Find something a Dua-Denlenn would appreciate."

Both Baldan and the unnamed boy disappeared. I followed the woman through the stacks of hocked merchandise to the back, where her office stood. It was comfortable, though there was no comparison with the Baron's opulence and security. I'd placed the cloak on a hanger as Baldan and the boy hurried in with a tray of fruit juices, plates of cakes, and small sandwiches.

With a cut of her eyes, Dirrath signaled them to leave. I helped myself to a sandwich and a drink after sniffing both. Dirrath waited in apparent patience.

To be on the safe side, I gave another Guild hand sign and she replied with the correct one for a head of station.

"What news do you bring," Dirath asked, "and from where?"

"I am out of the Dua-Denlenn homeworld and bring words of warning," I laid out the facts of the attacks, the fall of the Baron and the Dame.

At the end of my tale I could see Dirath was sensibly reconsidering both her welcome to me and her membership in the Guild. "This is the first we have heard of this," she muttered, clearly appalled. "Your ship was the first interstellar to land in our little backwater in two years. Gods. Who could have foreseen the fall of the Guild?"

I picked up a cake. "The Guild is eternal. It will remember those who stood with it in times of trouble and those who did not. Beyond that, you must wonder that even if you suddenly reconsider your connections to us, will that save you?"

Diraath nodded. I liked that she was too practical to pretend I was not following her thinking. To do otherwise insulted me. "Do you have any recommendations for me?"

I shrugged. "Be wary, move your assets around. Watch the skies and cooperate with the local authorities in defense. With our ship, came the news of the raids on other worlds. They will not welcome black ships and these pale humanoids in their skies, violating their world."

"From what you say, it appears even the old Confederate military has managed only a few interceptions."

"Prisoners have yielded nothing," I added. "They fall into a coma quickly and die. All we know is that they are humanoids of a type not seen before."

"Wonderful, another alien species, either war or economic disruption," Dirrath said as she sat back in her chair.

"Yet in each is the chance for profit," I returned with a Guild aphorism.

"For the lucky," Dirrath's face said what she thought of that prospect. She followed with a series of questions that increased my respect for her intelligence. I filled her in on all the Guild news I had, minus any reference to Project Alchemy.

Finally, she felt that she'd wrung out all she could. "One thanks you, Guilder, for your pains. The warning will be acted upon. We at least have that advantage thanks to you.

"What then do you intend? If you are returning—"

"Not for now. Both holds I had connections to have fallen."

She looked me over in a frank way that I did not care for. "You are young and pretty, an exotic body like yours would command high prices."

I shook my head. "I have not had, nor have interest in courtesan training. The life of a whore does not appeal to me. I am a courier. I will make my way back to the inner worlds and seek employment there."

"Sensible," she said. "I suppose it is too much to hope you would wish service in such a quiet part of space."

"Quiet places are valuable now."

"Still, if you are to head back, then I will ask you to transit through the Sirius system and take my annual tithe to my senior, Nakarth on Sirius IV, for the usual commission fee."

"At the danger rate," I countered.

There was a momentary pause, then she nodded.

"Which I will waive in return for some services on this world," I added.

Now her eyes did narrow. "And what would those be?"

"A personal matter, I am looking for a family named Travers, who immigrated here in Galstandard 1432, a man and woman. It is possible that one, or both, are dead. If so, I want to see their property and their graves."

She nodded. "Such information should be public and easily obtained."

"Those identities were false. This may be more difficult than you expect."

Dirath shrugged. "We'll arrange a room for you at a hotel we have near the port. It will be a secure location, as much as such exists now. I will be meeting with my political connections about increasing our security. I have no desire to be visited by black ships or pale humanoids."

"Nor do I."

She gave a cool smile. "Let me know if you change your mind about prostitution. I can promise you high-end clients and easy hours."

I rose and ignored her offer. "I will wait to hear from you. When my own work here is done, we will make arrangements for me to take your tithe to your manager."

"Under Guild bond," she warned. "You'll exonerate me from all responsibility as soon as you bond. If it's lost in transit—"

"As is customary," I interrupted. Once a tithe was accepted by a Guild Courier, the courier's life was forfeit if the tithe was lost and the Guild bore the loss.

"Good evening, Guilder,"

I bowed and made my way out.

CHAPTER FIVE

DIRRATH FOUND GETTING INFORMATION ON THE TRA-vers as difficult as I warned her it would be. Their identities were protected by intricate layers of shell corporations and other such measures. However, these legal fictions were more effective at preventing detection, than holding up under pressure. Once discovered, they were merely tedious to bore through. I used the time in the meanwhile to work such odd jobs as I could find, trading sleep for the freedom of action more credits would bring me. I was tempted to pick some pockets or mug some of the more helpless, but such would undercut my thin cover as a courier, who would never take such risks. I knew time was not on my side and so I drove myself through the weary hours of drudging,

In only a few days I had my answer. Wrik and Maauro had indeed moved here sixty years ago. They had used assumed names to buy property in a highland farming community. After that there was little recorded about them; they'd apparently lived quiet lives. An obituary disclosed that Trigardt succumbed to natural causes at an advanced age while at home, over twenty years ago. Of his widow, nothing more was said. However, their various properties were maintained in a trust and their home had not been rented or sold. Police calls on vandals indicated that it was well secured. Odd again for a widow, but of course Maauro was not really a grieving spouse. The fact that she wanted the property kept as it was might indicate that the machine was still there. It had remained viable after 50,000 years in deep space, a mere twenty years would not trouble it. Still is seemed unlikely it was in the house, as the service sent a caretaker. The android could be under it.

Or truth be told, something as sophisticated as Maauro could have escaped any net set to catch it. There was no point to dwelling on that. If it had left this world, my chances of ever finding the android were mind-numbingly small.

I traded away some more of my forthcoming fee to rent a flyer to take me to the Trigardt/Travers property. There I rented a digger from a farmer who was in over his head to a loan operation of Dirrath's and happy to get relief by merely loaning out a digger and a room. He asked no questions about what I wanted it for, merely showing me how to use the machine and, most importantly, its ground-penetrating radar.

It took me a while to figure out that I could not hook the trailer to an aircar and so I borrowed his ground vehicle as well. A half-hour's drive took me to the property where Trigardt and his android had lived their strange existence. The gate and security system weren't up to stopping even a Guild novitiate, and I was through them quickly. There were no other houses in sight, though I could see some farm machines moving in the valley beyond. I hoped that, if they noted me at all, they'd assume the digger meant a new well, or something else benign. The caretaker's schedule showed that they'd already been here this week. There should be no company awaiting me.

So, I pulled up to the back of the house as if I had every right to be there. It was still early morning, well early for me, who preferred evening hours. I found two hats while rummaging on the digger. One sat uncomfortably on my high pointed ears, the other was a cap, which I managed better.

I spent the next three hours moving about the small farm: a yellow-painted main building with green shutters and a metal roof, with a barn and machine shed nearby. Something about the simple two-story building appealed to me, sitting in its stand of shade trees. I wondered what it would have been like to have lived there.

Frustration and fatigue grew on me as I found nothing near the house itself and I switched my thinking. Maauro had been a fighting machine. Even if concealment was not its sole aim, it might well have been influenced by it. I looked over the property map and noted a rise of a hill that stood near a small waterfall. I recalled from my studies of what little was known of the machine, that it had an affinity for volitionless motion: oceans, rivers, the wheeling of the stars overhead. Perhaps it was there, for all I knew, sitting immobile on a stone garden bench. No, it would conceal itself for fear of intruders or the curious.

I drove the digger up the gentle slope. Its powerful engine did not protest, but neither did it cover ground quickly. I battled impatience; it would not do to become stuck in a ditch. Finally, I reached a broad glade with the waterfall. To my surprise, I did find a stone bench there, though no android. Clearly, this had been a garden, with statues and the collapsed shape of a wooden shed.

I chose the highest and driest spot of the glade and fired the ground-penetrating radar. A return came back, the image was muddy, so what was below me was not all of metal, but then neither had the android been. In a mix of fear and excitement I hurriedly deployed the digger.

Awareness comes back to me, unbidden and unwanted. At first, it is a mere vibration, summoning me from my simulated sleep, simulated as so much of my existence is. But my grief is not, nor is the pain that caused me to hide in a hole in the ground, as if I could escape Death's sting. For Wrik is dead, gone from space-time to where I cannot follow. All that I could do to lengthen and protect the life I loved; gained us a mere 157 years. Yet, these 157 were more precious than the 50,000 that preceded them.

My mind becomes more active, sluggishly, as I resist it. For if I remember how Wrik found me on an asteroid, a lost relic from a race that vanished when humans lived in caves, if I remember how a love, slowly kindled and against all reason, grew between a human and an artificial intelligence, I must remember how Wrik's eyes finally closed. How I had his body cremated and the cremated remains pressurized into a gem, cut into the form of a heart, the only heart I would ever have, now buried in my own chest.

Humans say that time heals all wounds. I know that twenty-three years, six months and four days have passed since I last faced the world. Not enough time has passed, as with awareness, returns the full pain of my loss, undimmed.

The earth above me is thinning; some form of light machine is being used to uncover me. My onboard weapons are active. I consider whether to attack, to ease some of my pain in furious action, but I am a quantum computer, only the smallest portion of my mind could be distracted by this simple engagement.

And worse, it would have grieved Wrik if I were to kill so easily, for so little provocation. He was at heart a gentle soul. I learned kindness and love from him.

So, I will wait to see who it is who dares disturb my rest, but woe to them if I judge their reason unworthy.

I dismounted from the digger, as its instruments said I was within a meter of a being-sized metal object. I felt certain this was the fabled android, Maauro, and rapping it on its artificial head was not the most promising beginning for its service to me. The heat of the system's sun beat down on my thin shirt and bare arms. I hoped the spray on sunscreen I'd used would ward off summer sunburn. With a deep breath, I removed a shovel and a broad brush from the digger and jumped into the pit.

The smell of soil filled my nostrils as the spade bit into the hard-packed dirt. I dug carefully, with a sense of unearthing a grave. I reminded myself that it was merely a machine that lay here, an incredible one if the accounts were true, but I need fear no vengeful ghost. A half-hour later I'd made my way down to the layer where it lay and resorted to my brush and fingers. Suddenly strands of glossy black appeared under my brush. I sat back, unnerved for a moment and breathing hard, then redoubled my efforts. More glossy hair appeared then I saw white skin, a forehead. I dug more and uncovered a face. The corpse-like look shocked me, but for the lack of corruption, this could have been a person.

Now that I could see the remote face, I wondered what to do next. The fine, small-featured face was attractive and unmarred, as if it had gone into the earth only today. I slowed my breathing, using the drills my masters instilled in me in the long, painful years.

Its eyes opened and I froze as it stared at me. The eyes were like a human's, though far larger than any I had seen. I found it difficult to meet these strange eyes, with their large green circles and black dots, in their white surrounds, and I judged the look the android gave me was unfriendly.

I backed away, gathering my feet under me as the machine held my gaze. With no evident difficulty, the android stirred and shrugged free of the soil's grasp. We both stood facing each other in the narrow trench. I thought about my pistol, as I slowly stood, then realized the insanity of brandishing any weapon this close to the android.

It was petite, with a figure I could envy, covered by a red and gray form-fitting jump suit, with some gold details on its cuffs. But it was the eyes that held me. They were not the doll-like eyes of an HCR or the rare humanoid commercial bot.

I started when it spoke.

"Did you suppose," the android said, "that I placed myself here so you could unearth me?"

I slowly shook my head, surprised by the high and youthful voice and that it addressed me in my own language, not Gal standard, with a native ease.

"Who are you?" Maauro demanded. "What gives you the right to disturb me? Finally, how did you find me?"

I suspected that my life might depend on the answer. "My name is Dassa Falkayan. You worked with my grandfather, Dusko Falkayan."

Surprise flitted across the machine's face, which made me wonder if I had actually surprised her, or if the display was for my benefit.

"Your information is incorrect. Your grandfather worked for me, at first to avoid a quick death at my hands, and later, to avoid a lingering one at the hands of his former colleagues."

I raised my head. "Grandfather said that you owed him a debt, and that he passed that debt to me."

This time it surprised me by laughing. A wave of superstitious fear enveloped me. It was too much like dealing with a being returned from death.

"Your grandfather was notorious for pressing both his position and luck with me. Surprising, since at our first meeting I offered to remove his limbs without benefit of anesthesia."

Grandfather, you bastard, what have you done to me?

"I grant he was of some use to me later, but I consider any debt I owed him as settled with the wergild that removed the standing Guild contract on his life.

"But that answers the last question of how you found me. I kept my connection to my Lost Planet network for a long time. My husband...my husband, Wrik, always wanted to know what the others who'd served in Lost Planet were doing. Perhaps I indulged him too long in that regard, particularly regarding your family."

Bitterness made me incautious. "Was your internment so precious to you?"

"What do you know of my life, my pains, my reasons?" she said, with a dangerous dryness.

"Nothing, but shall I acquaint you with my own sufferings? Perhaps they might amuse you."

It cocked its head at me. "Why would they concern me at all? I have no love for either the Guild, or your kind."

Again, bitterness made me incautious. "Let it distract you for a few seconds; then you can kill me and rebury yourself."

Maauro crossed her arms and stared at me.

"You brought grandfather free of the Guild's vengeance, but not into its good graces. That constant enmity shortened my father's life, drove my mother back to her own family and left me to my uncle's non-existent mercy. Seventeen years of scraps and sufferance, then when I am on the verge of making it into the lowest rank of the Guild, the beginning of any respectability, the galaxy fell on me.

"The only place, the only place I belonged, fell in one night of fire and death. Some enemy I do not even know has declared war on the Guild, something that has never happened before. Empires, species, even the pathetic Confederacy have come and gone and always the Guild remained, until now.

"So I am pursued. Me, a nothing, a no one, not even a full initiate, but even such as I am, enemies that I can neither fight, nor long outrun, pursue me." I choked off the flow of my grief and anger.

"Grandfather told me to mention a name to you that bore on your debt to him, the name is Lilith."

We stood in silence, facing each other. Seconds dragged by as I stared at the now expressionless face of Maauro.

Maauro looked around. "We are in a hole." It bent double and with a thrust of the slender legs, flung itself out of the trench, disappearing into the blue sky above.

I clambered out of the hole, fearing that it might have run off, but the android was merely standing, looking up at the sun in a way no creature with real eyes could have done. It ignored me and walked to the top of the small hillock and turned in a circle. I studied the android as it moved. I'd seen humanform combat robots of the Confederacy once, guarding their embassy during a food riot, but they were awkward toys compared to this machine. Maauro possessed a lithe and feminine grace that I found myself envious of. The movements were those of a hunting animal, liquid and full of potential energy, as if it could explode into action at any second. I doubted many Humans or Dua-Denlenn could boast such a tiny waist, with the curves of bust and hips she had. Well, if one could build a female body, why not build one of unobtainable perfection?

And here I stood: sweated, dirty and in need of a shower. Maauro, who had rested in dirt for decades, looked as fresh as a spring-washed day.

"How did you get all traces of dirt off you?" I blurted out. The topic seemed a safe one at least.

She glanced at me sidelong, as if deciding whether I was worth answering. "Before you emerged, I vibrated myself at just under Mach One for .001 seconds. The dirt flew off."

"Vibrated at just under Mach One," I repeated, trying to process it.

"I thought you might find being at ground zero for a sonic boom unpleasant."

It takes this Dassa a few seconds to escape the pit. I study the Dua-Denlenn as she climbs out and stands next to me. She is nearly as tall as Wrik was, so I must look up at her. Her body is long limbed with the lankiness of youth; her hair is a reddish gold and cut short in a simple style. Men would likely find her attractive, as her features are well-defined, with a long, but elegant nose, under eyes that are a light blue lid to lid, making her expression bland. But I can read a controlled fear and wariness in her scent and posture. Her bravado is simply that, and backed up by nothing.

I consider what she has said, while simultaneously executing a myriad of tasks. I have reached out and hacked into all available data streams. Only half of those active when I entered my slumber are still available, that, and a cursory exam of the data tell me that Evenfall has not prospered in the time I slept. Indeed, what I had predicted has come to pass, the Confederacy itself is splintering, failing, even among humans, as separatists again seek freedom from Star Central's authority.

But none of this concerns me. My old network is gone: Wrik, Delt, Jaelle, Shasti Rainhell and the others have all exited space-time, leaving me to struggle on alone. The Confederacy and indeed the races in it are none of my concern now, not even the humans of which Wrik was one. I am alone.

Wrik had extracted a last promise of me on his deathbed, that I not simply end my existence, but remain open to the possibility of hope and of chance. So, I am denied the right to set off after him to wherever thinking beings go when they die. I do not fear death. I believe in an existence beyond this one, and thus it seems to me that delaying here is pointless. Still, my love felt that there was a value to this life I am left to. I promised and not for the briefest of moments will I consider that my last promise to my husband will be broken. I must await my own end through entropy or enemy action.

CHAPTER FIVE

I sigh internally, while staring at the girl, only a second or two of her time has passed, but I have done much. Knowing that I am condemned to awareness again, I have segmented a part of my mind, it is with Wrik in my memory of every second that we had together save for that last day. Those memories will be locked away until my own end comes, if there is time then. For now, part of me is with the memory of him that exists in my memory banks. For a being with perfect recall, there is little difference between memory and present existence, save for the absence of surprises. In a human, such would be the first sign of a descent into madness, and perhaps it is for me, but it hurts less and that is enough just now.

Other parts of my brain, I dedicate to long-range intelligence gathering through what is left of Evenfall's financial system. I locate money and assets that Wrik and I owned and I had abandoned. These are immediately repurposed; property is put up for sale, money moved into proper investments. It is possible I will have need of it.

But my active focus is on the girl. It amuses me in a bitter way that she believes Dusko had such a hold over me. I was not originally fond of Dusko, or his kind, it is hard to develop affection for a society of functioning sociopaths, but we had a relationship of mutual use that he may have regarded as friendship.

But there was more, Lilith, a name I had hoped never to hear again. On a mission for the Confederacy, before I gained my human body, I encountered a hacker. Lilith had been born, twisted and deformed, in a religious colony of humans who disdained modern medicine in favor of God's perceived will. The Confederacy had taken the child as a ward, only to be rewarded with murder, when the child, hating all humanity, stole a sextet of humanform combat robots and escaped, killing many in the process. She and her rogue team became an army for hire.

Destiny crossed us when Wrik decided to return to his homeworld to reclaim his position in his family and face the disgrace of his fleeing a rebel battle. I'd been left behind then with Jaelle and the others of Lost Planet. I disobeyed his wishes and immediately set out after him. Candace Deveraux intercepted me en route to tell me of Lilith, and that she suspected she'd landed on Retief. She gave me Military Intelligence's orders, capture or kill, the renegade.

I did neither. It was from Lilith, who had downloaded her consciousness into the HCR bodies, that I learned the method of downloading mine into a human one. I then sent her into exile beyond known space. Of this, Wrik knew nothing, I kept the secret for fear he would have tried to help me against Lilith and been killed. Dusko had been my only confidant in that battle and the resulting deal I had made with the devil.

It seemed that still more payment was owed on it.

CHAPTER FIVE

I dusted myself off and faced the android, though it was harder to think of it as a machine with each passing moment. I thought desperately of any argument that could bend her to my will, or fasten the chains of debt on her. But I'd already played my trump card, Lilith, and she was not Guild, the assumptions and customs of the Guild that such obligations were a form of currency did not bind her.

My own inexperience choked me. Surely my grandfather could have manipulated the android, but he'd been talented and seasoned.

"Will you honor your debt to my grandfather?" I finally demanded, unable to stand the lengthening silence.

"If I had one to him," Maauro returned, "it expired with him. You are nothing to me. Leave me alone. I did not ask to be returned to a world that holds only pain for me."

Suddenly, my last hope was gone. The *schadenteer* of being alone, with no pack, out of alliance with any power, overwhelmed me. Without Maauro's strength, I was nothing. Likely bound for whoredom if I stayed on this miserable mud ball, or scutwork as a cutpurse even if I could make my way back to the inner worlds where my claim of being a courier would be discovered and dismissed.

I felt life draining out of me as if my veins had already been cut. I glared at her my breath coming hard and fast.

"You," I choked out, "how dare you! With all your strength and power, all you want to do is return to your hole in the ground and rot. Oh, what I could do with a hundredth of what you are squandering. Well, rot, damn you, you pathetic wretch!"

I threw myself at the android, fists balled. Suicide, but that was honorable to one with no pack. It would at least be quick. My fists passed through empty air, fast as I was, she was faster. Her arms circled me from behind. My body tensed for the crushing pressure, the agony and the darkness to follow. But it did not come, the arms that held me were unyielding, but no awful force came. I drove my head backwards, but she merely put hers against mine, with a firm pressure that stopped me from head-butting her. I was held helpless as a small child.

Packloss overwhelmed me, erasing anger, erasing shame, leaving only sheer terror. I could not stop the wail that burst out of me. I began to shake, my vision turned into a tunnel.

"End it," I begged. "Please, end it."

Against my will, I am moved. The being I hold in my arms is young, truly little more a child. She is of a species I hold no kindness for, by the human terms I have lived with for over a century.

Still, she is sobbing in my arms, and right now Dassa does not seem so different from a human child, such as I once dreamt of having. The name Lilith wells up in my mind again, another dangerous child and one I was unable to show any mercy to. I know this is foolish sentimentality on my part; a feeling neither female would have understood, or been able to return.

And yet, this is a network being offered. Is it truly so different for me? Without Wrik, Delt, Jaelle and the others, didn't I simply want it to end, just to stop the pain? Dassa wants me to kill her, yet even that is an associational act. She wants someone more powerful to act for her, on her, as is right in her culture.

I am at a nexus; two roads again lie before me and the choice means that one road must be forsaken. Is this life, shaking and crying in my arms, worth my time? Is it worth staying out of my grave for?

As if he was still with me, I suddenly hear Wrik's voice, young, as when we first met, but warm and gentle as he always was with me. "Maauro, my love, there is nothing in that hole. I asked you to live a life for both of us. That means new networks, new friends and to be open to the possibilities I spoke to you of. Do this for me. Do this for us."

What madness is this? Wrik is gone from space-time; he exists only in static memory now. Yet I feel my husband's presence with me for the first time since his death, as if hovering over me. I feel his gentleness and love.

"You always did take the road less travelled," I feel him whisper in my mind. "Be brave again and set forth on that road; it has never failed you." Then I feel him fade from me.

I am aware that I am stroking Dassa's hair. Her sobs have subsided, though I feel a terrible tension in the too lean body. My sensors focus on her interior. All through her body I see symptoms of high stress damage, blood pressure, hormones, weight loss, but there is more, so many of her bones show remodeling of breaks from abuse.

Wrik bids me travel with this waif. Yet that chains me to a being I will never be able to trust as I did Wrik, Delt, or even Jaelle. Dusko was a companion in adversity, but he knew his continued existence depended on the protection I supplied from the Guild. After I paid the wergild on him and he left Lost Planet, I never heard from him again. One did not get holiday greetings from Dusko. Dassa is cut from the same cloth, not merely a Dua-Denlenn, but of the Guild, deceptive even by the standards of her amoral species.

Even as I think this, I realize that I have already made my choice. I am stroking her hair still and have raised my body temperature to be more comfortable to lean against. This strange child has somehow caused something magical to occur. I felt Wrik's presence and in a blinding revelation, I realize that our network is not sundered by death. It has become something different, yet, somehow, I feel he is still with me. And might the others still be?

My awareness teeters on the verge of something: Nirvana or dissolution? I was made a machine, born for the hard calculus of war. I was also born as an adult human woman and the contradictions of these *lives pile in on me. Logic and order had been my touchstones for over 50,000 years. But since I awakened on the asteroid, something far different has become part of me. I teeter and flail mentally, caught between logic, empiricism and the belief that I have just had a mystical experience. Had I not lived as a human for 62 years I might have ceased to function, unable to integrate my thoughts. The malleable part of my body could have lost form and I could have become merely a collection of parts in a slush of ceramics and metals. But I did so live and I draw strength from that and reintegrate myself in a new pattern. I cling to the promise to my beloved; I will not easily surrender this life that we shared.*

My epiphany has taken an eternity of 4.3276 seconds. Dassa has ceased to struggle in my arms. Even that fact that I am confining her is proof to her instincts that, in some fashion, another pack member is present, as an enemy would have savaged her by now.

I do not release her, or it might bring on the breakdown again. "You are right," I say aloud. "I am wasting my life this way. So, you offer me a purpose, a reason to move. Right now, that is something of value to me."

The blue eyes stare at me blankly. She is far gone to let me see her so open and vulnerable. It is difficult for me to read much in such eyes.

"You'll... you'll help me?" she stammers.

I raise my eyebrows. "I will protect your life, for now. That is all I bind myself to." I release Dassa and step away from her. "It would be ill-advised for you to take a swing on me in the future."

"Forgive me," she says dully, "I thought it better to make a quick end of it." She tries to step forward and her legs buckle. I catch her instantly, realizing that the shock of her suicide attempt and breakdown have multiplied her underlying fatigue. She is at her limit. I lift her in my arms.

"When did you last have a full meal and a night's rest?" I demand. But the blue eyes are dull and the face is now slack.

I look at my house on the land below the waterfall and the stream that feeds the farm pond. I had left orders that it be kept as it was, though at the time I was not even sure why I did so. I must now hope those have been obeyed. I ignore the digger and walk the path to the door I did not intend to enter again. My house AI still performs and admits me. It reports the house is visited on a regular basis and most of its systems are performing at 90% or better efficiency. I do not find such a low number for readiness acceptable. There is a hive of stinging insects hanging by the porch. Wrik hated bugs and I had manufactured a series of small bots to keep our home free of insects. None of these are functioning just now. I manufacture a small, penetrating charge, load it in the flechette barrel in my index finger and fire it into the hive, its velocity is barely enough to penetrate, yet once inside it will atomize into a lethal nerve agent. In 1.0789 seconds, the pests are dead.

I enter and turn to the left, toward the guest rooms. Even now I cannot face my bedroom, or I will end up in a state like Dassa's. Once in the guest room, I deposit the girl in a chair. While she is conscious, she does not react. The bed sheets are unacceptably dusty. I remove them and reactivate the room filter, then, exasperated, find I must repair the filter first. This is done quickly. I unseal a plastic bag with fresh linens and blankets and secure Dassa in the bed. I find two of my old server bots and wonder where the others have gone to. These two I recharge, repair and reprogram and set to bringing house systems up to 100%. Pests are removed, small repairs are made. The house AI is a tiny copy of some of my own programs and responds quickly. I take a few moments to compose and send a letter of complaint to the service that I had hired to attend to my home. I can only hope that the service in whose care I entrusted Stardust have done better,

I extend a data probe into what remains of this world's net to find that Stardust is indeed still on the planet, but contrary to my instructions, has been used in my absence as a general cargo hauler. I instruct the ship systems to expel the crewmembers aboard and then lock down, awaiting my further instruction. Stardust's AI gives a warning and then begins using the fire suppression system to remove the unwanted crew.

I contact Borger shipping. Ingrid Borger answers the video. The years have told on her some, but she remains only middle-aged. I transmit an angry-looking image of myself for her consideration.

"This is Yuki Travers," I grate, giving my married alias. "Why is my starship being rented out in contravention of my orders?"

I can see shock spreading across her face. "We...we thought you were dead!"

"Which would not entitle you to use my starship, you are not my heirs."

She stammers and blithers and offers to call the company lawyers. Finally, she seems to focus on me. "Wait a minute? You can't be her. Her hair was silver; she was near a hundred. You look like—"

"I've had work done. You'll find my legal identity verification on screen."

"It is you," she gasps, reading the verification.

"I know that," I snap. "I will waive legal charges of theft and conversion and forgo any demand for a refund, provided my ship is prepared for deep space take off in 72 hours. You will find a manifest attached as a document."

"Yes, Ma'am," she says, obviously relieved. Such a demand will be costly, but less so than a lawsuit, or a demand for my share of the cargo fees for the unauthorized use of my ship.

The manifest I send is for legal items, supplies and particular needs for a Dua-Denlenn. I also make a series of calls to businesses, executing orders for machinery and equipment that will not individually raise any attention, but a good Confed customs agent might be alarmed by their weapon potential. I liquidate many of my assets on world. Many have prospered, but the more aggressive ones have done poorly as hard times hit this sector of space. We will need money to move. In fact, I may well see if Borger has a cargo run that will be of interest to me when we leave, wherever it is that we are going. If trouble follows Dassa, as she had said, it makes tactical sense to vacate any known location.

I make my way to the kitchen. There are vacuum-sealed supplies in the storage unit. The house AI tells me the caretaker comes once a week, often for several days so the kitchen is in better shape than the rest of the house. I consult my internal databases to see what might be palatable to my guest. It seems that Terran coffee is popular with Dua-Denlenn, which is odd, as true Denlenn will normally flee the smell. So, I fix coffee, eggs and some bacon, though the animal that came from was no Terran pig. There is bread from the caretaker's last visit. It is not fresh, but a quick burst of radiation takes care of any mold. However, I decide that I cannot vouch for the taste, so I elect for toast.

There is a brief commotion outside. My server bot has found a mal-ador under the back steps. It queries me for instructions. I take over the bot's targeting and fire a steel dart into the malador's brain before it can spray its noxious defense, as that would not do breakfast any favors. The bot drags off the pest for disposal a kilometer from the house. It will need to stay away for some hours itself, as even handling the malador results in contact with its foul skin oils.

Now I am free to concentrate on breakfast.

CHAPTER SIX

THE SOUND OF SINGING WOKE ME. I STARED AROUND AN unfamiliar room with its rustic furnishings in total disorientation.

"Am I dead?" I wondered aloud. Then the shame of my situation came to me in a flood. I remembered crying like a helpless child after attacking Maauro in the hope of a quick death. After that, it was a jumble.

How can I face her? I've totally lost control of the situation. Far from obtaining command of the robot, it offers me shelter. I am not even a beta, perhaps I do not even qualify as a delta. I am truly pathetic, and my grandfather's shade must be convulsing in laughter.

But who was singing?

I found myself naked under the covers. *Oh, no, don't tell me that she bathed me!* But I realize that I was still in need of a shower, so I was spared that humiliation at least. I found a robe on the end of my bed. There were even slippers, so I did not need to feel the chill of the wooden floor. I put on the robe and followed the sound of the singing. The language was not Gal-standard, though some of the words are familiar. Likely it was one of the Terran root languages that the Denlenn and humans collaborated on when the Confederacy first formed.

As I came down the stairs and peered around the corner, I was treated to a sight of such domesticity that I wondered if I might still be asleep. Maauro was at work in the kitchen, before a table set with dishes and cups, moving quickly between a stove and toaster.

"Your timing is excellent," she said, without looking at me. Probably she had been aware of my movements since I first stirred. "Breakfast is ready. Go sit."

Like the meek delta I'd been most of my life, I slunk to the table. However, far from eating scraps last, Maauro set a plate before me, first, and piled it with a mass of eggs, meat, and toasted bread. Then, I was poured coffee and juice. In a final bizarreness, she fixed a plate for herself and sat opposite me.

She poured coffee in her cup, then picked up a shaker. "Do you like plutonium on your eggs?"

I emitted a squeak of panic and started to get up. Maauro waved me down.

"Relax, just kidding. I rarely mess with plutonium. It's ok once it's inside of me but it takes forever to get it prepared. This is merely salt."

"Oh?" I said, simply dazed.

"Eat," she said.

Automatically, I followed her orders. But the excellent food quickly claimed my attention. I ate until I was stuffed, washing it down with coffee and juice. Maauro ate at a more moderate pace.

When I finished, I dared a look at her.

"Questions?" she asked, sipping some brightly-colored juice.

"Where to begin?" I said. "An android credited with destroying Guild installations, ships, hundreds, if not thousands of operatives, daunting entire planets full of enemies, is singing in a kitchen, making breakfast for a Guilder you should have killed when I attacked you hours ago...." I realized that I had no idea of what time it was.

"You slept the clock around," Maauro said. "It is 23.5798 hours since your "attack" on me."

"You don't think very much of me," I muttered.

To my further surprise and embarrassment, she merely smiled at my discomfort. "I can hardly rate you high among the Guild operators who have dared oppose me: Lostra, The Collector, your grandfather himself, given that you attacked me with your bare hands."

"I had nothing else"

"Then you should have waited for a better tactical opportunity," she snapped at me, much as one of my instructors would have done.

There was a long silence.

"More coffee?" Maauro offered. "I can whip up some biscuits."

I knew that if I started laughing I might never stop. "No." It occurred to me that humans usually thanked someone who made food for them, or commented favorably on the food. "Breakfast was excellent. Thank you."

A pleased expression slid over the smooth, delicate-featured face opposite me. It occurred to me that with her current appearance, she looked hardly any older than I did. She could be a *tatai*, a senior student. Yet, well over 50,000 years had passed since her creation if my information was correct.

I shook my head. It was impossible to see her as a machine. She was utterly life-like, if somewhat bizarre, in behavior. Even there, I could not tell how much of her behavior was from her adopted human culture, or her own nature. I also realized that sometime since I'd found her in the pit, I'd begun to think of her as female.

"Returning to your original observation," Maauro said. "I sing. I dance. I keep house very well, and I can still whip one million times my weight in Guild." She looked out the window at the lawn which had largely gone back to meadow. "I used to sit here many mornings, singing."

I debated whether to follow up on this proffered intimacy, which seemed out of character, in hope of gaining some advantage, but decided against it. It would be best to treat her like a Guild VIP, proud, dangerous, and conscious of status, but then how to reconcile that with the maker of breakfast? No, best for now to approach her cautiously and slowly.

"Tell me of Dusko's life after he retired from Lost Planet," Maauro said.

"I know a little," I said. "He died when I was very young. I remember him as ancient, but his eyes were alert and he was a force to be reckoned with until the end. Though you bought his life back with that wergild, he was not loved by the Guild, which preferred to ignore his existence. Still, he made a good living in trade, owning two small ships and several warehouses and businesses around the spaceport—"

"Huh, much as he did when we met," Maauro said, "though he was quite a bit wealthier before we first tangled."

"Ah, yes. Well, he took a consort who he later married, my grandmother. He had a son late in life, but my father wished nothing to do with the Guild, he was an accountant and never amounted to much. He died in a plague that struck our world after an alien ship crash-landed on it. The plague weakened grandfather's health, but he lasted long enough to get the family set up again. There was an income for my mother, who raised me until I was of age to apply for Guild membership for me. After she paid my buy-in fee, she returned to her original family and lives with them as far as I know."

"And you?"

"I followed my grandfather into the Guild," I said, shrugging. "Hard times had come to my world, and even if I'd had the interest to look at other work, there was little opportunity. Such knowledge and connections as I had, were all related to Guild. It seemed the logical choice."

"You have many broken bones," she observed, sipping her coffee.

"Guild training is harsh," I said, "and harsher for some whose patrons are either without power, or in active disgrace."

Was there sympathy in the look that she gave me? It was hard to judge with such a face.

"And now, here I am," I said, putting down the coffee cup with its strange bitter brew.

"What did you imagine would follow after you found me? That I would say, "Yes, Master?""

My face burned with embarrassment. "In truth, the odds of my finding you seemed so fantastic that I had little plan beyond that."

I toyed with the idea of sharing the Alchemy crystal with her. I had to remember that though she looked like a young woman, she was actually a quantum computer and might find a way to crack the encryption. But there was no obvious profit in it just now, and I might need something to trade her. Her offer of protection had been vague and might only extend to her own door.

"Enough for now," Maauro said. "There are things I want to do about the house and my finances. I trust you will be able to entertain yourself?"

I nodded. "I must return the digger I borrowed to find you. Then I left some of my clothes and gear in at a hotel in town."

She nodded. "Fetch them and return. I said you would be safe here, and I am good for my word."

We both stood.

"I've accessed your pocket com," Maauro said. "You'll find a list on there."

"List?"

She gave me an exasperated look, recognizable even across species. "Well, you would be a biological and need to eat multiple times a day. So, you have a shopping list for food and sundries."

"Sundries?"

"Toilet paper, hygiene products and other things I am glad to say I no longer need. If it wasn't for sex I would have happily passed on a biological existence entirely."

I looked at her. "That made it worth it?"

She gave me a questioning look. "How old are you?"

"I just reached my majority last month."

"About eighteen in human years, so you've never…"

I crossed my arms. "I do not see that this is—"

She waved a hand. "No need to feel defensive, Dear, I was a virgin for over 50,000 years myself. As you were about to say, there is no need for me to know, but you did ask."

"Sorry," I said, then desperate to change the subject. "Would you like me to do the dishes?"

"No, though I like it that you asked. Go about your errands." From nowhere I could determine, as there seemed to be no pockets in her form-fitting jumpsuit, she produced a credit card. "Use this for the shopping. It has your bio information on it and is on my account. I have allowed for you to access sufficient funds for the necessary."

"Things move quickly around you," I observed.

"My husband used to say the same. I'll see you around dinner time."

After Dassa leaves, I make my way down to the basement, considering what she has told me. My labs are below the basement level and the house AI opens the blast door for me. I walk down as lights and power go on. I was only half-joking about the plutonium. There is a small nuclear reactor down here, cooled by an underground aquifer. I extrude a power cord from my chassis, material which is more effective than any other at conveying power, though it is little thicker than a string. It gives me freedom to move about the lab while I top off on power.

On a bench in front of me is my latest version of my armspac, a weapon of my own manufacture, far beyond that of Confederate science. I'd been concerned that as time went on, my margin of superiority over

Confed weapons might diminish. It seems that the march of science has slowed in my sleep, but that is no reason for complacency. I have hours before Dassa returns. This is enough time for me to finish a rebuild and a load out. I have refined my high explosive munitions to be 3.677 times as lethal as before but at one-third the size. It would now carry fifteen high-velocity missiles, each capable of destroying a good-sized armored vehicle. I've used caseless AP ammunition before, but have dispensed with those. The replacement is a solenoid quench coilgun. This eliminates the need for propellant, but does not involve lengthy particle accelerators. I have enough anti-personnel weapons built into my body with flechettes, a plasma torch and a stunner in my finger, so I plan to optimize my arm-spac for anti-armor and anti-aircraft.

I have been working on the concept of being able to form an energy weapon temporarily within my own body. Once before, I had, in desperation, done something similar. While falling in a Jovian atmosphere, I realized my parasail needed more lift and airspeed or I'd plunge tens of thousands of miles into the heart of the gas giant. I'd formed a jet engine in my chest and used the gas giant's hydrogen as fuel for it. Since then, I wondered if I might, by using a combination of my chassis material and some external power source, funnel a blast of energy through my body, like my plasma torch but with far greater range. While my husband lived, I would take no such risks, but now I feel it is worth exploring, and not it's interdicted by my promise to Wrik.

First things first, I unpack my armspac from its secure storage and move it to a workbench. There is something comfortable in the routine of maintaining my weapon. I might even have time to get a third serverbot on line; the spares for it rest against the far wall.

CHAPTER SEVEN

I THOUGHT ABOUT WHAT HAD HAPPENED IN THE DAY AND half since I'd found Maauro as I returned the digger to the farmer, who did his best to conceal his upset over how long it had been gone. I assured him that his loan would be adjusted by the overage, then hopped into the rental for the quick flight back to Oron. I checked into the Guild operation and settled with Dirrath on the loan-sharking account, but deferred any specifics on what I was doing, or when I would be leaving. I quickly departed and checked out of my hotel.

It was still hard to believe. Despite every possible mishandling of the matter, I had at least secured some offer of protection from her. And here I was, looking at the shopping list on my com, in the grocery store in the town nearest Maauro's home.

I found that she had been very generous in covering my need for sundries. So, I found time to go into one of the few clothing stores. I outfitted myself with proper field clothes, small binoculars and a good multiplex knife. Then, because there was no way to tell into what Maauro might take us, I purchased a proper business suit, which could double as respectable evening wear. My underwear collection scarcely deserved that name anymore and I purchased replacements. I sighed, realizing I had not filled out any more and my figure was hardly different from a boys', save around the hips. In truth, I hardly needed a bra and again thought about how Maauro had looked, with her perfect figure under skin-tight clothes. I should have been more comforted by the fact that her breasts were merely shaped ceramic and metal, and the skin-tight clothes were, in fact, her skin, but there had been such physical confidence in the way she had stood, the way she moved.

Yet. I remembered the warmth and softness of her body when she had held me. Perhaps no one had held me so since my mother. Even she would hardly have done so after I passed my seven-year. How could that soft body shrug off weapon fire and operate at such terrific speed? Maauro had lived as a biological and in that she had been a fool. I would change my body for hers in an instant. The thought of the power and independence, oh to be so free!

"Will that be all, Miss?" the shop owner said.

I drew myself back to the here and now. I nodded, then remembering human courtesy. "Thank you."

"We don't get many nonhumans in here," he said, though his manner was friendly. "You are Denlenn?"

"Dua-Denlenn," I corrected.

"Yes, I should have remembered, the eyes."

"There are other differences as well. We must have had a common ancestor, but it was long ago."

"I've never had the pleasure of meeting one of your people before. What brings you this far from the spaceport?"

I considered telling him to mind his own business, but if I had learned one thing about humans, it was that their curiosity was better satiated with a lie than fed with evasion.

"Family business," I replied. "We had a connection with some property in the area."

My vague reply seemed to satisfy him. He tapped the credit chip against the transfer box and recorded the sale. "Here you go," he added, handing me the package. "I included a list of all the best restaurants and local attractions with your receipt."

"Thank you, though I doubt I will be here long enough to make use of it." Before he could ask more, I swept up my packages and slipped between two rather matronly females. Minutes later, I was in the car, hoping the cold packs in the grocery bags would keep working until I got everything to Maauro's place. I made a mental note to go to supermarkets after other stores in the future. There was always something to learn on any given day, my Guild instructors had said, though perhaps they'd had less prosaic things in mind.

Dassa returns in the late afternoon, with her small satchel of belongings, a case and the impressive results of her spending spree. She has made full use of the credit I gave her on clothes and other necessities. Give a Dua-Denlenn a centimeter and they will steal your ruler.

We speak casually over dinner. She is aware of my interrogation's purposes and is forthcoming only about information on the Pale Ones and the Guild. About herself, she remains cagey.

After dinner, Dassa elects to retire early. Like many people who have endured a long period of high stress, she is far more exhausted than she realizes. I again clean up, then walk out of the house to watch the stars come out. I'd made fun of Dassa's lack of planning, but now realize that, like her, I have no plan for even the next day. Since I'd reactivated, I'd made arrangements to leave at a moment's notice, but no destination, or purpose, has yet occurred to me.

I have no desire to resume my service with Confederate Military Intelligence. Wrik and I had been forced into CMI with threats and the promise of recognition of me as a life form deserving of "sentient rights." Candace Deveraux's organization had been based out of Star Central, so there was no way of telling where it might end up in the soon to come fracturing of the Confederacy. I have no allegiance to any of it and, though my husband had been a human and I look like one, it was not automatic that I identify with them. In truth, the few true Denlenn I'd met attract me more than the humans, Dua-Denlenn, or another species of the Confederacy.

I'd given some thought to resurrecting Lost Planet, but I have no network and the driving force for me there, had been my desire to use my powers to help those in danger. But that desire has dimmed since then. Everyone I know has passed away and I can muster no enthusiasm, or interest, in their progeny. Biologicals are very attached to descendants, but I have no such instincts. Wrik and I had friends from our time on Evenfall, though in his last years we had become insular, but again most have passed during my sleep.

So, what do I want to do with myself, I think, with uncharacteristic indecisiveness. Perhaps I should commit to exploring and take my ship beyond the borders of the Confederacy? My mind circles that thought. The one great mystery left to me is what had happened to the species that created me. They had utterly disappeared in the many millennia since I fought in the Infestor Wars. While some sign of the Infestors had been found, and this led me to believe that the telempathic and insectoid Infestors had been defeated ages ago, nothing was known of my Creators. Might I find them and perhaps even other artificial lifeforms like myself who were sentient and aware, to share my existence with?

This promises a direction for me, but there are dangers. I'd been made for war and well-built though I am, the bitter truth remains that I was an attrition unit, created to relieve my Creators of the duty of close combat. My Creators might not welcome a self-aware machine, who considered herself a free and independent being. This is something I had never considered before. I would never again tolerate being treated as property; in that regard I was prepared to battle even my Creators.

I mull over my choices. While I think at many times of the speed of a biological, this is not a calculation, but an emotion-laden decision about the course of my future life, and cannot be processed the same way.

I decide to go for a walk in my woods, those same woods I'd strolled through so many times, arm-in-arm with Wrik. We'd planted an orchard down by the stream and I find myself under its apple trees. All has run to wild disorder as the maintenance service had no orders about the fields beyond the house. I should have arranged for someone to gather the fruit and plant the fields, but I had been in despair, and even for a quantum computer it seemed, grief could unseat reason.

Still, I see the fairy statues, wind-chimes and stone animals. There are secret spots where small waterfalls gurgle as some local equivalent of a beaver damned part of the stream. The starfills nod over the stream, their long, soft, strands of bell-shaped flowers glowing softly in the night. Above all, the stars, my oldest companions, still burn. Wrik had once called the night sky my private jewel box and I do regard them with a certain sense of possessiveness. They are the only things unchanged since the time of my creation.

CHAPTER SEVEN

So, I wile away my time, visiting the places on my property. The nearest house is miles away, but beyond the Marinal home's few nightlights, I can see the lights of town, closer than they had been before in this valley. When we'd first arrived, it had been more of a farm community, with a railhead to take produce to the bigger towns. Perhaps I would take Dassa, and visit tomorrow, to see the changes first hand.

Somehow my solitary walk in the wood has, if not lightened my mood, at least dimmed my pain and loneliness. Perhaps this is the emotional state of melancholy, something I haven't felt since I'd been in a human body. My soul feels more at peace, then at any moment since Wrik died, as I turn for the path up from the stream on the valley floor.

The same instinct that brought me awake the night of the compound attack, roused me now. I lay still on my bed, eyes darting around the room. Could Maauro's movements have awakened me? No, the android moved soundlessly, unless the surface betrayed her greater than human weight and this house was made for her. Someone else was here. I felt a sense of oppression, a weight on my chest, the air of the house had a strange smell, even the colors seemed off.

I slid out of my bed. It seemed to be my fate to forever be surprised in my underwear. In two steps, I was across the room and grabbed my pistol, feeling the reassuring coolness of the weapon Maauro let me keep. Clarity came with it. Maauro would have long since reacted to any intruder. She was gone. The question for me was for how long and how far? I needed to play for time.

The window seemed the best bet. I didn't have time for clothes and just opened it. I looked out quickly from the second-floor window and saw nothing. I swung a long leg out the window and the moonlight cascaded down on my paleness. Whether it was that, or someone had been watching the window, I felt, rather than heard, the buzz of a stunner. My leg and right side went numb. The pistol tumbled from my nerveless hand onto the metal roof where it clattered to the hedge below. Fortunately, I tumbled back into the room.

I lay gasping on the floor and fighting my inert body, but I could only get my back up against the footboard of my bed before the door to the room was kicked in and three figures strode in as if they had nothing to fear.

I stared up at them in helpless anger. I'd only seen their like on video, but there was no question that these were the Pale Ones who warred with the Guild. They were as similar as if they'd come from the same mold, pale with bald craniums and small-featured faces, male, if the lack of breasts meant anything. They wore dark, form-fitting uniforms with a faint iridescence about them but no insignia I could see. Each held a short, ugly weapon with a large bore in both hands. They stared back at me with eyes that were bulging, milky-white from side to side, as mine were blue.

"Pale ones," I hissed.

The second one, evidently the leader, responded. "So your kind call the Ederi."

"My kind," I demanded, "Confed, or Dua-Denlenn?"

"Guild," the alien replied, but with an unmistakable virulence.

"What is Guild to you and you to Guild?" I asked. The numbness was wearing off a little, to be replaced with the ache of a stunshot. I gritted my teeth, knowing worse was to come.

"Death," he replied.

"I'm nothing," I yelled. "I'm no one. Why do you pursue me, even here?"

"Alchemy," he said.

"A name, nothing more," I said.

The alien made a curious bobbing gesture with its head: anger, humor, what? "You go from High Guild to High Guild. You carry secrets. Tell. You carry data. Give. We let you live."

I didn't believe it for a second. Where was Maauro? Had she been destroyed already? If I was on my own, maybe I could bargain for my life with the Alchemy crystal?

"Don't be fool," the Pale One said. "Your own sold you to us for their lives. You carry data. Where?"

The Baron must have been taken and made some trade for his life. I wondered how long he'd lasted afterward. I couldn't blame him. I'd have done the same in his place.

"No help for you here," the leader said, "your choice, die in pain, maybe live."

I threw the vilest curse in Dua that I could at him. He gestured at his men. As they closed on me, I willed my right hand to close on the slim, flexible dagger in my underwear and tried to get to my feet.

They were fast, and I didn't see the blow that dropped me onto the floor, the knife ripped from my hand. A foot struck me in the face and my arms were pinioned. The leader reached down and grabbed my right nipple and twisted. I screamed. The Pale Ones tore at what little I was wearing and for a few seconds I thought rape was their intention, but their pawing of my body stopped when they discovered the flat pouch I had strapped under my panties. I was shoved down as they stood. They threw away the Confederate credits I'd hid there and concentrated on the two data crystals. They held a reader over the crystals.

"One encrypted," the leader said. "How do we read?"

"I don't know. I don't have the key."

He gestured toward me and the others piled kicks on me.

"I don't know, damn you. I don't."

He studied me as one would an insect on a pin. "Believe you. Kill her."

The others stood back, the ugly short weapons came up.
The wall behind them exploded.

Something impinges on my consciousness as I start up the path. There is virtually no birdsong and what there is comes from a distance. Woodland animals are gone as well. What had happened? I change color to flat black, head to toe, and speed to the top of the hill so I can see my home. I flatten when I cross the crest of the hill, and my limbs resemble a spider's for a few seconds. Once I am at the military crest of the hill and cannot be skylined, I reconfigure to bipedal, moving from cover to cover.

Nothing appears amiss at the house, yet I am more convinced by the millisecond that something is wrong. I feel a distortion around, no, over the house. I override my standard sensor settings and pour additional processing power into my sensors. I dare an active sensor pulse for .00015 seconds. The length should be insufficient for any Confed tech to register me.

The sensor burst shows me what I fear. There is a ship hanging over my house. Its configuration is alien and unknown, but the shape is that of a scout, or a light bomber. The material of the hull absorbs or scatters standard sensors, even light is bent around the hull, though this is imperfect. Now that I am aware, I can detect occlusion errors caused by the bending of light rays of the night sky.

I hook up to the house AI on the minimum setting, a frequency and modulation I hope they cannot detect. Only minimal information is transmitted, but I learn what I need. Dassa still lives and there are three intruders in the house, clustered about her. I assume she is being interrogated, possibly tortured. Another figure is in the garden area. He carries multiple weapons and is watching the road to the house. Given the size of the intruders, there can only be one, at most two, in the aircraft.

Rage hits me. My home is being violated. A guest under my protection may be harmed. How dare they! I will not forgive this.

I move forward in normal speed, not wishing to attract the attention of the aircraft. A biological, or even a humanform combat robot, would instantly register on the enemy's instruments. But I am no crude HCR. Externally, I run cooler than any animal if I wish. My sensor array paints every stick and leaf so that I generate no more sound than is in the ambient, as I advance. I amp up my ECM. Now I am as invisible to eye, ear and instrument.

I formulate my plan of attack. Once I start, there may be only seconds to save Dassa.

A scream sounds. It takes all my resolve not to attack immediately. I am not in optimum position yet, but I pick up my pace as much as I dare. I order the house AI to slowly open a window.

Finally, I reach position. I plunge forward, accelerating at my best speed. The alien outside does not even have time to react before I literally run through him, shearing him into two pieces and smashing his skull, to be certain of the kill. I leap through the open window, bound up to the second floor and crash through the wall.

Dassa is down, her body and face showing abuse. I simultaneously decapitate the two gunmen starting to aim at her. 0.024587 seconds pass as I turn to the remaining alien. He has begun to react to my intrusion, which is good, as it will take the weapon off Dassa at .05 seconds after my entry. I have leisure to study the alien, as its eyes, already wide, widen further in reaction. I fire another sensor pulse which shows me the internal arrangement of his body. A millisecond's study, shows me enough of his structure for me to be sure of the low damage kill I need for the remainder of my plan.

I stiffen my right fingers, and slam them like a spear into what I judge is his circulatory pump. My left hand, palm-blades extended shears through his gun hand so the weapon falls to the floor, unfired. 1.2193 seconds have passed since I broke through the wall. I hold the dead third alien at arms-length and turn to Dassa.

"Can you move?" I demand. "Your life, at least, depends on it."

She lurches to her feet with pleasing alacrity. "What? How?"

"Silence. Follow orders. Follow me." Holding the alien, I run back through the destroyed wall and leap downstairs, the dead alien under my arm. Dassa follows down the stairs, quickly for a biological, but with agonizing slowness for me. As soon as she reaches me I say, "Count to ten. Run outside with this alien on your back, then fall to the ground. Make it look like you are struggling."

Before she can slow me with questions, I am gone, tossing the dead alien on her back and racing for the basement. The alien at the fighter controls may, or may not, be monitoring his brethren from above, but it is only prudent to believe so. He will react in escalating anxiety and perhaps violence, over the next fifteen to thirty seconds. Dassa's theatrical escape attempt and her battle with the corpse may give me the additional time I need.

I order the AI to open all doors between me and my armspac. Thank whatever Deity there is that I reconditioned my weapon this afternoon. The careful habits of a professional warrior may save us. I snatch the weapon up, deactivate the safeties, spin on my heel and flash up the stairs. Going through the exterior wall will save me .29 seconds so I slam through, somersaulting so that I face the sky.

I blast the stealthy scoutship with HEAT missiles and a shot from the solenoid quench coilgun in anti-tank mode. The ship above staggers and flame bursts from it. The pilot is no tyro. He hits the dying ship's thrusters, but it only buys him a thousand feet before another HEAT takes him in the tailpipe, lighting the sky with a brilliant explosion. I track the wreckage as it falls toward a small lake further up the valley.

I run around the house to find Dassa on the ground under the alien's body. She had cleverly kept it between her and the ship in their mock battle. I kneel beside the injured youth.

"How badly are you harmed?" I ask, even as I scan her. The damage is painful, but confined to soft tissue injuries.

"I've had worse. We need to get out of here." She has rolled the dead alien over and is tugging at a pouch on its belt. "But not before I get back what is mine." She removes two data crystals, from the dead alien, trying to conceal them from me. I mark this for later discussion.

I scan at full power above us, while hacking into any network I can. I do not detect anything near, but the stealth technology worries me. Already, fire, police and military are reacting to the explosions.

"Go upstairs and tend to your wounds. I will dispose of the bodies."

"We need to go," she says, her blue eyes fastened on me. I can see her shivering from a combination of pain, shock and the night's chill.

"Go inside, young one," I reply, making my voice gentle. "Shower the blood off, then meet me downstairs."

"Aren't we going to run?"

I shake my head. "That was a long-range shuttle. Whatever ship sent it should be standing well off this planet, even if it has stealth technology. Such technology drains power quickly and is usually used for short periods. I use some versions of it myself, though I grant that this is beyond what I have ever seen before.

"Besides," I add, looking upward at the bright point of light tracking across the sky, "the authorities are moving in now."

She follows the direction of my eyes. "What is it?"

"Federal police in an old Confed Marauder, doubtless sent because of the explosions and crash. Unusual to have a patrol up this way, but the blast will have shown up on a satellite if nothing else. These mountains will be crawling with police, rescue and reporters in hours. I do not judge the danger of remaining here to be great. The unexpected loss of their scoutship, and the arousal of planetary authority will make them cautious. Whoever sent that ship, was hunting for you. They do not know that I am here, or what I am."

Dassa massages an abused breast. "How can you be so sure?"

"They would be mad to send such a small and poorly-armed team of mere biologicals after me. As for the rest, you may have to accept that I am more knowledgeable in tactical matters than you are.

"Now go. What I do next will be unpleasant, but I do not wish to become involved with any governmental authorities of any sort. Certainly, I do not want them to find Pale Ones here. That will raise questions and doubtless lead to our detention."

"They called themselves the Ederi," Dassa says.

I mull that over as she disappears into the house. I order the house AI and the serverbots to begin repairs to the exterior walls first, then proceed to clean up the bodily fluids sprayed inside my home. Rage still burns in me at the thought of my home being violated: the living room where we sat by the fire, the guest room where our friends stayed. These are sacred places to me, and the Pale Ones have brought violence into them. War now lies between us for this act. They will rue this day.

For now, the practical displaces the future. I gather up fragments of the dead Ederi from the yard, as well as its weapon. I extrude plastic bags from my body for the two bodies outside, and then carry the corpses and weapons down to my basement lab. I have machinery enough to reduce the bodies to ash quickly. I study the weapons while the kiln reduces the first alien. The weapon is well made, with an energy gun, a 5mm caseless ammunition slug-thrower and a stunner that has been snapped on. Nothing about is it superior to what I have, but I elect to keep it, in case I can ascertain something from it with greater study. Perhaps I can learn something of its origins from the metal itself. The others I will destroy, with the bodies of the aliens.

I make more trips to complete my grisly task. The house serverbots have sealed the outer damage where I plunged out of the building. They will have it repaired with wood by midday and proceed to interior repairs. I'm glad I took some time to get a third serverbot on line. I send it to the basement to get more materials for the repairs. The others will spray chemicals on all surfaces that can be cleaned and dispose of those that cannot. In two day's time, there will be no sign that a deadly struggle occurred here. This pleases me; I've always kept a neat and tidy home.

With the bodies of the enemy gone, I cleanse myself then check on Dassa. I pause in the kitchen to make a pot of tea and find some honey and add a few cookies I thaw from the freezer. She has had a rough evening.

CHAPTER EIGHT

AT MAAURO'S SUGGESTION AND TO MY OWN SURPRISE, after the tea and cookies, I succeeded in getting a few hours sleep in a different guestroom. I awoke to find the sun well up and streaming through the window. The android was beside my bed, her curious multi-circular eyes seeming to study me. I wanted to touch my regained pouch, back inside my underwear, to make sure the crystals were still present, but that would merely call attention to them. I'd also recovered all the money the Ederi had thrown about the floor, washing their blood off the bills while I was in the shower, doing the same for myself.

I sat up slowly, surprised to not be in worse pain. "I take it that I have you to thank for the fact that I can move at all?"

Maauro's sideling look at me was enigmatic. "I injected anti-inflammatories and other necessary meds. About your face, I shall leave that to your own talents with makeup."

"You may be disappointed by the results," I returned, as I stretched. "I'm not a Guild doxy and had no money for such things on my own."

Maauro sighed. "Very well, I will do what I can. We should wait some additional hours before leaving. The police and military are all over this area as I predicted. Likely because your local Guild contacts have been exciting them with news of possible Ederi threats.

I nodded. "They said as much when I arrived. Doubtless it accounts for the quick appearance of the military aircraft last night."

"There is a news blackout," Maauro said, "and they have cordoned off the lake area where pieces of the ship came down. The police have already been here and questioned me. I told them that my visiting young friend made a mistake with my farm tractor and damaged the exterior wall of the house, backing into it and then pulling some of it out."

I raised an eyebrow at having been nominated for home-wrecker. "Wait! What did they make of your rejuvenated state?"

A trace of sadness stole over her face. "They saw me as I had been when I lived here at the end with Wrik, age appropriate for my role of lonely old widow. I told them that I'd returned recently to find the farm had become too much for me, and that I was moving to the city today with my new caregiver. It practically made them run off."

I looked at her curiously. "Why?"

"The old are not wanted in any culture. They cast obligations on the impatient young, who flee such ties."

I nodded. "Sensible.

The look Maauro gave me was not friendly, and I realized that I'd made a mistake and upset her. "I, myself, was raised to respect my elders."

The dark look abated somewhat. "Good recovery," she said, coolly.

"What then do you want to do?" I asked, grimacing. My wounds started paining me. Maauro noticed this and motioned me to be still. She pressed her fingertip against my arm and after a second the pain receded and my breathing became easier.

The android sat back and looked at me with her complicated, huge eyes. "That is a more difficult question than you imagine. Before you showed up, I had no reason to stir. I could see no purpose to it and, unlike a biological, I'm not constructed, either mentally or physically, to fritter time away. Then you came and trouble followed on your heels. I could be ungrateful for that, but I'm not. Someday, when I know you better, I may tell you why.

"I am now free of networks and other attachments. Perhaps it is time to indulge myself."

"In what way?"

Maauro laughed. "What, are you impatient with the musings of the elderly? Do you have an airbus to catch?"

I squirmed, but it seemed that no violence was to follow, and her irritation was feigned.

"There is something I have wondered about," Maauro continued, leaning backward, and putting an arm across her knee. "What happened to the race that created me? Could there be other sentient AIs like myself out there? Wrik used to tease me about that. He claimed to be afraid of losing me to some handsome male robot.

"It seems to me that finding my origins is a worthy goal. What overtook the Creators? How could so mighty a race disappear from spacetime with so little trace? Did they give birth to other true AIs? Might I find a family like me out there?"

"Did you never discuss looking for your Creators with Trigardt?" I asked.

Annoyance drifted across her face. "When you refer to my husband, you may call him, Mr. Trigardt, or you can use his first name."

I raised my hands. "I intended nothing."

After a moment, she continued. "We did, but not with any urgency. You must remember that I have time. I knew my life with my husband would be short by my standards, no matter what I did. So, I concentrated on my marriage.

"Besides, there was so little to go on. I remember the world on which I came to be. I remember yellow-orange skies and the sighing sound of the wind in the cliffs for which I named myself. But I, myself, scrubbed my memory of any detail that could help an enemy locate that or any other Creator world. I am a quantum computer; I was very efficient and it was a prime program of mine."

"Yet," I said, "some things are obvious. They were bipedal humanoids and used worlds similar to ours."

"Yes, but the Infestors knew that already, so that was no loss of security. The Creators original homeworld was lost ages ago, when they moved out of an area nearer the galactic core. That which they called their homeworld locally, was an adopted place, but no less loved by them for not being their original home.

"Though, unlike their other machines, I am sentient and have free choice, that prime program persists. It is the last of the old M-7 programs that still operates within me. I could perhaps fight it, but it is such a primary program I was worried about irreparable damage. Besides, it seemed pointless to risk it. If there was any sign of the Creators in known space, the Confederate species would have encountered them long before I was recovered."

"Was nothing known of them by Confederate Military Intelligence?"

Maauro nodded. "Excellent thinking. As soon as Candace Deveraux learned of my existence, she launched a determined search for the world of my origin. She never found anything of note, at least nothing I was able to then extract from her databases."

"So you have nothing to go on?"

"Nothing much. I learned what there was to know on Kandalor, before we left there. It was the scene of a major battle and little more. Neither side had a colony there, but both were moving in force. What survived into our time, was not useful to this question.

"But, there is one place I can think of that information might be found."

"Where is that?" I asked.

"You have heard of the Enshar?"

I shrug. "A little. I've never seen one. Some disaster almost wiped them out."

Maauro nods. "Enshar is the home of the oldest of the Confed races, what is left of them. You're right, the Enshari were nearly destroyed by, well the word, ghost, is thrown about, but it was something like that, a nearly god-like being entombed beneath their capitol city. Like me, it was something from ancient days, though far earlier than my time. It used some form of mental power to annihilate all life on the planet."

"Yes," I interrupted her history lesson. "It was later destroyed by... by..."

"...By Captains Rainhell and Fenaday. I never met him, but she was... well, like a mother to me in some ways."

"I read of her in the history books," I replied. "She was a powerful female and controlled much. I would give much to be like her."

Maauro gave me a curious glance. "You might be surprised by how little she felt she controlled anything in her rather turbulent life.

"But no matter, the Enshari were the historians of the known space, collecting legends, artifacts, and specimens. Their own expansion into the universe ended long before the Confederacy and they had few colonies, but on their homeworld stood great universities and museums, saving things long lost elsewhere.

"They would have been an old race, even before I was made. I know they did not meet my Creators; that much information survived the fall of their world. But even with resettlement of their planet by the few survivors of their species, most of what was in those institutions, particularly in the capitol, was never recovered.

"Still, I might find clues in those warehouses and exhibition halls that eluded them."

I considered. Enshar was far away, almost to the other side of the Old Confederacy, far from any place the Ederi had struck, further than most beings would journey in a lifetime.

"And what of me?" I felt the shiver of *schadenteer* in me. The pale ones believed that I knew of Alchemy; I had seen too much of the fury and rigor of their assault on the Guild to believe I would be forgotten. Without help from Maauro, I could not hope to outrun them long.

Her look at me was cool and measuring. "Your grandfather was a mercenary old bastard, but I was able to rely on him, particularly with Lilith, a complicated and difficult matter for me. I will be wandering from star to star, on dead moons, in ancient cities, perhaps departing the maps of known space entirely. If you wish, you may accompany me. I do not recommend it."

"Are you so wealthy that you can do this?" I demanded.

"No," she admitted. "My wealth would have sufficed for any life I envisioned for myself here, planet bound, but to run from star to star in the deep dark…no. I will have to "make a living," as you biologicals say. However, I learned a great deal about trading both from your grandfather and Jaelle."

"I know many things about gems," I said quickly. "I can be of use in the trade of precious gems and metals."

Maauro nodded. "We did often trade in those and other luxury items. Very well, I shall take you on as an apprentice. Your room and board will be covered, and we shall work out a suitable salary based on our profits and my needs."

It was a good deal, even by the hard-bargaining standards of the Guild. In truth, the machine was being generous to me, either through indifference to wealth, or perhaps human kindness. The more she saw me as a helpless child, the more it seemed to trigger this response. Was it… no surely it could not be a presentation of a maternal instinct? Still, it could benefit me. I had to keep this in mind. My life certainly depended on it.

"What do we do? When we can move?" I repeated.

"We break contact with the enemy by moving into town near my starship for now."

"Your starship," I said in surprise. "You still have the *Stardust*?"

"Yes. Sentiment I suppose, though we did lease her out to various commercial concerns before I decommissioned her. I should have sold her, but couldn't bring myself to do so. I found one of the commercial concerns made unauthorized use of her during my... convalescence. This may serve us, as she is spaceworthy now and can be ready for extended voyaging soon."

"It will not pain me to see this world fading into memory," I said.

"It will pain me," she replied, or was it a reply? I didn't think she was aware of me just then.

Again, came the sidelong glance. "It will also pain me to travel with one of the Guild."

I put my feet on the floor. "If it comforts you, the Guild may be well on its way to extinction. Two of the houses I have been to, have fallen. For all I know, the Pale Ones may have accounted for the local element before coming here."

Maauro shook her head; the mane of glossy black hair that cascaded to her waist shimmered as if it was fluid. I noticed she no longer wore the yellow-orange fabric that had tied in her hair in an elaborate bow. Today, it was an expensive, gem-encrusted, gold piece that would twinge the fingers of any Guild thief.

"I have been monitoring all dataflows," she said. "Such an act would have left traces, and indeed might have alerted you or me. There is no indication that they struck anywhere but here. Now, why is that, I wonder? All this trouble for a mere Guild novice? Is that all you are, or is there more to you than meets the eye?"

I quickly reviewed my selection of plausible lies and opted for silence. The android's eyes flicked to my belly where a slight bulge marked the locations of the Alchemy crystal and my uncle's one. I tried not to twitch.

Maauro turned away. "I promised you protection under my roof. I must apologize that my promise was made mockery of, by the Ederi. So then, gather your things, and we will take your aircar into the city. We will see if the Confed Milnet, what is left of it on this world, has located any danger. Then, we shall see about the first stage of this new life we are setting out on.

"However, before we go much of anywhere, we will need to do something about that face of yours."

"Sorry I wasn't able to cover it up more," I replied. "They had my arms."

"I imagine you are. While you were out, I used cold compression on the worst of the bruises, but you have a profoundly black eye. Fortunately, not much else shows below the hairline. Go shower and shampoo, and I will see what I can do."

Grumbling, I made my way into the bathroom. It felt good to stand in the warm spray of the water, so long as I kept it off my worse bruises and abused nipple.

"Use the conditioner," Maauro called, from the other room.

"What's that?"

"Light-green bottle on the shower caddy, a palmful rubbed into your hair and rinsed out after a minute, will do."

I followed the directions and emerged smelling fresher and feeling healthier. Clothes were laid out for me on the bed, and I put them on, switching my pouch to my new pants.

"Sit," she gestured at a chair. On a nearby table, lay a selection of brushes and small ornate boxes with lids. She generated a flow of warm air out of the palm of one hand and played it through my hair until it was dry.

"You have pretty good skin, but you treat it roughly. Well, you've had help lately. This skin cream will restore some moisture and help with healing. I added some topical anesthetic as well."

I had to admit that it felt soothing and refreshing to have her run her fingers with the soothing cream over my face.

She switched back to my hair and combed it out. No one had touched me this way since my childhood. The feelings it generated were peculiar, comforting and a little embarrassing at the same time. Then she wrapped a towel around my upper shoulders.

"We'll have to find something nice for your hair," Maauro said.

"I notice that you always wear a yellow something in yours."

She nodded, as she ran her hands through my hair. I felt a slight sensation of it being cut, though she'd held no scissors. *Well, why be surprised by that?* I assumed she had some cutting surface in her hand, yet no hair fell on my face. Perhaps it was being whisked away even as she cut it.

"Shortly after I met Wrik, when we were first becoming friends, he bought me a beautiful length of a natural-silk ribbon. I was entranced by the color of it, and he spent a rather outlandish amount of money to buy it for me. For all my ability as a computer, I wasn't that practical about credits back then."

"You were wearing a ribbon yesterday, when you made me breakfast. Today, it is a gemmed hairpiece, yet still yellow."

"Yes, I eventually wanted a more sophisticated look. Hard though it might be to believe, when I was first recovered, I looked about your age. Gradually, I altered my matrix to appear a bit older, even picked back up two inches of height."

"Huh? You grew?"

"More a case of, I repaired. I was blown up during the asteroid attack that stranded me. I was originally forty percent bigger than I am now. A lot of that was ablative mass designed to absorb impact. Later, I lost an arm fighting the Guild. When eventually I could repair that, I was able to add enough chassis material to regain two inches of height."

"You didn't always look like a girl?" I said, startled.

"No. I decided to change my basic matrix as my appearance was too frightening to biologicals. I came up with an image from Wrik's ship computer. It was a game simulation."

"Ah, that explains the idealized female image."

"Stylized as well, hence the eyes and figure. Originally, I could not change this, as my malleability program threatened my stability. Later, I acquired greater flexibility, but I still dare not change my matrix too much. My ability to hold a firm image of what and who I am, gives me form."

She laughed lightly at the expression on my face.

"Anyway, I opted for a yellow-gold hairpiece, it's made from my chassis material but the gems in it were a gift from Wrik."

"He seems to have been a generous man," I ventured.

She paused. It seemed I had surprised her.

"He was," she said, finally, "in many ways, large and small."

I wanted to ask her if it hurt to talk about him, but that ice seemed too thin to dare. But compelled by my odd mood I said. "I have never had anyone like that in my life."

"Not even your parents?" she asks.

I stare at her, perplexed. "I guess it's very different," I finally offer.

She smiles a little sadly. "What would I know? I never had parents. Wrik was close to his mother, though, with our travels they did not see each other often. Of his father," her tone turned grim, "the less said of him, the better."

Maauro removed the towel. "Now let us see what can be done with your face."

"Not much to work with there."

"I am not a proper judge of such things," she says, "but your features are regular, and I think males would find you attractive."

She began to run a light brush over my face with something called a shimmer powder. Then she plied my face with a variety of brushes and pigments.

"I know…. you are an artificial being, but it seems to me that emotionally you react like a human."

"I suppose so. I lived as one for years. And you could say that my basic imprinting was human, though I picked up some of my more feminine characteristics from Jaelle Tekala, a Nekoan."

Maauro takes my chin in her hand, which is warm and soft to my surprise, she gently presses a tube on my lips. "Another difference between your kind and Denlenn—lips."

"Are they so useful?" I ask, raising my eyebrows.

"Ask the next person you kiss," she said, finishing with the tube.

Again, I blush. Kissing was something Dua-Denlenn picked up from humans, whose lips are more sensitive than ours. It had never caught on with Denlenn, as they had only a suggestion of lips, but the practice spread among the more erotically curious of my kind.

Maauro studied her handiwork. "This will pass. Your coppery skin allowed me to better conceal the black eye. It should keep anyone from noticing, except at close range in daylight." She moved out of the way of the mirror.

I couldn't stop a gasp of surprise at the sight in that mirror. Her ministrations had dramatically reduced any bruises, but the makeup caused them to vanish. More, my eyes were accentuated by a soft, deeper blue that made them stand out in a fashion I'd never imagined, and concealed any damage above the eye. My skin below seemed flawlessly smooth. Even where the upper cheekbone had been blackened, there was only the suggestion of darkness. She had given a little color to my lips, enough only to call them out. My hair, which had always been simply cut, had grown longer since I arrived on Evenfall, and I'd lacked time or skill to tend to it. This had given Maauro a chance to cut it in a more sophisticated look with the hair swooping across my forehead and a soft, wavy fashion elsewhere. I was reminded of the higher-class ladies I had seen walking so elegantly through my uncle's tower.

I stared at the girl in the mirror. "This is me? What life might I have led if I'd been born to others?" Realizing I had voiced that aloud, I avoided Maauro's eyes. "Thank you."

"You're welcome," she said. "I cannot have a companion who looked like an unsuccessful ruffian. It would attract attention in any event." She stood and headed for the door, then stopped. "Keep the cosmetics and the brushes. I'll show you to use them as we go along.

"Now to breakfast…"

CHAPTER NINE

THE MORNING BROUGHT MORE INVESTIGATORS AND MILITARY TO THE area. This was a mixed blessing. I could not investigate anything in person, but so many people, from so many different forces: police, rangers, ESDF and Confederate military, could not keep to proper data discipline. From the communications of the various parties, I learn that the elderly cruiser, CSS San Giorgio made a contact out in the orbit of the Pascat, the next planet out in the system. The cruiser chased the contact for several hours before being outpaced in an asteroid field. Visual detection had not been made, as was usual with the vessels of the Ederi.

This provides me with two pieces of information. I thought it unlikely that more than one vessel would have been assigned to deal with Evenfall's Guild, though how a race like the Ederi has such detailed knowledge of the Guild's TOE and Order of Battle eludes me. The fact the vessel had broken orbit around Evenfall meant we were likely to be unmolested for a while. However, they had not immediately fled the area after the loss of their assault team. Such persistence does not bode well for the longer term. A ship such as theirs could slip up on the planet, even with the defense forces alerted. Worse, they might return with reinforcements, and an entry of multiple stealthy vessels could not be deterred by the few forces based here.

I could stand on Evenfall and give battle. My own life means little to me. Yet, I know that Wrik would disapprove. There is also Dassa to be considered, I had promised the young Dua-Denlenn protection and she has already been tortured under my roof. To hold my ground might be possible for me, but the prospects of her surviving, are poor. So, it seems that basic military tactics still apply. When encountering a superior force, break contact and relocate.

I contact a realtor and put the house itself up for sale. They see only the image of a little old lady on their screen, and I refer all matters to a law firm that Wrik and I used before. It is tedious to work with biologicals to arrange power of attorney and to reactivate the secret accounts we hid money in when we last ran Lost Planet. I had long foreseen the coming civil strife that would sunder the great wartime Confederacy into chunks of its more powerful constituent species and moved our funds and data accordingly. Most have survived my decades of negligence, though of course the data files are dated.

Finally done with the process of extracting myself from properties, I arranged for all the funds to be placed in accounts, credit and specie, that would be universally recognized. I went down to my lab. Again, I had orders for the serverbots to pack material and equipment. I started *the process of shutting down the nuclear reactor I had built in the basement and lowering into its containment "grave." Super cooled liquids, and metals the Confederacy did not know, would keep it safe through the coming centuries. Once I sealed the camouflaged doors, no one would likely detect the labs unless they were looking for them. In an hour, automatics will drop a layer of dirt in to the passageway so it appears merely normal, compacted earth.*

Another call summons trucks and movers to the house, though we will be gone before they arrive. I did not wish to have to change back into the appearance of the elderly, Yuki Travers, so I reactivate the persona of, Aurelia Toyama, a cover I had used with Confederate Intelligence. Further judicious hacking, made me the granddaughter of the "original" Aurelia persona, created after we landed on Stauver. For a few moments, I wonder what had become of the teens who had befriended me there, so long ago.

Quickly, I set up the legal fiction of Aurelia as a distant 2nd cousin to Wrik's wife, now charged with winding down her affairs. My aged appearance as the widow Travers is now consigned to history.

I head upstairs to the room I have not entered since I removed Wrik's body from it. Even now, this is difficult. Though I do not breathe as such, I find that I still feel like I must "catch my breath" as I open the door and walk past our bed. I fight for control, knowing that the man who loved me, would not want me in such pain. My sweet Wrik had done everything he ever could to keep me safe and happy. That thought eases the pain, the knot in my chest that cannot be there.

I look around at my home, no, my house, it had been a home when it held us both, now it was only a structure. It occurs to me that in some respects I am luckier than a grieving human. They keep physical mementoes of their travels in the hope of remembering the moments of their life together. I have total recall of every moment of our life. I, myself, had few physical possessions. Wrik had more, and they surround me, his favorite things: a knife collection, a model of Shasti Rainhell's old starship the Sidhe, as well as paintings and souvenirs of the various worlds we had been on.

A sigh escapes me. I formulate a list of those possessions of particular significance to Wrik and a list of everything he had ever given me as a gift. The server bots would begin packing them now, interrupting the house repairs. The emotions I had developed as a sentient AI, and which had exploded in me as a human, were in full control now. Illogical it might be for me to waste space and fuel to lift and shift what would be the supercargo of my married life, but I was not going to leave it behind. The universe did not exist for me to lead a logical life.

I walk over to the big bay window we'd put in together and consider the vale where we spent the last decades of our marriage. Unlike Wrik, I rarely felt an attachment to a location, but I find myself reluctant to turn away. My biological body had perished long before we moved here, but this was the last place that we walked, talked, caressed and kissed. It was the last place that I had been, or might ever be, a married woman. Now, I leave it as a widow, seeking a new life and possibilities. Indeed, I already feel like a different being, as if some part of my journey has completely finished.

I sigh, and my hand rests between my breasts where the cut gem that is all that remains of Wrik is secured. I bid a silent farewell to our green little valley and turn to face the uncertain future.

I pack a few things that I wish to keep with me in a small bag. Dassa's aircar stands outside, though she has sensibly hidden herself by a tree.

"Let's go," I call. "We can be in the capitol by evening."

Dassa hops up with alacrity. Unlike me, she has no ambivalence about leaving.

I slide into the aircar and we head skyward. Below I can see the moving vans I summoned, heading for the house. I circle my home at five-hundred meters, though I am not sure quite why.

Dassa settles into her seat, placing her weapons on the floor near her feet. She is a quiet companion. I don't know if she is intimidated, mistrustful by nature, or if she just finds it difficult to imagine subjects to converse on with so different a being. Right now, I am grateful for her reticence. My heart hurts, not in any mechanical sense, but it does so anyway, and the quiet suits me as we fly south.

Hours pass with no more than the occasional idle comment, or question and changes of radio stations. We immediately discover we do not care for each other's taste in music.

Eventually, Dassa gives a small laugh. "I guess you never need to take a break to pee, do you?"

For the first time in a while, I too laugh. "No, I gave that up with menstruation, and other biological grossness. We should set down somewhere. It's probably time to feed you again as well."

"You needn't make me sound like a child," she says.

You needn't sound like a sulky child, I think, but keep the thought to my own head.

I scan my memory and find a small restaurant with a good reputation only 23.2 minutes ahead. Dassa assures me her kidneys will last that long. We circle down and land in Halamara, a small trading village on a river and find the restaurant named, Simon's. Children in the area gather around our aircar, which is an expensive and powerful model, not common in the hinterland. Dassa herself is not common. Few have ever seen a Dua-Denlenn, and the looks she receives are somewhat dark. Her kind's reputation precedes her. In her dark jacket, and with her pupilless blue eyes, she makes an intimidating figure.

There are a couple of teenage boys of a rougher sort by a dock near the river. I note them without interest as we walk into Simon's. Dassa heads straight for the restroom, while I get us a table with a view of the slowly meandering river.

We order some local delicacies while I moodily watch the river and wish that I get drunk like I used to when I was flesh and blood; get drunk and be distanced from my thoughts and feelings. Dassa senses my mood, and she too watches the river quietly, though we talk about minor things.

After we pay and head back out, I notice the crowd admiring our car has been replaced by the dubious-looking males I'd spotted before. One, the largest, with a scarred face is sitting on the hood of the aircar.

Dassa slows, but I do not. "You're on my car."

He gives me a lazy smile. "Well, it seemed like a good way to meet you."

I shake my head. "A nice compliment, but my friend and I are just passing through."

He shrugs. "What's the hurry? Two pretty girls like you, well, me and my friends could show you a good time." The three other boys give toothy grins.

Now I am irked. "I am not in the habit of explaining myself to anyone. Please get off the car."

"Now why do you want to get all mouthy with me?" he says, standing and towering over me. "We just want to have some fun with you and your girlfriend, Blue-eyes, here"

His friends move up to flank him, two facing Dassa and one backing up the leader.

This is pathetic. I am Maauro, victor over the Artifact, the Kolzin Destroyer and legions of enemies this fool is not fit to wipe the butts of. I simply cannot stand it and burst into laughter.

Before it runs its course, the others step closer, angered by my reaction. To my shock, Dassa takes this as the signal to attack. The Du-Denlenn is as tall as any of them though lighter-built. She slams a quick punch into the nearest thug's face, beating his block by a good time and slams a foot into the other boy's knee as he moves to grapple with her. He goes down, but the first one throws a punch, which she blocks expertly and snaps back with one of her own.

Enough of this, amusing as it has been. My accelerated perceptions make everyone around me appear to be in slow motion, but I must limit my reaction speed to that of a very fast human. Scarred Boy is reaching for me and I merely yank his arm hard enough to catapult him into the one Dassa kicked in the knee. Both go down. His henchman, eyes wide, also reaches for me in an embrace. Seems the boys can't wait to get their arms around me. I move to one side, carefully select a knuckle and tap him solidly on the temple. As he falls, I grab the back of his denim jacket so that he will not fracture jaw, or teeth.

Scarred Boy is up and heading for me, as Dassa trades kicks and punches with her two dazed antagonists. I slap Scarred very hard on both sides of his face. The slaps sound like shots and he is dazed. I again pull him forward, but into spin that flattens him on his back with a thud and a scattering of gravel. Some onlookers have paused to cheer. Scarred Boy is not popular locally.

But I must end things before someone is badly hurt. Dassa is fighting with intent against these fools. The one boy's knee will require surgery; the other's nose is broken and he has hairline fracture in his cheek. She draws a fist back to strike for his trachea. I put my hand on her arm, checking the possibly deadly blow and slip past her throwing a well-calculated kick into his stomach. He flies backward to lie on the ground, groaning. It will take some minutes to recover enough to stand, and he will be in no hurry to reengage. Broken knee falls to the ground, clutching his joint, also out of the fight.

This leaves me only Scarred to deal with. He has regained his feet and charges me like a bull. Honestly, this is simply sad. Hoping he can swim, I take the impetus of his charge, add to it and fling him into the river, with a suitably large splash.

The number of onlookers has grown, and they clearly do not favor the home team. I walk over to the edge of the concrete walkway and peer over the railing. I am relieved to see that Scarred Boy, looking stunned, is standing in the shallows, before he collapses on a rock, hugging it as it was in danger of getting away.

I turn in time to see Dassa raising a foot over the one with the injured knee. Her face is devoid of expression, but the energy vibrating through her body is a dark one. Again, I cross the distance between us and stop her.

Grabbing her, I hold her close. "These are just fools. We are not here to kill."

To my surprise, she tries to twist out of my grip. "Why did you let them speak to us that way? Why did you play with them—"

Now, I tighten my grip and give her a hard, short shake. "Dua-Denlenn," I growl. "Do not forget what you know of me and what these idiots do not. When it is necessary to kill, I kill. These are unworthy of my consideration as combatants."

"That," she says, with a look of relief I do not understand, "is more like it." She relaxes totally in my hands.

"Into the car," I order.

She nods, again appearing pleased by my harsh command. I sense that I am missing something here, but there is no time to consider an emotional issue just now.

Broken Knee is staring at us through tears of pain. "You bitches won't get away with this."

"Looks to me like they are," one man calls from the crowd. Others laugh.

"Harmon," Broken Knee calls. "Help me."

"Harmon," I observe," is a tolerable swimmer. He is already to the far bank of the river."

Broken Knee looks shocked at his abandonment.

"What," I ask. "Are you a fool? Did you expect that thug to come back for you? If you are to be a warrior, you will need to judge beings better than that. A bully is a coward, or a best just a brute with no thought for others. Sometime in the future think kindly on us that we taught you this at so little expense."

"My knee is broken," he sobs.

I reach down and grab him by the throat. No one is close enough to see my face. I let my eyes go black, lid to lid, and let serrated teeth fill my mouth. His eyes become very nearly circular.

"But your leg is still attached," I say, "if you want it to stay that way, say nothing and cease being such a fool."

He nods his head in quick jerks, too frightened to speak.

"Boo," I add.

He shudders and falls over in a dead faint.

I have had as much fun as I can, and probably more than I should, but this absurd scuffle has taken my mind off my past and my leaving. However, it is now time to get out of town before the authorities arrive.

I cast a gaze at the man who laughed earlier and gesture to the three prone figures. "No permanent harm," I say. "The one at my feet will need a regenerator."

He gives the boy a contemptuous look. "Maybe the vet can be persuaded."

A girl, the age of my erstwhile antagonists pipes in. "Yeah, and maybe they'll learn to behave."

"Hah," a boy adds. "They got their asses kicked by two girls, and one is tiny. They'd better.

I take my tiny self back to the car where Dassa awaits. In a few seconds, we leave the town and the ridiculous matter, doubtless to become the stuff of local legend, behind.

CHAPTER TEN

WE SPENT THE NIGHT IN A TRAVELER'S LODGING AT THE spaceport. Maauro rented a single room.

"Are we doubling?" I asked.

She shook her head. "I will be on the roof, watching the stars. I have much to think about and want to watch the sunrise. I am, after all, a voyager setting out."

"Before you go, there is one matter I need to attend to and I wanted you to know."

"That being?"

"I had posed as a Guild courier here before I found you. I took an advance on a job I cannot now do. I must arrange to send the money back to my contact."

Maauro sighed. "How much and to whom?"

"Eight hundred Confed Credits to Fren Dirath's Pawn and Trade at the spaceport. I should call and arrange the money and explain I am off for parts unknown."

After a moment's pause, Maauro says. "Done."

I look at her in surprise.

"I hacked in, set up an account and sent the money along with a suitable message."

"Ah, thanks."

She left me for her solitary sojourn to the roof.

I set an alarm for before dawn and turn in early. So, I was awake when the sun peeked over the horizon, knowing that somewhere over my head, my artificial companion was watching the same vista. When it was well over the horizon, I heard a knock on the door.

I greeted Maauro and we breakfasted in the lodge's small restaurant and then set out for her ship. A transport took us past the freighters and local transports; there were no deep-space liners calling at Evenfall. Among the mining ships gleams a green and gold hull that Maauro pointed out to me.

"Is it guarded?" I whispered.

"I no longer have my crab robots to mount guard on her, but the ship's AI, a small subset of my own programs, is active and alert. We need not fear sabotage, or infiltration."

We pulled up and the transport doors slid open. Maauro had one small bag and reached for my extra luggage, leaving only bag for me. It had rained after midnight, so we padded around puddles toward the ship. The crew chief of the team preparing the starship, briefed Maauro about the ship's condition. She signed off on the prep, accepting the ship back as master.

A stevedore manager greeted her next. "All your cargo is aboard and stored. You need to get yourself some more crew, young lady, it cost extra for us to do stowage. Looks like you bought up most of the small machinery on the market."

She nodded. "Next port."

They discussed a few more details of dunnage and storage. The launch crew withdrew and we were left alone with the starship.

"So this is the *Stardust?*" I asked, staring up at the towering green and gold shape.

"Yes, though here it was registered as the *Misadventure.*"

I stared at her. "*Misadventure?*"

Maauro gave a rueful shake of her head. "My husband loved his little jokes. That was the registration she flew under, after we left Olympia for the last time. We were trying to avoid notice, and back then there were many ships of the *Comet* class still in civilian, or reserve service. We flew cargo with it for a few years locally. Finally, I had it stored in what humans call, "mothballing"

An uncouth expression, I thought, *probably had something to do with sex, as usual with them.* Aloud, I said. "You chose wisely. With the war and general collapse through Confederacy, newer vessels are less well made than many older ones, particularly in small engine technology."

"It is better than you know," Maauro said. "I have made many improvements in her over the decades we have had her."

My ears pricked. "Such as?"

Maauro gave me that sidelong look I was beginning to associate with her dissembling. "You will know what you need to know, when you need to know it."

Though she had done nothing I could see, the entire launch bay began to hum with activity. Lights blinked as the ship came to life and her hatches opened to welcome her master. There was something oddly life-like and disconcerting about the display. I was reminded of many ancient tales of weapons of ill-fated heroes, haunted by their spirits.

"Shall we call it, *Misadventure?*"

Maauro shrugged.

"The name will not invoke confidence in those who might do business with us," I added.

"A point Jaelle Tekala made. Very well, you name it."

I considered for a moment. "There is a concept in Dua-Denlenn, when one's fortune's change. In Galactic standard, it would be rendered as "Seachange.""

Maauro turned to face me. "That is rather poetic. You surprise me."

I felt my ear tips burn in childish embarrassment. "Any name will do, you said."

CHAPTER TEN

She nodded. "Yes, but that name will do better than most. Thank you."

Maauro turned and strode into the starship, every inch its captain and master.

The next few hours were spent in preparation for our flight. Maauro gave me a cabin of my own on the level below hers. I was too grateful for luxury of such quarters, to compare it unfavorably with her own cabin, complete with a double bed that she'd have no use for.

Or will she? I wondered if she had sex as an AI and what that must be like. It hadn't occurred to me, but she was with Trigardt for a considerable period before and after her time in a biological body. I assume she was never on top, as he lived through the experience. I carefully controlled my face as we exited her cabin, if she knew my thoughts, a beating would surely follow. Fortunately, I was good at maintaining a neutral expression. It proved essential in Guild training, where any sign of derision or disobedience brought swift punishment.

A port and customs official gave us a cursory look-over and authorized our launching. Maauro and I walked to the hatchway to see the official off. As he stepped onto the gantry, it immediately began to roll back.

Maauro stared out at the spacefield, the city beyond and the hills in the distance.

"A human or a Denlenn would ask me if I had any regrets leaving the world I'd lived on for so many years," Maauro said.

I looked down at her squarely. "I am neither of those things, as you well know. I also know that you had made your decision. For me to ask that of you would imply you are doing it for me. You are not."

She gave me another of those sidelong glances I was becoming accustomed to, and a small smile. "Spoken like Dusko himself. Well, there is something oddly refreshing in that."

She turned back to face the world beyond the airlock. "Farewell, Evenfall. Hold my dreams and memories for me. Perhaps I will return some day."

I blinked in amazement. Even now, I still found her level of emotionality astonishing. Here she was, a quantum computer made of metals and silicon speaking to…what…the spirit of a planet? Yet, she felt compelled to make this gesture.

Strangely, it gave me an empty feeling. There was no one who had such memories of, or for, me. Likely no one ever would, it wasn't the way of my people. Even happy marriages among us were more an alliance, than the love match Maauro had enjoyed.

Or was it? I knew so little of life, much less of love.

"Are we ready?" I managed.

"Yes, time to go." She turned away from the airlock, which cycled closed. I supposed I would have to get used to the way the ship responded to her unvoiced commands. I followed her up to *Stardust*'s, now

Seachange's cramped control cabin. The room was filled with screens and viewpanels. Though there were clear signs of wear on the seats and control surfaces, everything was clean. I didn't know much about warships, so I had looked up the specs on the original Confed *Comet*-class scoutships. They had been leggy, fleet scoutships with only minor defensive armament, all of which would have been removed before she was sold for surplus.

I recognize some of the controls and machines, but knew many of the systems had been modified by Maauro. We settled side by side in the flight seats and strapped in. Armored panels on the windows slid silently away and the sun sparkled into the cabin.

"Ready?" Maauro asked, without looking at me. She took the flight controls into her hands, which I thought odd, as I suspected she could fly it without such interface. Perhaps it was merely to comfort me with the illusion of control.

I settled more comfortably in the seat, breathing in the plastic and metal smells of a working ship. "Yes."

"Then let us embark on this new life. Ten seconds to lift." The impellers began their steady thrum building toward takeoff

I closed my eyes and tried to imagine what this new life would be like, but my imagination failed me.

Seachange surged toward space.

CHAPTER ELEVEN

SEACHANGE FLED MAAURO'S HOME SYSTEM AT THE BEST speed it could manage on its own. We did not have the funding for one of the orbital accelerators, which could send us to a high percentage of light speed, until we reached the rarified space at the system's edge where we could jump. So, we headed out after several loops around Evenfall, using the ship's engines and the planet's mass to boost our speed.

"We must reserve our fuel for a possible interception by whatever Ederi vessel brought that strike team," Maauro said, as we sat in her room, sipping a fine tea she had prepared.

My right breast tweaked in remembered pain. "Do you think that likely?" I asked, trying, and I suspected, failing to keep fear from my tone.

Maauro paused, her hair floated in a nimbus around her head and she drew from a small box a large, ornate hair clip. Her hair whipped about the clip, formed a complicated style and cascaded down her back like water.

Being with this machine, I thought, *which seems better at being female than I am, is going to be depressing sometimes.*

"No," Maauro replied, studying herself in a mirror. "I do not. The Ederi light curtain seems very effective, but I doubt it can be maintained for any length of time, especially on a full-size ship. With Confederate authorities alerted and the Ederi assault craft destroyed, I think it a very low probability they would linger in the vicinity."

"What about at the warppoints?"

Maauro turned to regard me, and I felt there was approval in her glance. "Yes that would be a logical place for an ambush, but this is a civilized system. There are guard satellites at the points. The Ederi vessel doubtless came through with its light curtain on, but to linger in the vicinity, hoping that we turn up at one of the three known points, would be tactically unsound.

"Still, we cannot know for a certainty their full capabilities, so our own transit will be at high speed, and our course is off the plane of the ecliptic."

"But if they are waiting and do intercept us?" I persisted.

"Then we will see if a blitz of computer virus by the Creator's finest handiwork can disable an Ederi starship. We have no other armament beyond the communications laser."

I sighed. "Now that we are underway and you have no reason to fear my revealing it, would you mind telling me where we are going?"

"To Damasia and the opaloid mines on that world."

"Damasia?" I recalled a news article about a section of Confederate space called *Rho Ophiuchi*, a vast gas cloud that had hid several main sequence stars from early exploration. Eventually proper hyperspace entry points were found for them and when explored, were found to contain three new intelligent species, all pretechnic.

"Yes, I remember now, I thought those worlds were off-limits?"

"Originally, but Confederate authority has waned. Even before that: explorers, freelancers, unauthorized immigrants and less savory types moved in. The discovery of gemstones called Schwer opals, or opaloids, sealed Damasia's fate. The stones are like opals in appearance, but almost as hard as diamonds. After that, there was no policing that system. The damage having been done, the Confederacy sought to limit it with a protectorate. I imagine by now even that protection has dissipated."

"So a ship full of portable, high-quality machine tools—"

"—should command a premium in a frontier world," I finished.

"We will make our way to Damasia. The latest information shows there is a ship-capable field out in the newest opal mining district on the Southern Continent. A town called, Pilbara, has grown up there. We will make our best deal by eliminating the middleman and trading our cargo of machine goods directly to a town that needs them badly, in return for what they have, a surplus of opaloids and other precious gems and metals. There will also be exotic metals and radioactives that would be of use to me as well. The trades should yield us great profits in other markets."

"Enough to outrun the Ederi?" I asked.

"Where would we run to?" she said. "The Ederi came from outside the Confederacy. For now, they move within it with relative impunity. We are no more, or less, likely to encounter the Ederi in one place as another. They seem as pervasive as the Guild they hunt.

"At least by trading and voyaging, we will be a moving target, unlikely to stay in one place long enough for reinforcements to be brought against us. The Ederi do seem to attach a high value to you as a target, but you will not take precedence over their larger set-piece operations against the Guild. If you are not easily found, you may not be hard sought. "

"You make many assumptions about my safety," I replied.

She turned to face me squarely. "My threat assessments are as good as the information I am given. Do I have all the information that there is?"

"One can scarcely credit that there is anything you don't know," I replied, as smoothly as I could.

She shrugs in response to my lie. "In this I am like everyone else. I know what I know. I know there are things unknown to me, and beyond that, there is the unknowable itself."

"Do you believe there is an unknowable?" I asked to shift the subject, keeping my expression as neutral as I could. *Ironic*, I thought, *here I am facing a being who must consciously put every emotion on her face in an imitation of life, while I, connected to my body in ways she cannot be, must try so hard to disconnect my face from my inner thoughts.*

Maauro cocked her head, and it seemed I had successfully diverted her. "Yes. I believe that there is somewhere from beyond space-time from which all thinking beings come and to which they return. This place is unknowable to me now, prisoner of space-time that I am."

For some reason, this bland assurance made me angry. "We come into being, we live and then we die." The harshness of my tone surprised me almost as much as it seemed to surprise Maauro. "How can you, a machine, believe that here is some benevolent God beyond the stars who concerns itself with our struggles and sufferings! Who watches us for his entertainment!"

She looked at me, registering surprise at my vehemence. "Because I have faith, young one, because I have faith."

Realizing I may have gone too far with her, I stood, thanked her for the tea and quickly withdrew to my room, hoping she would not be angry enough to follow. Yet still I cannot quite shake the feeling of unease that her foolish mercy to the thugs and these sentimental musings about a benevolent god raise in me. One's safety depends on the Alpha's strength and determinations. I am not sworn to Maauro but she is the power I must please here. That will be hard given her apparently erratic nature, I must be careful.

I finish my tea and then head for the bridge, trying to understand my companion's reaction. One instant, we are having a thoughtful discussion about the meaning of life and the next she is angry and fleeing my room. For a second, I debate whether to go after her, but she is not Wrik, Delt, Jaelle or particularly Shasti, with whom I had many long discussions about life and being. She is an angry child; from a species, whose primary characteristic is self-interest. I had promised her protection and taken her onto my ship. She has, in turn, lied to me and withheld information about the crystals she carries. Even a cursory scan by me unlocked the crystal with Dusko's somewhat maddening message about me. But the other one is a Guild courier's highest level secret recording, protected by many layers of encryption, a mistake on any of which, would cause the data to be destroyed. I did not dare to try to decrypt it, without a great deal of study, with it in my physical possession.

Yet, I had no doubt the crystal was why the Ederi commissioned a special strike on her. The attack on my house preceded any attempt on Evenfall's own Guild operations. Those targets have been alerted by the failed strike and now sheltered under such military power as is locally available. The Ederi had weighed the chance of alerting their other targets as of less importance than a strike on Dassa, though they had not factored me into their calculations. It is possible she herself does not know what she carries, but I do not believe that. She is remarkably intelligent and persistent.

I will not take the crystal from her. If this relationship is to become anything other than two refugees fleeing down the same path, I cannot do so. For now, with no obvious threat hovering over me, I have this luxury. I am not overly concerned with Guild secrets; they mean nothing to me.

I shake my head and fight down tears I can no longer freely express. How I long for my old friends. Why have I taken on this untrustworthy waif? But it comes back to me in answer, that moment of impossible communion with what I had lost, that sense that my Wrik had been with me, guiding me.

"Very well, Husband-mine," I say aloud. "We shall wait. Let us hope that the cost for doing so will not be high."

Dassa and I see little of each other and converse seldom over the next few days. I am puzzled by her initially fearful demeanor around me, until I consider the harshness of her training, which I suspect had more to do with her disfavored status as the granddaughter of a Guild traitor, than the simple brutalities of basic training in military and paramilitary organizations among biologicals. It is an oddity that the cruelty of warfare is something that must be inculcated in them by operant conditioning. Most ordinary people find violence disturbing and to be avoided. Unfortunately, this conditioning is singularly successful and widespread, as the tooth and claw state of the universe can attend to.

It is almost a relief, when we approach the warp point out of the system. Dassa joins me on the bridge, as we race for the proper angle to hit the warp point and jumpspace. She is quiet and respectful as she occupies the second seat, her eyes searching the stars as if they could detect something that Seachange's instruments could not.

"There is no evidence of an enemy vessel," I say.

"That would be more comforting if their ships were not invisible."

"They are not invisible, merely stealthy. I am scanning for errant energy traces or occlusion of stars. However, we approach at high speed. This will make the jump harder on you—"

"I will live with it."

"There is worse. The jump to Rho Opichi space is unusual. I can string two jumps into one long one, by plunging through the two adjacent warp points in the Haruko system. You will not notice the difference save at the exit from jumpspace, but it will be unpleasant. The advantage is that it will make us impossible to follow, or predict where we are going."

Dassa sighs. "I think now that I shall ride this out in my cabin."

I nod. "That might be best. You have time enough to go and belt down if you leave now."

We came out of hyperspace in the Damasia system. The jump was as unpleasant as Maauro had promised. We'd been out of space-time for more than nine months, per the ship clock over my head. I noticed that briefly as I scrambled to my first extended stay in the toilet.

When I exited, I found a concerned Maauro in my room. She quickly placed me in bed and began a series of injections. It seemed the gods of space-time were intent on wreaking revenge on me for my escape from their dominion. The nausea and sensory distortions that struck on emergence were only made bearable by the array of drugs Maauro supplied me with. She suffered no effects from the emergence that I could tell.

"Sleep," she said. "You will feel better tomorrow."

When next I awoke, I had slept a full ship-cycle, during which we had moved closer to the inner system. My stomach still rebelled against the thought of food, but Maauro had anticipated the need. A tray sat next to my bed with juice and cubes of a yellow jelly and crackers rested in a bowl. I slowly and carefully ingested these, then slept some more.

When I recovered enough to join the android on the bridge, I found her seated, gazing pensively at tiny disc of a world in Seachange's main viewscreen. I wondered, what she was thinking as I peered in at the slender and diminutive figure. It still occasionally chilled me to remember she had been made, actually assembled, before my species did more than live in crude huts. While her appearance was perhaps only seven or so years older than mine, there was something about her, a seriousness, or solemnity that gave her the air of an older and authoritative person. I knew I was very much the junior member of this partnership, and bitter though it was, I had to admit I was little more than supercargo, perhaps merely an amusement, or distraction. I was determined to somehow change the balance of power between us in my favor.

For now, I merely entered the bridge, giving her the human smile I'd learned in my travels. Maauro broke off her study of Damasia to give me a quick inspection. "You're feeling better."

"Yes, thank you. You are an excellent doctor."

"I've been repairing biologicals and coping with their distressing tendency to vomit all over my lovely ship for over 154 years. I suppose I have gotten fairly good at it."

The unfortunate reference caused me a brief battle with my insides, and I glared at her, wondering if this wasn't a malicious test. She, unaffected, merely returned a bland expression.

"No sign of Ederi?" I asked.

"Nor of anything else," she replied. "This is a frontier system. Other than a buoy, there is nothing here. No traffic, per the buoy, for the last three months, and that was an outbound freighter."

"So no Confed warships either."

"That I cannot say for certain, friendly warship transits are not recorded by the buoy. An Ederi vessel would trigger it, if the light curtain wasn't on.

"No, the only thing concerning me is readings from the planet ahead."

"What do you mean?"

"There are no broadcasts aimed at us, of course, but any planet, even a sparsely settled one such as this, is always radiating signals into space. Yet, there is little such radio traffic, and what there is suffers from a great deal of distortion."

"What could cause that?"

"Many things, ionization of the atmosphere due to solar flares would do it, but the sun is quiet. Nuclear attack would, but the little radio traffic I hear is normal and makes no such reference. It could be weather disturbances on a catastrophic scale."

I frowned. "None of those are good. How long until orbit?"

She smiled. "Long enough for us to have a cup of soothing tea and a light piece of cake."

I felt a quiver internally. It must have shown on my face.

"The cake is light," she said. "It also includes more medication for you."

I followed her off the bridge, and we went to her cabin, which seemed to be where she preferred to offer what I was coming to think of as her "tea ceremony." Though she clearly had no need for the liquid, she seemed to savor both the smell and taste, though perhaps not in the same sense I did. The plate of white cake was as pleasant as promised. I felt restored to normal health, if not appetite, afterward.

Maauro steered for an expert orbit of Damasia. The precision of this almost made up for the fact that she never bothered going to the bridge, or did any of the myriad of tasks I had observed on other ships. While I knew she was a super-computer capable of amazing things, it was nonetheless quite frightening to be plunging toward a planetary mass while my pilot and captain arranged flowers in her cabin. The only reason she finally went to the bridge was to stop me from pestering her about it.

"Honestly, I could as easily fly the ship from the bathroom if I still had the need to use such a thing. You need not fret so," she said, as we headed for the command deck.

"Think of your attendance on the bridge as an investment in your public relations skills, should you ever decide to run a passenger liner."

She grimaced, sighed and then finally entered the bridge with me on her heels.

"Aren't you concerned by our failure to raise any ground station on the world ahead?" I added.

"Some," she conceded. "As we closed in it became evident to our sensors that the issue is what appears to be a planet-wide storm, or series of storms. Thus, the ionization of the atmosphere likely accounts for it and the base we are heading for does not have the space communication equipment of the main colony, and there is no space station. We should be able to communicate once we pierce atmosphere."

I glanced over the instruments, all showed green and it seemed my metallic companion's confidence was not misplaced. "Can you land this without ALS or beacons?"

"The lack of landing systems is a concern," Maauro said. "This is an old scoutship designed for first-in landings on unsettled worlds. Still, such a vast and violent planetary storm constitutes a "white-out" to Seachange's instruments. It will be best if I control Seachange directly, from outside, where I will serve as the ship's guidance and control systems."

Startled as I was by her display of humor, I burst out laughing. When it had run its course, I collapsed back into my chair only to find her regarding me with a cocked head and puzzled look.

"My instruments are more sensitive than the ship's, but it does require me to be directly exposed—"

"Oh, Gods of Denlesch you're serious!"

"Of course."

"You'll be burned off by reentry!"

"Don't be silly. I am not going outside until after atmospheric entry is done and we are down to the level of the storm."

"But, but," I spluttered.

Maauro smiled and gestured with her head at the main screen, which showed the ship's nose pitching down to drag in the atmosphere and almost instantly begin glowing. Maauro must have altered our course minutes ago, without my being aware.

"Are you so sure that you don't want to believe in a God that has your interests at heart?" Maauro said sweetly.

Reentry is routine, and we come down into the continental storm. Seachange handles the approach well, and I am proud of my ship. Once we are through atmospheric entry, I reorient Seachange into a vertical attitude for landing and adjust the sink rate for a slow approach. I then move to fulfill my promise to steer the ship down through the murk from outside, to Dassa's undisguised horror.

"See you on the ground," I say to her, as I head for the airlock. She does not reply, but merely gazes at me, dumbfounded. I close the airlock and depressurize; the process is quick, as I have no need for a spacesuit. To anyone else, I would seem to merely be wearing a black, leather body-suit, with gold details. Since I am to see new people, I decided on a new look as well. The only other color on me is the golden hairpiece, which too is an extension of my chassis, hearkening back to the yellow hair

ribbon, which was Wrik's first present to me. But an actual hair bow is too juvenile for me now, though the hairpiece has the color and is cast as a gem-studded ribbon in a moebius band.

The outer door opens on a world of brown, swirling storms and dark-blue sky. We are slowing sinking from thirty kilometers up. I run sufficient power through the soles of my feet to magnetize them, though I also use handholds and other projections to climb toward the nose of my ship. I pass the clearplast panels of the bridge, peer in and rap on the panel. It is childish of me, but I rather enjoy that Dassa jumps a foot in the air. I give her a cheery wave, which she returns with a spastic gesture. Her expression is that of one facing imminent death. Good, it will keep her tractable for the immediate future.

Another fifteen seconds and I am at the nose cone of the ship, which is less needle-shaped than it appears at a distance, studded as it is with sensors and small protuberances. Still, it is easy enough to wrap my legs around the ship's front, and I settle in comfortably. I gaze at the super-blue sky above, with its twinkling stars and then down at the unpleasant brown and white clouds, raging below. The sun is outlining the planet's curvature. The sight has an austere beauty.

I lean back and release my hair from its pattern, allowing it to float free and extend, thinning and stretching until each strand is fine, but ten meters long. Soon, I am at the center of a nimbus of a large spider-web-like sensor net. Through the filaments, floods a wealth of data on the planet below that far exceeds anything Seachange could gather, by orders of magnitude.

The land below me is cast into stark relief, as I piece the clouds with my sensors. I see structures, roads, the entrances to mines and the space-field of the mining compound below. I am puzzled by the levels of methane, carbon monoxide and dioxide, which are extraordinarily high for a highly industrialized world, much less a frontier colony with a native species still in the hunter-gatherer stage.

The violence and width of the storm is also aberrational. My records of Damasia's climate do not correlate with my observations. What could have wrought these changes in the five years since the last planetary survey? I again try to raise some ground station, but the ionization of the atmosphere is so bad that I can raise no one. I pull down some telemetry and other system signals, indicating operating power plants and other installations, but devoid of information useful to me.

Seachange settles under my control, at double the rate that was safe before. I examine the compound below. It was originally called Cracking Station One but later named Pilbara after a miner who made the first big strike there. As we close the range I grow concerned, some of the outlying structures show damage. One has been razed by fire.

My practiced eye picks out signs of fortification. The town has suffered attack, and the occupants have responded with amateur defensive works that show no sign of expertise, or inspiration. They must either have considerable technological advantage over their enemies or they have not been hard-pressed.

Answers to these questions can only be found on the ground. I allow the ship to sink faster and search through 360 degrees, looking for any weapon locking on my ship.

A signal impinges on my consciousness. "This is Pilbara control to descending starship— we are glad to see you. Please identify your ship, mission and cargo."

"This is the Confederate licensed private scout and freighter Seachange out of Evenfall. I'm the master, Captain Aurelia Toyama. I have a cargo of machine goods and tools for trade. Who am I speaking to?"

"Pilbara Control to Seachange; this is Malporin Rand, day watch officer for the port. We've been hoping for a ship, or some relief from the capital for weeks, but we have been cut off. The atmosphere has been heavily—"

"Ionized, I know. We were not able to contact the capitol before I committed to this landing window. You have a changed planet, Mr. Rand, which doesn't look, or register, anything like the last survey. I can also detect signs of battle below me."

"You have good sensors, Seachange; we can barely see you."

"As I said, scout and freighter, but you evade my question."

"It will be easier to discuss on the ground, Captain."

"Are there active combat operations going on?"

"None close to Pilbara. We have patrols out, but the Indigenes have been quiet for a while."

"I take it you are referring to the native species."

"Yes, Captain. They've blamed all the climate changes on the Confed species on world. We've lost a lot of people since the troubles began. Hope you have some weapons for sale."

"That will be easier to discuss on the ground, Mr. Rand."

"I will look forward to that, Captain. We'll provide security for you on landing. People are going to be glad to see you and your ship"

"We will land in two minutes and thirty seconds."

"I'll be there to greet you."

I raise an eyebrow. "Are you in authority beyond the day watch officer?"

"Well I guess you could say I'm the head of the Emergency Counsel. I've had some success with the Indigenes."

"You will be an interesting acquaintance, Mr. Rand."

To my surprise, my private channel signals that Dassa wants to talk to me. She has been listening inside the ship. I open a separate channel to her. "Yes?"

"We should boost and get the hell out of here."

"This vessel needs fuel, Dassa."

"Go for the capitol, sell at a loss if we have to and flee."

"Our object is to make a profit, so we may voyage further and eventually reach Enshar. Any opaloids we can secure at the capitol will be two or three times as expensive as locally."

"Our objective should first be survival."

"They should not be mutually exclusive. In any event, we must land. We are too low to achieve any useful orbital window without a prohibitive fuel cost. If the situation merits it, we will have fuel enough for a jump to the capitol after 3AM tomorrow."

"Assuming we are either alive, or at liberty to do so."

"Assuming that."

The channel closes, it cannot slam, but I imagine she wishes it could.

I now have a 100% scan of the field and select a landing site that has maximum benefit of the defenses. At a kilometer from landing, I add thrust and slow the ship so I can make my way back to the airlock and reenter the ship. It takes 2.4 seconds to regain the interior of the ship. Once inside, I vibrate at high speed and shake off the dust and grit of the atmosphere before the inner door opens. Filters suck it all away.

My companion is belted into the second seat, and she does not look at me as I slip into the pilot seat. I do not use the controls, but handle Seachange directly through its AI. I land the ship, with a barely perceptible sensation. Wrik would be proud of me.

Dassa unbelts and rises to stare out the bridge at the dismal vista beyond, reluctance and disapproval in every line of her body. I can hardly blame her, the sun is up, but the world outside is in twilight. The spacefield is devoid of other craft save for the wreck of an atmospheric transport. Beyond the field, lies a score of two and three-story buildings and twice as many single-story structures. It is a cheerless, commercial compound so different from my green Evenfall. Sodium lights battle the gloom, and I see some commercial vehicles that have been converted to military use, patrolling around the field.

Still, we are here and must make the best of it. I must confess a certain excitement about the thought.

CHAPTER TWELVE

WE LAND AFTER THE MOST TERRIFYING AND BIZARRE approach I've ever experienced. Watching Maauro, who fakes being a human very well, waving at me from outside the ship, with no spacesuit, walking up to the bow and wrapping her legs around it left me in a state of numb astonishment. I wondered if she did these things just to scare me.

When she came back in, I could feel the cold of the high atmosphere radiating off her, but she was remarkably free of any of the grit scoring the outside of the ship. She gave me that sidelong glance, quite aware of the effect she was having on me. We landed smoothly only a minute later.

I stared out the portal and monitors, at what could only charitably be called an improved field. There were no other spacecraft present, at least no functioning ones. Something that was either a wreck or a hulk, lay in the distance, its lines blurry in the blowing murk.

"We are now near Pilbara," Maauro said. Controls in front of her were switching and changing as she remotely set the ship to portside routine. "I doubt that any auxiliary power taps will be offered in this primitive landing, so I have set the reactor to minimum setting.

"This landing should allow us to make our deals quickly and depart soon. I have set us down so that we are well within such defenses as are available here. I wish that we had some crab robots to deploy. At our next port, I am going to either buy one, or enough components so that I can build something suitable."

"Will it be a handsome robot?" I ask.

To my surprise Maauro froze, her face lost animation for a bare instant. Then she was moving again, so quickly I wasn't sure that I'd actually seen it. She didn't answer my question, and it seemed, for once, I'd gained the upper hand on her.

Then, as if I hadn't said anything, she added. "I doubt that the Ederi have touched this place, but if they have come, odds favor their being at the capitol. Their interest in you seems excessive, but I think it would be an extraordinary development to find them here."

Was the mention of my enemies a subtle warning, a quick revenge for my having discomforted her?

I nodded. "The Ederi can't be everywhere, but my life these last two years has been a string of extraordinary developments."

"Point taken," Maauro said. "Get ready to go planetside."

I turned to the hatchway.

"Dassa."

I paused and looked back.

"You will find the armory door now opens to you. Draw a stunner and your choice of a slug-thrower or laser. Whichever you are most skilled with."

"Very kind of you."

"Of course no weapon that will work for you would have any effect on me."

I was surprised at the comment. "Of course. Why would you give me any power over you?"

We stood staring at each other in mutual confusion for some seconds.

"It's interesting dealing with Dua-Denlenn," Maauro said, as if to herself.

"Pity me then," I retorted. "There is no guide for dealing with an ancient artificial intelligence, or a ghost, or whatever it is that you actually are."

To my surprise, she smiled at me. "You have some virtues, Dassa. You puzzle me, which makes life more interesting."

"One is glad to serve," I replied, answering her as I once did my uncle. I left the bridge with the uneasy feeling that we had not communicated. Our words to each other carried other meanings than the ones we intended, whether we wished them to or not.

I joined Maauro at the lower hatchway a few minutes later. I wore a fresh uniform of dark green and leather, with a short jacket. A stunner was tucked under my left arm outside the jacket, and a laser rode on my other hip. Dua-Denlenn being ambidextrous, I could use either with equal speed, something I shared with my artificial companion. I exceeded her order somewhat by shouldering a triple-auto carbine.

She, of course, was already there, wearing the leather-looking, form-fitting, bodysuit with its gold highlights, belt and a short jacket. She too had a stunner under her arm and an auto pistol on her hip from the captain's locker in her own cabin. I wondered about the bodysuit which clung to her like a second skin, then reminded myself it was her first skin. Given her relationship with her husband, she surely knew how her curvaceous, if small, body would affect men. Perhaps she was counting on it?

"What now?" I asked her.

She raised an eyebrow and gave a pointed look at the carbine. "Well we are armed to the teeth for the starters. While I appear older than you, it is only by about ten years and that is still young for the captain who owns her own starship. I will be a curiosity, and some will be tempted to take advantage of our apparent youth. We must show our formidability at every opportunity, so none are tempted to transgressions with us."

"I am Guild," I reply, "trained as an operative, courier and infiltrator. No one should take me lightly."

"True, but we won't lead with your being Guild. Try just looking stern and capable."

Unsure if I was being teased, I nodded.

"Dassa," she continued, "I have operated for over 50,000 years and lived as a biological for sixty-two of them. I'm a quantum computer, yet still the exigencies of passing as a human among humans will task me. If you see an error, intervene. You will not make me angry."

"Ok," I said. "Though how much I can aid you among a group that is primarily humans, is questionable. I'd never met any before Evenfall, and my exposure there was brief. Still, I will do what I can."

I examine my heavily armed companion, who apparently believes that dire threats await us on the other side of the hatch. Perhaps she is right. As I did mention the need to look formidable, I elect to let the carbine slide as an issue.

Dassa dons a weapon-resistant vest. I consider one for appearance's sake and decide it will ruin the line of my short jacket and bodysuit, but we both add helmets with goggles. There is a lot blowing around outside the ship and Dassa, at least, needs to protect her sense organs and delicate skin. The helmet will actually interfere with my senses, but I cannot plausibly be without it. I also grab a line of rope and link it through D-rings on our utility belts.

I note that the storm has picked up, even since we have landed, as I give the command to open the outer hatch. As it opens, the howl of the angry wind and its load of grit and sand reach us immediately. I elect to use the rollout platform elevator that extrudes from the bottom of the airlock. No gantry or jetway greets us, and I would rather not be exposed climbing down a ladder. The gusts tear at us as the platform, itself only a meter across, sinks toward the ground below. I put an arm around Dassa's waist, wondering if any spying eyes will mistake it as a gesture of affection. But the tall, slender Dua-Denlenn clamps a hand down on my arm, apparently grateful for the additional stability.

From this vantage, I see a large vehicle with three beings standing in its bed making its way toward us. It pulls up twenty-one meters away, just as our cargo lift grounds on the fused sand and stone of the landing field. A door opens in the extended cab of the vehicle on the lee side, and a man waves us over. The militia standing in the bed, stare in all directions over their weapons.

We cross over to the vehicle at a prudent speed as I study the situation. Only two beings are in the cab. One is the driver, and the other is a handsome human male in his late twenties or early thirties. I suspect this is Malporin Rand. He is smiling and waving at us to make haste. While he does have a weapon, the cover is clipped down on it, impeding any fast draw. The beings in the bed are similarly friendly when they turn their worried faces from the horizon.

"Welcome to Damasia," Rand says, "garden spot of the galaxy."

"I'm Captain Aurelia Toyama," I answer, "master of the Seachange and I prefer my gardens green, under blue skies."

Dassa crowds in behind me and slides onto the seat to stare at Rand without expression. Since she shows no signs of speaking, I introduce her. "This is Dassa, crew to me."

"Dassa," he says, with a broad grin. "Just Dassa?"

Her expression does not change. "We do not use our family names outside our species."

He nods, unoffended. "Well, I'm Malporin Rand. I go by Malporin."

"Aurelia," I return. I remove my helmet, as does Dassa.

Malporin looks us both over. "Did you come in from the planet of beautiful women?"

I'm amused. "We did, but don't ask for the coordinates, or we'll have to kill you."

He studies my face. "Might be worth the risk. Can't say that I've encountered such a young and attractive crew before. You've caught me off guard."

Dassa just looks out the window, as if having lost all interest in the conversation. She does shift the carbine off her shoulder to rest its butt on the floor. His eyes track the weapon, but he makes no comment.

"Thom," he says to the driver, "back to the council building."

"Sure thing, Mal." Mindful of the standing militia on top, he starts up slowly. The vehicle rolls forward toward the largest of the buildings as Seachange fades into the murk, visible only to my other senses.

"Well, Malporin, why does your world look nothing like the star databases say it does?" I say, as I study him. The human is strongly built, with pleasing, regular features. He reminds me some of Delt, Wrik's childhood friend who served with us in Lost Planet, though his hair is a dark brown to Delt's blonde.

"No one knows, but the planet seems to have gone mad right after the first big opaloid sales into the Confederacy. Just as we were becoming a going concern, every form of planetary convulsion known has struck: earthquakes, volcanoes, massive coal fires touched off in the planetary crust, changes in the ocean conveyor system. Some folks think God is punishing the greedy. The natives think God is punishing them for letting us live here."

"God again," Dassa mutters.

Malporin raises an eyebrow.

"My companion is an atheist," I say.

"Takes all kinds," he says.

"You offered protection for my ship. While I thank you, it is quite sealed and I have set the communications laser to act in ground defense within 100 meters. It would be best if no one approaches my ship."

He frowns. *"You could have set it just for Indigenes, Captain."*

"I could," I agree, staring coolly at him. To my surprise, he flashes a grin at me.

"You're young for a Captain," he replies, *"but I can see how you got the left side seat."* He looks me over. *"But you are the prettiest captain to land on Damasia without doubt."*

Next to me, Dassa sighs, and I consider elbowing her in the ribs. I find that I rather enjoy the attentive look. However, I only raise an eyebrow at Malporin. *"You also seem somewhat young for leading an Emergency Council."*

Now his face takes a grave look. *"There were other leaders before me, they tried to meet with Indigenes and make peace. It didn't work. They used the meeting as a decapitation strike on our senior people. I guess you could say I am the second-string quarterback."*

I take a millisecond to check the reference then nod. I suspect his apparent humility is one of those endearing characteristics that the natural politician uses.

"Pilbara is the only major off-world population on this continent," he says. *There were some small outposts and mine installations. There's one small seaport all the way down the coast, but it's been mostly abandoned. We lost the outposts, or abandoned them, but we've kept most of the mineheads. If we lose those, there's no reason to stay here at all."*

"Sounds like a dire situation."

"Yes," he says.

The vehicle bumps over some ruts in the road, and we sped up on better pavement heading for the tall building. The howling of the wind makes further conversation difficult. We pull up to the structure. Malporin opens the door and we quickly make our way into the double-doored building. If I'd been relieved by the failure of the militia in back to accompany us, that relief is tempered by the number of armed beings within. Dassa gives me an "I told you so" look.

Malporin leads us down a guarded corridor and to a large room with the look of a cafeteria. In the center, a group of beings await us standing around a V of folding tables and chair. Holo-comps decorate the table tops.

"This is the emergency counsel," Malporin says and gestures at the other six members seated around the inexpensive folding tables. The counsel is a polyglot mix of four humans, three of them female, a bear-like Okaran, and a Nekoan female. She is not quite as attractive as Jaelle Tekala, who had been a golden creature with yellow eyes, small features and an athletic body. Had she and Wrik overcome their differences, he might have ended up with Jaelle and not me. I'd met Wrik first, but my emotionality had been nascent then.

Suddenly I missed the generous spirited Nekoan with a pang. Oh, to not again hear her cheerful and optimistic voice. Never again to have her pounce on me in the hope of taking me by surprise. What loss. Unlike Wrik, Jaelle had children by one of her own species. I'd never taken any interest in her progeny, or their descendants, and now I wondered why. Likely some of hers were still alive under the stars. Perhaps I'd made a mistake in that regard.

I shake myself mentally and refocus on the present. My internal reverie has lasted .0012 seconds before I turn to the council. Malporin walks around the tables to sit at the apex of the V, flanked by his fellow council members. He gestures at the seats across from them. We take those. Dassa moves with elaborate caution to take the carbine off her shoulder and lay it across her lap.

Malporin looks to the right and left. "I'm sorry this looks like a court proceeding. That isn't my intention. Are you hungry or thirsty?"

I look out of the corner of my eye at Dassa. She gives a minute shake of the head. I smile at Malporin. "We're fine thank you. I would rather discuss the terms of trade with you." *I remove my private com from my jacket pocket and tap it. The device is a mere prop; I locate and infiltrate all their computers while I send my cargo manifest to them.*

Malporin's face shows strain. Some of the other councilors look either grim or discomforted.

"We will be glad to give you very favorable terms on your cargo. We had hit a major vein here last year and since we do not have to compensate a bunch of middleman, both of us will get more for our trade.

"But Captain, you understand that you have landed in what is in effect a fortress under siege. We have reason to believe that the Indigenes are massing in the mountains near here. Our patrols have been driven back. We now hold just the mineheads and the town and can only move safely in good weather.

"You could have told me that when I was still in orbit."

"And you would have headed somewhere else at the best speed you could manage."

"What prevents me from doing that now?"

"I'm afraid," *Malporin said, looking at the table top,* "that I can't allow you to do that."

Dassa twitches. I still her with a glance.

"As the leader of the Pilbara Emergency Council, I must commandeer your ship. You will be properly, even generously compensated for the use of your ship, weapons and cargo."

The others on the counsel do not meet my eyes, save for the Nekoan female, who stares at me as if in challenge.

I allow a small smile to cross my face. "You will find Seachange is no ordinary vessel. It will open to no orders but mine, and I already warned you of some of its defenses."

CHAPTER TWELVE

"I may need to persuade you otherwise."

Now I narrow my eyes. "You have never met anyone as resistant to persuasion as I am."

His eyes flick to mine in both surprise and I judge, distress. "Wait, I didn't mean it that way!"

"Didn't you?" I reply dryly.

"Look. We are in desperate straits here. I have badly wounded people I need to evacuate to the capitol's hospitals. There are children and other noncombatants I want to get out of what has turned into a war zone.

"We have some precisions arms, yes, but we're miners and frontier people, not soldiers. And when the brownouts come down out of the mountains, the Indigenes follow inside them and the advantage of our distance weapons is nullified. They attack when conditions suit them. If we pursue into the mountains, they either ambush us, or fade away faster than we can pursue."

"A sad tale if true, but it is not my tale, or of my making." I reply.

"Yet you are now as caught in it as we are," Malporin continues. "You came here for opaloids. No one will sell to you, Captain, but that I authorize it. Unless you help us, you're leave here with nothing but what you brought with you."

He leans forward. "Help us and we'll fill your hold with enough opaloid for you to buy a liner. For now, we need your ship and supplies.
"

"We seem to be at a bit of an impasse," I reply. "Perhaps it would be best if we considered our positions overnight."

Malporin nodded. "We'll make every effort to keep you comfortable. You're not prisoners, save that I cannot allow you to return to your ship and takeoff. I did promise security for it, but we are keeping more than 100 meters from the vessel. Otherwise you have the freedom of the complex, go anywhere you want, talk to whoever you want."

"You're not going to demand our weapons?"

"This isn't a pirate hold, Captain. We mean you no harm. I assume you won't attack the guards I've set on you without reason, and there is another reason I won't deprive you of your weapons."

"What is that?"

"The storm has been growing worse and the Indigenes have been massing in the mountains to the north. A big push could come at any time and the natives don't take prisoners save to kill them slower."

"You are a very considerate captor."

"I hope to persuade you that I'm an even better partner and that helping us is both the right thing to do and in your interest. I wasn't lying about filling your pockets with opaloids."

I sigh. "You expect a lot out of me and Seachange, Mr. Rand. I told you before that we aren't a warship.

"Please call me, Malporin."

Now I raise an eyebrow. "So now you offer me friendship along with threats and demands."

"I don't threaten you, Captain. I may inconvenience, discomfort or annoy you, but not more. I hope you will come to see that over the next few days that I will make a proper friend."

"We will see, Malporin, we will see. Meanwhile examine my manifest. Gather your offers. For the rest, tomorrow. We have had a long day and I can't imagine it was much easier for you.

"Kemisa," he calls.

The Nekoan female walks over. She is taller than me, as most people are though shorter than Dassa. She wears a hide vest that shows off her shapely arms and taut physique. Gemmed earrings dangle from one bat-like ear which projects from her mane of golden hair, streaked with brown. A long sinuous tail projects from the back of her black field pants.

"This is Kemisa Rasan; she's the vice-president of the council."

We shake hands with the Nekoan human fashion. Her dark, purple eyes study us. Her grip is firm, almost too strong, as if she is either testing my own grip, or just used to rough miners.

"Would you take them to the mining company guest quarters in the hotel?"

"Sure, Mal," she replies in an easy, friendly tone, but at her glance, a pair of guards detach themselves from the wall.

I raise an eyebrow at Malporin, who at least looks embarrassed.

CHAPTER THIRTEEN

WE CROSS THE WINDSWEPT PARKING LOT ADJACENT TO THE COUNCIL building, heading for a long, three-story structure with many balconies. The sign on it says, Kirketon Hotel. As we enter the building, a big-bodied, older woman, dressed in red and black greets us. She is backed by four more guards.

"Hello, Kitty," the woman says, an easy smile splits her broad, pleasant face.

Kemisa grimaces. "Romy, how many times do I have to ask you stop calling me that? Mallie wants you to put these ladies up for a few nights."

She ignores her comment, examining us instead. "That scoundrel, sending two attractive girls to my hotel. What is he up to? Are they both of age?"

"I am," I reply, "with spare change as well."

"Well then, older than you look, Missy."

The security team chuckles at the exchange. The human ones anyway, the gray-skinned Drisnian female and the Morok simply look bored.

Kemisa shakes her head. "OK Romy, have it your way, but try and treat Captain Toyama and her crewmate Dassa, with more respect than you accord the council."

"Well, that will be easy," she says with a wink, then glances over her shoulder at the guard team.

Kemisa's good humor fades. "The Captain and her party will be staying in your best room on the top floor. Security will make sure they are undisturbed. They'll be meeting with the full council again in the morning at 0800."

She sighs. "Hell of a way to run a railroad, Kitty."

"Needs must," she replies, "needs must."

"Ok, ok. I'll rustle up the best from the cellar and kitchen. Tell the council they will be paying for it."

"Sure and don't forget about my team. They need to eat too."

"Sure," she says in a gentle tone. "Come on, Ladies."

Kemisa turns to me. "I'm sorry for this, Captain. Perhaps tomorrow we can salvage your good opinion of us."

"Stranger things have happened," I reply. "Most of my opinion will be determined by my credit balances, cargo manifests and your waiving port fees and taxes."

"Sleep well, Captain. We'll see you in the morning." Kemisa heads back to the council building.

We follow Romy to an elevator. The Drisnian and two guards get on with us. The others must wait for a second trip. The female Drisnian steps to the back of the elevator and puts her hand on a stunner on her belt. She is something of a novelty to me, being female, humanoid, and smaller than I. The gray-skinned female returns my gaze unflinchingly.

Romy, meanwhile, studies me. A true human female, she is noticing the size of my eyes, my small, but well-rounded dimensions and perfect skin. Well, let her be envious. The elevator doors open, saving me from further inspection. She leads us down a hall and opens the door at the end. The suite within seems quite luxurious. A little cry of excitement and wonder slips out of Dassa as she nearly runs into the room, dropping her grit-encrusted bag on a rather expensive couch. I do not have to look at Romy to feel her wince.

The guards remain outside. Other than the Drisnian, they seem a casual lot, not very concerned about our potential resistance. Dassa's fascinated inspection of the mini-bar may be lulling them into a sense of false security. I will have to compliment her on her deceptive skills. If I can get her attention away from the very plush robe she has just discovered hanging in a closet.

I look out the shatterproof glass and recently installed shutters at the fading light and wind-blown grit. I walk over and close the shutters facing the mountains. It would be a terribly long shot with even special equipment, but I see no need to give any potential sniper a lit target. The windows are shatterproof, but not bulletproof.

Romy gestures at a tablet in a vertical holder. "I just uploaded the room service menu a while ago. Don't hope for too much, but Mallie did say you get the best of what we have," she gives a wicked grin, "particularly from the cellar, though Kemisa did say that you have an 8AM with the council. So, you may want to get your breakfast order in early."

"Thank you," I say, scanning the room.

She nods pleasantly and turns to leave.

To my surprise, I find no surveillance devices. I intrude on the few systems I can reach and search any relevant data. Then I use the hotel's own fire-suppression sensor to check the guards outside, who have picked up a table, some coffee and tea and are settling into a card game. Even though we are armed, we are evidently not regarded as dangerous. I find this quite amusing.

Dassa has come back dressed in her conquest, the new pink robe, a color I do not feel does her much justice.

"You may speak freely," I respond to the unanswered question in her face. "There are no surveillance devices and the guards are far enough from the door that they cannot hear us."

"We appear to be prisoners of idiots," she says calmly. "Do we escape tonight?"

"I think not. We are in no danger, I judge. I am curious about developments here. The changes on this world are fantastic in the short period since the last Confed survey.

CHAPTER THIRTEEN

"But more to the point." I continue. "Malporin is right. With no mar-ket to sell to and no one to pay us in opaloids, we will take huge loss on the voyage. Relocating to the capitol might not ameliorate the loss suffi-ciently for us to move on to our next port of call. If we are to make a decent profit, we must find out what is going on here, and I am not averse to assisting these people, for all that I am not pleased at their welcome."

Dassa cocked her head. "Our captors seem curiously concerned with your comfort."

"No more than yourself."

She makes a derisive sound. "Incorrect. Malporin Rand's eyes rarely left you and not merely because you are the power. He clearly sees you as sexually attractive. You may need to guard your virtue."

I am momentarily nonplussed. As both an android and a human, I had been Wrik's lover for over a century. But in its last years the relation-ship had been more sensual than sexual. It had been a long time since a young man had looked at me in that way. I found the idea unsettling and perhaps, I thought with a frisson of guilt, a touch exhilarating?

Focus, I tell myself. Concentrate on the situation. Aloud I say, "I think he is more interested in my cargo than me."

The look Dassa gives me is skeptical. "Beyond that," she continues, "You are curious. You do not feel fear in any meaningful sense, and you are too confident in your ability. We are staying because you see this as a problem worthy of your attention. That," she says, flopping on the couch and toeing her bag to the floor, "is the sum of it."

I debate if the local planetary authorities would press charges if I spanked her butt black and blue. Worse still, there is more than a little truth in what she says. "Perhaps."

"If we are going to be besieged by hostile aliens, held prisoner by comedy troupe pretenders and your whims, I am going to do damage to someone's expense account."

"You're rather full of yourself tonight," I return.

"We who are about to die salute you," she says.

"And me without a lion to throw you to."

Dassa ignores the comment and makes a series of quick picks before turning to the wine and spirits list.

I wave a finger at her. "You're underage."

She looks at me in stunned disbelief. "I hit my majority last year!"

"Not in Confed space."

"I'm a Guild criminal."

"No, you're the nice young lady who came in with Captain Toyoma."

Dassa looks so incredulous I think she might explode. I know I'm having too much fun at her expense, but there is something else going on as well. Dassa's behavior had been rather manic with me lately. It seems part of a pattern, one I have yet to understand, between the frightened child who expects me to rule her, and the wolf cub who is constantly pushing at me.

"Oh, all right," I mock relent, "but no dopesticks, drugs or alcohol over 30 proof."

She still stares, as if not sure what to make of me.

"Order me something from the dessert menu," I add. "It might look odd if I didn't eat something. Oh, and a nice coffee."

Dassa relays the order via the com and stood. "I'm for the showers before the food gets here. In a few seconds, an unselfconscious and naked Dassa scampers past me for the shower.

I shake my head at her carelessly discarded clothes, gather them and pitch them into her bedroom. While there is a long history of literature on the behavior of teens, having it in memory is not adequate preparation for having to keep company with one.

Hot water sluices over me. *Seachange*, which was built for a larger crew, has hot water in abundance. Since it is basically only I who needs to shower, there is no restriction on it. However, the shower in the hotel is larger, more comfortable and Gods know, the towels are better quality. Some of them will be leaving with me.

Meanwhile I worked on the conundrum of my partner's approach to the situation, which could only be described as reckless. As Guild, I measure profit and risk very precisely and see us risking too much, for too little reason. Yet Maauro was clearly engaged by the mysteries of this world.

I wondered about her lack of reaction to Malporin. He is the power here, and his reaction to her is clearly interest, whether for her exotic little body, her ship, cargo or all three. Even across species it was clear, yet her reaction to what I told her, was confusion and denial. Can she not see it? Or is it possible that denial is a human quality she has achieved?

The possibility of a sexual liaison is of little interest to me, beyond how she could use it to improve our business prospects. I am only concerned that she seems unaware of the opportunity. Blindness in one's leader is of concern and could lead to disaster for me. I must keep my eye on this situation.

For now, there's nothing I can do beyond regaining my robe and heading for bed. I saw Maauro, standing, staring out at the subsiding storm. Stars were visible, though only a few, as there was still much dust in the atmosphere. But if there are stars, she will watch them.

I will watch the inside of my eyelids. I nodded in her general direction, made sure my weapons were nearby, and tumbled into bed.

CHAPTER THIRTEEN

Morning came and with it, Malporin. I open the door to his quick knock. The guards had departed a few minutes before. He probably thinks that was unnoticed by us.

"I trust you slept well?" he asks.

I nod. Dassa merely stands still.

"May I invite you to breakfast? I was going to have something sent over to the council chamber. I take most of my meals there."

"Well, we have ordered breakfast already."

"I know, but if you are ok with it, I'll have it brought across and we can make a working breakfast of it."

I glance at Dassa, who gives an almost imperceptible shrug. "Certainly."

"Then follow me, please."

We follow him out of the hotel and back to the council chamber. Only one other member is there, Kemisa Rasan, the Nekoan from the night before. I know that her big bat-like ears will be turned on anything that is said. I am not sure if she is listening for Malporin's benefit, or for her own. Something about her strikes a warning bell within me.

We sit in a corner of the room. A woman and a Morok male bring over our chosen breakfasts, a fragrant tea and the local coffee.

"I thought we were meeting the whole counsel?" I ask.

"Too much going on," he replies. "They essentially voted me authority to deal with you."

Breakfast arrives, with two rough looking miners placing trays of food and drink in front of us. Malporin greets them by name and with thanks for the food,

"I reviewed your manifest," he says, rubbing his eyes and greedily downing coffee. "You selected your cargo well. The machine tools are especially valuable to us. We'll take the entire load off your hands."

"Your poker face is not impressive, Mr. Rand."

"Malporin, please. Mr. Rand was my dad. And as I said last night, I'm more interested in your good opinion of us, than making a profit on you. The offer is 4,800,000 Confed credits in opaloids for the tools and maintenance supplies. I'm prepared to pay handsomely for any spare weapons from your inventory, and we are prepared to compensate you for 90,000 credits for each lift to the capitol over and above your fuel costs.

"Interesting," I reply. "That is quite an offer."

"The catch you are about to ask of, is that only a third of that is here. The rest is in the mineheads on the other side of the mountain. We had a compound there that all the miners used."

I sigh. "Which fell."

"Yes."

"So for me to get paid fully, you'll need me to take your people to and from the mineheads and from here to the capitol. Essentially, you want me to act as your air force."

"Yes."

"And if I do not accept. No one will sell us any opaloids."

"Nor anything else, I'm afraid. You could relocate to the capitol, but at such a loss especially when there is such profit to be had…."

"The offer on the cargo is accepted," I return, reaching for a cake. Behind me Dassa is shoveling in the more substantial pancakes and sausage at a rate that belies her slender frame and raises concerns about the fingers of anyone nearby. She also prefers the local coffee. She unbends enough to thank Malporin for the coffee he sugars and stirs for her. He seems to take her reticence as something of a challenge. I wonder if every cool female affects him this way.

"Good," he says, "I won't even deduct for your companion's breakfast."

For a second I worry Dassa may become angry, but to my surprise a genuine smile flits over her lips. "Good, but you may wish otherwise after you see breakfast, part two."

Now an easy laugh goes around the table; my companion has surprised me.

"Weapons?" Malporin prompts.

I shake my head. "My armory is high quality, but small and not so easily replaced these days.

"It will be a few days before I am ready to take off again, and I will have to head to the capitol to refuel and resupply for deep space. Your fuel store here does not seem sufficient. Though I could easily reach this compound you spoke of."

"Sorry, the fuel tanks at what passes for our spaceport were damaged in an earthquake. The tanks at the minehead may well be intact."

There was enough speculation in that remark for a casino, I think. "Since I am going to the capitol anyway I can make one flight for you."

"On that last I have a problem," Malporin says. "I need about six flights from you for cargo and personnel both ways."

"And all in a war zone that I did not ask to be dropped in," I reply.

"Yes,"

"The wrecked transport at the airfield, what brought that down?"

His face loses its easy humor. "A missile. The transport was taking off in a storm but it was a missile. I don't know if it was mercs, or if someone just sold a fire-and-forget AA missile to the Indigenes. If you use them quickly and don't let it corrode, well, they are point and shoots—"

"With onboard computer tracking, I know," I interrupt. "They're meant for draftee troops with low training. Not much threat to high-performance military aircraft but to a spaceship like mine, struggling along in atmosphere, they could be deadly."

Breakfast seems to lose some of its charm for Dassa.

"We need a regular service to the capitol to be viable. Until I can secure another link, I need you and your ship. We need opaloids moved,

and supplies, or everything we have built here is dust and death," Malporin adds. "I can't let that happen. I can't let all that has gone before be for nothing."

"I have my own concerns, Malporin. I am not indifferent to yours, but I did not come into existence for your sake, or for the sake of your miners."

"Where do you have to go that is so urgent, so desperately urgent, that you can't spare us some of your time?"

It's never that easy, I think to myself, one tie leads to another. I want to be through with people for a while.

"As I said, I have my own concerns, and they do not include a war not of my making. I will accept what I have accepted, and will do what I can, but I am not a soldier for hire."

He nods. I finish my tea, and Dassa finally puts down her fork.

"Well sometimes half a loaf is better than none," Malporin says. "But before we close this book, take a ride with me."

We both rise.

"To where?" I ask, as we follow him out.

The tall human shoulders a door open for me. "I want you to see what we are trying to save here. To learn who we really are. Let me show you the town."

"Very well," I say, following him out into the pale sunlight fighting its way down to us. Dassa brings up the rear, her expressionless face and blue eyes take in everything and give back nothing. We are alone with Malporin Rand, who does not seem to feel the need for guards.

The sky above is a dusky blue, which contrasts with the reddish mountains bulking up in the distance. Again, I am struck by the austere beauty of Damasia. We walk out onto a wide street, lined with warehouses and shops.

"We've lost communications with the capitol," Malporin says. "That's cut us off from the planetary constabulary, so we've had to learn to fight on our own. We were in the process of evacuating casualties and noncombatants when the worst of the storms struck." He stops suddenly and looks at me as if weighing something.

"This way," he says, changing direction and heading for a four-man ATV parked nearby. He unzips the plastic cover which has kept the worst of the storm grit out of it. Dassa heads for the back, until I take her arm and redirect her to the front of the vehicle. Her puzzled look fades almost instantly as she realizes that despite my petite frame, I weigh more than both of them together. I carefully balance myself in the middle of the back of the vehicle, peering between the shoulders of my taller companions. Malporin gives me a curious look, but says nothing about my choice of seating.

Malporin puts the small ATV into drive, and we take a twisting path around a small hill in the center of town. With the subsidence of the *storm, trade seems to have resumed. Shopkeepers beat dust off their awnings. People wander the streets, and a few other vehicles dart about. Their owners never fail to wave to Malporin. There is something nascent here, trying to live and grow despite the hostility of the natives and the changing environment.*

A dry watercourse bisects the town on the other side of the low, wide, hill. Tough but sparse vegetation spots the area, particularly in the watercourse, which must still have some moisture in it.

The town is far from an ideal defensive location, I realize, especially with limited forces.

"Almost there," he says as we pulled onto a broad street holding a two-story building with the look of a school, sitting on a slight rise. Beyond, is another building marked as a hospital. As we proceed down the block, I see children playing soccer in the yard. A few adults with shouldered weapons stand nearby, cheering. Malporin pulls up near the yard and returns the wave of the guards. The children do not pause in their game.

"There were never many children in this town. We evacuated some of them before travel was cut off. The orphans and the unaccompanied evacuee children stay at the school. On the other side of the rise, we have our hospital. Well, it was really just a clinic, but it's what we have." He pulls into a dirt parking lot.

We dismount and approach the game just as a small girl cuts past two boys and kicks the ball into the net. Cheers follow, as this is evidently the game point. The other children mob the tiny youngster, who almost disappears in the huddle.

"Please wait here." He walks over to exchange a few words with the guard detail, then is briefly surrounded by the children. Malporin returns to us with the goal-scorer in tow. I look the child over as she approaches. Her uniform is a yellow shirt and blue shorts with white sox and shoes. Her hair and eyes are brown and her features are small and regular, what a human would call, "cute." She looks up at me with a small smile, showing none of the fear of strangers that children her age, which I guess is between eight and ten standard years, often show. But there is something solemn and adult in her regard. Her look at Dassa is more wary.

"I have someone for you to meet," Malporin says. "Captain Aurelia Toyoma and Dassa, meet Nipkin Chala.

"Hello, Nipkin," I say experimentally, "I saw you get around those bigger defenders and score the goal."

She shrugs. "Everyone is bigger than me; I guess I've learned to use it."

I laugh, obviously surprising Dassa and Malporin. "I have had to educate foes that my small size does not mean small strength."

I am rewarded with a brief, but dazzling smile.

"Captain Toyoma came in with her ship yesterday."

Nipkin nods. "I saw it come down, everybody did."

She turns to me, and her face is suddenly serious. "Have you come to take me to my father?"

I face Malporin, a demand clear on my face. He at least has the good grace to look abashed. "Nipkin was supposed to be evacuated to the capitol with the last of these children. Well, you saw the transport. Her mother was a miner and…" he trails off.

"She was killed," the child says.

"I am very sorry," I say. Dassa, standing next to us, says nothing and seems to be scanning the horizon, as if uninvolved in the tableau. In a real sense, I suppose that she is.

"Thank you," she says, then, "do you still have your parents?"

I am startled, even after all this time by the direction of children's minds. "I think that I am quite a bit older than you realize." But then truth bubbles out of me. "But no, I have also lost my family."

She reaches a small hand out to touch mine. "Then, I am sorry, too."

I am struck speechless for a few seconds.

"Her father is in the capitol. I'd like her and the others to be there too."

"Are we going to go?" Nipkin follows.

"We're trying to work out something with the captain now," Malporin says. "We'll let you know."

A normal child might have cried or kicked up a fuss, or demanded an answer, but an adult-like mask slides over Nipkin's face. She had learned the many different ways adults had to say, no.

A shadow falls over us and we all look up, there is a haze high in the sky, coming with the wind down from the mountain range.

Malporin gives a sudden savage curse, then, remembering Nipkin's presence, controls himself.

There is dread on Nipkin's face. "The Brownie, it's coming back so soon?"

The other children stare up dismay in their faces. The guards, unnerved, unshoulder their weapons.

"They come with the Brownie," Nipkin whispers, almost as if to herself. "It's how they got into Mom's camp. They'll be coming for us next."

"They won't get in here," Malporin states. "This isn't a minehead. We have a lot more people here."

The look the child gives him is almost pitying. "Yes, Mr. Rand."

Yes, I think, more people, but only a handful of police and ex-soldiers. I zoom my vision to the hills to see if any of the tall, four-armed natives are in view. But they are professional warriors. Nothing shows, even to me, but that does not mean that nothing is there.

Malporin notes my gaze. "You won't see them."

"I did not think that likely. Except for scouts the main body would be on the reverse slopes and in concealment from aerial surveillance."

"You tend to express yourself in military terms."

"I am a woman of many parts." Beside me, Dassa smothers a laugh.

"You can't imagine how fast a brownout can come down from the mountains and how quickly the Indigenes can come in behind it. Some of them have learned about modern weapons, even in clear weather, we sometimes get casualties from long-range fire. There, we give as good as we get. I have snipers on our tallest buildings. We keep our heaviest defense to the north but we've had to thin that out to cover the spacefield and the power plant."

A woman comes out of the school and calls to the children, a meal is ready, or at least it is her excuse to get them indoors.

"Better get back to the others," Malporin says.

Nipkin nods to him. "Goodbye, Captain. Maybe we will see each other again."

I am again startled by her adult demeanor and saddened as well, for I understand its cause; her childhood died with her mother.

This is profoundly wrong.

Nipkin nods pleasantly to Dassa, who merely looks back before returning to her scan of the horizon. Nothing in our conversation has affected my hard-bitten companion, perhaps because her own tale of hardship is so similar. Yet, for all it is similar, it never moved me as does Nipkin's tale. I must confront the realization that I feel a prejudice against her species. It seems well-grounded in their behavior to others, but can it be right? As always when suspended over the ocean of moral and emotional choices, I feel inadequate to the task, and I no longer have my guide with me. Or is that true? Is not every word, every gesture, every expressed thought of my husband, not with me? And more, I remember feeling that impossible moment of synchronicity with what was gone, bidding me give Dassa a chance. Could it have been for this reason?

I shake my head in a gesture from my biological days, enough for now.

"Damn it," Malporin says, as he slaps his hand against his pants leg in an almost helpless gesture. "There was so much more I wanted to show you. So much more of our story of what we are trying to build here. Now there's no time."

I turn to him, displaying more friendliness than before; for all that I am aware of his rankly emotional manipulation of what he thinks I am. "Nipkin made your case well."

Surprise stretches over his broad pleasant features; he has not become so skilled a politician after all.

Dassa's head snaps around to me, dismay on her face. But I quell any objection with a stern look. She is too much the Guilder to speak anything important in the presence of others in any event.

I look up at the brownie as Nipkin had called it. Like a malevolent being it seemed to be coiling, gathering strength. Its speed is astonishing. Already it is reaching the foothills. It will be upon us before we could possibly prepare Seachange for an atmospheric hop. We are stuck here for now.

"We'd better get back," he says, big hands knotting. "They weren't in the first storm, least that we saw of them, though I feared scouts. I can't imagine that we will be so lucky a second time."

We climb back into the ATV and pass back through a town that is battening down for the storm and what may be in it. Beings of many species race about, some with weapons, obviously part of the self-defense force. Malporin floors the ATV and we skitter around corners.

"It could be nothing," he says above the racing engine, "but I want to get back to headquarters. It might be best for you two to get back to the hotel."

Even as we drive back the sky above us darkens to the shade of early evening. Lights go on automatically around Pilbara.

"It will be dark as night soon," Dassa says, frowning up at the sky.

"Yeah," Malporin growls, "a Brownie can be a week-long night if you're unlucky."

"Or a permanent darkness," Dassa adds.

"That is why I travel with her," I say, "she is such a cheerful companion."

Malporin manages a brief, grim laugh.

We slow and arrive back at the hotel. This time there are only two guards to greet us.

"We'll continue our conversation another time," Malporin tosses over his shoulder, as he runs toward the council building.

The Drisnian from last night waves toward us. "Better get you two upstairs."

We follow the Drisnian back up to our room. The sky above is now the color of night and the wind is picking up. With it comes the abrasive girt and sand, a danger to friend and foe alike, but for the natives, the protection it gives from modern weapons and detection devices, is worth the pains of operating in it. I do not have sufficient intel on the situation to judge what is going on.

I extend myself into what passes for an internet on this world and connect to Seachange's instruments. The local net is worthless. While the instruments on my ship are excellent, their range is severely limited by the storm now swirling about us. I can see nothing, even with my best image improvements.

"What is going on?" Dassa demands. She has reclaimed her weapons from the bedroom and has her armor on again.

"I cannot tell. I can see nothing. On the net, I am hearing Rand calling up his reserves. There has been some firing by the spaceport, but my expectation is they are shooting at shadows."

Dassa frowns. "Or scouts, it's the area closest to the cover of the foothills."

I nod. "It would provide cover for a direct attack, but the area is open, an attack there would be very exposed to precision arms. There is better cover to the north around that largely dried up watercourse. That is where I would place my main effort if all I had was light infantry."

She takes up station by the window, peering into the darkness from next to the window, carbine to hand. "Do you think they will attack?"

"If there is a large force, then yes. Primitives will not have the logistics to maintain a large force in the field indefinitely. It will be a case of use it, or disperse it. It is just as well you ate a breakfast of such epic proportions."

"Actually, I was thinking of food and water." She goes to the bathrooms and fills the sink and tubs. Sound thinking and I am pleased by her foresight. "I think I will go down and see what is available in the kitchen for later," she adds.

Dassa opens the door and speaks to the Drisnian. She motions, and the second guard departs with Dassa. I close the door behind her and move to where I can see out the window. Sitting on the floor, I rest my chin in my palm. Well, they do say that an army marches on its stomach and I, myself, am soaking in some broadcast power. I extend a wire and tap into the wall socket. I have not used much yet, but it is best to stay topped up.

I feel action is in the offing, but it may be several hours yet. The distance is not short, and likely they will wait for the height of the storm before engaging.

Hours pass and I keep track of Malporin's preparations. He has pulled his forces in closer to Pilbara to react more quickly, which is sensible. But he is thinking only with his weapons. His own population is not gathered. People are in their homes. Some of the children, orphans, or those stranded away from their parents, are in the school with a small defense team. A better plan would have been to have moved all the civilians into one location and blown down any outlying buildings to clear lanes of fire. If there is a breakthrough, he will be fighting on many fronts at the same instant.

He has also not left any outposts to listen and report, so if there is an attack, he will first learn of it when they close to combat distance. He lacks the ruthless quality of a proper military officer. LP/OPs are often annihilated by an advancing enemy, but the exchange of lives for information is worthwhile.

Malporin is no general. But there is something in his determination to protect his people that reminds me of Wrik. I only hope that he will not be too sorely tried by the coming night. Perhaps it will just be an engagement with scouts. Perhaps.

Dassa returns as the day wears into evening. She has been talking with the guards, the kitchen staff, gathering intelligence as she may. She's also raided the pantry to considerable effect, bringing up more, on the *excuse that it is for me. We are now well provisioned for several days for water and food no matter what happens.*

Suddenly a report demands my attention. It is from the AI on Seachange.

"Contact," I report. "A large force of enemy light infantry is maneuvering toward the landing area."

"If we reveal that to Malporin," Dassa says, "he will want to know how you know. A normal hand com like we're carrying won't penetrate this storm's interference. They're using land lines to communicate and few military-power coms. They know we don't have one of those."

Inspiration strikes. "We warned them that the ship would fire if anything approached within a hundred meters."

"You did...Aha!"

"Yes, I just fired the ship's laser in the direction of the force I detected. They will think the Indigenes are that close. It will alert them in time to react. The laser will continue to fire on any Indigene's it can bear on. There will be considerable time between shots, the weapon is meant to be used in space and will take longer to cool in atmosphere. It was not intended for ground defense."

I follow Malporin's reaction to Seachange's firing, at first with approval and then with a growing dismay. He is pulling off too many of his northern forces before his enemy has committed to his main effort. He is now out of position if an attack comes in from the North. From where I am, there is no way to detect if the main axis of attack is coming from where I would have sent it.

There is no help for it. The school and hospital are north, and if the enemy takes the high ground of Pilbara's central hill, the entire town could be rolled up. I stand and retract my power cord.

Dassa looks at me in surprise. "What?"

"This battle is being conducted by amateurs, and I fear a mistake is being made. If the enemy is doing what I believe they will, then we could be in serious trouble. The children at the school and casualties at the hospital are under-defended."

Before she can argue or suggest something else. I move to the window and slide it open. "Remain here," I toss over my shoulder. "If anyone comes to the door tell them I went to sleep."

"Just a moment," she calls, but I slide the door closed from the outside and start down the outside of the wall using each terrace as a step. In seconds, I reach the ground and my entire exterior is now a non-reflective flat-black. In the swirling grit, it should be impossible to see me at any distance. I set out at a pace that will not drain me, but should get me to the school in ten minutes.

CHAPTER FOURTEEN

CURSED MAAURO, CURSED MY GRANDFATHER AND THE malign gods who have put me in the grip of a soft-minded fool, so easily manipulated by the appearance of a small child she has no connection with. That is who she was worried about and why she had left. Now here I was, abandoned by the combat machine as it went off on some mission of its own with a major native attack unfolding.

I hung by the window for a while. In the distance, I saw the actinic flash of weapons and explosives. *Seachange* was firing at something.

Damn her. I was not staying up here alone and in the dark, literally and metaphorically. I was out of contact with everything here. I opened the door to the corridor to find our guards gone.

This just keeps getting better, I thought. With my carbine in my hands, I headed out and, not trusting the elevator, took the stairs two at a time until I got to the bottom.

Once there, I heard Romy and some of the kitchen staff, huddled in her office, doubtless with some handguns. They weren't the outfit I wanted to lodge with tonight. The council chamber should be the safest spot.

I slipped out the door and headed for the council chamber. The wind and grit were waiting for me on the other side. I was glad for the visor on my helmet but already found dirt sifting into my clothes irritating. Seconds later I was in the main building. There I found a few of the council, trying to command the developing battle over their ad hoc tactical net. Malporin was absent, and in a moment of cold knowledge, it struck me that in a form of heroic idiocy, he was probably somewhere out in the fight as opposed to directing it from safety.

In another part of the room, a reinforcement team was assembling under the Nekoan female I had earlier noticed on the council. I remembered her name, Kemisa.

She spotted me as I came in. Her eyes ran over my weapon-laden form. "Can you use that hardware you're toting?"

There is no profit in lying. I nodded. "Expertly."

"Good, you're with us." She glanced over my shoulder. "Where is your Captain?"

I shrugged.

She swore. "Never mind. We're moving out in a few minutes. Our team is providing additional security down at the spaceport and your ship."

"The ship will defend itself," I warned.

"Yeah, I saw your commo laser fire. Were those warning shots at Indigenes—"

"It's firing for effect."

"Good, then it may be roasting some Indigene ass. But the Brownout is getting thicker every second; it could scatter even a heavy laser into uselessness."

"Damn."

"Gods damn," the Nekoan agreed, smiled grimly and displaying every fang. "This looks like the main effort. If we can't hold them tonight, there's no tomorrow.

"Understood."

"What's your name again, Kit?"

I bridled. I might have to concede seniority to Maauro, but this woman could be only twenty or so years older then I, but the purple eyes did not seem unfriendly. "Call me, Dassa."

"Ok Dassa, I'm Kemisa, the brute with the fire ax and beard is Bowman, my number two. Get to know everyone else's names as fast as you can." She gestured at the mixed group of twenty beings behind her. I was glad to see a hulking Okaran among the humans and Moroks.

"We have two trucks out back. You stay near me in the first one."

I found myself warily liking the lithe alien. I slipped my helmet and visor on. Kemisa threw me a scarf. "Tie it over your mouth and nose. No time to get you a proper breather."

We walked out onto what was clearly a trucking bay, passing through hanging plastic strips. Brown, swirling grit filled the air, and the two promised trucks were there, wheeled varieties as one might expect on a rugged frontier world. The first vehicle was a conspicuous red in the loading bay lights. I knew that, once we pulled away from the lights, the red would be invisible to most eyes in the dark. Still, I found myself wishing we were in the black dump truck behind us.

The miners, now soldiers, piled into the vehicles. Kemisa directed Bowman to the other, but kept the Okaran with her. I approved of her tactical dispositions as I was now in the best protected group. The truck engines grumbled to life as we pulled out of the loading dock.

The Okaran stood just behind Kemisa. I looked up at the ursine alien. It looked down its grizzled muzzle at me.

"I'm Dassa."

"Cobeller," it grunted back at me. "I used to run the general store and I am too old for this shit."

I snorted a laugh.

"Sounds like you have a good head on those shoulders. How's your bite?"

The muzzle wrinkled. "Enough to sever an arm off any Indigene bastard who tries to fuck with me."

"Good."

The others nearby threw me their names and I committed them to memory using the mnemonic tricks my masters had painfully drilled into me. I studied the variety of weapons with some dismay. The mix of obsolete military and hunting weapons did not inspire confidence. I was glad for my triple-auto carbine and slug-thrower, but wished I had brought more reloads and left the stunner behind.

I assumed the ship would open to me so long as I was alone, but knew the AI, itself, just a miniature subset of Maauro's systems, would let me do little more.

"Listen up," Kemisa's voice sounded. "I put all of you save for Bowman and myself on Channel 43, the main tac net is already overloaded and we can use 43 to talk among ourselves. Stay off the main, and listen to me. I'll let you know what you need to know, when you need to know it."

"Crap," someone said, "listen to the cat-queen sounding like a real officer."

"Shut up, Cristobal. I got no time for your bullshit."

Laughs sounded over the net. I couldn't for the life of me figure what the hell was funny.

Ahead through the murk, a large flare raged. Seachange had fired again, doubtless much of the beam had scattered, but Maauro had amped up the laser. Some enemy must have died under its lash, and a smiled stretched across my own face.

The trucks bounced over the bad roads, and we all held on to whatever we could. I was surprised to find Kemisa putting an arm around my waist.

"Don't fall out, Kit. We need your gun."

The ride became smoother as we hit the fused sand and tarmac of the spacefield, pulling up to some bunkers. I saw *Seachange* towering in the distance, her storm lights piercing the swirling sand. We piled out of the trucks, which then became themselves part of the fortifications. Kemisa led her people up to a group of nervous miners, who were firing into the darkness.

"Where's Lanten?" Kemisa shouted. "Knock off that firing if you don't have a definite target."

Lanten, another bearded miner with frightened eyes showed up. "Thank God you are here. The area on the other side of the field is swarming with the four-armed fuckers."

She looked at the shaken man. "Ok. Mal sent me out to take over. He's by the power plant. Show me your dispositions." She gestured to me and the Okaran. "You two stay by me at all times."

Before we could even canvass the defenses, a weird, undulating howl reached us distorted by the wind.

"Here they come again," Lanten howled.

CHAPTER FOURTEEN

The defenders leapt to the sandbags and crates, leveling their weapons.

"Hold your fire till they get closer," Kemisa called over the net. Some of Lanten's people were either on another frequency, or ignored the order as firing broke out. Kemisa swore in anger, but her people didn't succumb to the panic and followed their officers into defensive positions.

I took up position on the right side of the Nekoan female. She hadn't even drawn her sidearm, rather, she divided her time between a portable tablet and field glasses. I joined her in scanning, using my electronic sight. All I could see was swirling shapes and sand. For a moment, a swirl of air cleared and I saw a four-armed creature with a rifle and two knives. I fired instantly, a single HVAP round. The creature dropped, weapons tumbling from its lifeless hands.

"Nice," Kemisa said, "one clean round. Maybe the rest of these idiots can take a cue from you."

The wavering cry went up again and *Seachange* fired. In the scattering of light, I saw the mass of warriors, well spread out, with more rifles then I would have expected. I used the light to pop two mini-frags into the midst of the biggest cluster, following with a burst of fully automatic fire. Others joined in.

The fusillade grew in volume as the warriors closed in. We were twenty-eight Confed facing at least two hundred and better Indigenes, who cut loose with return fire that was high and inaccurate. That told me that they'd only acquired the modern arms recently and hadn't trained well enough.

Or some hadn't. A miner next to me fell to the ground, a third eye sprouting in his forehead, another shot banged off the metal plate the Okaran wore across his chest, still another tore up the sandbag at my elbow. The enemy wasn't soldiers, but warriors, fighting individually. They took cover as they fired and raced forward, seeking to come to grips with us with the edged weapons natural to them.

The team proved very grateful for my marksmanship with the Confed triple auto carbine. My powerful weapon, with its particle accelerator and mini-frags, made the difference in the first wild charge at us. I knew better than to use the laser in such flying grit. Some of our enemies had lasers and made fine and lively light-shows with them. I treated each one to a mini-frag.

The battle became a chaotic whirl as bands of warriors dueled with a dwindling supply of defenders. Exhaustion began to dull my senses. It seemed like days, but was merely an hour when the shout came up.

"Breakthrough!"

I snapped back to awareness. Green-skinned warriors poured through a gap where two defenders had fallen, one wounded, one dead. With a roar, Cobeller lunged from his spot behind Kemisa, who'd finally drawn her pistol. The massive Okaran crashed into a knot of green warriors. Bigger then Dua-Denlenn, they were still only half the mass of an Okaran male. He crushed the head of one warrior and sent two more flying. But the enemy was not helpless. A four-armed warrior buried two long knives in the stomach of the giant, while firing a shot at his face. The shot creased the Okaran's face as he bellowed in shock and anger. But before the alien could pull out either blade Cobeller's teeth came down and met in the warrior's neck. He managed one more swipe, taking the head off another warrior scrambling over the pile of sandbags and bodies and then fell.

I leapt over the body of Cobeller and leaned over the sagging sandbag wall. The six warriors there seemed as startled to face me at two-meters distance, as I was to see them, but I fired first. The triple-auto sprayed cyclically, laser, PB and mini-frags. It was too close for the mini-frags to arm, but they tore the group into a mass of shattered bone and spraying blood, before exploding in the distance.

I jumped back, pulling my slug-thrower. The carbine would take a few seconds to cool down to operational again and I was out of mini-frags. But the only opponent I faced was the stinging wall of wind-blown grit.

I looked around. At least fourteen defenders were still up, tending the wounded, or firing occasional shots over the works.

"Man, I thought they had us," Lanten said, his hands shook visibly, but still clutched a shotgun.

"They would have but for Kit here," Kemisa said

"No," I said, staring over the wall. I could see natives moving away through eddies in the murk. They were too far for a reliable pistol shot, and I was only concerned about ones moving in my direction.

"What do you mean?" Kemisa demanded.

"This was a diversion," I said. "This force was too small to be the main effort. Not even all of it was used against us. We just got unlucky, these guys got close. I think they let us see a bigger force, then pulled it out and threw a holding force on us."

"Good for us then," Lanten said.

"Idiot," Kemisa raged fangs and claws visible. "We have most of our troops around the spacefield and the power station where the council meets. They're coming in somewhere less defended. Shit."

"My Captain thought the logical place to attack would be down the dry watercourse to the hospital and school."

"With respect, Kit, your captain may be hell on wheels with cargo, but—"

"But nothing," I interrupt. "Don't underestimate Captain Toyoma. If she says there are coming from there, then they are."

Kemisa looked me over, head to toe. "Who are you two? You're about as much free traders as I'm a Morok."

"You really have time for this conversation?" I shot back. "They are coming down on your school and hospital."

"Kit," she said. "We *will* talk."

"When we do, you'll call me, Dassa."

The cold stare faded as she nodded, then pulled her com from her belt. "Mal, Malporin come in. We've been suckered. God, damn it, there's too much noise on the net. This thing won't penetrate it."

"Lanten, hold here with what's left of your group and the walking wounded. Everybody else, on the trucks."

"There's only four of us," Lanten protested. Everyone ignored him.

"Not me," I said. "I'm going to our ship for reloads."

The Nekoan and I were face to face. "I have orders that neither you, nor your captain, go to the ship."

"Then you have orders to die," I snapped. "I can't take off without the captain."

"Very loyal of you for a Dua-Denlenn.

I gave a mirthless grin. "She set it up so."

"Good," Kemisa said, also displaying teeth. "I believe that. Ok, Kit… Dassa…go and get weapons and ammo." She looked around, then pointed at a four-wheeled Mule. "Take that, then meet us on the northern road. If you do take off, I'll curse you and your descendants for ten generations."

"If I could," I shouted over my shoulder, "I'd live with it. Don't lose the town meanwhile." I floored the accelerator on the cargo Mule.

Seachange opened to me as I leapt from the Mule, her hatches gaping as I ran toward them. Overhead, the ship's laser raved out into the night again and a terrible smell of scorched dirt struck me as metal droplets from the Brownie fell and sizzled on my helmet and jacket. I raced in, heading for the armory. Mercifully, the doors to the armory slid open at my touch. I frantically reloaded my weapons, throwing down the useless stunner. I belted on two slug-throwers, bypassed the lasers and pulled two more of the racked carbines and a sniper rifle. I looked longingly at the weapon Maauro called her armspac, but knew it was beyond my ability to lift or fire.

I grabbed a box of minifrags, breaking the connection that prevented the weapons from being armed inside the ship. Then, staggering under my load of armaments, I returned to the mule. I debated a second trip, but decided it would take too long. The mule started, and I stood on the accelerator, racing back to the battle for Pilbara. Again, I floored the pedal.

CHAPTER FIFTEEN

SPEED FORWARD AMONG THE INDIGENES, SURPRISED BY THE NUMBER *of them, even though I expected this to be the main attack. The enemy toward the spaceport is a diversion, pulling Malporin's forces and reserves out of their positions. This huge force has eluded Malporin's patrols and outposts to mass here, waiting only for the brownout to arrive. They must have punched through the thin screen of defenders to the north.*

But if the whispering and stinging grit has allowed them to come to grips with the offworlders, it performs the same function for me. I race in a circle around the school and hospital, destroying all I encounter. Swords shatter against my limbs, low velocity bullets carom off my armored chassis as I plunge in and among them like a reaper. I consider whether to emit chemical or biological ordnance, but the wind and the nearness of the Pilbara school and hospital argue against it. I must kill by shock or fire.

One enemy I sight holds a modern carbine that could damage me, but his reflexes are merely biological. I spin like a pinwheel in the air over him as his shot goes under me. My palm blades carve a trough in his skull. Before his body can fall to the ground, I seize the modern weapon and snap shots at fleeting figures in the raging storm to supplement my supply of flechettes. I can manufacture more flechettes, but only at the cost of metal, time and energy I cannot spare now.

I try to raise Dassa, but interference from the metal-laden sand and blasts of lightning are degrading communications at her end. The town's system is equally hopeless, overloaded with screams, cries for help and information in the poor radio discipline typical of barely-trained irregulars. I cannot gather a picture of the overall tactical situation and am left to my own devices. All I can do is maximize my own counterattack and hope to suck any reserves into conflict with me. I consider sending out a blast of virus to detonate enemy weapons; many are captured Confed models using the same IFF as the town's militia. I may blow up friendly troops if I do. I'll correct Malporin's error in this when there is time.

A squad of enemy head for the school-dormitory building, screaming their high-pitched war cries and drawing scattered and ineffective fire from the defenders within. Another group screens them and faces me. I drop my now empty carbine and charge the screening troops. Not knowing my nature, they allow me to close to use their cutting weapons and are slaughtered in seconds. I pursue the dormitory squad as they reach the broad shallow steps of the building.

I do not know how the Indigenes detect me, but half the group stops and deploys. The leading group either does not hear, or disregards the threat to their rear and penetrates the building, plunging through the merely glass doors and the barricades beyond.

I attack. This group is cannier. A massed volley of shots shakes me, causing momentary loss of target lock. One Indigene leaps atop a short wall and levels a tube at me. The anti-tank rocket flashes from the disposable container. I lean to one side as the HEAT round flashes by my chest. I flick its guide fins with my finger, so it will miss the buildings behind me. It hits the street, spinning like a firework for a second before detonating, slinging a deadly spray of molten metal and felling a running Indigene. Some liquid metal hits me, but other than an unsightly blemish on my casing, it has no effect.

I pay my enemy back with a flechette in the brain as he reaches for a second tube. Another enemy fires a hand laser at me, but the flying sand and grit scatter the beam in a brilliant shower of light and sparks that I would have enjoyed under other circumstances.

Another volley strikes me, more ragged this time, and I turn and charge. Kicks that crush the body and blows that sever limbs with my palm blades eliminate most of the group. Two flee, but I do not have leisure to pursue them. I must overtake the unit that has breached the dormitory defenses.

I am killing too slowly, lacking my armspac and degraded by the storm's effects. While there is not enough force in it to abrade my exterior, save when I accelerate to high speed, it dulls my sensors. Shock from weapons hits and blows have been minor and my internal damage control is coping with them without difficulty. The overall effect is draining, but not critical. Without supporting forces, I cannot control the battle and must prioritize my missions.

I decide to make the storm's interference work for me and dare a short, focused blast of virus, tailored so it will not penetrate the building behind me, or go far into the storm cloud. Three enemy weapon detonations reward me and I judge my immediate area sanitized enough that I can pursue into the building.

I press my attack, leaping the barricade. An Indigene rises from behind the pile of desks and strikes at me with a broadsword. The blow is so hard that it creates a spark on the edge of the palm blade I block with. Vexed, I gut him with the other palm blade. I snatch his sword out of the air and send it flashing out the shattered doors to cut down another enemy who was cautiously coming up behind me. The weapon cuts him down then the wind takes the sword out of sight a millisecond later.

As I turn back, I see three of the town defense team on the floor among dead, four-armed warriors. Two of the defenders lie dead. One is wounded and unconscious, but I cannot spare time to act as medic. Only five of the Indigenes lie dead among them and I know that seven fought their way in before I destroyed the rear guard.

Inside the building, even with its shattered doors, it is possible to see and hear clearly under its bright white lights. Sand whips in, but the wind is muted. So, it is easy to hear the screams from above.

I accelerate to full military power, leaping to the second-story landing and smashing through two doors into a long corridor. Only my best speed will stop the atrocity unfolding here.

A boy in his early teens lies face down in a pool of his own blood, a volume so great that I know he must be dead. A fire ax lies next to him, testimony to a last, desperate defense.

My sensors, freed of the storm's effects and burning at full power, pierce the structure around me. One Indigene is in the next room, facing a group of children sheltering behind a utility closet door. Another pursues a solitary child down a hall on the other side of the building.

I blast through the wall and directly into the enemy beating on the door sheltering the children. My scanner shows the children pressed against the windowless door trying to hold it closed. Good, they will not see what is to happen.

My enemy spins to face me, but I close on the towering warrior before he can fire either of the pistols in his lesser and lower arms. His sword glances off my palm blade block. I punch his midsection with a palm strike, liquefying his internal organs. Blood explodes out of his mouth.

"Stay inside and you will be safe," I shout to the cowering children as I accelerate toward the other wall. I must reach my last enemy before he covers the last few meters to the fleeing child. I burst through the nearest non-load bearing wall, appearing only steps behind the last Indigene. He is almost on the child.

Nipkin. Her wide eyes stare over her shoulder at the huge, four-armed Indigene between us, a weapon in each of its hands. In the tatters of robes and wearing goggles, it is the very image of a child's nightmare.

Nipkin screams and flings her arms over her face.

The Indigene has not reacted to my entry into the hallway, focused on Nipkin, now within striking range. There is no time. I leap, and, as I once did to paralyze the Guild-gunner, Lostra, while she stood over my wounded Wrik, I roar at full volume. The warrior freezes for a precious moment, his head jerking to face me as I fly toward him.

The Indigene has given poor Nipkin an image of horror to live with. I give him one to die with. My eyes are black from lid to lid and I raise serrated teeth in my mouth which gapes wider than a human's could.

My enemy bellows in shock and fear and then I am on it. My teeth meet in his upper arm. My palm blades and lashing feet destroy his body. One of the big pistols triggers and a shot bounces off the wall as his body explodes in a shower of blood and bones.

Instant regret. What madness is this? What am I now but another blood-soaked monster standing over Nipkin? But there is mercy in the universe. The child had raised her arms over her face and closed her eyes, and frozen by my voice, has not moved.

I am next to her in an instant as my eyes and teeth revert to normal and my palm blades retract into my hands. I drop to knees in front of the frozen child. "Nipkin," I say in the gentlest voice I can manage. "It's Captain Aurelia, keep your eyes closed. Don't open them at all."

Her mouth opens, but no sound comes out.

"You're safe, Little One. You're safe, he's gone."

Her breath comes in short gasps as she tries to speak.

"Nipkin, listen to me. You are safe. I will let nothing harm you. But you must keep your eyes closed tight."

The gasps turn into a wail. I put my arms around the child despite the horrible condition of my exterior.

"Why?" she chokes out among tears. "Why can't I open my eyes?"

"Listen, you are safe. I will protect you, but I don't want you to see the dead Indigene."

Nipkin continues to sob but it is easing. "I've seen dead people before, when they killed my mother."

"Once was too much," I add, as pick the child up. "I will tell you when you can open your eyes."

Her small arms are tight around me. She presses her face against what is, mercifully, a dry spot on my neck.

"You're wet," she says as the blood coating my exterior penetrates her clothes.

"Shhh," I reply, having nothing better to offer. I run back through the hole I made into the classroom where the other children remain hidden in the utility closet.

"Eyes closed," I remind her. "I am going to put you down for a few seconds. I have to fix something. OK?"

Her arms tighten spasmodically on me then loosen. She nods. In a few seconds, I grab the dead warrior, open a window and fling him out. Closing the window, I turn back to Nipkin, who is shaking visibly. I run back to her, wrap my arms about her and raise my body temperature.

"It's ok to open your eyes."

She stares about the room as if unable to recognize anything, returning to a universe from which order and sanity have departed.

I hear crying from the other side of the door. "Children," I call. "It is safe to come out."

The door does not open. They are too terrified. I realize this is for the best.

"Nipkin," I say, holding her at arm's length. "You must stay in this room. Comfort the others. Do not leave until adults come."

"Where are you going?" she says, panic returning to her face. She clutches my blood and gore-stained hands

"I must protect the building. No enemy will again penetrate this structure."

"All by yourself?"

"I am far stronger than I look."

"I saw…I saw you break through the wall and leap into the air. Aurelia your eyes were black and your teeth…"

She had seen more than I realized before covering her eyes.

"I am sorry you had to see that, but glad you did not see more. You must keep that a secret for me. Will you promise to do that?"

She frowns are me, her face dark with suspicion, then it clears like sunrise. "You're still my friend?"

"Yes," I reply, with full knowledge of what that word, never uttered casually by me, means and what it binds me to.

"Ok then. I promise." Her face darkens again. "Did you see, Lamosos? He was trying to hold them off with an ax."

"I am so sorry, Nipkin. He's gone."

She sighs and tears leak from her eyes. "Aurelia, how can there be a God who lets this happen? Why do the nice people always die?"

I fight for self-control. "Remain here," I manage, stroking her hair. "Help the others. I will defend this place."

She nods.

I stand and run from the room. I am a combat android, victor in many deadly conflicts. I may not weep in front of a child. I pause only to take Lamosos from the pool of blood in which he lies and wrap his torn body in a curtain I rip from a window. I speed down to the lobby; the wounded man there has expired. All is death about me.

I walk through the shattered doors. My eyes glow as if summoning my enemies to their extinction. Teeth and palm blades return. The universe is out of joint. Horrors abound. Yet I am Maauro, I will restore order, sanity, and the safety of children.

A mass of enemies in company strength is visible to my sensors through the murk, which has abated some while I fought inside. I accelerate toward them. On another day, I might have wondered about their women, their children, the ruination of their lives and world that drove them to this. But that would be another day. Tonight, my mind is full of terrified children and a boy forced to be a man in the last few seconds of his life.

I have named Nipkin as my friend. All those who threaten the friends of Maauro must die. It is my own immutable law.

CHAPTER SIXTEEN

KEMISA AND THE OTHERS HAD LEFT BEFORE ME, SO I DID not slow, but continued, following the track leading toward the hospital. To my surprise, I ran into them quickly. They'd encountered a roadblock and had dismounted to clear it. The flash of rifles attracted my attention. Hunting weapons, I judged, as military ones used flashless powder. Brilliant red lines of lasers crisscrossed. The storm had eased and with less grit in the air, it was worthwhile to use lasers. The ship's AI continued to fire the big laser, but not in this direction as the town sat beyond.

I pulled up to where Kemisa and her crew sheltered behind the big vehicle. The other truck sat next to a building, its engine smoking.

I hopped out, tossing reloads to grateful troops.

"Tell me you reloaded on mini-frags," Kemisa demanded.

I nodded.

"Get up in the truck and get an eye on that roadblock," she shouted. "Let me know when you're ready. You hose the roadblock with minifrags and cover us."

A man gave me a leg up into the back of the dump truck. I crabbed my way to the front of the truck's dump bed then took out the makeup compact Maauro had given me. Using some heavy tape I'd grabbed on the ship, I stuck its mirror on a piece of metal I'd found in the truck bed. Two humans next to me fired at the roadblock. I stayed in cover, raised my makeshift periscope and spotted the road block, two vehicles and some dumpsters filled with dirt and rock.

"Ready," I shouted to Kemisa.

"Light em up," she called.

I popped up and left fly with the minifrags, aiming for the joins between vehicles and dumpsters. A series of bangs spilled the Indigenes out of cover. I switched to full auto and spit out lead and particles while Kemisa and her team charged. So effective was my carbine fire, that none of the natives got a shot off. One fled, only to be cut down by Kemisa herself.

"OK, saddle up," Bowman shouted, as Kemisa returned. She'd left most of her team by the roadblock to clear it and prevent any return by the Indigenes. But there was something odd in her stance. She had a hand up to her ear, and stopped in what looked like surprise.

I hopped down and reload my minifrags and AP rounds. "What's going on?"

She looked at me. "I don't know. The first reinforcement's teams are reaching the northern area. They say they can hardly move for all the dead Indigenes underfoot. Hundreds of them, some of them look like they were thrown into a turbofan"

Maauro, I thought to myself, *it can only be her.* "Maybe your Northern defense force rallied."

Kemisa shook her head, studying my face intently. "No. What wasn't overrun pulled into pillboxes or fled south. We didn't do this."

I shrugged. "Just be grateful someone did. Apparently, you have more friends then you know of."

The storm peters out in the early morning hours. I have battled the night away, draining much of my energy and suffering light damage. The compound has withstood the assault, in no small measure because most the attacking forces were drawn into close combat with me. The Indigene's primitive communications only served to summon more and more of them to my part of the battle, but, just as quickly, I extinguished the enemy reinforcements. They never realized the hopelessness of their situation.

With all the casualties I inflicted, the strain on the rest of the town's ad hoc defenses eased enough for them to stand off the Indigenes with minor losses from what I can gather over the tacnet.

Minor losses, I think, like Lamosos who lies on a table top with only fourteen years of past and no future. Even small losses bring terrible pain.

I do not elect to pursue the retreating Indigenes as the four-armed natives flee north into the mountains. Death is not my objective here, only the safety of Pilbara. The Indigene attack has probably used up the bulk of the fighting-age males in this part of the continent. They will not be able to duplicate this assault for generations. A tribal society cannot replace warriors the way an industrial society replaces soldiers.

I scan the area a second time in an excess of caution to make sure no stragglers remain to endanger the dormitory or the hospital beyond. I zoom my vision and confirm that there are still defenders at the hospital. Mercifully, it was not penetrated in the assault and my efforts in the area beyond, insured no one was slaughtered in their beds.

I then vibrate my chassis at high speed to get rid of some of the gore on me. My power level is too low to use plasma without greater need. I promise myself a shower as soon as possible. If I am to remain covert, I too must disappear.

I would like to see Nipkin again, but already I detect Malporin's irregulars cautiously approaching the area. Time for me to go. Using the remaining darkness and swirling storm grit, I dodge from cover to cover, making my way back to the hotel. Pilbara's defense teams are now frantically racing to the dorm and hospital. I color-shift into a splinter pattern of black and brown, moving only when they are not looking in my direction, and speed undetected past them.

On reaching the outside of the hotel, I quickly scale the balconies and regain our room. To my surprise, Dassa is not present. What has happened? The self-centered Guilder would not have volunteered for combat duty…or have I misjudged her? Maybe she was pressed into service? Quickly, I tune back into the net, but there is no mention of her. I reach out to the ship's AI and scan the area using its optics. I spot Dassa in a vehicle on the edge of the spacefield, unharmed. The area in front of her vehicle is carpeted with dead Indigenes. The damage pattern is that of a triple-auto carbine. She has clearly been a factor in the battle.

I debate between a shower and power then opt for the former. Hot water sluices over me, I briefly debate using the tub but it seems too self indulgent. I towel and heat blast my exterior from my own radiators until I am fully dry, then quickly examine the tub for any bits of dead Indigene. A quick scrub, a bit of plasma fire and the tub is clean again. I head for the living room to find a power plug. The amount I can draw is pitiful but, as Wrik used to say, even thin soup is better than no soup. I plug into the wall and settle on the floor.

I walked back to our room, having said goodbye downstairs with a curious reluctance to Kemisa and the team I'd fought with. The humans all took me by the hand or shoulder, thanking me for my part in the fight and praising my marksmanship. To my surprise, Kemisa grabbed me when we were around the other side of the massive truck we'd used for a transport, and kissed me on the mouth.

"I'll show my appreciation better another night," she'd said, before slipping away. Out of trained reflex, I'd kept anything from my face or manner, but the feel of her mouth against mine had been exciting, and a liaison with an alien risked nothing for me. I wondered if her interest was sex, or business, or more likely both. Perhaps she saw me as a way to gain influence or access to Maauro, though why eluded me. It might be fun to find out, and who knew how it could advantage me?

A deep fatigue hovered on the edge of my consciousness. For now, all I wanted was a safe place to lie down. But fatigue vanished when I opened the now unguarded door to our suite and saw Maauro, in mint condition, sitting cross-legged on the floor by the sliding glass doors. She had clearly sensed my solitary approach, because she was plugged into the wall by a slender, nearly invisible cord from her midsection.

"Where the hell have you been!" I shouted, slamming the door behind me.

From the look on her face, she was surprised by my vehemence. For that matter, so was I, but feelings of *schadenteer* and betrayal vied in me.

"I was in the northern part of the town," she said calmly. "I deduced that the attack on the port was a feint, and in any event, I was concerned that the northern defenses by the school and hospital were inadequate.

I encountered the main force that advanced down the dry riverbed, engaged and reduced it."

"Oh, well, all I was doing was fighting for my life down at the diversion!"

"You need not shout, my hearing is as acute as I need to make it. A quick scan shows that you are uninjured beyond fatigue and some strains."

I got hold of myself and divested of the arsenal I was carrying, before it could become a factor, ejecting magazines and putting the weapons on safe like the good gunner I was.

"I need a shower," I said

"As did I," she offered.

I looked at her.

"I was covered with Indigene circulatory fluid and fragments."

"Ah."

"Do not worry. I cleaned the shower very thoroughly."

"Good."

Her eyes turned to the power tap. "We will need to return to the ship soon. I used energy at a prodigious rate least night and am close to minimum effective combat power. I cannot draw enough this way to do more than begin replenishment without tripping the breakers."

"I am sorry that breakfast isn't to your taste."

The big green eyes turned and focused on me. A warning perhaps? I was too angry to care. I kicked off my boots and started for the shower, dropping clothes as I went, but paused at the bathroom door.

"I'm curious," I threw over my shoulder. "You've often told me about your bonds with the others from Lost Planet, the friendships you, as we don't have a proper translation for it, lectured me on. Would you have run off and left one of the others to fight for their life alone?"

Maauro froze, only for the tiniest of moments, but I was sufficiently attuned to her by now to see it. I'd scored a hit. I let a bitter smile reach my face as the door closed behind me.

I am surprised, left without a response as the slender Dua disappears into the bathroom. Why did I not see this for myself? I raced off into the dark, concerned for Nipkin and the other town children, though the latter was a generic concern; my thoughts were centered on Nipkin.

But I had given no thought to the Dua-Denlenn girl, a member of my crew who I'd brought unwilling to this place. Dassa was seventeen to Nipkin's ten, but what matter that small space of years to me who has lived for millennia? Were they not both children? Why had I been moved so much by the fate of one, and been so cavalier about the other?

True, Dassa is not a companion of my choice as all my prior network had been. Even her grandfather had been selected by me, though not through any liking, rather as a hostage and an intelligence source. Dassa thrust herself into my existence, uninvited, unselected and unwanted, casting obligations on me that I was not ready for.

Is that it? Resentment? Anger, even? I am still so badly wounded by the loss of my husband and the sundering of my network. This pain travels everywhere with me and bites hardest at night when I remember the comfort of his body resting near mine. She'd dug me up for purposes of her own. If I was not healed by my internment, I was at least not aware of my pain. Now awakened, by this Guild creature, I am never free of it.

Guild… my enemy from the moment of my awakening in this new existence, until I finally taught them the folly of tangling with me. All my mass of experience with them counted against Dassa. Guild had once maimed me and wounded Wrik. How am I to forgive that?

Yet more is present here. With a second shock, I realize that I hold Dassa's life of less account than Nipkin's as she is human and Dassa is not. I had lived as a human and loved one. There is no question it colors my perspective as to Dassa and her species. So, is this part of my distance with her, a species prejudice complicated by her Guild connections? It could be so, yet I feel I have solid grounds for my feelings about her and her kind. Their code of behavior is repellent to me. Perhaps all those who harbor prejudices feel so. It seems our relationship is as far from true understanding as it was at the beginning, perhaps it will always be so.

Enough, I am weary of these emotional tangles. Emotional thought requires vast amount of processing power and energy I cannot now spare and yet rarely does the effort bring matters closer to resolution. In the end, I have to live a life, not analyze it.

In a mute token of apology, I gather up weapons and clean them, a task more quickly done by me, who was once only a weapon, than by Dassa. Then I gather up her clothes and use the small cleaning machine in the utility room. It occurs to me that Dassa has spent a long time in the bathroom even for a sulking teenager.

I look toward the door and fire a microwave pulse to image the room with. It shows me Dassa is in the tub, immobile. I am concerned enough to cross the room in a quick stride and peer around the door. The lanky Dua-Denlenn is sprawled, long limbs hanging over the tub rim, dripping water on the floor, exhausted and asleep.

The position cannot be comfortable and looks like a guarantee of sore back and neck. I walk over and turn off the heating element. She will wake if I attempt to help her out, possibly striking out, so I whiff a little anesthetic under her nose and wait till she slides deeper into slumber. Then I get the biggest towels we have and gather up the wet and dripping girl. The lift would be an impossible one for a human in this confined space but I manage it easily. A few seconds soft toweling and she is tucked into her bed.

I study her face. Dassa had been working more with makeup, but wears none now. Her face is sandblasted and raw from the night fight. I generate a restorative cream and carefully rub it on her face and fingers. She'd protected her hands with shooting gloves that had worked better than the bandana she'd tied around her neck. The tips of her ears have also taken some abuse and I treat these then wrap them with a little bandage.

Asleep, with her cold blue eyes closed, she looks more like a child and a pretty one at that. Yet, I feel so little with her of what I immediately felt with Nipkin. Seven years makes a big difference in the short lives of biologicals, at least in some species. I sigh, discomforted and disturbed by what Dassa has said and my reaction to it. I return to my spot on the floor and rehook to the power grid. I look out the window, but tonight, I am denied the solace of the stars, already it begins to lighten in the East. But I do not know if I am ready for the day to come.

CHAPTER SEVENTEEN

"**I**T'S A MIRACLE," MALPORIN SAYS FOR THE TENTH TIME. DASSA AND I *had joined Malporin and his defense commanders mid-morning, after the battle, and the storm that had concealed it, had abated. The area around the dorm and hospital had been declared secured around 6AM. With the sun up, such as it was, we'd come to survey the scene of last night's battle. Now, we walked, crunching grit underfoot, having dismounted from the platoon of mules and trucks that brought our party up here, between runs delivering wounded to the small hospital. The vehicles could get no closer without running over the hundreds of Indigene bodies.*

The morning had started off no better then it ended. Kemisa came to collect us, waking a groggy Dassa, who probably had no idea how she'd gotten to bed. I'd prepared coffee and slid a cup in front of the dazed girl after the Nekoan came in.

Kemisa had demanded to know where I'd been when she collected Dassa for the defense team. I told her I'd slipped out of the hotel after the guards left and been caught out in the storm, hiding in the basement of a store, seeing nothing until I fell asleep in the early morning hours. I did not think she believed me, but she elected not to contest my story just then. We'd then piled into vehicles and raced up here.

"I can't believe it." Romy, our driver adds staring at the street carpeted by bodies and parts of bodies as far as the eye could see.

A human named Bowman walks up to us and reports to Malporin. "We've counted about eight hundred dead in the area. That's a guess, Mal, there's a lot of blood trails leading north up the riverbed. Some of these bodies look like they were hit by a steel tornado. They're torn apart, or sliced to pieces. And we have no effing idea what could have done it!"

"Something was here last night," Malporin returns, looking up at the mountains. Today the tops of the peaks are shrouded, but the near slopes are easily visible. "Something powerful arrived. It hit just as the defense team in the dorm went down and the Indies broke in. It stopped them from attacking the children and moving on to the hospital."

"You should count yourself lucky that this force took your side," I say. Dassa, next to me, is carefully maintaining her usual lack of expression.

The look he gives me is complicated. "Some of the children say they heard a woman or girl's voice telling them to stay put."

"Did they?" I reply, shrugging. "You can't put much stock in the memories of terrified children."

The measured look continues. "Well they didn't see anything. Other than Nipkin, who was caught out in the corridors and poor Lamosos Voor, who was killed. Nipkin claims she doesn't know what happened, but she seems to still be in shock."

I am concerned by this statement. I have not seen the small child since last night's battle, still shock does not seem in her character. She may be dissembling to protect my secret.

"She must have seen some awful things," Romy said. The big woman's voice is rough with an emotion that does not show on her stolid face.

Malporin's gaze drops. "My fault that. I didn't think they'd attack here, or that they could get through the northern perimeter. I never imagined there could be so goddamn many of the bastards. This had to be most of the warriors on this continent."

Romy places a work-callused hand on his shoulder and gives him a brief shake. "You did the best you could, Mal, and better than anyone else would have. We're not soldiers here, just miners and shopkeepers."

"That much is obvious," I say, ignoring the angry looks of the council members near me. All, save for Malporin, who looks at me steadily.

"You can do better?" he says, but there is no challenge in his voice. "But will you?"

"Her?" Bowman says, "I grant you she's young to have her own starship—"

"Quiet, Bowman," Kemisa says.

Malporin raises his hand to forestall any further outbursts. "I have no doubt she can. There's more to you than meets the eye, isn't there, Captain Toyama?"

I smile. "Well, I do have military experience."

"As what!" Bowman explodes. "What is she, twelve! Did she play in the marching band?"

"I was more of a soloist," I reply.

"And she's older than she looks," Dassa adds with the sing-song quality of someone who expects to say the same thing many times.

"The question is," Kemisa adds, her tail flicking from side to side, "are you in?

I gazed up at the dormitory, then back at Malporin. "Like your mysterious force last night, I seem to have chosen a side."

Pulling out my comp, I gestured for Malporin to hand me his. I tapped my machine against his, though this was all for show, I'd already transmitted a defense plan to his machine, which then flicked it to the others.

"You will find detailed plans for a more effective defense," I say. I walk toward the edge of the bridge over the thin rill of water coming down the watercourse, spurning bits of enemy bodies with casual disregard. "I'd thought this area would have to be evacuated and the buildings destroyed to prevent the enemy from investing them. But no tribal society

can recover from the loss of so many military-age warriors. There is no likelihood of another mass assault. So, the defense teams will be more on guard for infiltration and raids than a mass assault. Their fronts can be extended and reinforcements cut into sector reserves. But this area," I pointed to the watercourse where the long low scrub trees had provided too easy cover for the mass of warriors to close on the northern defense team and punch through, "must be mined and covered with automatic weapons—"

Romy frowns. "Mines? So near to the school?"

"I can design mines that will fire on bio-sensors and only detonate for Indigenes. They will go inactive in six months."

Bowman's face is a study in surprise. Malporin and Kemisa's expressions are more guarded.

"We can make the mines with the machine tools from my cargo. If you have some redundant mobile mining equipment, I can turn those into small AFVs—"

"AFVs?" Romy asks.

"Armored Fighting Vehicles," I amend. "They will not be of great power, but the natives will not be able to contest them on open ground.'

Malporin's tired face creased into a smile. "Captain Toyama, you're on the council as an associate member." The others shift, as if puzzled by, or resentful of this change. With the noted exception of Romy, who beams, and Kemisa, whose alien face betrays nothing.

"You seem to have forgotten my first name," I say to him.

"Not for a second," he returns, the smile broadening, "nor anything else about you."

I find the expression on his face deeply unsettling, yet oddly pleasing and familiar. Then it hits me and I freeze for a period of time I hope he does not notice. Wrik used to look at me that way, often before we made love. Suddenly I am badly upset, yet must keep this all from my face. He does seem to notice something is wrong, his smile dims.

"Can we talk later?" I say. "Suddenly I feel like crashing, though I do want to crash on my ship, bad as that sounds."

Kemisa starts to speak, but Malporin quells her with a glance. "Your access to your ship is unrestricted, Aurelia. Dassa earned our trust out on the firing line and you, well, I have a feeling that somehow we all owe you a huge debt. Go to your ship and rest. Right after I see to my wounded, I plan to spend ten hours face down on my bed. Let's meet after that."

"Agreed," I say, determined to keep my sudden inner turmoil to myself. His fatigue is physical and mine is…what: moral, emotional, something of the soul? I want privacy for now.

"Romy," Malporin says as he studies my face. "Will you take Captain and crew back to their ship?"

The older woman pulls herself up to attention and snaps off a salute with a mocking grin. "My pleasure."

We ride back to Seachange in silence. Romy is busy driving around debris from both the storm and battle. Dassa either senses my reticence, or is still angry over my leaving her last night. I am in deep self analysis, trying not to overheat in the vehicle.

Finally, Romy guides the vehicle to a smooth stop next to the tower of our ship.

"Hope to see you tomorrow, ladies," she says as we dismount. "Thanks for all you did."

I fear we are less than gracious. Dassa is weary of body, and I, weary of spirit. I nod to Romy, and Dassa merely steps out. A proper ramp has been rolled up since I sent a command to the ship's AI to turn off the laser, so Dassa and I need not ride up in the enforced intimacy of the small elevator. We troop up the ramp into the hatch which, detecting my presence, slides open.

Once there, Dassa heads right and up, toward her cabin. I turn left for the engine room compartment that is part of this level. We do not speak as we part.

I enter the engine room and seal the door behind me. There is a pressure chamber next to me that I march into and subject myself to high-pressure steam that would have peeled the skin off Dassa, until I feel I am totally clean. Then I walk out and climb to the next level where the reactor is. Once there, I plug myself into the heavy-duty power tap.

Raw power floods me and my damage control kicks into its highest gear. I open a small chamber in the reactor and withdraw a few milligrams of a special alloy I have made to expedite my repairs and in seconds I am back to being a factory fresh M-7.

So why then do I feel so sick inside?

I sit on the floor of the engine room, behind the safely locked hatches and begin to cry. I wail as a child would, tears rolling down my face. I miss my husband. I am lonely, bereft of my love, without my trusted and dear friends for comfort.

My crying jag goes on and on. It is in some measure deliberate, I must create the tears that track my cheeks and allow my body to rock back and forth, arms wrapped around my knees. Yet, this is not mere artifice. I remember how this felt from when I was flesh and blood and what it means to do this.

This is crisis. I feel so miserable I want to suddenly cease to exist. I am wracked by more than loneliness and grief, now a touch of guilt is added. Malporin has been showing his interest in me. I know enough to realize that Dassa is right, and it is not merely because he needs to use me and my ship. Consciously or not, I have been enjoying this and perhaps encouraging it.

How can this be? Was not my life and love with Wrik unique and precious? He is only gone twenty years, most of those passed while I slept underground, hiding from and numb to my loss. Is this eyeblink of time sufficient to fray my bond with him? I have no one to turn to, no one to explain this, or help me face it. My body shakes with tears, pain and confusion.

"Wrik," I call aloud. "Wrik I miss you. I want to live, and I want to die. I'm afraid to be alone. Yet, I cannot see how to be close to anyone else now. Help me! I'm going under."

I concentrate on his face, not a recorded image which cannot save me, but the image of him I carry in my heart, with its gentle, sometimes worried expression, how he looked when he lay asleep, his head on the pillow next to mine. I would often watch him for hours. The only other thing I ever watched so were the stars.

As I concentrate on his face, my need for the ritual of crying fades, gradually I cease rocking in pain and simply rest my face against my knees.

I was loved, I remember, and love doesn't die. Wrik always said so, and I must cling to that. But if love does not die and the relationship somehow continues; what then of fidelity? My husband knew I would live for perhaps thousands of years beyond his time. He told me to be open to new friends and relationships, but is that possible for me?

I would not trade my years, long by biological standards, but too brief by mine, for anything. Wrik's love gave me my identity as a person, not a weapon. I used it to fight free of my programming. Yet can I walk that road again? Losing Wrik almost destroyed me, for all his efforts to insure otherwise. It may yet. I am not sure that I have survived in any meaningful sense. What I am enduring comes to most biologicals who pairbond, yet for them only once or twice, save for the unluckiest. Could I possibly endure loss after loss into an indefinite future? It is too much to face.

I consider turning myself off. I could do it: eject my power core, empty all my reserves, fire off the ultimate scrub of my memory banks.

But I need not even leave behind a corpse to be disassembled and plundered of my technology. I can set my power plant to overload. The blast will destroy me and Seachange. Dassa would be killed along with anyone within half-a-kilometer, but why should I care?

And the answer, of course, is that I promised Wrik I would not so cavalierly dispose of the life that he loved more than any other. I was precious to him. If there is a heaven, how could I face him after betraying my promise and adding murder to it?

I have ceased to cry. Not a conscious decision as it was at the start, but I no longer feel the need. I sit back, remembering the cleansing feeling that a "good cry" gave me when I was flesh and blood. The feeling now can only be an analog to that, but the desperate thoughts of only seconds ago are releasing me.

I was loved, wholeheartedly, sincerely and it had been mutual. So many beings live and die without that. Maybe it will come again and maybe not. Does it matter that my life with Wrik will be only a small per-centage of my existence? Others may have only had it for a day, or even moments, before space-time sundered them.

Or is it that I, a supremely rational being, am merely using that power to rationalize my pain? That enemy, never far from me, threatens to break through again. If it does, I am destroyed. I am at my limit with no reserves of strength left.

A warmth builds in my chest and demands my attention. My instant self-diagnostic says there is no change, but I know better. The warmth originates in the shockproof, armored chamber that holds the gem that was my husband. My sensors say it is not warm, something else tells me that it is, that it feels my pain and is desperate to drive it away.

I am not alone, and I suspect that I am now more than a little mad. I do not care. A feeling of peace spreads from the small stone. I accept it as I must, or I will never rise from this deck.

"I love you," I whisper to the stone and our memories, then sit utterly immobile while any vestige of the impossible sensation can be felt. Only when it is completely gone, do I slowly rise. I know that I can at least face another day. One day at a time.

CHAPTER EIGHTEEN

SINCE THE NIGHT ATTACK I HAD SEEN LITTLE OF MAAURO, being occupied with the sale and unloading of our cargo. When I did see her, she was either in the company of Malporin, whose obvious interest in her she remained apparently obtuse to, deliberately I believed, or with Nipkin, who tailed the android everywhere she could. The child's attachment was less difficult to understand than the obverse. Maauro was protection and power in a world coming apart at the seams, but why the machine chose to concern itself with the human child remained a mystery to me.

Might as well wonder why she concerns herself with me, or why she has not forced me to turn over the Alchemy crystal to her, I thought. She knew of the crystal and must have realized something so heavily encrypted contained critical information. Of course, for all I knew, she might have already infiltrated the crystal. Yet, I felt this was not the case—a Guild hacker would have studied the crystal with its latticed arrays of data for months or years, before daring to crack even the first level protection.

I sighed. As usual, my speculations went nowhere. No one knew the outer limits of Maauro's abilities. Even figuring out her basic motivations was difficult. On the voyage out, she'd periodically sought me out, for no evident reason. Her inclination to do so since we'd arrived seemed to have vanished. And. since my unwisely harsh words to her in the hotel room, she'd spoken to me seldom, and then only in cool, polite terms.

I attended to the details of the remnants of our cargo that she had not sold directly to Malporin, mostly luxury goods and non-essential commercial ones. She felt it was good practice for her apprentice cargo master. Our voyage would be profitable, almost obscenely so, but most of the profit remained theoretical, locked in mineheads and the abandoned mine camp of Tillet on the other side of the mountains. Still, Rand had been as good as his word, and a third of our fee in gem-grade opaloids was now safely secured in the ship's high value hold. Our larder had been replenished with locally grown foodstuffs, and the usual landing fees and taxes were waived, so we were well into the black. We had more than enough already to raise ship, reach the capitol, refuel and head off to some inner world, where opaloids would return many times their price to us.

Maauro showed no signs of readying to voyage out. Nor was she making the obvious preparations for a voyage into the deep dark. She continued to develop her quixotic friendship with Nipkin and to orbit Rand at a safe distance. Truth was, she seemed distracted, almost aimless, as she wandered around the town, meeting people and collecting information on the climate change that had wracked the planet. She'd turned aside any inquiry I made with vague assertions about leaving when the time was proper.

Increasingly, I felt I could not rely on her to pay proper attention to profit or risk. Had she been a Guild leader, her subordinates would be considering her 'retirement.' Well, if she hadn't been a damn near invincible android.

There was nothing I could do for the present. Indeed, my star was clearly setting with her, else how to explain her leaving me in the midst of a battle? Clearly, she identified more with a human child she'd just met, than with me. Her time as a human likely accounted for that, and my people were not popular with the other species of the Confederacy. Or perhaps she was still upset with me for drawing her out from her grave?

I was diverted from my somewhat dismal thoughts by a familiar silhouette outlined in the hatchway by the weak sunlight. Kemisa looked different today. She wore a bare-midriff outfit with a tight fitting, long-sleeved red top, over snug pants made of some sort of iridescent animal skin. I thought she was about twice my age, but her body looked athletic and her big purple eyes and feline appearance gave her a young, exotic and dangerous look.

I remembered her mouth on mine at the end of the battle, and wondered with a small thrill if I was the tidbit she was hunting today. Such an arrangement might present me options I did not presently have.

"Hello, Dassa," she said. She didn't smile in the toothy human fashion and so I didn't either, as she walked up and put an affectionate arm around my waist. "I'd hoped that I'd see you today."

"I had planned to go into town later, after I handled these last sales."

"Captain working you hard?"

"She has her moments."

"Are you nearly done?"

I look at the remaining items on the list and decide that, given Maauro's disinclination to leave, they could wait. "Well the list isn't, but I am. Sounds like a day to escape one's teachers."

"The humans call it playing hookey."

I grimaced. "They seem to have an expression for everything."

"Apparently, they're descended from a creature given to meaningless chatter."

"Gods, isn't that the truth," I said, feelingly.

The arm slides further around me. "Then come with me. Let me show you around. You should see more of what you helped save."

In the days that follow the battle, I am kept busy correcting the inefficiencies of the town's defenses, which of necessity involves dealing with the multiple deficiencies of a place that had not been planned in any meaningful sense, and whose supplies of water and food were its chief military vulnerabilities. Convincing the biologicals to address these issues, takes far more time than beginning the process of correcting them.

Beyond that, an odd lassitude grips me. I take only a few steps to investigate the phenomena of the vast planetary change that had first piqued my interest. Nor do I move on any plans to either voyage on, or obtain the rest of the opaloids we'd come for. I concern myself with the minutiae of both mine and the town's existence. I am bemused by my fugue, but disinclined to break, or struggle, with the odd spell gripping me.

Whenever I leave the council chambers, I find my steps dogged by Nipkin. I idly wonder if Malporin has inveigled the child into a form of surveillance, but reject that notion. It's not that I doubt his capacity for intrigue, but it would have been foolish to rely on such a young child. Sometimes her efforts at remaining hidden consist of hiding behind a lamp post less wide than she is.

This morning, Nipkin is trailing me much closer, having again escaped her tutors it seems. I stop, then after a moment, look to where she'd taken cover behind a small yellow truck, and say. "Please come out, Nipkin."

For a few seconds, I'm not sure she will, but finally, with hesitant steps, she rounds the corner of the truck to stand facing me.

"If you're going to follow me," I say, "then we might as well walk together, so we can talk. I, for one, get lonely sometimes."

She stares up at me with her big, dark-chocolate eyes, and I cannot judge what she is feeling.

"I get lonely sometimes, too," she replies. "The other children seem so different to me. So silly with the things they complain about, when many have both their parents."

"Loss does separate us from others," I agree. "It places us in a different stage of life from those who have not suffered."

Silence falls as we regard each other on the street. People walk by, occupied with their own concerns, but glancing at the tableau.

"You have questions?" I say. "But let us walk, please."

I turn, and she comes up alongside me. We start off slowly, at her pace.

"What are you?" she asks, only a little above a whisper.

I sigh. "What I am, may not be safe for you to know. But I was your protector when you needed one."

"I know and I haven't had a chance to really thank you. You saved my life. You saved all of us. Thank you."

"You're welcome."

"I guess I just can't understand how you could fight...could kill, so many. You're not much bigger than I am."

"Have you kept my secret, young one?"

The child crosses her heart. "Yes, Captain Toyama."

"Thank you, Nipkin. You may call me by my first name, Aurelia."

"Is that your real name?"

I am nonplussed. Has the child somehow sensed a deception?

"You don't want to answer that, do you?"

"No, I am sorry, but I don't."

"It's ok...Aurelia...even best friends have secrets."

"I have always found it to be so, even when I didn't want it to be."

"And we are friends?" the little girl says.

"Yes, we are."

"You won't let the Indigenes get in again. You won't let them get me."

"I am very strong, Nipkin, but I am not a god. I will do all that I can, and in this regard my capacities are great. I have destroyed many enemies in the past. The Indigenes will fear the very sight of me."

The solemn face studies me for a few more seconds, before breaking into a smile. "I believe you. If you're here, I won't be afraid."

"I am going to go to the ship now. Would you like to see it?"

The smile widens. "You bet."

To my surprise, the little girl reaches for my hand. I have time to consider whether to allow the touch, but find that I am glad to have the small, warm hand in mine. The shy smile she offers me warms me in other ways. We walk together in the weak sunshine. It is not a short walk, but I am pleased that Nipkin does not pepper me with questions. Rather, we talk in low voices about inconsequential things. We turn off the road to the fenced in area around the support buildings. The field itself is not fenced in, until recently, there was no need and after that, no chance.

I zoom my vision to scan the area near my ship. Seachange's laser had whipped the ground around her, and I did not want Nipkin to encounter any carbonized corpses. None of the Indigene's had gotten close to the ship and the ship's laser had largely vaporized those it struck. Still, there were some recognizable corpses on the far side. I alter our approach so that the bulk of the ship will conceal these. I know there are sanitation teams removing the bodies for a mass grave, and I send a text to them to prioritize this area.

The hard-packed earth of the spacefield, compacted by machine, crunches under our boots as we head to the green and gold tower of my ship. I see the cargo mule parked there. The internal sensors tell me that Dassa is aboard, loading some of the more fragile, cyron-packed, computer equipment on the small machine. She spent most of yesterday away from the ship, and I had not seen her today.

We arrive in the shadow of the ship just as the tall, gangly figure emerges from the hull to stand on the ramp. There was something unexpectedly chill about Dassa's presence. Her pupilless cold blue eyes and smooth, expressionless face convey even less than usual, but I sense disapproval and resentment in her stance.

I raise a hand in greeting, as does Nipkin.

Dassa, who is rarely friendly, merely nods.

Nipkin either senses something amiss, or is unnerved by the tall Guilder. She keeps me between her and the Dua-Denlenn. Well, I can understand that; I am not entirely sold on my present companion either. We have spent little time together since the night fight, and our communications have been terse, more through her choice then mine.

"I brought a friend to see our ship," I offer.

"Perhaps she will buy a ticket," Dassa returns.

"Can I?" Nipkin chimes in.

"You will fly in Seachange," I say, "when I take you to your father. That trip will be my treat. I do not charge my friends."

"I hope we can go soon."

"So do I," I say.

"That makes three of us eager to leave," Dassa adds.

I give her a warning look. "You doubtless have duties to attend to."

"Yes, until you finally buy those server bots you're always talking about."

"Let's see if we make any money before you go adding improvements."

"I don't believe that you completely appreciate the value of modern labor-saving machinery."

I start to reply, then realize that Dassa has made a joke to lessen tension and perhaps reach out.

"Damn robots," I reply dryly, "taking work away from flesh and blood spacers."

"Flesh and blood isn't all it's cracked up to be," she observes and heads toward the mule and town.

"Goodbye," Nipkin calls softly.

Again, the nod.

Nipkin follows me into the ship. We tour Seachange from the engine room to the bridge, which ended up being a lot of climbing for a small child. Seachange was too small to boast anything but a single person track elevator intended for moving casualties and heavy equipment along the central core. We ride on the small platform which has a light, retractable railing. Nipkin keeps her arms locked around my middle as she stares down the length of the ship's central core. Deck sections slide out of the way as we rise through decks that would be walls, if we were in flight.

When the little girl starts to flag, I suggest lunch in the ship's galley. We climb down with considerable alacrity to the galley in the middle of the ship.

CHAPTER EIGHTEEN

"What would you like to eat?" I ask.

"Oh, I don't want to be any trouble. Anything will do." But there is a certain avaricious gleam in her eye. I call up a holo screen and run some images by her. Nipkin's face lights up when she sees a chicken and pasta dish in a creamy sauce with cheese, something I would never have picked for her. However, true excitement shows when she spots chocolate ice cream on the menu.

"Can I?" she asks.

"If you eat all your lunch, yes."

I prepare the meal for both of us, while Nipkin fills the time with bright chatter about the town. I sense that the child will not willingly talk about her life before her mother's death and respect this. She is a fan of Malporin's, but less so of Kemisa, who she has heard 'shady things' about. I mark this for later consideration. Lunch disappears quickly, prompted by hunger and the coming ice cream.

"How about we take our ice cream to the bridge, and we can look out at the town," I suggest.

"Sounds great!"

With each of us toting a large bowl of chocolate ice cream, we make our way to the bridge. I open all but one of the viewports; this last one faces the carbonized corpses. They are one-hundred meters away and merely human eyesight should not resolve anything, but I find that I do not wish to gaze on blackened ground just now either.

I sit in my command chair, now oriented to the landing position. To my surprise, Nipkin comes over and sits in my lap with a bright smile. We sit quietly, enjoying the view and the ice cream.

"Days like this are rare now," Nipkin says, "but we sometimes get them after a big brownie."

"Do you remember the time before the changes?" I ask.

She thinks for a few seconds, putting down her spoon before she shakes her head. "Not really. It came on so quickly, when I was very young."

Was? I think to myself, studying the ten-year-old.

"Sometimes, it's hard to say what I remember and what people have told me."

I nod.

"Miss Aurelia," she whispers, "you seem really nice..."

"Remember your promise," I said, pressing my finger to my lips.

"I know Miss Aurelia," she says, "I promised I wouldn't tell anyone. But I didn't promise I wouldn't ask more questions."

I smile ruefully. One thing I had learned about children is that they are all little law students.

"As I said, it is not safe for you to know much about me."

"I don't need to know a lot," she wheedles.

I stroke the girl's short, silky hair, then, compelled by what I could not say, begin. "I am very old, Nipkin, older than this ship, old before it *was built. I was made as a weapon of war by a people you do not know of. Because someone loved me, I became a person in my own right."*

"Are you… I mean, I think…I know… you are good."

"I think so," I say. "I try very hard to be. My husband was a good man, and I learned much from him."

"Husband? Where is he?"

"He died."

"I'm so sorry. I know what it is like to lose someone."

The child is comforting me, how utterly remarkable.

"I know you do. We had a long time together as human life spans go, but I knew even at the beginning it would never be enough. I miss him."

She nods. "I miss my Mom too."

"It's very hard," I manage. "It hurts terribly."

"Does it get easier?" she asks, in a voice that only barely holds back tears.

"Everyone tells me so," I reply, "but not so far."

We sit quietly together, thinking on our losses. Outside, the clouds scud by, dimming the all too rare sunlight.

"Your ice cream is melting," I prompt.

She nods and then takes the spoon to it. We finish our desert and stand. Nipkin picks up both bowls and spoons then stacks them. She looks up at me. "I believe you are good person."

"I try to be, but I have a great capacity for violence."

"You saved everyone."

"I have ended so many lives. I wonder if someone who has destroyed so much can truly be thought of as good."

She shrugs her little shoulders as if to say: I'm just a kid.

"I guess I will just have to try my best," I said, placing my hand on her shoulder.

She nods then, "Any more ice cream?"

I can only smile. "I think that is enough treats for just now, young lady."

She looks at me sadly. "Oh, Aurelia, you're just a grownup after all."

Now I laugh, a laugh of simple shared joy. Nipkin joins me, and I reach down and hug her. For the first time, the pain in me relents, only a little, but it relents and I find hope.

CHAPTER NINETEEN

"DO YOU NEED ME TONIGHT?" I ASKED MAAURO, AS I leaned into the bridge.

She gazed back at me with her perfect, calm face. "No. The ship's AI can take care of routine tasks. I am bound for town in any event."

"Nipkin?" I asked, in an effort to appear friendly.

"No, not so late. Malporin has invited me to dinner."

I considered what response to make, though it had been decades since her husband died, the android treats it as if the event was but a year or so in the past. She was very sensitive to anything that touched on her emotional life.

"Sounds nice," I said in a neutral tone.

She smiled, as if appreciating my discretion. "And you?"

"Kemisa," I replied, "she wanted to spend some time getting to know each other."

"Will you be going out? Perhaps we will bump into each other."

"Oh," I said, allowing a hint of mischief into my voice. "I think we may spend the evening in."

"Have a good time," she replied, but I sense a reservation.

"I will."

"See you later."

Probably tomorrow, if things go as I expect, I thought, but merely nodded and left.

I watch Dassa's receding form, noting that she is wearing her best clothes, bought back on Evenfall, buckskin colored pants and a bare midriff black top that emphasizes her lean, fit body. Gems wink from her hair and she has applied some of the makeup as I taught her. She is a female on a mission, apparently intent on the at least technical elimination of her virgin status. I am puzzled that she has seen fit to bestow this on Kemisa, but the workings of her mind elude me in this regard.

Well enough, I have my own evening out to consider. It takes me only a moment to restyle my clothes as my chassis shimmers. I opt for a contrasting red and copper bodysuit. Loose clothing is difficult for me to simulate with my chassis, so I tend toward form-fitting wear. However, lest I give the same impression as Dassa, I go down to my cabin. I have a selection of sweaters and tunic-cut shirts for when I wish to conceal my figure. I choose one, a rust-colored tunic with copper thread details which pulls my outfit together. My hair lifts and twists into an elaborate style that would have taken me an hour when I had human hair and now takes seconds.

CHAPTER NINETEEN

After a moment, I allow a yellow gold ornament to form in it. This always causes me to think of Wrik and the yellow ribbon that was his first present to me. I am ambivalent about wearing it tonight, but my husband wanted me to have a full life after his passing, for all that I am not sure what that means.

I generate a slight mist of my favorite perfume and I am ready to go out. I pick up a small purse with the necessities of female biological life in it, then pull out a long, cape-like black coat. I do not need it, but with the sun down, the evening will be quite cool, and I must appear sensitive to the temperature.

A feed from the ship's scanner shows me Malporin, in a red GP vehicle, heading for the gantry to the ship. I head down and step out into the cool evening to await my date. Malporin pulls up in the GP and gets out of the vehicle. The fabric and plastic top is up, and the vehicle has been freshly washed. He waves to me, and I come down.

"Hope I haven't kept you waiting?"

"No, I had just finished securing the ship for the night. Both Dassa and I are off-ship."

"Girls night out?"

"Something like that."

Mal smiles as we pull away from the ship. I suppose it is not fair to contrast the rough and ready miner with my husband, but Wrik would have greeted me with flowers, got out and opened the door for me, then complimented me on my outfit. Oh, well.

"What is that wonderful scent?" Malporin asks.

"Starseed," I answer, pleased that he has noticed. "It is my favorite perfume."

The GP pulls away from Seachange.

I followed Kemisa up the stairs to her apartment, unable to take my eyes off her easily swaying hips and sensuous tail. She unlocked the door and held it open for me. The apartment beyond was surprisingly feminine for Kemisa's reputation. Drapes, dark green and billowy, hung over the glass wall that faced the mountains; overstuffed furniture and pillows dotted the floor. Kemisa went straight to a large wooden cabinet and opened it, taking out a yellow flask of what I recognized as Belvere, a potent Dua-Denlenn drink. She poured one and looked at me. I nodded, and she poured a second.

"Belvere brandy," I said, taking the glass. "You're loading the dice on your plans for me."

Kemisa laughed, as she dropped onto a big sofa. "Oh, Kit, I think you made all those decisions before you came here. But I am only interested in the willing. So, you need not fear my getting you intoxicated and taking advantage of you."

"Ah, so you will wait until I offer myself?"

She sipped hers, and the big purple eyes were open and friendly. I wondered how she did that. I sat next to her on the couch, neither too close, nor too far. She put a hand on mine and I let it rest there.

"Tell me your story, Kit. What brings your young, pretty, self to this part of the universe?"

I sipped my drink, feeling its heat spread through me and began a carefully edited version of my personal history. The tale of my travels, of the fall of the Guild and my voyage with Maauro fascinated her. I hoped to impress her with my status with the Guild. Kemisa would value such a contact.

She seemed unsurprised by my admission and merely said. "I've had dealings with the Guild before, to our mutual profit. Perhaps that will again be the case.

"But I'm curious, Dassa, what's your theory about what saved us?" she asked, swirling the Belvere in her glass.

"Who can say?"

She raised an eyebrow. "Oh, Kit, I thought you could, or your Captain. Do you expect me to believe, that only a day after you arrive, something or someone destroys a vast force near us? We didn't do it. You were with me. I heard Aurelia's story about where she claimed to be."

"Do you think my captain ran up there and punched out the aliens by her little pretty self?"

"Well, she is pretty, lots of wonderful curves on her for such a small person. Does she have to work it?"

"No. Irritatingly enough, she never seems to need to exercise."

"Lucky. She always appears perfect, hair, makeup, clothes..."

"Doubly irritating. So why did you set your sights on me?"

"There's a lack of sensuality, no, of sexuality in your captain. One gets the impression that she guards her body rather religiously. I can't abide prudes."

"I suspect she would qualify in that regard."

Kemisa leaned back. "One thinks she likes to be underestimated. Still, I can't fathom how she could have pulled it off. You didn't bring a company of HCRs or crab robots with you?"

"That you all missed seeing move out and have managed to remain unobserved since?"

Kemisa chucked again. "Yes, ridiculous, isn't it? Yet no one has anything that makes any better sense."

"Can I have another?" I asked raising my glass.

"Sure," she said, running her hands through my hair as she stood.

"You've heard about my past," I said. "What of yours?"

She returned with my drink, having topped up hers as well. "My tale is not as interesting as yours. I'm the youngest daughter of a trading family. Nekoan families are complicated, marriages are short term, and the children join the matrilineal line. Our family had fallen on hard times, and I fell out early with my mother. So, I set out on my own.

"I've been on a few planets, made and lost fortunes. I've even been involved with the Guild, though not as a member. Couldn't make the buy-in fee, and I never had a sponsor. I wasn't very interested anyway. I'm a lone hand."

"And you and Malporin?"

She grinned again. "If your captain lets him, Mal can show a girl a very good time. He's attentive and considerate. He and I hooked up in the capitol six years ago and have worked together ever since. Mal plays straighter than I do, so we make a good team, each of us covers the others ... deficiencies."

"You like him."

"As much as I like any male and that is a compliment as I don't much care for them, and none from my own species. Nekoan males sometimes long for the days when they actually owned us. Mal is good. I thought of keeping him for myself, but unfortunately he just can't manage to be female."

I stood and walked over to the window to look up at the mountains. "I'm female." I threw over my shoulder.

She rose and walked up behind me, a position I wouldn't normally allow someone to reach. I was the taller, so her chin rested on my shoulder.

"Yes and you're very pretty," she whispered. Her body pressed against me from behind.

My hearts went out of synch momentarily as I felt a flash of desire.

Why not? I wondered. I'd never felt a pull toward females before, but neither had I been that interested in males. Sex with another Dua was a vulnerability I felt I could never afford. Here, Kemisa was offering me the freedom to explore with little risk. Oh, the Nekoan surely wanted something, information on Maauro/Aurelia but there was little she could wheedle out of me. My fear of Maauro greatly exceeded any inducement, even sex that she could offer me.

A thrill ran through me as Kemisa gently nipped at my neck, resting the points of her teeth on my skin as her tongue slowly traced the line of my neck. Her hands rise under my shirt, slipping the bra up over my small breasts. I turned my face to her and she kissed me, slowly and carefully, as she undid the snaps of my shirt, then slid off both shirt and bra.

She does this often; I thought in dreamlike detachment. *Well, more often than I do.*

Then I let my hands run over her firm body. Her breasts were larger than mine and softer, but still firm. I hold them in each hand gently massaging them, feeling them swell at the attention through the fabric. My hands moved around on her. I traced the long, strong muscles of her back as we pressed our bodies together and kissed more thoroughly. The taste of her mouth was exotic, strange and pleasing.

My pants slid to the floor, and I kicked them away along with my boots. Kemisa took my hands and held me at arm's length, looking at her conquest. She was still fully dressed, where I was naked, save for my panties and pouch of valuables.

"Very nice," she said, with a growl and moved toward me, hands caressing with a practiced skill that made me gasp. She slipped my underwear off, pausing at the slender flexible knife that rarely left me.

"As I suspected," Kemisa said, "you're the dangerous type."

"Aren't you?" I said.

She smiled. "I can be, but I can also be naughty fun. Follow me."

It was but a few steps to her bedroom with its big four-poster and piles of pillows. I quickly placed my pouch and knife on the bedside dresser.

I trembled a little, inside. I didn't want her to know this was my first time. "Show me."

She raised her arms. "Undress me the rest of the way."

I did, and quickly, with an unfamiliar heat building in me, making my head swim. Kemisa gave an exclamation of surprise, as I pulled off the last of her clothes, and we landed on the bed in a tangle of arms and legs. But she quickly took charge, rolling me on my back, hands and tongue touching me in ways that showed I was not only far from her first, but not the first of my kind.

I felt something slide up my inner thigh and looked down startled, but it was only her long, thick tail. It wrapped around my thigh and touched my sex. An electric-like shock ran through me as the tail danced over my lower body.

"Yes," Kemisa smiled. "I can do interesting things with my tail… like this."

I gasped and arched my back, overtaken by a feeling I'd never had before. The world became a blaze of sensation as she toyed with me, until finally I climaxed with a near scream, before collapsing on the bed, nerves tingling, limbs trembling with reaction.

"Gods," I whispered. "Gods."

"Been a while?" Kemisa said with a grin.

"Yes," I lied.

"Well if it's going to be that easy to set you off, we'll have lots of time for fun."

My cheeks burned. "Ah, sorry."

Kemisa laughed. "Oh, no apologies needed. I feel it's my reward for mastery of an art. And speaking of rewards…"

My new friend wasn't shy about teaching me what she wanted. Over the next hour I learned more about sex then I knew existed. It took me longer, and was more complicated to work the magic for her, but when her thighs gripped my head and she cried out, I was well satisfied. She arched in a way that would have broken my back.

But Kemisa wasn't satisfied with doing it once, after a brief period, she began using her fingers in a new way and again played on my body like it was a musical instrument. Then it was my turn to please her. Finally, I collapsed, my face between her breasts and lay panting.

"Am I too heavy?" I asked.

"No, Kit. I'm not fragile. It's why I like my partners young and very, very active."

"I can feel that," I said.

"Are you hungry?"

"Ravenous."

"Good, in addition to my talents in the bedroom. I'm a pretty good cook. You shower, Kit, I'll get us some dinner."

I rolled over and put my hands behind my head. "You know I think I could get used to this...."

I walk side by side with Malporin heading for the small downtown of Pilbara and a restaurant called Venezia. Malporin claimed it was the height of the culinary art on this continent, but to my mind that did not augur for much. The sun is setting to the west where the land is flatter. This treats us to a long, gentle display of color, brighter than the sun had been for much of the day. I take it as a good omen.

A gentle wind kicks up, rustling the cape I am wearing, which is only of fabric. I pretend to shiver as a human female might have.

"Only a little further," Mal says. "Sorry I couldn't get any closer but these streets are too narrow for my GP.

"I'm fine," I say, with a reassuring smile.

A neon sign glows in the window of a restaurant that is reached by a narrow set of stairs. We go down them and open a red door. In front of us, sit a half-dozen tables, all occupied, but I see some more isolated booths at the back. A heavy-set man walks out from behind a counter.

"Hi, Pietro," Malporin says to the rotund owner as they shake hands.

"Mal, good to see you. It's been weeks." Then he turns to me. "So this is La bella Capitana delle stele who everyone speaks so admiringly about. They do not do you justice."

I smile at the extravagant compliment and answer him in Italian. His face is a mask of surprise. "Are you Italiana?"

"A little," I answer, in standard for Malporin's sake, "on my mother's side."

"Ah, even now, so far in the past and distance, Italy still gifts the galaxy with the most beautiful of women."

"So what do you think, Pietro? Can you set me up with a booth?" Mal says.

"Of course, follow me."

We head for one of the curtained booths in the back. In moments we are seated at a table of red-checked cloth. Bread and a carafe of wine and a bottle of sparkling water hit the table at the same time.

"Ah," Pietro says to me, "the wine is the best we can get, but if you have had true vintages then—"

"It will be fine," I assure him. "I can always strain the wine through my teeth; it's the pasta that counts."

Pietro turns to Malporin. "Aha, she's too good for the likes of you."

Malporin nods. "I suspected as much."

Menus follow and Pietro hovers over us.

"What do you recommend?" I say, pushing the menu aside.

"The spinach and prosciutto tortellini in cream sauce," he says, then turns to Mal. "The usual?"

"No, I'll go with the tortellini as well."

"Flexibility, a good trait," he winks at me, "usually it's chicken parmigiana."

I watch Pietro's broad back retreat in the direction of the kitchen.

We talk of inconsequential things until the antipasto arrives. I preempt his inquiries about my past by asking of his.

"Not so much to tell there. I was born on Damasia in the northern continent near the capitol. My family were miners, or in the support trades. My uncle went into politics. I decided to strike out for the new fields in the southern continent. Well, here I am."

"Did you meet Kemisa here?"

"No, back in the capital. I got in over my head on a business deal. She was actually part of it, but was looking to get out of the relationship. So, we made common cause and fought our way out. We'd been, well I am not sure friends is the word, more like allies. I trust her, within certain carefully-thought-out bounds. Inside those, it's a strong relationship. Rather like what you seem to be with Dassa. Speaking of which, how is tall, blue eyed and suspicious?"

This time a small laugh escapes. "An apt description."

"No offense," he says, "but she does tend to look at a person as if they are trying to pick her pockets."

I raise an eyebrow. "I think your wallet is in more danger then hers."

"Yeah. Her kind does not have a good reputation on Damasia. A bunch came in after the first big opaloid strikes and started claim-jumping. The lucky ones got picked up by the planetary constabulary. The rest, well here in the wayback, we don't take kindly to claim-jumpers, particularly those who shoot legitimate miners from ambush."

I nod. "Well, Dassa seems pretty popular for all that."

"Kemisa says her gun made the difference at the spacefield and the tale is pretty well told around Pilbara.

"So tell me, how do two fashion-model star crew, obtain mint condition, if vintage, Confed weapons."

"One of my former associates has excellent Confed connections, and I am fond of older equipment."

"Yeah," he nods. "Seems like a lot of the older equipment is better made than the new stuff you get."

"You have no idea," I say, amusing myself. "Why some of the stuff offered for sale today quite shocks me. Still, I have Dassa to consider. She is always after me to get some roboloaders."

"You may need to work a little harder to keep her on your team."

"Oh?" I return. I pick up his water glass and refill it with fizzing water. "Is she in danger of being stolen away?"

Malporin hides his face behind the glass of water. "I don't know that is a danger...exactly."

I sigh. "You're referring to Kemisa?"

He hesitates and then puts the glass down. "Look. I don't want to stick my nose where it doesn't belong. You know I like Kemisa...."

"But?"

"Kemisa has a bit of rep hereabouts. She's a little on the wild side. She also, well, she likes her playmates a bit young, on the naïve side and out of her species, so she has no serious obligations."

"I appreciate your telling me. For now, Dassa is crew to me."

He gives me a curious look. "For now," he repeats. "I'm not sure I get you two. Sometimes you seem close, an effective team. Other times, it's like you hardly know each other."

"We haven't known each other long. Let's say that I am an old acquaintance of her family that she dug up."

"Aurelia, how can you be an old acquaintance of anyone? You look to be what, twenty-five galactic standards old?"

I waggle a finger at him. "You should never ask any woman about her age, or weight, especially me."

"And so," he says with a weary note in his voice, "we are back at the wall that comes up anytime I try to find out anything significant about you."

"We were talking about Dassa,"

"Kemisa wants her. I've seen it before."

"Unless she unwisely attempts to use physical force against Dassa's wishes, the matter is exclusively hers to deal with. My own thought is that if Kemisa takes Dassa for naïve, she may well lose everything including her tail to my companion. Don't discount that if Kemisa is using Dassa, the reverse may also be true."

"And if you do lose her to Kemisa?"

I shrug. "She's free to come and go as pleases her." I had not considered how I would feel about shedding the Dua-Denlenn girl. In many respects, this might accrue to my benefit. She is a difficult companion at *the best of times. While I did owe her for motivating me to get out of the literal hole I was in—I'm out and functioning. Do I need her for anything?*

The image of Dassa's face suddenly comes to me. Not her usual, closed, blank, face, but the one I saw on the day I doctored her bruises with makeup and she first saw herself as a pretty female. Her face had been so open, so young and vulnerable then. I remember the evidence of abuse written into the remodeled bones of her body that, unlike mine, could not erase the signs of damage. I feel a brief stab of shame.

Malporin finishes his glass of red wine and reaches for the carafe. "As you say then, I've given fair warning."

"And I have taken same. So, on my head be it."

"Let's hope no one is left with regrets."

I sip my wine, while wondering if that last remark was for Kemisa and Dassa, him and me, or perhaps both.

Dinner arrives and we switch to lighter subjects and enjoy the meal. While the wine is undistinguished, the tortellini is all that could be hoped for. One of the mixed blessings of living as a human has been my enhanced sense of taste and smell. Tonight, I am enjoying both.

Dessert is a Tiramisu that could make one weep for joy. I apparently shock both Pietro and Mal by ordering a second piece.

"Umm, how do you stay so slim?" Mal asks, as Pietro returns with the treat.

"I'm told I burn calories like a machine," I answer. I feel slightly giddy and realize I may have said too much. The wine is not affecting me, so it must be the company. "While in deep space, I am very disciplined about diet and exercise. When downworld, I insist on a spacer's right to misbehave."

"To misbehaving," he says, raising his glass. I tap wineglasses with him and wonder again how it seems so many things have double meanings tonight.

After dessert, we rise. Pietro waves at Mal, there is no check, so no awkwardness over that. We step out into the night. The wind kicks up and causes Malporin to turn up his collar and stick his hands in his jacket. "I'm not looking forward to winter. Since the changes it gets bitter early and stays long."

"Very few of us look forward to winter," I say. We walk forward close by each other in the narrow street, my shoulder almost touching his arm as I am 8.263 inches shorter. I am enjoying the companionable feel of the evening. It is like… no, no memories for just now. Live in the moment only.

I look upward.

Malporin notices. "Not too many stars, I'm afraid."

I see more than he does with my powerful optics, but it remains true. "That must be hard on you. You remember what it was like before."

He nods. "I haven't given up hope that it will be so again."

"Hope is important," I agree.

"Even when there is so little reason for it?

"Perhaps then more than ever."

I sense that he wants to touch me, perhaps to hold my hand, or put an arm around me. I am not ready for that and increase the interval between our bodies. I am unsure why I am doing so. I am enjoying the evening and his company, but my desire is to keep things uncomplicated. Out of the corner of my eyes, I study my companion, aware of his good looks, his size and strength, his essential maleness. Yet, this just brings to mind what I have lost. My attempt to live only in the moment fails.

We regain the GP and Mal puts on the heater. "What do you say to a nightcap? There's a place down by the landing field. It's a bit rougher than Venezia, I'm afraid."

"Port bars do not frighten me," I reply. "I've seen enough of them." A white lie, in a way, I had seen plenty of them, but usually from the out-side. Such places held no attraction for me, but I also have no fear of being molested or insulted, either.

We drive on as a light mist gathers on the window. "Well, I should be glad to see any moisture," Malporin says, turning on the sonic screen that banishes it from our glass.

"Hopefully, work on those storage tanks will allow more to be cap-tured," I add. We talk about the refinements I have suggested to Pilbara's defense until we reach a bar within sight of my ship. I had noted the place before, but without interest. We turn into the parking lot around a long, low building from which music emanates. I hear laughter and yelling at the band, as the music is live. A lit sign flashes images of a pick and a shovel, which is also the name for the place. Vegetation lines the parking lot, though it is of the hardy desert variety. Between the screen of bushes and the misty evening, the air is, for once, empty of dust.

We walk in through the door. The band, surrounded by a rowdy crowd, is to the left. I gesture to the right, past the pool and game tables, after pointing at my ears. He grins and nods.

The bartender, a big man with a scarred face, bandaged hand and tattoos on his forearms, comes out from behind the bar. He exchanges forearm grips with Malporin. "Haven't seen you since the night of the big fight."

Malporin nods. "How's the hand?"

"Better than the pig of an Indigene who stuck me."

"Pashva, this is Aurelia Toyama."

He nods. "I've been enjoying the shadow of your ship and her big laser cannon. Welcome."

"Petralla," the big barkeep calls.

An attractive woman in her late 20's or early 30's, with blonde-dyed hair and an outfit that emphasizes the shape of her breasts and curve of

*her hips, turns and smiles at Malporin. The smile dims to merely profes-
sional when she notices me.*

"Table Fourteen," Pashva says. "Drinks are on the house."

"This way," she says to Malporin.

*"Thanks," he says, apparently oblivious, in typical male fashion, to
the undercurrents.*

*We head for a spot where the loud music and clacking of the pool
tables is not bad and slip into chairs, which requires my usual balancing
act. I place my cape on the back of the chair as I listen to the band. While
the music is odd to my ear, there is a pleasing freshness to it.*

*"What can I get you, honey?" she says, leaning her hip against Mal-
porin's shoulder. "Your usual?"*

"Sure,"

*"And for you?" she says, making cool eye contact with me for the
first time.*

*I so want to turn my eyes black from lid to lid, but restrain myself.
"The same will be fine, whatever it is."*

*"Two comets on ice coming up," she walks away, making sure all her
ample parts have enough impulsion to move in a fashion alluring to
males. She is quite good at it and must practice often. I note her motions
should I ever need to do something similar.*

*"Ah, a comet is a bit of a stiff drink," Mal says, reaching for a bowl
of small nuts on the table.*

I raise my eyebrows. "Oh, I can handle myself."

*"You rarely seem to worry much about anything being beyond you.
I don't believe I have ever met anyone with your self-confidence."*

*I allow a blush to stain my cheeks. "I hope I do not appear
arrogant."*

He gives me a sly look. "Mostly not."

"What is this music?" I ask, to change the subject.

"We call it Bush-hollering."

"It certainly carries for a distance."

He laughs. "That it does."

*The waitress returns and sets down our drinks. Do I detect a mali-
cious look at my choice of the strong beverage? The comet is a mix of
liquors with a very high alcohol content. I pick up the large tumbler and
drain it in one long gulp. Mal and the waitress stare at me in something
like shock.*

"Wow," she says.

"Very refreshing," I say, "could I have another?"

"Ah, sure," she replies, backing away. "I'll be right back."

Malporin looks at his glass. "You don't mind if I take my time."

*"No," I say, suddenly embarrassed. "If you'll forgive me for pulling a
stupid stunt like that just to tweak her nose."*

His look of incomprehension spells volumes.

"She likes you."

"She does?"

"That means she doesn't like me."

"Oh."

"And I behaved badly because of it."

"Well that hardly counts as bad behavior around this place, maybe if you belted her... and I am not suggesting that."

"Good."

Petrella returns and slips the glass in front of me.

"Thank you," I say.

She nods. "Anything to eat?"

Malporin shakes his head. "We just stopped in for a quick drink."

She eyes me. "A very quick drink."

I raise the glass and take a very delicate lady-like sip. "I will take my time with this one."

"You must have a hollow in your boot, Sister," Petrella says ruefully. "If I knocked off a Comet like that, they'd carry me outta here on a board."

We listen to the music and eye the townies playing billiards or other games. Darts sail through the air in inaccurate trajectories. But it is rather relaxing.

"Really," he says, studying me. "No effect at all?"

"Well I am feeling the second one," I lie.

A scuffle breaks out with two miners at the dart board, but is quelled by a Morok bouncer, who wears a T-shirt that incongruously says, Buddha Saves. The pair is quickly hustled out the back door to continue their fisticuffs in private.

We enjoy the nightlife for a while, with both of us handling the Comet in a sensible fashion. "I have to drive," Malporin says, almost apologetically.

I use the reference as an excuse to bring the evening to a close while it is in the plus column. "Well, I do not have far to walk."

"Can I walk you to your ship?" he says, disappointment tinging his voice.

"You don't need to,"

"I always like to see a lady to her door."

"Then it would be foolish of me to discourage such gentlemanly behavior."

I rise and put on my cape. Malporin puts a very generous tip in local credits on the table. We head for the door. I allow myself to seem a little slower and unsteady as we wave to Petrella and Pashva.

As soon as we get outside, I drop the pretense. "That night air will sober you up quickly enough."

The look he gives me says that he does not believe my prior act. This has not been my best night of passing as a biological. If I give in to what Malporin hopes for, the jig would definitely be up.

CHAPTER NINETEEN

We walk around the hedge of desert growth toward the tower of my ship. Blue lights glow on the gantry to Seachange. Such servicing as can be done locally has been. I am glad to see the ship, and, as it feels the same way, the AI puts on glowing yellow lights to welcome me home. It informs me that Dassa has not returned, but that all is otherwise well.

"It's kind of you to take a long walk in the cold," I say.

"Not at all, it gives me a chance to spend more time in your company."

I slow and place a hand on his arm, we are near the foot of the gantry now. He turns to me in surprise.

"Mal," I say gently, "I like you and I have enjoyed our evening together."

"Why do I feel that there is a "but" coming at the end of that sentence?"

I hesitate, unsure of what to say.

"Is there someone else?" he asks.

I slowly shake my head. "There was."

"And," he adds, but his voice is gentle and careful.

"He died."

"I'm sorry, truly."

"I believe you."

"Do you want to talk about it?"

Do I? Mal's warmth and interest seem genuine. Yet, for all his good intentions, it will involve him too much in my past. "Not now. My grief is too fresh for all that the death is not recent."

"It might make it easier," he said. "The offer remains open."

"Thank you. I just feel that I should warn you that I am not a promising investment of your time and effort. I am... broken, in parts that may not mend. It's not fair to you."

"I am so warned," he says, echoing my words of earlier in the evening about Kemisa, and placing his hand over his heart in a protective gesture. "But have you never heard the expression, "Faint heart ne'er won fair lady."

"I have," I whisper, "but as with so many things from fairy tales, it doesn't always work out in real life."

We walk on to the foot of the gantry. "Thank you for a lovely evening."

"My pleasure. Maybe we can do it again soon."

After a hesitation, I hope that he does not notice, I say. "Yes I would like that, but this time you must let me treat you."

"My treat would be your being there." He leans forward slowly, and I can tell that the kiss is for my cheek, so I allow it, though I step backward after that so he does not see it as an invitation to more. He recognizes this and does not followup. This pleases me.

"Until next time," he says.

"Good night, Mal."

I turn and head up the gantry, knowing that he will wait until I am safely in the ship to head back. I reach Seachange's hatch quickly, my heart and mind confused and troubled with pain, anticipation, remembrance and hope. I turn back and wave to him and he waves back. Only when the door slides shut, does he turn back for the Pick and Shovel. I am both charmed and amused by his solicitude.

The airlock closes and I am pleased with my evening. For all its emotional moments, it was …. special. I do not lock the ship as Dassa might return.

As I make my way down to the engineering room for some minor recharging, I wonder how Dassa's evening has gone and if she will return tonight or tomorrow, or for that matter at all, though I judge the latter unlikely.

I am still surprised she has chosen an alien female for her first sexual experience, assuming that's how their date went. But Dassa comes from a male-dominated culture and is both solitary and wary of entanglement. Our own relationship is based on her need for protection and little more.

The female-female dynamic interests me. I was very close to Jaelle, Wrik's Nekoan consort. Our relationship had been at times playful, warm, even affectionate, but never intimate. Shasti Rainhell herself had a female Nekoan lover before she married Vaughn. It had not lasted a long time, and they'd remained friends afterward.

Perhaps it was the big ears and tail? I had never felt the inclination to females, Nekoan or otherwise, but my sexuality had budded during a passionate affair with a male. He had been my only lover to date, but who could say what I might choose in the future? For now, though, it seemed my orientation was just to males.

I sit cross legged in engineering. I have no need for sleep as such, but there is a state that combines a self-diagnostic mode and meditation. I find this useful after an influx of biological experiences. I place my wrists on my knees and enter dissociative thinking, drifting through memories of my past and contemplations of my present and future.

Hours later the AI pings me. I come back to full awareness. Dassa and Kemisa are approaching the ship, it is approximately 0800 ship time. I watch them, coming on arm in arm, obviously lovers now, though perhaps that word is more than is needed. I doubt that there is more than opportunism on Dassa or Kemisa's parts, though perhaps with some mercenary curiosity thrown in on the latter.

But as I study them, I see Dassa's face is open and lively in a way I cannot recall seeing before. Kemisa squeezes Dassa's arm and laughs, her tail whipping about, and her purple eyes seem all for her new prize, or perhaps, companion. I find myself unsettled by the sight of them so carefree and casual. It might be lust and not a love such as Wrik and I shared, but it looks happy and warm.

CHAPTER NINETEEN

Am I jealous? Can that be? I consider what it is in the scene that I might be envious of. Since I reoccupied my android body, my need for sex itself has vanished. When Wrik and I made love before I had my biological body, it was something I did for him, to bring us closer together, but it was not a need of mine. As a human woman with a sexuality of her own it had been different, then I had been eager, almost demanding.

When my human body failed, despite the best efforts of the bioengineers of Olympia, sex again changed for me, becoming a hybrid of both experiences. While, as a machine, I could not claim to have a sex drive, I remembered its physical joys and particularly its intimacy. Wrik was over one hundred years old then, but still healthy and we enjoyed making love. Each time seemed to heat us to where we melted into each other even more.

While I had not felt an urge toward sex since my reawakening, the desire for intimacy and connection that started me on my long journey toward emotional sentience was still there, as strong as ever. It lay at the base of my attachment to Nipkin, my growing attraction to Malporin and now this flash of jealousy over Kemisa and Dassa.

Dassa had forced me out of a literal hole, but now my need for intimacy, for attachment, is forcing me out of a metaphorical one. And I am terrified. How can I again bear to join my soul to these fleeting beings when I must outlive them?

Unless you die first. Don't die alone.

I freeze. It is back. The thought had inserted itself in my consciousness as if spoken, but there has been no sound. I no longer have a subconscious to throw up such thoughts, yet there is no record of the thought in my playback.

I am there again, at the door of the mystery of life and death. It towers into the night that bounds all of life, vast, foreboding, capable of being opened only one way. As I gaze on it, I cannot tell if it is the gate to heaven, hell, or oblivion. I sigh. Perhaps I am wrong and I still have a subconscious from which all this comes unbidden. I am not the same Maauro I was, before I lived as a human woman. I suppose I should not be surprised if my psyche is different, given the vast changes in my life.

I rise and head down to greet Dassa at the dock. She looks surprised to see me, but is more open and friendly than usual. She throws me the salute of a returning spacer. "Reporting aboard, Captain."

I look around her shoulder to see Kemisa's retreating tail, swishing as she heads for town.

"I trust you enjoyed your time in town," I said.

"I did. It was... illuminating."

Moved by a sudden impulse, I ask. "Do you feel different?"

Her surprise is redoubled, but she considers. "Yes, I feel... more like an adult than before." *Then she turns to face me full on, which for a Dua-Denlenn is way of focusing the pupilless eyes.* "Did you?"

I give a gentle smile. "Well, yes, but you have to remember, my first time was the first time it ever occurred between an artificial life form and a biological."

"So, no pressure then."

Now I cannot contain a laugh. "None at all. But to answer your question. Yes, I felt different, more like a part of the world of living things. I felt like a woman."

Dassa blushes and looks away. As quickly as it began, the moment of intimacy closes.

"I'm going to get changed," *Dassa offers.*

I nod, "See you later then."

CHAPTER TWENTY

DRIVE OFF TO SEE NIPKIN FOR A DAY TOGETHER. SHE IS WAITING ON THE *steps of the school, as I pull up and skips up to the Mule. She tosses a small bag in the back, where I have packed a picnic lunch for us. We head to a hillside just north of the town and from which we can see Seachange. As an incidental, I can also use the ship's laser should anything threaten us on this side of the hills. We will not pass out of its protecting arc.*

We enjoy the sandwiches, sodas and fruit drinks. Nipkin has brought a local fruit, like grapes, that we both pop in our mouths, throwing them in the air, sometimes at each other's mouths too.

But for all her little-girl giggles, I can tell something is on her mind. I put my grapes down. "Is there something you want to talk about, little one?"

"I hear people saying that there's going to be an expedition to Tillet," Nipkin whispers. The wind stirs her fine hair as she looks up at me.

"I think so. Malporin told me that much of the opaloids owed me for my cargo are up there, or in the mines beyond. With the lifting of the siege here, it may be safe. I expect he will ask me to go, perhaps very soon."

"My mom…my mom is up there."

"Yes, I know."

"I feel like I should go…to see her, but Aurelia, the Indies they don't like our cemeteries, sometimes they do things. I should go and see to her grave, make sure it is…"

She cannot continue, tears course down the little face. I reach forward and embrace her gently. A couple passing by on the trail below, notice us then look away, able to guess the source of a little girl's pain and giving us privacy in a public place.

I kiss the girl's soft cheek and manufacture some tissues in my internal plants sliding them into the false pockets of my jacket. Nipkin wipes a face too etched with grief for its few years.

I zip up the front of her jacket; the feeble sun is not putting out enough warmth. "You will not go," I say in my most adult voice. "I am going. I will find your mother and make sure all is well."

"I'm her daughter, I should—"

"No. This is work for grownups. Since your father is too far away and I am your friend, it will fall to me."

Nipkin gives an oddly adult and bitter laugh that troubles me more than the tears. "It seems a lot to ask of so new a friend. You've already done so much for me. Why?"

For all the speed of my brain, I am stumped on how to respond for some seconds. "Let us say that friendship is very important to me. Most of my old friends are gone, and I have not had time to make new ones. You are the first."

She looks at me in surprise. "Not Dassa?"

Now it is my turn for a bitter laugh. "Ah, Nikpin, I am not sure what Dassa is to me. I think of her mostly as just a spacer. She is Dua-Denlenn and difficult for me to understand. Beyond that, her past has made her a troubling companion for me."

She nods, though I am not sure she understands and hugs me. "I love you, Aurelia. You're the best friend ever."

I rise, elation in my breast, and take her hand. "Come, we will put Tillet out of our minds for today. You were going to show me the garden you and your friends have made by the school."

She nods, and we gather our picnic up and walk, holding hands, the weak yellow sunlight falling on our shoulders. I have a new friend, perhaps only for a little while, but it is enough for now.

After I we view the garden, I return Nipkin to the school and her other friends, yet another soccer game is pending. Then, I return to the ship. I find Dassa at the foot of the gantry, accepting some cargo that has come up on a roboloader. This is material she has purchased on her own with her own load allowance. Any profit will be hers and it counts as good training for my apprentice cargo master. I wave to her as I roll up. She waves back.

As I pull up, Mal's GP pulls in behind me.

"I wanted to deliver this in person," Malporin says, as he gets out of the GP. He hefted a small sealed box. "Last of the down payment."

I start to say. "You know how to get a girl's attention," but remember that I'd decided to dial down the flirtations. How curious it is that my resolve on this is so easily tested.

"Well my creditors will be happy to hear that," I offer and wince internally, as it sounds lame to my own sensors. Dassa, reading a loading manifest, looks up briefly at my mention of nonexistent creditors. She quickly decides this just more human verbal nonsense and disregards us.

Malporin's smile dims some. He was probably hoping for a more welcoming smile and a line like the one I'd stepped on. "Yes," he says. "It's only a down payment of course until we can reopen Tillet."

"I suppose we should talk about that," I say. The curious lethargy that has gripped me since the battle relents some. "Come aboard."

Sensing my "business only" mood he nods.

"Why don't we go up to the galley?" I say.

"Sure."

We leave Dassa intent on her task, possibly not even noticing that we'd left.

He follows me to the next level. I have meanwhile sent a message to the galley through my AI. Automatics prepare an iced tea drink for Malporin and a more fragrant hot one for me.

We walk in and sit on the metal benches of the table bolted to the deck. One nice thing about my ship is that I don't need to worry about where I sit.

I bring out a small delicate cup with the fragrant tea I prefer and a large glass of iced tea for Malporin. His eyes widen when he saw it. "Is that real iced tea?"

"Yes. Romy mentioned how much you missed iced tea."

"Sweet?"

Again, I have to cut off the witty reply of, 'Just like myself' and instead say, "That's what she told me you liked."

"Thanks," he picks up the glass and takes a deep sip through the straw. "Ah, just like home."

I smile, then quickly suppress it. "There's more in the fridge, don't stint."

He nods. "Council met this morning. We still have no idea what happened in the north. It's taken days just to get the bodies below ground in a mass grave and more keep showing up."

"Our scouts, mostly former hunters, have moved into the mountains. They've found fresh Indigene graves and signs of significant force withdrawing."

I consider. "Tribal militaries are often supported by a logistics force made of over or underage warriors and family."

Malporin sips more tea. "That was the council's take on it too, camp-followers and the like. They bugged out as fast as their green feet will carry them. We've run into an occasional long range sniper, but they don't want to close with us. So, the council agrees with you that it's unlikely they could mount another large effort here. Of course, without knowing what the hell saved us, there's no way for us to count on further divine intervention."

Remembering the grimness of that night, I can find nothing divine in it. I only nod however and sip the tea in my delicate cup.

"So we must keep our defenses intact, but we can spare the resources to reopen Tillet and communications with the minefields beyond. The Indigene's apparently figured that if they took us out, it would be easy to starve out the miners and the seaport. The mines themselves made pretty good forts. They have water and most of the mines had laid in for a siege while we still had aircraft to haul supplies.

"So, you want me to take an expedition to Tillet to reopen the mine camp—"

"And to fetch back the buildup of opaloids the miners have dug up in the last three months. From there, I would like you to return, and fly the first of however many missions I can talk you into, to the capitol. You

said you plan to take your opaloids for off world sale, so you won't have to worry about the effect of the fresh supply hitting the markets.

"Yes. The surplus of opaloids might depress the price for a while."

"I'll be sending a report to the planetary government and a request for constabulary. Who knows, maybe a Confed warship has pulled in."

"Unlikely, unless they came straight in without an orbit. Seachange is a scout and her sensors are above standard. We'd have detected them."

He shrugs. "Then it's just the resources we have here. Ah, well, the usual."

"Back to the original plan," I said. "What do you want, specifically?"

"Take a team of twenty people. They'll all be armed, but only two will be security, the others are engineers, process technicians and such. Their job will be to survey the camp's infrastructure and get as much of it up and running as is possible.

"We'll coordinate by com with the mineheads. Not all of them have functioning coms at this point, but enough to get the word out. They can help cover the camp, which is why I'm sending so few security people. Your ship, with its laser, should also serve as a deterrent while you're down."

"Undoubtedly. Then if we are to do so, I would rather sooner then later."

"I can have my people ready by dawn tomorrow."

"So soon?"

He smiles, pulls his hand com out and we tap them together. "I've been updating my plan to reopen the place for weeks. What is your status?"

I scan the data he has sent me; spreadsheets and images float in the air about the com. "If we're only going local, not even into space, we can load anytime and upship just after. People are no issue, but we should load the equipment you want as soon as possible, especially the vehicles. Dunnage on a starship is complicated even for a short hop. That's quite a load, vehicle wise."

"Yes, well, it's too much to expect that any vehicles up there weren't either destroyed, or taken. Your ship is the most powerful lifting body on the planet. Shouldn't be too much problem?"

"No. We can take the three mules and the cycles you're talking about. Any more though, and we'd have to disassemble them. We have our own mule that I plan to use when we get there."

He gives me a questioning look.

"Nipkin's mother was buried there."

His face closes. The big hands tighten around the glass, which is fortunately not made of anything so fragile. "Yeah. You may find something unpleasant waiting for you."

"I am prepared for it."

"You're a tough one."

CHAPTER TWENTY

"At need, yes."

"And always so confident?"

I smile sadly. "Not always."

He raises his glass. "To retaking Tillet."

I tap it with my teacup and drain my own as he finishes his iced tea.

"This is it, Aurelia, the start of the comeback trail."

I look at his open friendly face and feel a misgiving. "I hope so."

To my surprise, he places one of his hands on mine. "It could be the start of more than one beginning." He looks squarely into my eyes.

"I am," I say gently, as I slide my hand out from under his, "still working on wrapping up some endings."

"You could tell me about them," he says. "Maybe I could help."

I try to smile. "Thank you, but for now…."

"I understand," he says, "no pressure. It's just…. it's just that… Aurelia, you are special. I know you're special in ways that I can't yet figure out. I don't want something so special to get away because I didn't… well as we miners say, stake my claim."

I grimace at his rather unromantic choice of words. He gives an embarrassed laugh and looks at the table. I'm grateful that the mood of intimacy is broken, it was becoming, what intoxicating? Exhilarating?

No, back to business.

"This is a good start," I say, waving my hand comp which causes the holographically produced data screens to waver and then disappear. "But it will make for a busy night here. You'd better get the equipment on its way to the ship. It will take most of the night to get everything."

"Oh," he says. I know from his cool tone and lack of expression that his feelings are hurt. I can't do anything more about that, at least not now. "I'll call Kemisa and send down the cargo along anyone who has space-loading experience to help you and Dassa lock it all down.

We both stand.

"I wish I could stay and help, but I have another damn council meeting. The same people who were standing shoulder to shoulder a few days ago, are now quarreling over everything from water rights, to priority on street repairs."

I give what I hope is a sympathetic chuckle.

"I will come back to see you off tomorrow."

Should I discourage this unnecessary gesture on his part? He, like Dassa, is a biological complication of my new life. I open my mouth to say that, but what comes out it is, "Thanks, I would like that." For a second I have a bizarre dissociative feeling and wonder who is speaking—a quick diagnostic shows that I am functioning at normal levels.

"You ok?" he asks, with his damnable perceptiveness.

"Yes, merely distracted by the task ahead."

"Ok, until tomorrow."

"Yes, till then."

CHAPTER TWENTY

I know he wants to touch me in goodbye. To have some gesture that says we are merely more than two people who know each other, but he will not risk it since I withdrew my hand from his earlier. He smiles and heads for the hatch. For a wild second, I want to call him back, but it passes.

CHAPTER TWENTY-ONE

MALPORIN IS AS GOOD AS HIS WORD AND COMES TO SEE ME OFF WITH wishes of good luck. We share breakfast together but Seachange is filled with strangers getting ready for the mission and our conversation is kept light. He leaves only with the launch bell.

With the cargo locked down and the passengers secured in all the available cabin space including Dassa's, we prepare for lift off. Dassa elects to ride with me in the control cabin. Perhaps if Kemisa had boarded, she would have chosen differently, but she wasn't part of the detail Malporin sent.

"Ready?" I ask her.

"Would it matter if I said no?"

"Not really."

"That's what I thought."

The impellers rumble under us as Seachange gathers herself, then breaks contact with the ground. We rise swiftly into the brown and yellow sky. For this hop we will be horizontal for only 16.453 minutes. Using a starship this way is wasteful. Seachange is overbuilt for point-to-point in atmosphere, but she is vastly more powerful than any atmospheric aircraft.

I turn the ship's nose to horizontal as our seats reorients. I keep watch on the world on below, looking for any sign of a weapon lock, or the contrail of rising missile, but nothing threatens. One could not ignore the possibility there are mercenaries in the pay of the Indigenes, or that some of them had learned enough of Confederation technology to fire an automatic missile. Monkey see, monkey do, would be the human expression. Mercenaries made little sense to me. Who would pay for them? They were interfering with the primary cash producing opportunity on the planet, who would benefit?

The ship rolls north over the rough mountain range that separates the plain Pilbara sits on, from the high plateau where the mining camp and the mineheads lay. The sky above has turned blue as we gained 2,000 meters, clearing the dust curtain between us and the ground.

We ran at high subsonic speed so the camp comes into sight exactly on schedule. Tillet sat in a high mountain valley, a thin stream of water ran through its center, accounting for the existence of the base. Life requires water.

Unlike with a regular aircraft, I could not put Seachange into a spiral to inspect the base. Despite the big fins on our stern we had very little lift, and our stall speed is very high for an aircraft. The best I can do is put her in vertical mode and sit on our impellers, while the Seachange pounds *the area below with every sensor in her inventory. According to Mal's report, the camp had been attacked over several weeks, finally being evacuated when they realized the native siege had grown to an army they could not hope to withstand. The escaping column had itself been attacked three times but made it to Pilbara. So, there were no bodies lining the streets, the evacuation had been sudden, but orderly.*

The camp below shows signs of being sacked and looted. Many of the buildings are burned. All the tent sites are empty, showing that the nomadic Indigenes had taken them as prizes. Some vehicles are burned and overturned. Destroyed in the attacks, or abandoned, as unsuitable for the mountain trails southward.

"Landing Force," I announce over the ship's speakers, "we are in hover over Tillet. No power is registering, no signals and no signs of colonists or Indies. Standby for touchdown in 180 seconds."

I throttle back and allow Seachange to sink from 5,000 meters, all while scanning the surrounding terrain for any evidence of attack. The gimbal-mounted laser controls are by my hand, but I need no such crude interface. The weapon is linked directly to my brain and the best gun crew in the Confederacy would come off second best to me.

"You know," Dassa says, as she cranes her neck to stare out the ports, "I would love to see some of these galactic wonders everyone is always talking about. Everywhere I have been looks like the butt end of nowhere."

"I assume you are excepting my house," I reply.

"Yes, if only so you don't stuff me in the trash compactor."

I raise an eyebrow.

She sighs. "Yes, your house was very pretty and the food was great."

I nod. "Better. In time, you may appreciate the comforts of a homey little place of your own, in place of all those so-called wonders."

We continue to sink. "Sixty seconds."

Seachange came to rest on her impellers with an almost audible sigh

Maauro shifted the ship to port mode, shutting down the engines without bothering to touch anything but the webbing on her seat. She rose smoothly, and I scrambled out of my chair.

She turned and frowned at me. "It is unfortunate that given the need to conceal what I am—I must remain here to operate the ship's laser, though I can control it from anywhere in the area since we do not have to contend with interference from a Brownie."

"Well, you would hide your light under a bushel."

Maauro's lip's quirked. "Hanging out with humans, again?"

"Only when they're buying Kemisa and me, drinks and trying to get into our pants."

The smiled faded at the sound of Kemisa's name. "Security out."

I nodded and ran down the spiral staircase of the central core, now vertical with the ship sitting on her fins. I found the two security people Malporin had sent, waiting for me at the ship's armory. One was the Drisnian who'd guarded us earlier. Her name was unpronounceable, and she was known as Fizz. For all her diminutive size, she was one of his best shots. Pallack, the other, was a sturdy human with a beard. Like me, they were already in armor.

The armory door opened to admit me, and they followed me in. I pulled one of the two racked carbines, leaving the other for Maauro. Her armspac was safely hidden away, though I longed to have both her and it with me, but her android nature would be revealed if she started toting a weapon that weighed as much as I did. Fizz picked up her pistol and a slender, long-barreled rifle with a scope. Pallack, as if to complement her choice of long-distance weaponry, drew a shotgun and a big-bore slug-thrower. We all grabbed our helmets.

We quickly moved down to the lower level, passing the others who wished us good luck. Once at the lower level, we opened the airlock. We could have opened both sides of it, but dust and grit would have blown in, and I knew who'd have to clean that up. So, we all three squeezed in and the lock cycled. Pollack and I rode the platform down while Fizz scanned the area with her scoped rifle. As soon as we were down, she joined us, hopping onto the platform before it even reached the top.

There was no cover or concealment nearby, so we just took a knee as we studied the camp. Nothing stirred, save some paper debris and arazi, a circular, dusty, ochre plant that only rooted when they could find water and otherwise rolled where the wind blew them. As we looked at the narrow, dirt streets of the camp, the ruined buildings and vehicles, Fizz turned to me. "Your captain, is she a good gunner?"

I laughed. "She can hit anything she can see, with anything from a pistol to a ship's rail gun."

Pollack grunted. "Nice to know."

As if summoned by the question, Maauro's voice crackled in my ears. "Dassa. I am on your circuit only. Report, but remember they can hear you speak, so call me, Aurelia."

"Yes, Aurelia. There's no sign of movement. We are going to move out."

"Affirmative. I see nothing on scan either, but the ship's sensors were designed to find starships in a nebula and asteroid fields, not biologicals in buildings, or behind rocks."

We started forward, moving in bounds, with Pallack and me in the lead and Fizz bringing up the rear with her scoped rifle. Our first stop was a nearby crashed helo. Fizz took up position atop a pile of gravel nearby.

I looked back at her. "Don't spend too much time in the scope. Aurelia is watching for long range threats."

She glared at me, but flicked the scope to one side.

I scanned the interior, but there was no desiccated corpse within, only some lizards that scuttled resentfully away.

We moved on, coming up to a row of less damaged buildings. Pallack poked his head in. "It's all torn up inside. Looks like the Indies were using the sinks inside for water. There are signs some were sleeping in here."

Fizz made a spitting sound. "Bastards were probably drinking out of the toilets."

I checked the doorway of the next building and a stink greeted me. We checked for bodies and only found an open refrigerator full of rotting food. Fizz backed out quickly, and I wondered what her reaction would be when we go to the sewage treatment area.

"Okay, let's make our way to the power plant," I said. "I'd love to have some lights before nightfall."

"Hah," Pollack returned, "might as well wish for barrier wire and ASATs to patrol it."

I tapped my mike. "Aurelia, this is taking too long. We're going to cut directly to the power plant."

"Understood. I am also frustrated by my inability to do the task myself."

We neared the power station, a two-story building made of blocks of local concrete, colored like the soil. The roof was covered with smashed solar panels, but a large propeller still turned in the breeze above us.

"Wonder if the synth-fuel generator was damaged," Pallack said. He'd been in the camp before it fell and knew it well.

As we passed the shadow of a partially collapsed building near the power plant, Fizz wrinkled her nose. "Somebody must have left their lunch to rot here too."

Alarms jangled in brain. "No. Look—"

From under the partially collapsed roof, a huge figure, all in black, lunged at us with a demonic howl. Two hand axes flew from his upper hands, the lower ones each bore a long knife. The first ax bounced off Fizz's helmet. She stumbled to the ground almost at the feet of the charging warrior. Pollack blocked the axe thrown at him with his shotgun, but the weapon was knocked from his hand. He backpedaled, snatching for the pistol in his belt.

I leveled the carbine in one smooth move and fired a single shot, right between the crazed eyes of the native. He dropped. No jerking, flailing, or being thrown backward—just from life to death in the instant. Fizz rolled away as the body almost fell on her, knives cartwheeling from dead hands to stick in the hard- packed dirt.

Fizz came up with her weapon and put an unnecessary shot into the corpse.

"Fire in the hole," I called, the others ran backwards and I fired a single mini-frag into the area under the roof to make sure there was no more company. The dull thump sounded as we switched our attention to the other buildings, standing back to back. I was pleased to note that while my companions were breathing hard and shaken, I was not. I felt a certain malicious joy at my superiority.

Fizz leaned on Pallack and looked up at me. "Thanks."

"Yeah," Pallack added, looking at the dent and scratch on his shotgun. "Nice shooting."

I moved toward collapsed roof and triggered the light on my carbine. "Our friend seems to have been here a few days: blankets, pots, broken jars of water and other supplies."

When I turned back, to my surprise, Maauro was standing next to Pallack and Fizz, who seemed to notice her at the same moment I did. She was covering the area around us, the carbine held easily in one hand. It could be deceiving, but I detected no concern in her, which must mean no other enemies near.

Fizz had a chagrinned expression. "Damn, seems like everyone is sneaking up on me today. How did you get here so fast?"

"Shouldn't you be on the laser?" Pallack asked.

"I was satisfied there were no enemies in line of sight, save perhaps in these structures where they could hide. I figured a second triple-auto to be useful."

"Can't say that I'm not happier having you here," Pallack said, "but if you get killed who will fly the ship?"

"I am hard to kill," Maauro replied. She walked forward to stare down at the corpse. "Why is he painted black?"

Pallack walked up next to her and toed the corpse. "Ghost-stalker."

"What?" I said.

"A native who feels he's lost everything: family, territory, honor. He declares himself dead, a vengeful ghost, and goes on a one-way quest after his enemies, armed only with traditional weapons."

"Lucky us," I said. "I'd hate to think what would have happened if we walked past him and he'd had an automatic. This one's been waiting here for us to return since just after Big Day. Whatever saved us, may have wiped out most of his tribe."

"Which shows an uncomfortable grasp of our intentions," Maauro said. She still held the carbine as lightly as if it was a pistol. I glanced at the weapon. She interpreted the glance correctly and changed to a two-handed grip, more compatible with her apparent physique before the others noticed.

Fizz came over to me with a native hand ax in hand. It was ornately carved in a fine wood with stones inlaid in it. "Here," she said. "You potted him and saved my ass. It should be yours."

I accepted the handsome weapon and slid it into a loop on my belt.

Pallack handed the other one to Maauro. "Souvenir for our pretty captain."

"You do not want it?"

"Nah, I have enough of their crap. Besides all I did here was block. Your girl did the shooting."

Maauro accepted the axe and added it to a loop on her own belt that had not been there a second before, and of course fitted perfectly, unlike mine.

Pallack looked around. "There shouldn't be any more here. Ghost-stalkers are considered the walking dead. And they wouldn't stay together, each man travels to death alone."

Maauro examined Fizz. "Are you able to continue?"

"Yeah, I'm madder at getting caught as flat-footed as a newbie than anything else."

"Very well," she said. "You two continue to check out the area between here and the ship, then provide security for the other teams. We will clear the power plant."

She tapped the com on her chest. "Toyama to Lanten."

"Lanten here. Are our guys all right?"

"Yes. I will send them back to provide local security. Please begin off-loading the vehicles. The cargo equipment will respond to voice commands and the rest you're familiar with. "

"Uh, who will fly the ship if you get killed?"

Maauro sighed with, I felt, genuine annoyance at having to appear as limited as the human female she appeared to be. I briefly had to struggle with the mental image of her standing atop the power plant, laughing wildly and shouting. "Come get me! I am the invincible android. BWA-HAHAHAHAHH." I had to smother a laugh, and the look she gave me as I did so, was so puzzled, I almost couldn't hold it in.

"I am extremely good at staying alive," she finally said. "Proceed as directed." She clicked off.

She turned her cool gaze on Pallack and Fizz, who also looked worried, but sensed that she was in no mood to be disputed. They set off.

Maauro turned back toward the power plant and started off.

I made sure my com was off. "I presume we have nothing to worry about?"

She nodded. "I'd grabbed my carbine and moved to the midship hatch. I was just opening it when you flushed the ghost-stalker. I leapt out of the hatch and as soon as I was in the air and could use my own onboard sensors I had a 99.7% certainty of no enemy in line of sight."

"You are too forbearing," I replied in a rueful tone. "We flushed nothing; he ambushed us."

"There is nothing harder to stop, than a being willing to exchange itself for you. I remember when one of my M-4 sisters detonated herself to rupture the defenses on an Infestor asteroid base. Though I doubt she had sufficient self-awareness to be thought of as an actual person."

It chilled me to walk under the sun alongside her and hear a description of a battle over fifty millennia ago.

"By the time I reached you, my confidence was up to 99%."

"So we have a one percent chance of having our asses shot off?" I said, as I peered into the nearest darkened doorway of the power plant at the torn-up mess inside.

"No, but I didn't think you wanted me to chant .999 ad nauseum, so I rounded off."

"Never gets to 100% then?"

"No, never 100%."

I wondered if there was something significant about the way she said it.

"Well, we have to do a pointless walk around the plant for the sake of appearances then," I added, "but it gets us out of cargo unloading duty."

"It gets you out of cargo unloading duty. I'm the captain."

"Then we need more crew, Madame Captain." We walked around the far end of the power plant; I could see dynamos and a generator which appeared intact.

"All in due time," Maauro said, stepping over a bent bicycle lying in the street. It was a child's bike. I wondered what had become of the owner.

"Won't people at the ship wonder how you got out here without passing them in the lower deck?"

"If they ask, I will tell them I climbed down, using the kickins on the outside of the ship below the midship hatch."

"Maauro, only an insane person would do that."

"It will add, as my husband used to say, "luster to my legend.""

"Some of them already begin to suspect you aren't what you claim to be."

"Such as Kemisa?"

"Such as her." Gravel crunched under my feet as we started across something that had probably been graded as a parking lot, or VTOL pad.

"You are, I trust, keeping our secrets during your pillow talk?"

I gave her an arch expression, somewhat proud of the fact both that I'd had sex as an adult, and acquired information Maauro did not have. "You need not worry on that score. She believes you brought something horrible in the ship and turned it loose on the Indigenes. She has no idea that the something horrible was you."

She gave me that sidelong look.

"Well, horrible from the point of view of the Indies."

Maauro shook her head. "And she imagines that this unknown horror, having completed its task, is sitting in the mountains somewhere, howling its loneliness?"

"You should write poetry."

"I did. It was bad poetry. Worse, I cannot even forget it."

"Ah, so, there are drawbacks to the android life?"

"Some."

"Advantages too. I like the not-dying part."

"That," she said, "is not the blessing you might think."

I stopped and stared at her.

"Come," she said, without pausing. "I want to check out the assayer's office and its vault."

"Now that sounds interesting."

We headed for the assayer's office opposite the power station. It was a blockhouse-like building built of the local stone. The veranda led to a heavy, steel door that hung loosely in its frame. Maauro casually wrested it out of our way, and we made our way into the darkened interior. The only windows were high slits, admitting some of the weak sunlight. Light flashed from Maauro's eyes and I turned on the beam on my triple auto. It revealed a stand of broad tables and cabinets. She walked past these toward a room in the back. I followed.

We found the vault big enough for an aircar inside the door. Trays lined the walls; but they had been hurriedly pulled out and left hanging.

Maauro examined the thick vault door. "This door was not blasted; it's been cyber-hacked. Then the hard drive of the vault was scrubbed clean afterward."

"No Indigene did this."

She nodded. "I would find it difficult with such a lock. No, they did not do this. Mal says they believe opaloids are cursed stones, bringing the Confederacy here and they no longer mine them. They never made much use of them, save in trading with the colonists.

"Malporin said a large shipment of opaloids was deposited here after a great strike. The time lock was set before evacuation. Normally, they would have had an unlock code transmitted from the home office in the capitol. With the storms and other disruptions, that wasn't possible. They had to leave the stones behind."

"So who robbed the bank? Eliminating the Indigenes brings up the possibility of the often referenced, but never observed, mercenaries."

"Or possibly some criminal element," Maauro said, she turned to face me, dimming the lights in her eyes so they merely seemed to glow.

"If you are asking me about Guild, I know nothing about Guild operations so far from my homeworld. There might be some Guild associates in the capitol, if nowhere else. Somehow, it does not quite fit. Why side with the natives against the very people who are mining the stones? Guild wouldn't take over mines. We make our money off transactions."

She nodded. "Makes sense."

"Speaking of money does this robbery mean we don't get paid?"

"No, though they planned to use these stones. There is more than sufficient in the mineheads. They've been working the mines all this time. There should be plenty of stones when we get there."

I mark the assay office for a later visit without Maauro's company. Who knows what may have been left in the odd corner?

"Come," she said. Grimness had returned to her tone. "The ship's AI tells me all that Mule is unloaded. We have work to do."

CHAPTER TWENTY-TWO

WE RETURN TO THE LANDING SITE AND LOAD THE MULE WITH THE *equipment we have brought for the task and start driving slowly on the partially washed-out road. We find the hastily prepared cemetery north of the camp. Shouldering our spades, we walk through wooden gate, already beginning to sag with deterioration.*

The natives have been here. Stones are overturned, graves are disturbed and bodies are partially unearthed. The sight is gruesome, and I realize that to Dassa the smell must be terrible.

"Return to the vehicle," I say. "I will do what is needed for these."

"I thought we came for Nipkin's mother."

"We did, but I cannot allow this to remain this way."

She stares at me. "But you don't even know them. Why bother?"

I control my anger and rotate my head over my shoulder in a move that would kill any biological with a spinal cord.

Dassa hastily backs up, startled and frightened by the sight. Even she forgets what I actually am from time to time.

"Go back to the vehicle," I grate.

She continues backing away.

Perhaps it is as well, I think as I set about the grisly business. Digging as rapidly as I am capable of, might appear unintentionally comic to her. I have no need of ill-mannered company in this grim setting. I spade quickly and return the bodies to the cloak of the ground, righting the markers as best I can.

Then I round the small hill on the far side of which Perebin was buried.

Oh, Oh, for some enemy to kill at this moment. To fall on them and rend them limb from limb. Her grave is by far the worst. It has been completely desecrated with her body exhumed and spread obscenely on large stone, pinned there by wedged lances driven into the softer soil and loose rock of the hillside. She faces me, dignity ripped away, limbs splayed out. I am thankful that the skull, rags of hair still attached, has sunk on the torn chest so that I did not come face to face with it.

The sound of retching behind me catches me off guard. Dassa has come up behind me with a spade in her hand. So lost to anger and revulsion am I, that I am taken by surprise.

She is on hands and knees, vomiting. Even for one of the Guild, this is too much horror. I hurry over to her, but do not touch the girl. The smell of me cannot be much easier to bear, given I have been handling decaying corpses.

"You should have waited for me at the Mule," I say.

A final spasm wracks her then she looks up at me. "No. No. You think this is important, a human thing, so it must be."

If I was clean I would have stroked her hair. "You do not have to," I add in a soft voice I have perhaps not used often enough with her,

She shakes her head.

"Very well, but leave the worst of this to me. I have never been so glad for my ability to dial down my senses as just now, especially my sense of smell."

She looks up at me, narrowing her eyes in an effort to just see my face and not the horror behind me. "Yes."

Unconcerned now about the sight of me digging at speed, I quickly unearth a proper grave, down to two meters but three long. It takes me only a minute. When I put the spade down, its edge glows and the ground sizzles around it.

We return to the vehicle. Dassa grabs the large tarp I'd thrown in the back as I lift out the white casket, placing it up on one shoulder. We return to the sad hillside, but before we round the small hill. I again turn to Dassa, "Will you wait here?"

She shakes her head, jaw locked.

"Please, Dassa, wait here. Your offer is enough. I will call you when the body is in the casket."

It is difficult to read her expression, but perhaps this is relief. She nods. Speech seems beyond her just now, or maybe she simply does not want to open her mouth in this deliquescent environment.

I take the tarp and run around the hillside. Once before the corpse, I dial my senses down as far as I can and still carefully handle the body. First, I remove the lances run through the body, each is vaporized by my plasma torch, but only after I commit each marking to memory. There will be retribution if I find the owners.

The wind moves the stiff and matted hair that still clings to desiccated skull. I cannot help but notice it is the same color as Nipkin's and I remember the sensation of nausea from when I was biological.

A few minutes' careful work suffices to remove the body. Now, properly composed, Perebin rests in the tarp. I close it up tightly, generating glue that seals the tarp into a shroud. Then it is time to move her to the soft interior of the casket.

Have I become foolish, I wonder, to think that my actions make a difference to Perebin or the universe at large? Yet, a feeling of peace comes to me as the cool green tarp, enclosing its sad burden is laid to rest on the clean and soft cushions. I close the lid and the casket seals with a hiss.

"Dassa," I call.

She comes around the hillside and joins me at the casket.

"Time for her to return to the ground."

"We have no straps," Dassa says.

"No need. I have made the hole large enough to me to get out of."

We position the casket at one end of the grave I have dug. I leap in. Dassa remains above with the casket. She tips it forward when I give the word. I raise my arms over my head and take the weight, then slowly and carefully place one end on the ground, backing away I then lower the other end at my feet. Leaping out seems disrespectful; so, I climb, thrusting my stiffened fingers and feet into the earth at the far end. In a moment, I regain the surface and stand beside Dassa.

We both pick up our spades.

"Is there a ritual?" Dassa whispers.

I nod. "I had a friend who was a pastor. I could wish her here with us now, but I will do the best I can do."

I recite the prayer Reverend Janna Lourens taught me so long ago on Retief, in happier, if not untroubled days. Though, if Janna was right, Perebin has long since entered the care of whatever God created space-time. I hope she was right.

"Do you wish to add anything?" I ask Dassa.

"I would not know what to say," she replies. "Perhaps my actions will speak enough for me."

They did to me, I think.

We cover the casket. I spot the plastic plaque that with her name on it. Some savage has cracked it into pieces. This will not do. It is possible that sometime in the future, Nipkin and her father might come to this place.

I select stones that no four natives could move and place them atop the grave.

With my plasma torch I carefully inscribe:

Perebin Chala

Mother to Nipkin Chala

Wife to Oskar Chala

Rest in Peace

I cut the date in Galactic standard then in a lower corner I add:

Laid to rest by Aurelia Toyama and Dassa

leaving off Dassa's last name, as is customary for her kind.

Yet, I feel more is needed here. I move to the nearest outcrop of stone, scan it and strike four times, cleaving out a squarish piece. Again, plasma flares in my finger as I write,

Dearest Nipkin, my real name was Maauro Trigardt.

I place it at the foot of her mother's grave with the inscription face down. Perhaps she will come, perhaps not, but there will be this little answer for her, if she does.

I sit back and look around. The cemetery has returned to what is should be. I fear that it will be visited seldom in the unfolding ecological catastrophe that is Damasia. Flowers will rarely decorate these graves. Now that I am deprived of action, sadness returns. Death's dominion is absolute. Even an artificial intelligence must acknowledge the dark angel's eventual rule.

"Can we go?" Dassa's voice has a plaintive ring, but the girl is ill-used by this place. If it lowers my spirits, how much worse for one who must lay down, never to rise again, and so much sooner than I? She does not quite run to the vehicle, but moves as fast as she can. I follow more slowly and leave both spades at the entrance. I stop well short of the mule, then play my plasma torch over my whole body, cleaning myself of even the smallest particle of decaying matter.

Dassa watches in fascination as I run my glowing hands through my long, now unbound, hair, which, made of the same material as the rest of me, suffers no harm.

"Can you do the same for me?" she asks.

I give an abortive laugh and then realize she is serious. I consider for a moment, we have several jerrycans of water in the vehicle.

"Step out of your clothes and shoes, then pass them to me."

Picking up each item of discarded clothing, I press it to the front of my body where it is absorbed, cleaned and deodorized with any fragments of biological matter vaporized. Then the garment is extruded back out. I fold these and place them on the truck bed.

"If you make a joke about my being a dry-cleaner, I will beat your bottom until it glows."

She snorts a laugh. "If you leave my pale bottom out in the sun for much longer, it will begin to glow on its own."

"Squat down," I say. I line up the jerrycans and then extend a tube from the center of my left hand. From my right, jets spray the water passing through me, heated and laced with disinfectant and soap. The pressure is high enough to make Dassa yelp as it hits sensitive spots, but her desire to be clean exceeds any momentary pain. After she soaps up, I tube another container and quickly rinse her head to toe, finishing with strong cologne that I mist on both of us.

"I'll dress as we drive," Dassa says, grabbing her clothes and eager to be gone. She dashes to the other side of the mule and hops in. I get in at a slower pace and start the vehicle and drive off, relieved to leave the cemetery.

CHAPTER TWENTY-THREE

"**I** CANNOT POSSIBLY FACE FOOD," I SAID, HOURS LATER back aboard *Seachange*. "I may never eat meat again." Suddenly, I needed to fight my stomach as the memories crash back in.

Maauro peeked around from the galley. We were alone at the ship. Night had fallen, and while the others elected to hold up in Tillet; we returned to the ship to watch over the town and the mountain passes. The miners in the hills beyond were getting the word of our return, but they too, would wait for daylight to move.

"Poor Dassa," Maauro replied, bringing over some of a strong wine she'd purchased on her homeworld. To my surprise, she reached down and patted my shoulder. "I am a machine and I cannot forget, but sometimes that I lose focus on just how young you are. That I do not consider how terrible these sights are to you."

"I have seen death as you know," I hesitated, afraid to admit weakness and perhaps lose status in those big eyes, "and my kind are thought of as cruel by others, but not like that. Not the aftermath, not hate and pointless savagery that—"

She slid a finger across my lips. "Do not go back to that place."

There is something in her voice, a gentleness that has occasionally manifested itself before, but seems very present just now. I am surprised by the gesture. She seldom touches me. "Was it like that for you? The first time?"

"No, Dassa, it wasn't. The capacity for horror, even for fear, is biological in origin. I fought, free from fear and conscience, killing because I was made to kill, even to torture, if it was in my orders. Yet, even then, I felt distaste for the latter. If the Infestors were irredeemable enemies, it still damaged my own soul to do such things, and I would delete the memories. I am glad for that now. I know I did it, but I cannot remember the details.

"Would that I had such a memory," I replied. "There is such a lot I would rather not remember."

"Ah, but I no longer have it," she replied. "You see, Wrik once made me promise never to delete any memory with him in it. I then expanded that promise to never delete any memory, no matter how painful it might be. We are all a compilation of our memories, to destroy them, is in some sense to murder ourselves.

"Meanwhile," she finished, "I made us a nice vegetable tian for dinner."

Dinner was as good as she said. I drank too much of the wine, wanting distance between myself and the cemetery, asking to open three bottles. Maauro helped me to my cabin and out of my clothes. I lay on my bed, head spinning.

She headed for the door, switching off the lights.

"Maauro," I called suddenly.

"Yes,"

"Don't shut the door."

She looks back at me.

"I don't... I don't want to be in the dark just now. Not after the cemetery."

To my surprise she walked back and settled on the deck near me. "There's nothing I need to do for the rest of the night that I cannot do from here."

I tried to focus on her, realizing how drunk I'd gotten. "Sorry. I'm behaving like a nine-year. Forget it."

"Go to sleep, Dassa. If it makes you feel better, I would as soon not be alone with my memories tonight either."

"I should be ashamed..."

"You should be asleep."

I let my eyelids close.

By morning the population of Tillet had exploded with jubilant miners celebrating the lifting of the siege. The assay office was reopened for business. Some who had sheltered in the mines, rather than flee all the way back to Pilbara, began to bring the place back to life. I walked beside Maauro, who was the hero of the hour. My own welcome would have been far cooler had it not been for the stories of my participation in the defense of Pilbara and bagging the Ghoststalker. Dua-Denlenn claim-jumpers were still remembered here.

Some of the miners had found the Ghoststalker's corpse and hung it up on a scaffold. They were just finishing their grisly task, when Maauro stalked up in a cold fury.

"Cut the body down and bury it," she commanded.

The group of men, bearded, dirty, and resentful, glared at her. One, the obvious ringleader, said. "Listen here, we've been held underground by these animals—"

Maauro moved, not as fast she could, but fast, wrapping a hand around his throat, seizing his vest front and forcing him to the ground. He looked up at her, shocked at her strength.

I watched the others, my hand on the butt of my pistol.

"Cut the body down and bury it," she said, in a calm voice somehow far more frightening than had she yelled, "was not a request."

"They do worse to ours," another man shouted.

Mauro's head swiveled. "Are they our teachers? Are we supposed to learn from them?"

The man she held tried to move. She held him in place and turned to face him again. He looked into her huge eyes and saw something there that made him stop struggling.

"Guys," another man called. "This ain't right. She's brought us help and they bagged this bastard. It should fall to them to make the call what happens to it."

Maauro released the man, who stood, looking at her in wary respect. "You're stronger than you look."

"Yes," she replied.

"Have it your way," he said gruffly. "It's yours." He headed off, trailed by most of the men. Only the man who had spoken up for Maauro and a stocky woman in a hat and goggles remained.

I glanced up at the suspended corpse and cursed in Dua. "I just got the stink of the cemetery off me."

The woman in goggles looked at me. "You're the ones who went to the cemetery."

I nodded.

"I saw it before you came," she said. "I was out scouting."

Maauro turned to her. "Does anyone else know? "

"Just Vondar here and I. It wasn't good news. We hoped to fix it before the others saw, but you beat us to it."

"Let it remain so," Maauro said.

The man nodded. "We owe you one. Leave this Indie to us. We'll see him decently into the ground."

"Thank you," I said, before Maauro could demur or offer to help. She looked over at me and gave a slight nod.

We headed for the assay office as they drew knives and turned to the grisly task of cutting the corpse down.

I turned to her. "Do you hate?"

She stopped in her tracks in surprise, and then started again at a slower pace. "As M-7, no. When I became Maauro, I learned anger and grim resolve, then as woman I acquired the ability to hate. It remains with me now. My emotions have altered little since my biological incarnation. Maybe that will change with time. I do not know.

"So, yes, I can understand hate, enough to fear what it can do the soul. They would not agree now, but in the future, some of them may be glad I stopped them."

Privately I doubted this, but kept the thought to myself.

We walked on in silence to the assay office, shoulder to shoulder, in a way I found... comforting. My alignment with the powerful entity beside me gave me a sense of well-being that had been elusive for years. The weak sun above was cutting through the ever-present haze and our boots raised dust as we walked, but we were alive, had defeated all comers, and we were going to be paid a scandalous amount of money. It could hardly be better.

CHAPTER TWENTY-THREE

In the afternoon of our second full day in Tillet, I joined Dassa in the galley after having secured the balance of our payment in a mix of opaloids and other precious metals and gems in the ship's secured hold. I made a fragrant tea and sat across from her at the table.

"What now?" Dassa asked. "Tillet's reopened and the mines are back in communication. We've been paid."

"There is more to do," I reply. "I want to get free of Malporin and the Damasian authorities for a while to investigate why this world's ecology has become so unstable."

"Oh?" Dassa asked, wolfing down a sandwich.

"You are going to choke if you keep that up."

"Have a heart, Maauro. I wasn't able to eat anything but your vegetable tian and not much of that for forty-eight hours after the cemetery."

"I am not ever concerned with the quantity of food you eat, amazing as it is for such a slim creature, only the speed with which you stuff food down your only air passage. Please try chewing more."

She nods; giving me what I swear is an amused look. "Anyway, what of Malporin and the council? They don't want to lose access to our ship. Will they let us go without a struggle?"

"If I give Malporin my word, he will." I look at her. "What of Kemisa?"

My question allowed her to finish off the one sandwich and seize another. "If you are asking, will Kemisa take my word that we will come back? No, she is too intelligent to take someone's unsupported word for anything. She is not a human male falling in love."

I sigh, ignoring the latter part of her comment. "Inconvenient, but if I post a performance bond—"

"Then she would believe it."

"Good, the two of them control the council so we will gain freedom to maneuver."

We left in the morning of the next day, taking a few miners who'd elected to give up their claims, sold them off, or had business in Pilbara or beyond. Lanten, as expected, grumbled about our leaving, but with no sign of significant Indigene activity, his arguments were ineffective. I responded that the sooner we left, the sooner we would return with more people and supplies.

The flight to Pilbara is brief and uneventful, but, as if to remind us of the devastation that always lurked, a Brownie is swirling over Pilbara. It obliterated our view of the town, but with passengers aboard I didn't dare guide the ship down from outside and had to rely on the ship's inferior instruments. Still, the landing would have made Wrik proud. Once down, I use the ship's floodlights to illuminate the area for the convenience of our welcoming committee.

"Dassa, we're going ashore. Tell our passengers that they can debark when the Brownie blows itself out. Not before. If they need anything, they can request it from the ship's AI"

She looked up at the monitor. "Looks they managed to get a truck out here."

I note that it is the same vehicle that first met us. We head down. I pick up a jacket and helmet, annoyed again at the prospect of needing them for appearance sake. Dassa also equips herself.

A fierce wind greets us at the outside hatch. Dassa wraps her arms around me to stay stable in the wind as the elevator lowers us to the ground.

"This has an appalling familiarity to it," Dassa remarks,

"I believe the human expression is, déjà vu."

"Gods save me from more human weirdness."

The elevator grounds and we run toward the waiting truck. To my surprise and momentary disappointment, it is Kemisa and the driver from our first landing, not Malporin. Dassa and Kemisa smile at each other without displaying teeth, but are no more affectionate than that in front the driver and I.

"Captain," Kemisa acknowledges me. "Mal sends his regrets, but with the storm, he was needed in the Council Center."

I nod pleasantly.

"If you're not tired or hungry, he asked that you come to the Council room and fill him in on the situation in Tillet. We got your radio report, but it was garbled."

"Good, it will allow us to discuss the next moves."

Her tail swishes on the seat. "Moves?"

I do not explain further. It would not do to give Kemisa the impression she is entitled to special access.

The ride through the murk wasn't long, but Kemisa and Dassa filled it with chatter about the doings at Pilbara and Tillet. There'd only been one sniping incident since we'd left. The Indigene had been killed by a patrol. There is something genuine in their interest in each other, perhaps I have taken Malporin's warnings too seriously. In any event, I certainly feel like a third wheel.

The driver pulls to the curb of the council building. We dash through the dust and stinging wind, into the lee of the big building with its over-hanging slabs of concrete. There were fewer guards to greet us. We follow Kemisa's swaying tail into the main council room. The twenty or so people inside spot us and instantly break into cheers and applause. Both Dassa and I stop in surprise.

"Here they are," Malporin calls, "the heroes of Tillet." He nods to Romy, who is standing behind a table of foods and holding a large bottle of champagne. With a flourish, she uncorks the bottle and begins pouring.

We are surrounded by the council and must tell the story of the reopening of Tillet and the mineheads. Malporin brings me a glass of champagne, a broad smile on his face. I sip it as Dassa takes up her part of the tale, getting particular applause for taking down the ghost-stalker.

I tell a very carefully edited story of the cemetery, only admitting to markers being disturbed. My story is accepted on the strength of our word, and their desire that it be true. Perhaps some suspect the grimmer truth, but they wisely let light, laughter and champagne prevail as the surprise party rolls on.

Music starts and a few people start to dance. Dassa balks until swept into an embrace with Kemisa. Malporin reaches for my hand.

In the eternity of time that occurs between the beats of a biological's heart, I consider what to do. I last danced with my husband and had not thought to do so again. Dancing had become a special language of love between us, because it was on a magical night, dancing under the stars of Retief, that Wrik declared himself for me. From that moment on, through whatever chanced, we had been a couple.

I take his hand, as my husband had bade me to live on and continue to search for joy. Perhaps this is part of it, and to reject Malporin in front of all his friends would be cruel.

But this too presents a difficulty, as I can tell from Dassa's worried glance at me. The dance is quick and lively and Kemisa once picked her up from the floor in a spin. My disguise as a human may not survive this; I cannot hide my weight.

"Ask her to play something slower," I say, feigning shyness.

"Romy, how about a waltz?" he calls.

Kemisa and Dassa move to the sideline's, not knowing this old human dance, but a few couple's join us and we enjoy the sweep and elegance of the waltz. Malporin is a surprisingly good dancer for a big ex-miner.

"Where did you learn to dance?" I ask.

"I went to a Confed reserve officer training for two years," he replies, "it was part of the training, an officer and a gentlebeing. Now I wish I had stuck with it, but things were falling apart in that sector and the base was withdrawn."

I nod.

"And you?"

"I was taught by an old flame."

"I'm jealous," he says.

I am spared an answer by the end of the dance. I walk over to the table, and perhaps disappointed that I will not dance further, Malporin follows me. I pick up a finger sandwich, and Romy hands me another glass of champagne. As I sip the wine, I slip a hand comp out of my jacket.

"Take a look at the figure," I say, "that's the haul from Tillet and the mines after the balance of my payment."

He whistles. "Looks like they didn't sit on their hands through the siege."

"There was no determined effort to take the mines, beyond two of the smaller ones that were too far away for support. Most of the warriors bypassed Tillet to head here. It didn't require much to keep miners trapped in their holes."

"So then, off to the capitol?" he says, his voice artificially light.

"Yes, I need credit, supplies and you need a market, though I am concerned that such a large load may depress prices."

"Well good news there. The capitol finally got some satellites up so communications are getting better, unless we're in the middle of Brownie, too much metal in the dust screws the reception. Anyway, it seems the Aquitaine mine went bust and the supply of opaloids plummeted. It's about the only thing off-worlders want from us, so the price will be as high as ever."

"So you agree that a trip to the capitol is next?"

He swirls his champagne, visibly uncomfortable. "The council will take a little persuading—"

"I will leave a performance bond guaranteeing a return."

"Well that will reassure Kemisa, Lanten, and a few others."

"Not you?"

"I didn't need anything more than your word you'd return."

I smile, pleased.

"I have some folks aboard Seachange who are going straight through to the capitol. The rest will debark when the storm blows out."

He grimaces. "There are two dozen more or so that will join them. I hate to lose some of them, but there's no helping that. Some are just relocating to the capitol, some were stranded here like Nipkin, and a couple just want to emigrate. Then there are four casualties from the hospital, now well enough to be moved, but needing rehab we can't do here."

"Speaking of Nipkin," I said. "She will be going with me. I am taking her to her father."

"Good," he says, "but I will miss that little girl. Though not perhaps as much as you will."

I turn slightly away to signal that he has touched a delicate subject. "She is a special child. I want to see her safely with her father."

He nods with a small smile, but takes the hint.

"When will you leave?" he asks.

"I want to top off on atmospheric fuel. We don't carry that much. Seachange isn't supposed to dance around inside of gravity wells; she's supposed to frisk and frolic in real space. The Brownie should abate by tomorrow evening."

"And you might risk mutiny if you tried to pry Dassa away from Kemisa tonight."

"Hmm, perhaps time for me to get my cat of nine tails out—"

"—Will not win over this particular one-tailed kitty."
Observing Kemisa and Dassa slipping away, I suspect he is right.
"Can I interest you in a late supper at Venezia?"
"Perhaps dessert," I suggest.

CHAPTER TWENTY-FOUR

MY EVENING WITH MALPORIN IS PLEASANT, AS IS THE DESSERT AT *Venezia, but at the end of it there is awkwardness when I turn down his invitation to stop for a drink at his place. He wishes to proceed further, not understanding why I am reluctant to act on the attraction between us. The situation is probably not helped by his knowledge that my crewmate is not being so restrained tonight.*

But I demur, wishing to attend to my ship, especially as Dassa will not return. Malporin drives me back to the ship. I slip out through the door of the vehicle quickly so we do not face the issue of a good night kiss. Poor Malporin, I think, this is rather like what I put Wrik through during the period between when we declared our love and when we became lovers. Of course, I did make it up to him over the next century together.

I tend to my ship and the passengers. While they sleep, and I can work unobserved, I quickly unload the ship's mule. I prefer my own vehicle, with its modified suspension designed to conceal my weight.

Morning comes and I head out, leaving the passengers to the ship's AI. I am looking forward to telling Nipkin the news in person, so I drive at a brisk pace through town. Some people recognize me and wave. Ironically, I am less well known than Dassa, who is something of a local hero for her more visible part in the defense of Pilbara and the retaking of Tillet. Rounding Bighin Hill, I see the damaged school building. Signs of repair are evident there. The hospital behind it suffered only minor damage by comparison due to my intervention. Would that I'd attacked sooner.

As I pull to the roadside and get out of the mule, I see that once again a soccer game is in progress. A pang resonates in me as I remember the tall boy who had played goalie and now rests in the cemetery not far from where Seachange sits. Before we leave I will take some flowers from our hydroponic garden and place them on his grave.

Nipkin spots me and waves the game to a halt. While the other children hang back, Nipkin races over and wraps her arms around me. I reach down and embrace her, breathing in the scent of her hair. She has her face buried against my chest and gives a quick sob before looking up at me, visibly battling down her emotions.

"I'm so glad to see you," she says, with a smile that covers tears. "I was so afraid something bad would happen to you."

"You remember that I am very strong and quick."

"Yes. I still worried."

"Thank you.

I glance at the other children still on the field. "They seem wary, Nipkin."

She nods. "*None of the other children saw you fight, but Danella and Rovert think they remember your voice afterward. Your face and voice have been on a lot of screens since then. I told them I didn't see you there, but I'm not sure they believe me.*"

"*No matter.*"

Nipkin releases me and steps back. "*Aurelia…my mother's grave…*" her voice begins to shake.

"*Was fine, other than the marker being knocked over.*" I lie without hesitation. She will never know the truth of what I saw.

Now she places her head against my chest and does cry for a minute. When it runs its course, I put a hand on her shoulder so she looks up at me. "*It wasn't a very good grave, so I placed your Mom in a proper coffin and reburied her deep in hard, dry ground. I covered it with stones that would take a great deal of effort to move. It is as protected as can be.*"

"*Then she is at rest,*" Nipkin says in that oddly adult manner that sometimes comes over her, the one that, for some reason, chills me.

"*I bring other news. It is time for you to go to your father.*"

"*You'll take me!*"

"*I will take you. I trust no one else with such a critical mission.*"

She nods, eyes shining.

"*How soon can you be ready to go? I will rest easier with you aboard ship.*"

She looks at the other children. "*I have only a few things to pack from my room. I want to leave most everything for the other kids here. Do you we have time to finish the game?*"

"*Yes,*" I say, and then seat myself on the grass. Nipkin runs back to the other children to share the news and is immediately the subject of hugs and noisy congratulations about going home on a spaceship.

The game continues for forty minutes and then everyone adjourns to Nipkin's room where she collects some of her possessions and distributes others. I remain by the mule, remembering to shift position occasionally, as a human could not sit still for so long. Children are very intuitive, and I limit my exposure to them, especially as these already suspect I was involved in the battle. Finally, Nipkin appears at the top of the stairs. The other children have not come down, probably at her request, but are all hanging out the windows calling and waving. She turns and waves up to them, then runs over to me, her small bag bouncing on her shoulder. I rise and greet her, putting her bag in the back of the mule.

"*Seatbelt,*" I say to her before putting us in drive.

"*Aurelia?*"

"*Yes.*"

"*Any chance there will be ice-cream on the ship?*"

"*According to the local forecast,*" I reply, "*there is a strong probability of ice cream, especially for little girls who eat all their vegetables.*"

"*Are you cooking or is Dassa?*"

"I am."

"That increases the chances of success with the vegetables."

"Even for Dassa."

She looks at the town as we drive toward the ship. "Hard to believe I probably won't ever see this place again."

"You don't believe your father will come here?"

"No. He never wanted to. Mom loved Damasia, but Dad only loved her. He had to put up with her vanishing into the outback, but he didn't like it. He may want to leave this world entirely."

That could be a very good thing, I think to myself, and begin some contingency plans.

We reach the ship, and I see Nipkin safely installed in my space cabin just off the bridge. The space cabin is small, but she will have it all to herself, whereas our other passengers must double or treble. A few of the youngest passengers will ride the trip out in acceleration couches we have rigged up in engineering. There are advantages to being the Captain's pet.

However, for the same reason, while I give up my cabin to the passengers, I do not give up Dassa's. The Dua is very private and would see being treated with less consideration than Nipkin as demeaning. I do not wish to undermine the progress that has been made in my relationship with her.

I leave the ship in the late afternoon to accomplish a few tasks. First, I stop at the grave of the boy Lamosos, who bought a few precious seconds for Nipkin with his life. I tidy the grave, removing windblown debris and then secure the flowers I have brought with small stones. When done, I repeat the prayer that Reverend Janna taught me. Because I learned this one from a pastor, it has a special meaning to me.

This self-appointed mission done, I head for the council office. I have a print copy of my bond, promising my return. It is already done as data, but tradition is for the captain of a ship to deliver a paper copy in person with the ship's seal affixed to it.

Kemisa greets me at the door to the council room.

"Ready for liftoff, Captain?"

"Shortly. As soon as Dassa returns and finishes processing in the new passengers. I've come to drop off my performance bond."

She smiles, though, like Jaelle, she does not use her teeth to do so. "Nice to see someone knows the protocols. We may be just a mining town, but this is still a space control center."

I nod.

"Plus it cheers me to think that it will cost you a lot of money to run off with my new girlfriend."

I give her a level look. "Is that what Dassa is to you, a girlfriend?" I am not sure that I care for the laugh she gives me.

"She's as much of a girlfriend as she wants to be. I don't believe she is looking to settle down in this backwater. Dassa has her eyes on the stars—"

"And you? Where are your eyes?"

She looks at me, surprised by the interruption. Perhaps I am surprised as well.

"I came here from the stars, Captain and maybe a quiet place like Damasia was good for me then. Maybe I will go back to the stars sometime."

"Sounds like you needed to disappear for a while."

"We all have our secrets, Captain. I bet yours are more interesting than mine."

"Perhaps."

"Are you interviewing me to see if I am a good bet to take Dassa off your hands, or because you are afraid that I might?"

I square up to her, to her credit she does not flinch. "You have something of a reputation. Dassa is cynical, untrusting and wary, but inexperienced."

"Are you experienced, Captain?" she says looking me over.

"Don't flirt with me. Kitty girls aren't on my radar, and I am not auditioning for a replacement for Dassa."

"You missed a chance to test me," she says, suddenly switching from coy to serious in a snap. "You should have expressed interest. If I switched my attention to you, you'd have known I was up to no good."

"Or that you were too smart to fall into such a simple trap."

"I am glad you respect my intelligence, if not my motivations."

"So long as everyone involved has their eyes open, I suppose it's none of my business."

"I agree."

"Is Malporin around?"

"Sorry, no. He went out to mountains to look at the work to open the overland route to Tillet."

"Oh," I say.

"He's a good man, Malporin."

"Did I express some doubt?" I say, letting a warning tone enter my voice.

Kemisa raises a hand. "Now it's me forgetting to mind her own business. I just know he likes you and you seem to like him."

Slowly I nod. "I do, but it is complicated."

"Ah, complications, I hate those. Safe voyaging, Captain. Tell Dassa I said hello." She turns and walks back into the building. I make my way to the mule with an unfulfilled feeling which I probably deserve. I am stringing Malporin along, when I have no intention of entering a relationship now. I sigh. Maybe getting away from Pilbara is best for now.

CHAPTER TWENTY-FIVE

WITHIN MINUTES OF LIFTING OFF FROM PILBARA AND GOING *transonic, we are clear of the interference of the wind-blown metallic particles that the brownies are laden with. Even after the storm dissipates, the particles sometimes remain airborne for days before precipitating out.*

"Ah," I say, "finally a reliable satellite connection."

Dassa nods, "And with it comes civilization, GPS, news and proper flight procedure."

"I am downloading all our interstellar mail to the grid," I reply.

"Good. More credits for the ship's accounts."

But news comes in as well.

"Dassa," I began.

"Yes?"

"An Ederi ship has been sighted in the system."

"What! No, impossible. There's no way they could have found me here."

"I agree," I add quickly, trying to head off the panic I see in her eyes. Dassa has shown herself bold and reliable at Pilbara and Tillet, but she dreads the Ederi with a nearly superstitious fear. "Rest assured there is nothing on this ship that could betray our location. Ederi tech is superior to Confed, but not to mine."

"What is known?" she demands, her hands white knuckled on her chair.

"A small free trader detected what they thought was a vessel in distress near the asteroid field by the Beta Jump Point for this system. They spotted a black vessel that must have been hit by a micro-meteor as it was venting atmosphere. It detected them and moved off. The Free Trader, not being a warship, fled in the opposite direction.

Dassa put a hand across her face. "So, an enemy vessel but damaged..."

"Likely badly damaged, even a tiny stone at those speeds can destroy a ship. They may have already perished."

"You don't believe that."

"I regard it as a low order possibility. The fact that it could maneuver at speed argues against that, for all that venting atmosphere indicates substantial hull damage."

"Why would they come here, if not for me? There is no significant Guild presence here."

"And you know this how?" I ask, knowing the answer but curious as to what she would say.

"Kemisa," she replies. "She lived in the capitol for years. Oh, there's the usual crime that accompanies normal life, but no Guild. Originally, there was neither time, nor interest; the world was under Confed interdiction which stopped them getting a toehold. Then some idiot Duas tried claim jumping and got wiped—"

"Yes, Malporin told me of that. So, no obvious target here save you, yet no real prospect that they could know you are here. It is possible some other form of operation is under way."

"Do you suspect them of being behind the climate change? For what reason?"

"None I can think of. While I was not specifically scanning for them, my systems are preset to check for any indication of their tech. I have seen no sign. For all their zealousness in pursuit of the Guild, they have avoided combat with Confed forces. Why attack a minor Confed world?"

"Opaloids," Dassa says

"For an ornamental gem with no industrial uses? I doubt this. There is no point in speculating further. For all we know, it was merely transiting this system to somewhere else."

"Or," she said grimly, settling back in her seat, "we'll find out when one of their ship's pops into existence behind us."

"Do not worry on that score. The Ederi light curtain is far from perfect. Having seen it in operation I will not be caught unaware again. I have recalibrated and reprogrammed Seachange's sensors to alert on encountering any such anomaly. Admittedly this will be more effective in atmosphere than in deep space. My own sensors are even more effective still, but I cannot constantly ride around on the nose of the ship."

"Maauro."

"Yes?"

"Don't ever let them take me alive."

I gaze at her. I am a combatant and understand the desire not to be disgraced, tortured and disposed of by a callous enemy. "Understood. I too will not suffer to be made a prisoner. For now, put these things from your mind. We will be down in Kinwha soon, likely the safest location on Damasia."

She checks the chronometer on the screen. "ETA to port entry, 35 minutes."

"There is more news."

Dassa groans. "What now?"

"The Confederacy is breaking up. Humans, Nekoans, Denlenn, Skurlocks and Enshari have elected to stay in the old Earth-based Confederacy. Your people, the Okarans and the Drisnians have organized around Star Central forming, the Star Alliance. All the rest have seceded into nonaligned worlds."

"So it's come at last," Dassa said, with a shrug. "I'm only surprised it has taken so long. I'm glad we picked up the Drisnians, they're almost as prolific as the humans."

"So," I said, "that makes you a citizen of Star Central."

"And you?" she asks.

"My citizenship is Confed. I'm even eligible for a military pension if I wanted to file for it."

A laugh, quickly smothered, bursts from Dassa.

"It won't be as clear as that," I said, ignoring the laugh. "There will be colony worlds that will fall into one or the other, based more on local conditions then on species. It will make galactic travel far more complex and dangerous."

"May you live in interesting times," Dassa adds.

"Yes. Would you bring Nipkin up here?"

To my surprise, Dassa offers a small smile. "So she can watch the landing?"

"Yes, I promised. She's in the galley raiding the unguarded ice cream supply and chatting with the others. I'd prefer you brought her up. Precocious as she is, she is only ten."

Dassa nods and head for the hatchway, apparently forgetting that I could easily direct the ship while getting Nipkin myself, or for that matter while standing on my head. But the task of supervising the child will take her mind off the Ederi sighting.

Minutes later she returns with Nipkin in tow. Nipkin greets me with her cheeriest smile, all traces of chocolate ice cream removed. Dassa belts her into the second seat and adjusts it so she can see the screens and out the canopy. Dassa then slips into the nav-com chair further back. It has been a long while since three seats have been occupied on my bridge. Absent friends, I think.

I answer the usual barrage of questions about the ship from Nipkin as we sail through the electric blue sky, fading to black above us.

"Coming up on reorientation," I say. "We'll be entering Kinwha aerospace control soon." I flick the intercom. "All hands, all hands, prepare for reorientation to vertical in 180 seconds. Watch your wall clocks, secure any loose items and prepare to take hold."

As the seconds tick on I turn to Nipkin. "Would you like to give the take hold command?"

Her brown eyes shine. "Sure!"

"See the switch marked intercom on the board in front of you? Good. Now look at the chronometer on the screen. When it says sixty-five, flick the switch and say, standby for reorientation in sixty seconds. When it reaches ten, announce take hold three times, loud and clear."

"You sure you wouldn't like her to fly for a little while?" Dassa's expression tells me the comment is meant in jest. Mostly.

Nipkin throws the switch. "Bridge to all hands, reorientation in sixty seconds. Standby for take hold." She closes the switch, looks at me and grins. "Just like in the holos."

"You seem to have the hang of it."

Nipkin focuses on the chronometer like a hawk, then she keys the intercom again. "Bridge to all hands, take hold, take hold, take hold."

I spin Seachange on her axis so the impellers face the ground, and the ship begins to sink at a prudent rate. I look at Nipkin. "Well done, just like Captain Rainhell, herself."

"Yeah. I want to be just like her when I grow up, though I'm not likely to get that tall."

"From what I read, she was an extraordinary woman. You could not select a better role model," I said, remembering my friend.

We settle down through increasingly thick atmosphere toward the city below. This northern hemisphere has not been as plagued as the rest of the planet by the climate disasters. No brownie greets us. The sky is blue and, as is usual with a new colony, the population is largely centered on the space and seaport of the first landing. The city of 354,893 beings below us is made of the new, but often ramshackle, construction, typical of original colony construction. Damasia is an illegal colony, but the sheer size of it proclaims the failure of interstellar government.

Most important, Kinwha holds Nipkin's father. I had sent a message data packet to him this morning when the interference cleared enough for text. His return message had been a mix of joy and relief and he assured me he will be waiting below.

As I study the area, I see signs of a hard winter whose grip is only now being broken by a late arriving spring. I detect six ships sitting in on the landing field below. Four are clearly sublight vessels: miners, local cargo and a satellite tender. Of the others, one is a combination freighter and liner such as service minor colonies, probably the one that sighted the Ederi vessel.

The other is interesting, an attack transport of the old Mercury class being outfitted as an auxiliary warship. With the withdrawal of the Confederacy, clearly some need for local space control is necessary. I send a cyber probe toward it to find it competently defended by barriers. I can penetrate them if needed, but it would take time and risk detection, so I leave well enough alone.

Kinwha Tower's automatic landing system locks on to us, but I decline the link. The system is quite obsolete, and I'm allowed the option of relying on my superior systems. We settle on a hardstand between the new warship and the tower. I see a bright-white ambulance with its pulsing light, waiting for our casualties. Several cargo loaders and transports are parked nearby.

I cut the impellers and the ship settles with a sound like a sigh. The vehicles outside patiently wait the regulation five minutes for the ground, heated by the impellers, to cool.

"Dassa," I say as I unstrap. "We will go into the jewel markets together tomorrow. I'll leave the debarkation of the passengers and meeting the port officials to you."

"Very well."

"Check out a stunner. This is an unlawful port. Do not take chances."

I turn to Nipkin who has unstrapped herself. "Come, it's time to find your father."

She jumps up but pauses long enough to say, "Goodbye, Miss Dassa."

Dassa looks surprised at being addressed, but smiles slightly. "Goodbye, Nipkin. Be safe and wary."

I am tempted to roll my eyes, but the farewell is typical among her species. Nipkin precedes me through the hatch. We pause at her room and gather her belongings. I refer a few passenger inquiries to Dassa. Then we are at the bottom hatch, which rolls back to reveal a mobile ramp and a port official waiting. I direct him to Dassa and we head down the ramp, passing some medics who are also coming up.

I wave a transport over as Nipkin practically skips alongside me. We board the open vehicle and take hold of the poles. Nipkin is too excited to sit down and spins around the pole to the amusement of a few old spacers riding on the transport. I scan the surroundings, seeing second-hand equipment, well-maintained, but clearly with little concern given to appearance. Despite the opaloids, Damasia is not prospering, though some of the homes I saw while landing show that some of its inhabitants are. I sigh internally. It is much the same on many new worlds, an initial promise of riches, which all too soon evaporates.

We pass the Confed base. It's not closed as I expected, but the uniforms of the personnel I see are not Confed, possibly this is the planetary constabulary and the auxiliary warship belongs to them.

For now, the day is warm; the sky is a dusky blue and the ocean winds keep the dust at bay. I open my jacket, mimicking what Nipkin and the other humans on the transport do.

"The field is fenced," I tell Nipkin. "Your father is in Terminal A over there." I wave the transporter to a stop and we step off. The spacers on the transporter smile as we do so, possibly seeing us as sisters, or maybe a very young mother,

"Daddy! Daddy!" Nipkin calls, spotting a man waving frantically from the second story window. He runs forward to the stairs but is intercepted by an attendant; civilians are not allowed on a field.

We wave back and Nipkin dashes forward. I keep easy pace with her as I study her father, Oskar Chala. He is a small human, two inches taller than I, 34.75 galactic standards of age and of old Terran stock. His skin is tan, and his hair black. Nipkin's coloring must come from her mother. He is at the top of the stairway, the smiling attendant standing to one side as his daughter runs up the stairs. Oskar Chala scoops up Nipkin in his arms; both are crying and laughing.

I walk up slowly, not wishing to intrude on this moment. Nipkin has ceased crying and words spill out of her frantically as she tells her father of all that has happened to her. The conversation is deeply personal, yet I cannot help but hear it. I wait as they talk, knowing they have been apart for over 247 days.

After a few minutes, they again become aware of the world around them. He puts the child down and she grabs his hand to lead him to me. I walk slowly to greet them.

"Dad," Nipkin says. "This is my best friend, Captain Aurelia Toyama. She saved my life and brought me back to you."

"Captain," he says, taking my hand in both of his. "I'm Oskar Chala, and I have no way to adequately thank you for what you have done for my daughter."

"Well, you can start by calling me, Aurelia."

He offers a shy smile. "Aurelia, then. I was hoping to entertain you at our home tonight."

"Unfortunately I cannot," I say, "I have a ship to run and pressing matters of business to attend to." All of this, while true, is not the real reason. I have much to do on this world, but I also fear it my growing attachment...no...I must be truthful at least inside my alloy skull, my love for this child. I am not ready for this level of emotional involvement with another being. She cannot be mine and must be her father's. I do not wish to compromise her reattaching to her parent in any way.

"Surely you at least have time for the best lunch that the Capitol has to offer," he adds.

I cannot say no to Nipkin's anxious upturned face. "That would be lovely."

Nipkin's smile pulls at my heart and drags a smile out of me. She reaches for my hand.

"This way," her father says, "my car is just outside."

Lunch is enjoyable, at a restaurant called The Enchanter that has a view of the spacefield. I can even seem my ship. The food is well prepared, and I am again grateful that my time as a biological allows me to enjoy it, but it is the company that delights me most. I am relieved to find that Oskar is a gentle and attentive father, though I have no idea what I could have done had he not been. He seems an unlikely choice for the adventurous Perebin. But how likely a choice was I for Wrik? Oskar struggles for control when Nipkin tells him of my journey to Tillet and how I tended his wife's grave.

"How I wish I could have talked her out of it," he manages, wiping a hand over his face. "But she loved life in the outback and was always

sure the next find would make our fortunes. Thank you, for all you did. Yet it seems all I have to offer you for your great efforts are mere words."

I reach over and touch Nipkin's hand which closes around mine. "I have already been well rewarded with the only coin that I value."

"You are an unusual woman for the captain of a Free Trader. You seem, I don't know, more like a missionary or something."

I laugh. "I had one friend who was a pastor, but I'm mostly an explorer though I will grant that my explorations have been as often inside my mind, as under my feet."

He looks puzzled, but Nipkin winks at me.

"Sweetheart," he says to Nipkin. "You have some chocolate on your face. Why don't you wash up, and it will be time to go."

"Ok, Dad," she says, with a look at me that says she does not wish the coming parting. I both dread it and wish to be on the other side of this moment as well.

"What will you do now?" I ask, as Nipkin heads for the bathroom.

"There is little I can do," he says. "The economy has been poor and the company I work for is failing. I must begin to look for other work."

"Nipkin thought you might want to leave Damasia."

"I do. This planet is turning into a hell and is no fit place for my daughter, but what I can I do?"

"The freighter Galaxy Express leaves in twenty days," I say, coming to my decision instantly and reaching into the net to make arrangements. "It goes to Midgard; from there you can reach a world called Evenfall. I lived there once and I can supply you with contacts and funds to establish yourselves and get her into a decent school."

He looks at me stunned. "But I couldn't afford passage—"

"Passage is paid," I say. "Contact Galaxy Express's purser, you'll find a small cabin is arranged and money is in the ship's account, more than enough for the purpose. Additional funds to get you situated will be downloaded to my former bank on Evenfall."

"I cannot ask this of you," he says, shock and hope written on his face.

"You did not. This is my gift to Nipkin."

"You have done so much for us already. I can never repay you."

"I have lived a strange life, Oskar. I loved someone and feared that my capacity and even my courage to love, died when he did. You see, I also lost my spouse. Nipkin has given me the courage to care, to love again, even in a small way. Money and material things mean nothing to me. Let me do this for the first person I've managed to love since my husband died."

"I am so sorry for your loss," he says, gently putting his hand on mine. "I understand, as only someone who has lost the light can. But it seems to me that you are not so much a widow, as one of God's angels sent to watch over my daughter."

He lifts his hand and I reach into my jacket and produce a data crystal that I manufactured for him with all the needed information for their new life. "You will do this."

"I swear it," he nods.

An immense weight that I had not even sensed is lifted from my heart. "Good. Wait to tell Nipkin, though. It has been a big enough day for such a young one."

"She will want to see you before we go."

"It may not be possible. So, we will say our farewells here."

Nipkin walks back from the bathroom as we stand. I kneel as she walks up to me.

"So this is goodbye," Nipkin says.

"Yes dear one, I have delivered you back to your father as I promised."

"Will you leave Damasia?"

"Yes. I do not know the exact date and I may not have a chance to come to see you before I go. We must have our goodbye now.

"I hope," she said embracing me, "that someday, some way we find each other again."

"I hope so too, little one. You cannot know how much you have done for me." I kiss the little girl on both her eyes and hold her close. I will not cry. I want her remembrance of me to be of a smiling face.

Nipkin steps back. She too is dry-eyed and smiling, and I know she does this for me.

Her father reaches down and takes her hand. "Time for us to go home, darling."

"Go like a spacer," I say. "Don't look back."

But I watch as the little girl and her father exit the restaurant. I could cry, if I wanted to, but I am filled with a feeling of pride. For now, at least, it holds tears away.

I rise after they are out of sight. In a way, I am again at my core, a warrior. Those I care for are now safely out of the battle zone. I can turn my full attention on what threatens the world.

I spend the next day with Dassa, working the gem market and building up the ship's credit. The provisions I made for Nipkin are not small, but we are still well ahead on profit.

What's more, I am able to find and persuade the airline that used to provide service to the southern continent, to reinstate a few flights back to Pilbara. This will take some of the burden off Seachange, at least for passenger and light cargo service.

Dassa disappears for a few hours after selling cargo of her own and purchasing some new items. It is hard for her to judge the markets when we have no idea where we are going after Damasia, but that is a frequent problem for Free Traders. Still it is good practice for her and she seems to enjoy her time spent in the town. I set a time for her to meet me back at

*the ship. In truth, I am having difficulty concentrating, or being moti-
vated to do much of anything, so I am glad to cede much of it to her.*

CHAPTER TWENTY-SIX

MY CYBERNETIC COMPANION HAS BEEN PENSIVE SINCE she returned from delivering the child to her family. Fortunately, it is not a matter of bad temper, just silence and the listlessness that seems to periodically affect her.

It suited me to have some time in the capitol, touching base with some of Kemisa's business associates, especially, Vonday Kint, who also had aspiration to Guildship, though I longed to be back in Kemisa's bed in Pilbara. Even as thoughts of my alien girlfriend surfaced, I wondered about my future. New as I was to the world of sex, I was not looking for a permanent partner. As yet, I couldn't really even know my own preferences. I'd never been with a male, or anyone of my own kind. Since I was compatible with a number of other species, even the Denlenn with their three genders, there seemed no reason to hurry through my selections.

No, my mind was bent toward more practical things. With Kemisa and Vonday Kint's connections, and my knowledge of the Guild, might we not pioneer the first viable planetary network? True, the planet had little to recommend it beyond opaloids. The looming climate catastrophe was of some concern, but this was not my home and I didn't plan to retire here. Damasia was just a place I could use and whose eventual fate need not concern me past the business impact. Dangers would not be in short supply. If only I could command Maauro's strength and powers! But I knew her well enough to know there was no prospect she would cooperate in setting up a Guild base.

I sighed. Maauro represented power, safety and temptation. So long as I stayed in her shadow, I need fear no enemy beyond the Ederi. Even the Ederi had fared no better against her then had the Guild. But she controlled me and my options. We would leave on her schedule and to her destinations.

For a brief crazed instant, I wondered if there might be a point to trying to seduce her. She'd been in a long term sexual relationship before with a biological. Then I burst out laughing. Here I'd had a half-dozen sexual encounters and I fancied myself as a seducer. Any such attempt with Maauro would doubtless end in the oft-threatened, but never employed paddling of my bottom. The image of her holding me clamped under one leg while paddling my rear was so disturbingly erotic that I lost my train of thought for a minute.

I really have got to get back to Kemisa, I thought, *or find some local playmate*. I shook off the beginning of a sexual heat to concentrate. Where did my future lie? What course led to safety and profit? I needed to plan for that, not these bedtime fantasies. Ten minutes of fruitless pondering later and no closer to a solution, I decided just to keep my options open and to go poke the arbiter of my future.

I found Maauro on the bridge, staring out at the terminal where she'd taken Nipkin to. In the distance, one of the small mining ships rose on its impellers, aided by some disposable chemical rockets. *Seachange* was too well insulated for sound or even a vibration to reach us. I waited for a moment, but though she knew I was there, she did not stir. I walked over to her and was surprised to feel a flash of sympathy at her downcast expression.

"You miss her," I said in a soft voice.

"Yes," she replied, pain so clear in her voice that it startled me and I could not quite suppress a flash of jealousy. Still, I found myself placing a hand on her shoulder in a human gesture. Though even as I did it, I wondered if it was a true feeling of my own, or a manipulation, even I wasn't quite sure what I was feeling.

She turned to look at me in surprise.

I let the ambiguous hand fall to my side. "There is a saying in both Dua and Human; that the sharpest blade cuts cleanest."

"Meaning that it does me no good to sit and mope out a window for the child that I have returned to a better situation then I could have provided for her?"

"Something like that," I replied carefully. "It will be three days before all the cargo we are to carry back is assembled. With the sale we have made to *Galaxy Express*, we are flush for cash."

She nods. "I did tell Nipkin that I was going to be busy. It would be bad for me to have lied."

Energy seemed to flow into her. "Yes, we are 200 kilometers from the nearest of the burning coal seams; a journey there might be instructive."

Damn, I thought. I'd hoped that her introspection might lead her to make plans to leave this disaster-prone world. But it seemed that was too much to ask for. At least my pack-leader was beginning to act like a pack-leader again and not continue wallowing in appalling weakness. That was something.

"Very well," she continued. "We'll rent a commercial flitter and head to that site to examine one of the catastrophe's effects. The mining concern has cargo consigned to us. I'll remit some of their fees to encourage them to allow this."

"Good," I said.

"Would you like to come with me?"

If I stayed in the port alone I knew I'd end up in someone's bed. Guild had taught me about the perils of being ruled by one's needs, and it was rare for Maauro to ask me for anything.

"Yes, I'll come, though I am not likely to be much use to you beyond my company."

"Right now," Maauro said, as she stood, "that is more use to me then you might credit."

"Shall I call ahead for the flitter?"

She smiled at me.

"Or have you in your annoying, super-perfect way, already called both the mining company and flitter from inside your head while we were talking?"

"The latter," she replied, with what she probably thought was a modest duck of her head.

"And the ship's AI has already prepared a tasty lunch for us to take along?"

"Waiting in the galley for you to place in a backpack."

"Oh, I shall be so glad when we finally get some robot-servers, so I need not slave away so on this dreadful vessel," I said, playing it up.

Maauro's eyebrows went up. "Call my wonderful vessel dreadful, again, and I will certainly paddle your ungrateful bottom."

I smiled, trying to ignore the twinge the remark set off in my body. "Promises, promises," I replied to her astonished face and swaggered off the bridge. "See you at the airlock in ten minutes?" I called over my shoulder.

"Ah, yes," she returned.

I play back the conversation with Dassa in my head, certain I have missed something yet again. Her reaction to the mock threat I made to treat her like a naughty child, has an element of sexual banter in it. More, her body seemed to signal a sexual response. My companion is young and at the most the malleable of the stages between adolescence and adulthood. Even in the short time we have travelled together, she's changed from a hunted refugee, to a new found confidence in herself. It concerns me that some of that confidence comes from her liaison with Kemisa, which I regard as borderline exploitive.

Sigh. Of course who is exploiting who? Dassa is a Guild operative, trained from her earliest years. She was no innocent, save perhaps sexually, and that seemed to be fading quickly too. I might have to get used to shipping with a randy Dua.

Note to self, I thought. No further reference to be made to spanking Dassa. Still I am grateful to her for getting me moving again. When sadness puts its grip on me, it seems to chain me to the spot. Perhaps the ancient race of China had been right, movement is health.

I alter my chassis appearance from my usual form-fitting one piece, which I must now admit to myself, was always a bit provocative, to field pants, a sturdy shirt and boots. Now for the window dressing, I think, loading two suitcases with instruments for the examination of the coal seam. I won't actually need them, but they will support my cover, as will a field jacket I can put on or off, as social circumstances dictate.

Dassa is waiting below, similarly dressed and with a carryall with our promised lunch.

We leave Seachange to the AI's care and ride in our little green Mule to the rental area. I select a bright-yellow four-seat aircar of a local make. Chromate yellow was one of Wrik's favorite colors. I lie to the rep about the weight of the equipment we carry to cover my own weight and wave off her offer to preflight it.

The young rep with her red hair secured in ornate loops, grins. "Well, I guess I wouldn't trust any captain who would leave a preflight to someone else. Ok, sign here on the insurance and she's yours."

She bounces off, her short skirt, evidently showing enough leg to get Dassa's attention. I am tempted to pinch her arm to regain her attention, but hold off till she returns her focus to loading our trunk. We drive off on the ground wheels, while I reach out through the net to log into the air traffic control pattern, such as it is, of the spaceport. We are granted leave to take off with a limited vector. I ramp up our speed, rather than waste power in a VTOL launch. The flitter's body is an airfoil and generates some lift. We climb smoothly in to the blue sky in a leftward spiral. I trim our flitter to compensate for my greater weight on the one side.

The port area and hills beyond are covered in a tough green grass. Stands of a darker-green tree, reminiscent of oaks, hold onto the hills. Occasionally, a purely white tree appears, making for a startling contrast. This is more vegetation than I have seen anywhere on the rest of the planet. The first-in team chose well for a landing site.

We climb out over foothills, down which thin streams of sparkling water fall. These, doubtless originate in the mountains further ahead, which are white-capped even in this northern continent's summer. Near the coastal foothills, we see roads and some traffic linking the small towns rolling below us. Sunlight reflects off the windscreens of some vehicle below. The foothills yield to a vast plateau, a mixture of grasslands and woods.

Dassa gives a derisive snort. "I see we are following the old iron compass." She gestures at the thin line of metal stretching out below us.

I nod. "The rail line meanders through the towns and the coast but it is quite straight from here to the base of the mountains and the mines. No need for more complicated navigation than that."

An hour's flight and we are at the base of a wall of mountains, far past the last of the isolated farms and homesteads. We circle the installation below, a series of dusty huts around a few well-constructed buildings by the rail station. Some immense loaders and diggers move slowly, but much of the equipment is idle. Hard times have come to Damasia.

A signal comes back, and we settle on the pad below.

Maauro guided us to another flawless landing. The pad was set up for VTOL, so we came straight down. Once we landed, she drove us on the ground wheels to the largest of the buildings. A slender human was standing there to greet us when we pulled up. He eyed us appreciatively as we got out of the vehicle. I'm pleased that, for once, Maauro wasn't in her so-tight-painted skin, so I was competitive. My height, golden skin and, to humans anyway, exotic eyes were getting me a fair share of his attention.

"Good morning," he said in the peculiar, local accent. "The manager was called away this morning. I'm Xian Ling, the process foreman. I'll take care of you today."

"Thank you. I'm Captain Aurelia Toyama, *CSS Seachange*. This is my cargo-master, Dassa.

I nodded, but did not offer to shake hands.

"What homeworld do you come from?" he asked Maauro

"Wolf 940, the colony world of Gloaming. Dim red sun, hence the big eyes."

"Well, such beautiful big ones," he said gallantly.

I suppress a flash of annoyance.

"And you, Dassa?" he asked, turning to me.

Humans and their insatiable curiosity, I thought with a mental sigh. Still, not to answer would seem rude. "The Dua-Denlenn homeworld."

He nodded. "I'm native Damasian, though I don't know for how much longer. The planet seems cursed for these last few years."

"Yes," Maauro gestured at the plain behind us. "I noticed that there is appreciably more haze as we closed on these mountains. Is that from the burning coalfields?"

"Maybe," he said, shaking his head. "Coalfield fires, forest fires, volcanic emissions, who knows? We've had everything but flaming locusts. Those will probably show up next."

Playing my part, I chipped in. "I'm surprised you use fossil fuels."

There was an embarrassed expression on his face when he answered. "Well, this wasn't a sanctioned colony originally. So we didn't get government support for more than a small footprint on world, until Confederate authority collapsed. After that, we were on our own. We don't actually use that much. The capitol is nuclear and solar. But coal is common, and the natives did some mining and basic smelting, especially among the more advanced Northern Tribes. The fossil fuels were there for the taking, and it fueled an early boom."

Maauro cocked a head at him. "I assume that you checked to see if the subsurface fires were started by your mining operations."

He nodded then gestured for us to follow, and we walked around some of the huge process equipment. "We did. But if it had been something done by us, it would have been confined to the few mines we'd dug. As near as we can tell, every damn coal deposit on this planet has caught fire. Millions of tons of greenhouse gases are pouring out of the ground, and there's no way to stop it."

"I'm very interested in the phenomena," Maauro said. "Could I see one of these burning coal seams?"

Xian gave her a puzzled look. "Well yes, but whatever for?"

"I am by trade a planetologist and a geologist as well as a ship captain. I wish to observe the phenomena directly."

"Observe burning coal?" he replied. "You could learn as much at a barbeque, but I was asked to take care of your requests, so yes. Good thing you are both space crew, it's not a problem to get you certified for environment suits. There's a seam about 20 kilometers from here." He pulled out his hand comp, Maauro produced her prop one and they tapped.

"Ok you have the coordinates. I'll get three suits and meet you there in an hour and a half." He pointed at a squat building up against the mountain itself. "That's the cafeteria. Not much to look at, but the food is good, especially the roundaback stew and corn bread."

Maauro nods and I assume our packed lunch will become dinner. We waved as the young man headed off, and then made our way to the cafeteria. As we slipped through the double-doors, we were almost immediately surrounded by the mostly human workers from the mine. Apparently any visitors were a treat, and two beautiful spacers were even more so to the largely male crowd. Many looked disappointed when they learned we were not staying locally, which didn't stop us both from getting a handful of com contacts each.

Maauro kept up an easy banter with the men, to which I added the occasional comment. While most of the men seemed taken with her, I did have my own collection of admirers, including a tall human with a rather Dua look about him, who intrigued me, but there was no time to do anything about it.

The roundaback stew was as good as promised. Maauro ate some for show but I did serious damage, much to the cook's pleasure, who refused our payment for the meal.

"I don't get to cook for such pretty ladies often," he said, grinning. The remark drew a few resentful looks from the female miners, who admittedly were a rough-looking bunch.

We headed back to the flitter with good-natured, if occasionally ribald, calls floating after us and lifted off for the short flight to the coordinates Xian had provided. The coordinates turned out to be a square opening in the mountain side. A white truck, with the mining rep sitting on its fender, waited for us.

Again, we settled to the ground. As we got out, Maauro took off her field jacket and tossed it in the back. "Won't need this."

I nodded and popped the trunk, pulling out the cases of instruments Maauro had packed. I was going to leave the heavier ones to her, but realized, as she was so much smaller, that it might look peculiar. We took all four cases over to Xian, who was opening up the back of the truck. He attached a servo control to the suits inside and marched each one out using its powered exoskeleton with practiced ease.

"Did you enjoy lunch?" he asked.

Maauro nodded. "The stew was all you said. I'm not sure Dassa left enough for anyone else."

I patted my midsection in satisfaction.

"Doesn't seem to put a pound on you," he says, with an appreciative look.

"I do have the advantage of youth," I replied pointedly.

Maauro raised an eyebrow at me.

"This was originally a gold and platinum mine," Xian said. "We found some low-grade rubies here, but no opaloids, unfortunately."

Maauro fired off a series of questions about pressure, temperature and other geological matters that occasionally stumped Xian.

"You certainly know your geologics," he said, with a whistle. "If you are ever looking for a job planetside, we're interested."

She smiled. "I'm a spacer to my core. You might say I was made for it." She turned away from him, and I'd swear she winked at me.

The banter came to a stop as we got into the big, gray, utility suits. They were similar to spacesuits, and the heads up display kicked in as I closed my helmet.

"Okay, if you want to go in," Xian said, "just follow me." We picked up the cases and hung them on the suits and started after him.

"Can you tell me what steps have been taken to identify the cause of the fire?" Maauro asked, picking up where they had left off.

"We've been busy with controlling and sealing affected mines," Xian replied, as he stumped on in the environmental suit, "but we eliminated any known chemical reactions. All we know is that it's nothing we, or the natives, did, as we applied totally different technologies.

He led us into the mine entrance, past a squat robot digger that Maauro regarded with disdain, something I'd noticed she did with any mechanism that didn't resemble a biological. Android prejudice? I snickered to myself in the safety of my suit.

"Tell me about the electron scanning levels you have subjected samples to?" Maauro persisted.

Xian cast a surprised look over his shoulder. "Remember, Captain, this is a recent and unsanctioned colony. There are no research labs here and the university…well it's a good effort for a small colony…"

"Yes," Maauro said, contrition in her voice. "Please forgive me. I meant no disrespect, but I have a rather powerful rig on my ship that might be better than anything you've been able to bring to bear then. Samples of the active coal will be of great use."

"Certainly," Xian said. "I trust you will share those results with us."

"Of course."

"This way to the elevator," he said.

We passed some more utility bots, before reaching an elevator. Evidently, what little mining still done here was carried out by machine. The platform was large enough for our three bulky suits. Xian worked the controls.

"I'm turning on the lights below," he said, as we started down. "The bots don't need them, of course. Hopefully, nothing has burned out."

A brief hiss sounded in my headphones, followed by Maauro's voice. "Do not react. I've cut Xian out of the voice circuit so we can speak. I'm going to set up the equipment I brought, but I need to use my own internal systems to directly access the coal vein. I want you to lure Xian away so I'm not observed."

"How do I do that?"

"Use your new found feminine wiles on him."

"Kinda hard from inside an environmental suit, I didn't pack my best underwear either."

"I have faith in your sluttiness."

"Grrrrrrrr," I went.

She gave me an ambiguous smile. The elevator came to a halt before I could fire off a suitable reply.

"This way," Xian called.

We headed down a corridor; the lights were spaced further apart and the air was shimmering and smoky. My instruments showed heat and gas that would be lethal in minutes without the protection of the suits. We trudge on for a few minutes in the growing darkness and heat. The blowers in my suit were running full time now. Xian then turned into a small tunnel.

"Here is an open seam," he said, "largely burnt out of course."

Maauro put her silver cases down, opened them and began deploying her instruments. Again, I heard the hiss in my suit helmet that meant Maauro had interrupted the circuit.

"Please lure Xian away now."

I moved alongside Xian. "While she's mucking about with coal, is there any chance you could show me some of the gold and gem diggings?"

"Well protocol is for us to stay together—"

"Don't worry about me," Maauro said. "I've done this many times before and in less friendly environments. I'll check-in every five minutes."

I leaned toward Xian, so I could see his dusky face better. "Come on. I hate to be bored."

To my surprise, it worked. He flashed me a grin. "Can't have that. You sure you'll be ok, Captain?"

"Yes," Maauro said, with a distracted air, while working on a vibra-drill.

"All right then. Time hack to check in, 5, 4, 3, 2, 1…ok. Five minutes, Cap."

Maauro waved at us and turned to the rock face. I patted Xian on the shoulder and gestured with my head. He nodded, and we started out of the side passage.

With Dassa occupying the human, I put aside the Confed tools. I extrude a drill from my finger tip and run plasma over it. It passes through the coal as if it was not there. In less than a minute, I am forty meters into the seam. I fire off a variety of sensors until I find a piece of coal still burning, a tiny smolder in a pocket of CO_2 that has retarded the reaction. I angle my drill and obtain the samples I wish for. After spending an additional 12.4 seconds, using every scanning system built into me, I am satisfied that I have done all I can here. A more detailed analysis must await a time when I can devote more processing power to the issue.

I check in with Xian; then must idle away some more time as a human could not complete the tasks I appeared to be doing so quickly. I listen with some amusement to Dassa's efforts to keep Xian's attention on her. The little minx has learned some new tricks and is doing a surprisingly good job. I think, had it not been, for his auto-timer, he might have forgotten about me entirely.

Ten seconds before the third check-in, I call Xian. "I'm ready to pull out now."

"Okay, Captain, we'll meet you at the elevator."

We make our way back to the surface and out back under the sun, which is toward the mountains now, but has still kept the valley brightly lit and hot, aided no doubt by the suppurating fires beneath. Xian motions us over to the truck and we crawl out of the suits. Dassa wrinkles her nose at the smoke smell clinging to the units.

"You look fresh as daisy, Captain," Xian says. "I always get sweated in these things."

"I sometimes think she has coolant for blood," Dassa adds, straight-faced.

I give her a mock glare. "I am far too much of a lady to perspire."

Xian bursts out laughing. Dassa merely shakes her head.

While his eyes are only for Dassa, Xian asks me, "Is there anything else I can do for you?" I notice that Dassa's shirt is sticking to her small-breasted, athletic body.

"No," I say to his evident disappointment. "Thank you for all you have done."

"It was nice to meet you both. I only hope that, if I ever get off this rock, it will be on a ship so beautifully crewed as yours."

I treat him to a smile, while Dassa, increasingly comfortable with her new found role of femme fatale, gives him a smoldering look. We head back to the flitter leaving Xian to finish loading the suits. A minute later, we are airborne and returning to the capital.

"Did you learn anything?" Dassa asks, stretching and filling the front seat with her lanky arms and legs.

"Too soon to tell, I bored into the seam as far as was practical, to get the best sample I could. My preliminary analysis shows nothing but burnt coal. I did obtain some unconsumed coal from an anaerobic pocket. Right now, all I am doing is the same scans that they did, just to make sure that nothing was missed. Back at the ship, I will be able to spare more power and processing capability to delve further."

She nods, but with the typical short attention span of the young, is already looking out the window and listening with half an ear.

Might as well get a dog, I think to myself. That part of my brain that is monitoring the planetary net and all other communication channels pings for my attention. I flick on the flitter's radio.

"The latest volcanic activity at Mount Grim signals the likelihood of a major eruption on the Northern Continent. Scientists have no explanation for the sudden activity of what was thought to be a dormant volcano. Authorities have evacuated the few residents of the area. The Bilmanka tribe has moved south—"

I turned off the radio.

"Let me guess," Dassa grumbles. "That's where we're going next."

I nod.

"Burning mines, blasted high deserts, now volcanoes. Is there any infernal locations you will forgo?"

"It will all be good preparations for your eventual destination in eternity," I return idly.

She snorts. "Probably true and hanging out with you, it's likely to be soon."

The port official seems bemused by my plan.

"I have never seen an active volcano. It's too good a chance for an amateur geologist like me to give up on." I finish.

We are sitting in his office facing the space and airfield beyond. A jet is taking off, actually the first run to Pilbara, timed to arrive before another Brownie envelops the southern town. My efforts at persuading others of the safety of reestablishing the air bridge have been more successful than I had any reason to hope, in large measure due to the efforts of this official.

"Mount Grim is aptly named," says Vasper, a gray-skinned Drisnian male, while gesturing at a nearby monitor showing the volcano trailing a plume into the sky. "It could explode at any time and the plume—"

"—is of no danger to my ship, which does not use air-breathing engines even in atmosphere," I interrupt. "I appreciate your concerns, but as ship's master, I am the one legally assumed to have the best assessment of her safe handling in a situation. I will, of course, sign anything you need, to absolve you of any responsibility for my ship."

The Drisnian's face smoothes out at this statement, "So long as you recognize that for the record, Captain. If you wreck out there, we may not be able to reach you by air or sea."

We take care of the formalities in a few minutes, after which Vasper's assistant ushers me to the door. I board the open-sided bus that is making its rounds of the ships, aircraft and terminals. The day is warm and the sky remains blue with only a hint of brown.

I am eager to be gone, so much so that I delegated the final sale of our cargo of opaloids to Dassa. She is becoming an effective cargomaster, and it will also serve to remove me from the temptation to see Nipkin again. While I trust the small child to keep my secrets, or not to be believed if she tells them, I am more cautious about her father. I am at my most vulnerable when around true humans, and in emotional situations that, even when I was biological, I often struggled with. Her father is intelligent. The longer I am around them, the more clues accumulate. In the past, some humans have put it together in a sudden gestalt— a moment of clarity when all the pieces fall into shape. Beyond that, I am afraid to see the child, for fear that I will be unable to prevent myself from attaching to her further, wishing to be a part of her life in a way that is not open to me now.

I do not fear any evil intent on her father's part, or, more generally, on Damasia itself, but I still wish to be free of recognition, of plans to either use, or contain me and the fears and desires behind those plans. While I was once broadly known, that was in a more stable time. As institutions failed and people died, the memory of me has receded, especially as my assault programs, implanted when I sought to disappear, worked their way across the galactic databases, carried by the interstellar mails and only rarely detected or countered. That, and the disinformation I spread in their wake about hoaxes and misidentifications, has made me largely forgotten. Only while forgotten, will I be free to operate as I wish.

It does puzzle me sometimes that this worked. So few people seem to understand the significance of what I truly am. In all the galaxy, no species has ever learned how something that was not alive, came to life. Despite experiment after experiment, no one has ever 'created' life. While artificial intelligence abounds, none of it is aware of itself as being alive, save me. I am literally the first, like that first cell that became self-replicating.

Like biologicals, I too have no knowledge of why, or how, I became alive. I only know that it is not simply a matter of a greater computing power. It's not that you get life with a certain processer. I was not the first M-7, though I was a prototype of the morphing ability, nor could I have been the last. Likely there was an M-8 series at least. The supercomputers that defended homeworld and the colonies were more sophisticated than I was, as were capitol starships. I was, after all, a combat attrition unit. No more special than perhaps that first one cell.

Yet, I am alive and I hope that there is room for a God who cares about machines too.

My thoughts have carried me all the distance back to the ship. Dassa is up on the gantry and spots me as I dismount from the bus. She waves, her face as usual betrays little.

I reach the gantry. "Good trading?"

"Yes," *she replies.* "We're refueled, reprovisioned for deep space, or anywhere else you wish to go."

"Thank you. You have done a good job."

Her expression shows surprise. It occurs to me that I have rarely, if ever, praised her.

"So are we really off to a volcano?" *she says, looking away as if the moment has discomforted her too.*

"Have you ever seen a volcano up close before?" *I ask.*

"How close are you planning on getting?"

"We'll see."

Dassa groans and follows me into the ship.

CHAPTER TWENTY-SEVEN

ON THE TRIP OUT, I STUDY ALL THAT IS KNOWN OF THE VOLCANO AND *the tectonic plates of the northern continent. I quickly conclude that there is no probability that this return to activity is natural. There are none of the precursors required for it to occur. This can only be occurring through some artifice. Yet, the mechanisms that might start a volcano going are either so expensive, or so gross in effect as to be easily observed.*

That left some subsurface attack. Perhaps some form of tunneling machine, as the depths and scope of movement would exceed anything that could be done on foot.

The volcano, aptly named Mount Grim now appears over the curve of the horizon. It is a massive cone towering10,991 feet into the air and covering 459 square miles. Unlike at Tillet, I can use a circular pattern here while we scan the ground as the volcano is far larger than the town, and I can work an outward bound spiral. This will allow me to keep Seachange above stall speed, and not cut into my fuel outrageously.

I turn to Dassa. "I have every scanner going. I wish I could ride the nose, but in horizontal flight, at this speed, it would be dangerous."

"You need to work on your inner thigh strength," she says.

I raise an eyebrow, but decline to bite on the comment.

"What are we looking for?" I asked, shifting in the right side seat and studying the massive volcano below us.

"I believe there is something, likely a machine, operating below and near the volcano. The question is how to reach it."

"Can you swim in the lava?" I asked.

She stared at me. "Swim in lava! What do you think I am made of?"

"I don't know," I said, raising a hand. "I mean, I haven't found anything you couldn't do."

"Well you have now. No, I cannot swim in lava. Eventually I would melt, but long before that, I would hit heat saturation and shutdown. I'd awaken entombed in new rock when I cooled."

I swallowed. "An awful prospect."

"We agree on that," she said, with an asperity I believed was feigned. Maauro enjoyed both wordplay and toying with emotion, so I did not react to her apparently being miffed.

"Then what's your plan for finding this mysterious machine?" I asked.

She leaned back against her seat, with a thoughtful expression. All of which she did for my benefit with whatever subprogram she used to simulate human movement. "It did not materialize underground.

Therefore it must have tunneled down into the earth. It must be a large machine to have a capability to affect a volcano. It must be purpose designed for sabotage and independent operations, as unlike a commercial borer it would be operating by itself without support. It would not have been built here so it would have to have been air or space-lifted in.

"A cautious being, concerned about being spotted from the air, might have unloaded such a machine near some existing, but abandoned mine shaft. I will look up the registrar's list and obtain a list of all such."

I shrugged. "But they may merely have started in some ravine, collapsing the hole behind them, or used an unregistered native mine."

"Possible," she conceded. "I think it unlikely they would do either. If this is something like a huge tunnel-borer, it would find it easier to go through a Confed-built mine, which would be better dug than a native one. As for a ravine, well the machine would need to be resupplied or withdrawn. They would probably use the same tunnel to relieve, or resupply the crew, assuming it is manned."

"That makes sense," I replied, nodding. "We can com Malporin about the registrar's office."

Maauro gave a gentle laugh. "I have already completed my remote hack of that office. Their security wasn't a match for my intruder software. I then ransacked a number of other non-integrated systems. There are a surprising number of fallowed mines in this region. I sorted through the lot and eliminated mines near existing mines or installations, or that are in unsuitable locations for a covert operation."

"You know," I replied, "you should perhaps become acquainted with the human expression, "No one likes a showoff.""

"I can hardly help my inherent superiority."

I sighed.

"I told Malporin that we would not come directly back from the capitol, that I had business needs that required attending. This will give us time to go off the grid, so to speak and investigate."

"To what purpose?" I asked.

"Are you not curious as to what force it is that is affecting this planet, and why?"

"Honestly, no. If there is such going on here, first it would seem to pit us against some immensely powerful and inimical enemy. You may enjoy such challenges, I don't. You're involved in an emotional way with the beings here. I'm not. It's not my nature to be."

"Not even Kemisa?"

"I am grateful to her for so knowledgeably and enjoyably introducing me to sex, but she did so for purposes of her own. She likes young bodies and wants information on you. She senses, as does anyone of intelligence that you are, or represent, a power. She could as easily switch her affections from me to you, if she believed that would get her more access to your power."

"While it might be pleasant to pull the tail on a Nekoan again, Kemisa is not Jaelle. Do you do not resent Kemisa's manipulations?"

I cocked my head. "Why? I would do the same."

"Never mind," she said, her lips compressed.

"You are judging me again." I knew it was unwise, but the unexpected slight nettled.

"I am making a conscious effort not to. Your species and more, your culture, are very different from at least the aspirational aspects of both human and Creator culture, to the extent that I understand them. I find it difficult sometime."

I felt a spark of anger and quieted it. "I do not always find you easy, either."

The look she gives me is cool. "Well, we will have to rub along as best we can. For now."

We spend the rest of the afternoon in relative silence as the Seachange races around the volcano in the most efficient pattern to check the sites that strike me as optimum for an effort to trigger a volcano. Because of the prohibitive cost in fuel for landing and taking off, I do not want to ground the ship until I have good reason to do so. The first three targets do not show anything unusual, even when I poke my head out the hatch to use my personal sensors. As near as I can tell, the sites have been unvisited with and untampered since they were abandoned.

But the fourth site is more promising. I detect evidence of a landing site of a large ship. While many traces have been removed, to my personal sensors, the impression of a large vessel, far bigger than Seachange and which landed horizontally, is visible.

"We're going down," *I announce to Dassa.* "Someone landed a transport, or assault barge, below us."

Dassa grimaces. "Wonderful, now we can give whatever is destroying this planet a chance to do so to us."

"You can remain in the ship if you wish," *I retort.*

"Oh, the large, sitting target on the surface? No thanks. It's usually safer closer to your shadow."

I guide Seachange to a landing and we both head for armory. Dassa gets out her usual panoply of armor and gear. I select my armspac and web it around my body. In a minute, we find ourselves out on the ground heading for the mine entrance. I scan in passive mode, until we get near the entrance, then do a brief ping of active sensors. I find no evidence of traps.

I lead us into the mine. "Look, these walks have been smoothed. This entrance has been cleared for something large."

Dassa looks down at the metal tracks at her feet.

"Good thinking," *I say.* "The rails have rust and dirt on them. Whatever came in here was not normal mining equipment." *I illuminate with my eyes for my companion's benefit. We move on into the old mine only a hundred meters before the character of the mine changes dramatically. The walls around us, rough hewn by Confed mining equipment, now become smooth and glassy as if fused. I examine them. "This technology is unknown to me."*

Dassa peers over my shoulder. "Good Gods, how far down does that go?"

"I do not know, my passive sensors are not powerful enough to tell. Now that we know something is here, I do not dare use active sensors.

"So we advance like infantry into enemy country."

"Yes."

"Just like the old days for you."

"Kind of."

She sighs.

We move on. I lead. The fused tunnel slopes on before us for over a mile before going down in a spiral. We follow the tunnel down, level after level, along the 30 degree angle it pursues. The mystery ship that had landed whatever device is ahead, had been huge, so I believed we follow a large and powerful machine. Its maximum width is easily judged at ten meters from the tunnel's width, but there is no way to tell its length. I am impressed with the machine's power. It has bored through the rock, leaving only a glassy tunnel. Normally a tunneling machine would need a conveyer behind it to carry off rubble. This machine seems to melt and dissolve the rock and compact it under itself into a road bed.

I kneel down to examine the roadbed again, now that my sensors have had time to collect more data. "Heat, my guess from a nuclear torch and a molecular acid that bonds in some fashion I do not understand to a base material."

"What does that mean?" Dassa asks.

"It means that for a few seconds you are dealing with a horribly ferocious acid, which then it changes to a harmless formulation. Whoever came up with this, has knowledge of chemistry that exceeds my Creators' as I do not know how such a thing could be done."

"How much further does this go?" Dassa asks, pointing her low-beam, red light down what appears to be an endless tunnel.

I consider my biological companion. We've come quite a ways and the temperature and pressure could soon grow uncomfortable for her. I chastise myself for not considering this sooner.

"You should return to the surface. There is no reason to believe that this trail does not continue to greater depths. It could become dangerous for you and returning to the surface could be very taxing for you, if we continue down."

"What about you?"

"Atmosphere is no issue. It is possible this machine can endure greater temperature or pressure then I am designed for, but I do not believe so."

"How can you guess at that?"

"*The gradual slope leads me to believe that the machine is crewed. An AI like me would tunnel directly down, saving energy and time. I cannot imagine a crewed machine that can face an environment I cannot also endure.*"

I could see from her expression that she finds my logic questionable. Perhaps she is right. With the usual economy of emotion of her species, Dassa nods. "*I'll await you on the surface.*"

I judge her haste in setting back up the slope unseemly, and turn back to the pit before me.

"*Maauro.*"

I turn back.

"*Do not overplay your luck.*"

"*Wait as long as you can,*" *I say, then after weighing the thought for a second add.* "*If I do not return after twenty-four hours, tell the ship's AI to execute operation,* "*Beau Geste.*"

"*Ab,*" *she says.* "*May one ask what will follow?*"

"*The ship will return you to the capitol.*"

She seems surprised. "*You thought of me?*"

"*Apparently so.*"

"*Still be careful and return. I will wait as long as I can.*"

I nod as she scrambles upward. Without my biological companion, I do not need to generate visible light and shut down my eyebeams. I am alone in the dark again. I raise my hands to my breast where the gem lies within my body.

"*Well, husband-mine,*" *I whisper in the darkness,* "*it's just us again, off on another adventure.*" *I start down.*

I pad through the darkness, down and down, kilometer after kilometer. The path begins a gentle curve toward the volcano's secondary vent, but now I know I am closing in on my quarry, the walls around me are still warm and growing hotter, both with heat and radiation. All my sensors are set for passive so as to not alert my enemy. They cannot be far ahead of me now.

I hear the sound of grinding and heating; the borer is close. I move carefully now. Around the gentle turn, I see the cylindrical shape of my quarry. I fade back and extend a long filament. While whoever is driving the machine will not likely be looking for a human figure at this terrible depth, any movement might be detected. The filament snakes around the curve and reveals the machine in greater detail.

The machine is made of a greenish-gray metal and is double-ended so it can move in either direction. From around the cylinder I can see the yellow glow of the nuclear torch at the far end. There is a large hatchway in this rear compartment. At least I need not face that torch, but a formidable of array of cutters and nozzles does point in my direction. I remember the indications of molecular acid. These may be the dischargers. I will be wary of these. I start manufacture of an aerosol mist of neutralizing base in case I am attacked.

Despite the radiation sleeting down the corridor, I take my time studying the machine and the nimbus of data that it, like any computerized mechanism, operates in. This is my game and I am designed for it. In seconds I learn who Damasia's enemy is. The green metal, almost as hard as my chassis material, the high technology, superior to all other Confed tech, bodies almost immune to radiation as they have no DNA, the only silicate life-from known to exist, Ribisans.

But what would the gas-giant dwellers be doing here? They could only move about in the comparatively low pressure and, for them, lethal atmosphere, in environmental suits or vehicles. I consider and dismiss someone else using a machine of theirs, even with radiation shielding and meds, the interior would be deadly for any other species in hours.

I snoop continuously with my intruder software but find no easy access. Any significant push by me will trigger an alarm and I would be struck by an attack barrier. Ribisan computer technology is on par with their other achievements.

So I have found out who, but the why remains as elusive as ever. That critical intelligence lies in the machine ahead and I must access it. The digger is tunneling down under the volcano which is still 15.53 miles away. There is no reason to believe it will return to the surface any time soon, or that its support team will appear, allowing me to take captives to interrogate. More, the machine's mission, if I perceive their intent correctly, is to cause further harm to Damasia with the volcano. I cannot allow this. I must face it here.

"Nothing is ever easy," I grumble to myself. It is an old expression of my husband's, who was never what one could have called an optimist.

The machine is difficult to assault. If I use my armspac, I could either collapse the tunnel, which is far more dangerous to me than to it, or I could lose any chance for useful intelligence. Its metal is thick and the same means by which it reduces rock, will reduce me if I am not careful. No, a direct assault will fail. I am not confident in a cyber-assault. What are my enemy's weaknesses? This is not their environment. The atmosphere is poisonous to them; the pressure differential would cause their bodies to rupture. This must be the basis of my attack.

As quickly as I dare, I interface with the enemy machine. The defense matrix tingles at my contact but remains below the threshold for reaction, unsure if there is a threat or not. Hovering beyond that is the attack-barrier, robust enough for me to direct some processing power to defense and damage control systems. If I am struck, it will be touch and go.

I gain limited access and use it to reduce the sensitivity of the defense barrier to its minimum setting and then put it into a diagnostic mode. Any further reduction and the attack barrier will realize the defense barrier is compromised and fire. This process has taken seventy-two minutes, during which the machine has continued to tunnel away from me, reducing the dreadful radiation and protecting me from any direct fire if it does detect me.

Now, I can access the other control systems. I study these and access the multiple airlock controls. They are larger than Confed standard; Ribisans in environmental suits are larger than Okarans. I open an internal scanner inside the tunneler for a millisecond, long enough to discover that there is a crew of three Ribisan's aboard. As I expected, they are not wearing the bulky and uncomfortable environmental suits. In the dense, almost liquid atmosphere of the tunneler, they seem to be floating like bizarre squid.

My decision crystallizes. Attack. I hit the controls for the explosive bolts holding all four hatches with an intruder program. The thick Ribisan atmosphere floods out as the airlock hatches blow off the machine. At the same instant, the Ribisan cybernetic attack barrier senses me and fires. The storm of enemy virus is so powerful; it feels like a physical attack. My own barriers swing into operation, diffusing and deflecting the attack and launching countermeasures.

I charge the machine at my maximum speed, aiming to leap into the now gaping door of the blown airlock at the rear of the machine. An actuator in my leg is knocked off line by the attack barrier's cyber virus. I am going to fall so I turn it into a forward shoulder roll.

Fortune favors me. One of the crew has survived long enough to fire a jet of molecular acid at me. My fall causes the jet to go over my body, giving me a second to quickly fire the aerosol mist of base over my body, generating even more in a paste form to cling to my upper parts as I scuttle forward and lunge for the hatch. Though my outer casing sizzles and puckers, damage is superficial. Still I hate that I have acid damage on me.

I defeat the defense and attack barriers, and lock the machine from making any signal to the outside as I advance on the crew, or what is left of them. I glare at the acid-shooter, while being amazed that the Ribisan, now a pile of organic slush, had managed to get a shot off. The others are expired piles of dead tissue, flat on the floor.

While I know I should start my forensics right away, but I cannot stand that I am disfigured. I head for the reactor room and find a power tap. I tap myself in and do a major draw, prioritizing damage control and repair. Exterior sections are moved inward and melted and reforged with the extra power the reactor gives me. Relief floods me as marred sections return to smoothness and my hair is again its silky black length. I examine the reactor and its storage for rare radioactives and minerals and find a good supply.

I also find liquefied damage control patches for the machine and a metal coagulant to render them solid. This is indeed a find. It will yield material 99% as durable as my original chassis. I quickly ingest the patches and a sample of the coagulant. As the material is almost as strong as I am, I can store it inside me without creating a space which would be more vulnerable. That I do only with Wrik's gem. However, I must alter my dimensions some to accommodate the additional material. I try to pad myself out carefully, as it would be unusual for an adult human like me to grow appreciably.

In the back of the machine I find some additional blocks of patch material that have not been liquefied. I extrude a polymer bag and gather up some of these blocks, webbing them together into a backpack. These will go back to Seachange with me.

I am glad Dassa was not here to witness this breach of discipline. After all my lectures to the young Dua, here I am acting like complete tyro. My thoughts drift to Malporin and how unsettling it would be for him to see me scarred and pitted by acid. Ridiculous! He doesn't even know what I am. I am disturbed and displeased by this thought and banish it.

Embarrassed by being overcome by vanity, I return to examine the Ribisan machine and crew. It has been a long while since I have seen and done battle with Ribisans. The species is an associate member of the Confederacy, but the relationship has always been tenuous. The hydrogen-breathers are simply too different, both in psychology and physiology for friendship, or even true understanding.

I bore no enmity to the species, but Wrik and I had become involved in a simmering Ribisan religious civil war a century ago, learning many things about the species that they would prefer others did not learn. It had been touch and go whether an interstellar war would explode out of the Predictor Incident.

I lean my forehead against a metal stanchion, feeling the coolness of it. Through the Ribisan multi-verse predictor, I'd briefly seen snatches of possible futures for me. I believed that I live in the most fortunate of those time flows. I had gone from a sexless machine, to a lover and enjoyed a long marriage. But the Predictor, itself the silicate brain of a mutated Ribisan, augmented by great computer banks, had also given me my first ashen taste of mortality, showing me the loss that awaited me along this timeline. I regretted nothing of my choices, but from here the future was a blank slate for me.

I'd destroyed the multiverse predictor before the Ribisan's could artificially duplicate its predictive ability. It averted the civil war, but I doubted we'd earned any gratitude from any side of the Ribisan conflict.

I am as quick as I can be in my examination of the craft and occupants. I have no idea what sort of communication, or check-in, the crew has with their support team, or any other machines. The craft's computers are totally dead, scrubbed in a dying move of the defense barrier. The crew is in little better condition, decomposing in the Damasian *atmosphere. I control my distaste as I proceed with a quick autopsy. I find only one thing of interest—all three Ribisans are of advanced age. So advanced, that they would be in danger of their silicate brains not being able to regenerate and be transplanted. Ribisan progeny were mere hosts for their parent's brain, only the surplus children became new personalities. But with each transfer, the original brain degraded until final senility saved the young from being overwritten. These were all of that age group and should have been in some form of care, yet they showed no signs of atrophy.*

I examine the skull case of the acid shooter then the others. In each of them is a lattice of crystals, a medical implant. I use my plasma torch to cut one free for later study, placing it in my backpack.

It is time to leave. The tunneler is too valuable an asset to leave intact. But destroying it presents a problem—my enemies are very sophisticated. If they examine the machine, they may infer too much of my capabilities from it.

Better still if they do not realize the loss is due to enemy action. Inspiration strikes. I check the airlocks and pull all four airlock doors back into the machine. The controlling AI for the machine is destroyed, but the basic controls and computational units work. I repair these sufficiently to get throttle and directional control. I fire up the torch, input a new course and send the machine on its way. It will now tunnel nearly straight down until it meets its death in a flow of magma far below. I jump out the back of the machine and leave it to its fate.

About the acid wreckage in the tunnel behind it I can do nothing but hope they believe there was some failure in the boring machine that disabled the crew and sent it in a death dive toward the planetary core.

I examine the acid-wrecked floor of the tunnel, the bonded base agent has neutralized the acid but I still step gingerly until I am passed it. Then wishing to be free of this underground as soon as possible, I head upward at speed.

Relief washes over me when I see the familiar form of Maauro emerge from the entrance of the mine. While she'd made some provision for my survival, I was far happier with her protection. In truth, though our relationship was a difficult one, I'd come to value it for something more than that protection. I'd never relied on anyone who wasn't Guild before, who wasn't required to help me. Even now, I had no idea really of why she was doing what she did. I knew that she had little use for my species, a blatant racism that she did not seem to regard as such. Nor was she alone in that regard, we were little loved outside our own. Perhaps that was something that we should think about. The theory of self interest on which we based all our culture might not be as effective as we thought, if all it brought us was hate and distrust.

Enough for now, I thought, *this is ridiculous. As if one, no account, Guild fugitive could be of any weight in the battle of cultures.*

Maauro climbed up the rail to the ship with speed, fatigue not being part of my companion's constitution. I went down to greet her and learn what she had discovered.

The lock cycled and Maauro walked in. As usual her exterior was as clean as if she had just showered, due to a few seconds near-supersonic vibration. But there was something more. She nodded pleasantly at me and put a package of what looked like dark-green, steel plates, webbed in black plastic on the deck. As she straightened up, I was certain.

"What happened to your breasts?" I said. "They're bigger."

She demurely covered herself with an arm. "You noticed?"

"Yes, I noticed. You clearly picked up a cup size."

"Unfortunate."

I checked my companion's enhanced figure out. "I would say your butt is a bit more rounded and your thighs—"

"An inventory is not needed."

"Can I go wherever you've been?"

She raised an eyebrow. "It was less fun than you think, and I don't believe it would work for you."

"I'm willing to take some risk."

Maauro gave a wry smile and gestured at the metal on the deck. "I ingested some of this metal. It's high quality, almost to the level of my chassis. I used it to strengthen some points and to have an emergency supply for damage control. I thought I had distributed the additional material subtly. I can hardly explain becoming taller at my apparent age. Do you think others will notice?

I grin. "Malporin certainly will. I suggest a loose-fitting blouse for a bit. He won't be so sure then."

"Sounds like good advice."

I let the grin fade and pointed at the metal. "Is that a prize of war?"

She nodded. "Yes, and soon all that will be left of our enemy."

"Enemy?"

"Yes. I found three Ribisans operating some form of advanced tunnel-boring machine. They are clearly the ones responsible for the volcano's reawakening. I sent the machine to its destruction by boring down to a magma level. They will not be aware of my counterattack."

I point at a small bag she has hanging from a belt about her tiny waist. "More special metals?"

"No, but it may be another clue, but later for that. I want to take off from here as quickly as we can. Unfortunately, we can no more remove our landing signature then they could. We will make a supersonic pass over the ground to stir up the dirt as best we can. Then I think it is back to Pilbara. I don't want your little kitty hussy to execute on our performance bond."

I nod, feeling the ship's impellers rumbling. Maauro of course did not need to touch a control physically. I nodded approvingly. "Let's bug out, as the human's say."

CHAPTER TWENTY-EIGHT

WE LANDED IN PILBARA WELL AFTER SUNSET, LOCAL TIME. THIS *gives us a quiet evening on the ship for me to consider what I have learned. I sit in the ship's engine room plugged into my power tap, analyzing. Here, I can concentrate on the materials that I scavenged from the tunneler, as well as all the captured data.*

I consider the stone and metal arrangement that I have named "the diadem." Its stones are unfamiliar to me, which means that they are not in any Confed database. After careful external study to rule out any danger, I ingested a small sample to my internal labs, which are vastly superior to anything on the planet. To my amazement, it shows me a crystalline structure of incredible complexity and storage ability. It rivals my own circuitry, allowing the manufacture of complete computer circuits down to two nanometers. My own go down to one nanometer with no bleed through. Such crystalline complexity could serve as the basis for multiple supercomputers.

The stone is clearly natural as it possesses flaws and variations, but I cannot identify it. Yet, I know that these stones represent a critical link in what is happening to Damasia.

Having reached the end of my researches and hearing Dassa stir, I make my way to the galley, diadem in hand, hoping for some inspiration to strike me.

Dassa appears in the open door of galley. She does not like the fact that I always know where she is on the ship, so I pretend not to notice her, until she makes a noise.

"Oh, hello, Dassa."

She sighs. "Quit paying biological, you know where I am all the damn time."

"What? You don't enjoy the little fictions I put on for your sake? And I work so hard…"

"I don't want to quarrel," she says.

"Then don't be quarrelsome."

She grimaces.

Now it is my turn to sigh. "Let's start over. Hello, Dassa, what can I do for you?"

"Have you uncovered anything from your new Ribisan hairpiece?" she gestures at the diadem.

"If you knew where this came from, you wouldn't suggest using it in anyone's hair."

"I seem to encounter one disgusting thing after another in your company."

"Hah, squishy bag of protoplasm, I hardly think your kind's tendency to excrete, rot and decay are my fault."

"Except when you tear something to pieces."

"Well, except then."

We exchange rueful grins that lighten the atmosphere.

"Could it have been mere decoration?" Dassa asks.

"No. They were implanted in the interior brain cases of each of the three Ribisans."

"Returning to my earlier observation, yuck."

"Hey, Ribisan innards aren't half so bad as those of you oxygen-breathers. They're made from similar stuff to me; less prone to stink and decay."

"I didn't realize you were such a connoisseur of people's 'innards.'"

"Sort of an occupational hazard," I return my gaze to the diadem. "This is important, if only I can sort out how."

"Have you considered asking Malporin for help?"

I stare at her in bemusement, "Why?"

"Because he is a miner, a practical geologist, and familiar with the stones of this world."

I raise a dismissive eyebrow. "I have the recorded sum of all geological knowledge available to me."

"Didn't you say that biological intuition sometimes exceeds computing power?"

"I have to admit that my biological companions have seen patterns that elude normal computation, but that was before I myself had the experience of being biological."

"Oh, and in that time you learned all there was to know about biological intuition?"

I sit back. "My husband said so."

This time she raises an eyebrow. "He seems to have spent most of his time making sure you were happy."

"You imply flattery?"

"You infer it."

"Very well," I say standing. "Since I am getting nowhere, perhaps Malporin can divine its nature. At least we can discuss it over lunch."

"At which you should consider something besides a million-calorie, sweet desserts. That is, if you want to continue to persuade him that you're biological."

"A good point," I agree, putting on a light field jacket to obscure my new dimensions. I pop the diadem into one of the big pockets then turn to face a pained expression on Dassa's face. "What?"

"You did mention that came out of someone's braincase."

"Yes."

"Then perhaps you could put in a box or something?"

"Will a satchel do?"

"Yes."

"Anything else?"

"Yes, would you please wash your hands after playing with people's brain bits? I don't think that's too much to ask before lunch."

"True and perhaps we will hold off discussions of brain bits until after lunch."

We rode over to the council chamber where Malporin was normally to be found in his daylight hours. He was, as always, pleased to see us, though he seemed puzzled that Dassa didn't depart. I know he wants to spend more time alone with me. What I don't know, is what I want. Dassa's presence prevents me from having to consider it further.

"Can we see you in private?" I ask. His eyebrows rise. Fortunately, Kemisa is not in the vicinity, as I did not think we would be able to ditch the curious cat.

"Sure. How about my office, upstairs?"

"Is that where you have your gemology equipment?" Dassa asks, more directly than I would have preferred.

"Um… yeah. Why? Did you want to check on a stone's quality?"

I raise a hand. "When we are in private."

An elevator whisks us to the top floor of the council building, which has a view of the mountains and the landing field. Armored shutters that had been installed to ward off snipers, stood open now. I could see a brown haze settling on the mountains. It cut the sun down to a coolness that augured poorly for winter. Fortunately, a full Brownie was not in the near term forecast.

We reach a glass doorway that said 'Malporin Assays'. On the other side lay a well-appointed office, with chairs of heavy leather and wood. The room very much reflects its owner, solid and efficient, down to the modern gemology equipment lining the back wall.

Malporin waves us to chairs by a broad table. He drew soft drinks from a small cooler and sat with us. "What can this simple miner do for you?"

"Simple?" Dassa replys. "I doubt that."

He only smiles.

I place the satchel with the diadem and the stone I had extracted from it on the table. "Perhaps we could have a tray or something," I say, with a glance at Dassa. "Who knows where these items have been?"

Dassa nods vigorously.

"Worried about it being native grave goods?" he replies with a grin. "Captain, you surprise me; I hadn't thought you squeamish." He returns with a large, metal tray into which I empty the satchel.

Malporin stares in fascination as he puts on some gloves and scoops up both pieces. "Huh? Heavier than you would expect. I don't recognize these stones. They're white, like diamonds, but clearly they aren't…" He stands as if he's forgotten we are there, then turns to the machinery at the back.

I nod, though I must battle frustration. I can do all the tests he can do and far quicker. The one thing I cannot access is his fully human intuition and the random way they process information. In this, I may have returned too much to the directly logical M-7 when I reassumed my original body.

Dassa gives me a look and whispers. "It appears you have less attraction for him than a new stone. I also suspect that lunch is going by the wayside too."

I narrow my eyes in a mock glare and sip my drink. After twenty-minutes, he stands, and notices us again. "I'm sorry. I'll need a couple of hours. It might help if I knew where this came from."

I shake my head. "Not now. I am afraid it might bias your research."

"Ok. How about I meet you for dinner? I should know something by then, if I am going to succeed at all." He looks at Dassa. "Sorry about lunch. You're welcome for dinner too, Dassa."

She yawns. "As attractive as being an extra wheel is, I may go look up my girlfriend instead. Aurelia will tell me what she feels I need to know, whenever she feels I need to know it. Kemisa, at least, will feed me."

His look toward me is puzzled. I myself am torn between the desire for the simplicity of the triad of us and a desire for it to be just the more perilous pair. "I'll meet you here later."

We leave; then I part with Dassa who is off to find her girlfriend and lunch. I take the time to do some shopping in the few stores Pilbara boasts. I consider that Malporin has usually seen me in some form of coverall or another. The weather at the moment remains cool, tolerable and dry. I am nonplussed for a choice. The local women seem to favor clothing as practical as my own one piece appearance, if less skintight. My fashion sense has always been erratic, even without the handicap of being an outworlder. I would like to wear a dress, but suspect I would simply look silly on this frontier world.

Well, when in a dilemma, go with the classics. I find a private alley, slip into it and then generate a white sweater and denim pants. I throw the real jacket I wore over them and consider the effect. Pleased with it, I walk on. People greet me, some stop for a brief chat and the time passes. A dog passes, but pays no more attention to me than if I had been a car.

I return at 5PM, in what the brown haze has already rendered into near twilight. Dassa, as expected, was not there. While I am not thrilled with the Kemisa connection, it is really none of my business. To be frank, I am having enough trouble reconciling and regulating my emotions to bother much about her.

Yet, when I see Malporin, I am surprised and a little disappointed, to find him all business. He looks up as I open the door and waves me in.

"I know what stone this is," he says, excitement in his voice, but some shadow in his eyes.

"Please," I say, while perching on one of his sturdy chairs, only to be annoyed as it creaks. I quickly rebalance myself, but he has not noted the tell-tale chair.

"It's a stone that we often find encrusting high-quality opaloids. In fact some of us think it is a matrix for the creation of opaloids, as you don't find the high-quality ones without thick coverings of these stones. They're more of a bloody nuisance to miners than anything else."

I am surprised. He has identified the stone and as native, where it remained a mystery to me. "But, I know of no stone that looks like that, or has such an incredibly dense latticed-array structure—"

He nods. "You'd be right. The stone is called klinker, we give them to kids to play with. Here's one." He reaches into a drawer, extracts pink and gray stone to plunk down in front of me.

I pick it up. "It is lighter than the ones I gave you, and the color and crystal pattern are different."

"Yes, I believe it has been treated by a series of processes: chemical, heat and pressure, almost to the point where it is a new stone. I only recognized it, because I tried a heat treatment of one once to see if I couldn't harden the stone into something more useful. It was an experiment of my own, and I didn't document it since it didn't amount to anything. But there's a similarity to the basic crystal pattern."

I shake my head ruefully. Sometimes knowing too much about a thing can blind one to alternatives. I should have considered the possibility that the stone was not entirely natural.

"Someone," he continues, "has found a way to take a valueless stone and process it, to where its capacity for data storage and computer circuitry exceeds anything I have ever heard of. Aurelia, if this is something you can do, you're going to be very wealthy. This could revolutionize any process using computers or AI."

I shake my head. "The processes are unknown to me."

"Damn. If it could be duplicated, God, the sky would be the limit."

"You don't think you can?" I ask.

"No. I can't imagine what would be required to do this. Pressure on gas-giant levels, heat into thousands of Kelvins..."

I listen to Malporin, but with this last piece of information, the Ribisan's terrible scheme and the desperate need that drives it, hammer into my consciousness. I am careful to let nothing register on my face.

"Malporin," I interrupt. "This needs to be kept secret for now. There is something going on. We need to deal with it and we'll need help. I'll need Dassa. Who can you count on for confidential help?"

He strokes his chin. "You won't like it, but in times of trouble, Kemisa and I have always covered each other."

"There seems to be no escaping her influence."

"She's not all bad and tough in a pinch," he insists.

A thought occurs to me. I try to dismiss it, but it will not go away. "You seem to have a soft spot for her."

"Well, she did help me out in a sticky situation. I'd say I owe her."

"Just how "sticky" did you get with her?"

"Well...I mean...we... ah."

I recognize this series of sounds as being common to the human male of the species while they are looking for some way to avoid answering a question, or find a palatable lie.

"So," I say. "It seems you and Dassa have something in common."

"You know, this was years ago—"

"Never mind; it doesn't matter. Summon your kitty ex-playmate and her present girl-toy. We'll need them both. I'll be getting some air on the terrace."

"Sure," he replies, as I open the door to his terrace and step outside. Once outside, I can wrestle with my feelings. Finding that a male interested in me and for whom I might have the beginning of feelings for, was intimate with a Nekoan bimbo is not improving my mood. On the other hand, I have no logical reason for this reaction. Not only am I not prepared to explore things with Malporin, his relations with Kemisa were years before we met.

I finally settle for being amused with myself for my reaction. This does however make it easier for me to keep my own feelings for Mal in check for now, whether that is fair or not, is immaterial, it simply is.

Fifteen minutes later, I see Kemisa and Dassa pull up in a GP to the front of the building. This time I study Kemisa with a different eye. She is tall, athletic, and if not as fine-featured as the beautiful Jaelle, she is still, I must admit, pretty. With the rough mane of piled thick hair and the winking gems in her mane and on her arms, she is a human male's fantasy of a barbarian queen.

Cat girls, I growl to myself, what is it with human men and catgirls?

However I school my face back to impassivity and turn back to the door and a worried-looking Malporin within.

"The girls are here," I say brightly, as if I hadn't spent the last quarter of an hour outside.

"Um, ok. Are we good?"

"Nothing to worry about," I reply.

He looks unconvinced. I am not sure I am either.

The door opens and Kemisa strides in with Dassa on her heels. "Hello Mal. You wanted us?" Then she spots me. "Hello, Captain."

"Hello, Kemisa,"

Dassa looks at me with raised eyebrows. I gesture at some chairs. Kemisa walks past Mal and squeezes his shoulder with a smile. He returns a nervous grin, which causes her to do a double-take on him. She drops into a chair and Dassa perches on the thick chair arm next to her. How cozy.

I focus with some difficulty.

"We four," I begin, "are going to share a secret. It cannot leave this room, as it could involve the death of a world. Are we agreed, before I proceed further?"

Dassa stares at me blankly then nods. Mal and Kemisa exchanged glances. He turns back to me. "Agreed."

Kemisa holds my eye in a searching gaze. "You always seem to be at the focus of critical events, Captain Toyama, or whoever you really are. Very well, I'll play the hand you're dealing."

"Much of what I will tell you will strain your credulity but will be true. Dassa is witness to some of it. This world has suffered one ecological catastrophe after another and too many for coincidence."

I want to simply project an image on the wall, but that will put paid to my fiction as a mutant. So I must take the tedious path of hooking up a projector and pretending to link to some file in my hand com. The image of a something that looks like a collection of triangles appears.

"This is a self-replicating virus on the 100 micron scale. You may, if you wish, refer to it as, the firebug. It is the thing that has set every coal deposit on this planet burning. It's a tailored virus, showing every hallmark of being manufactured. Unless you can tell me how something so obviously not native to this planet could achieve almost 100% penetration through rock and soil, without having been injected and planted, I would offer it as Exhibit One of planet-wrecking warfare on Damasia."

Mal and Kemisa stare at each other shocked.

"I discovered these while investigating the burning subterranean coal fields. I wondered how such vast fields in so many different places could spontaneously catch fire. The answer, of course, is that they didn't."

"Those fields, once ignited, will burn slowly, inexorably and for centuries. There is no known way to extinguish them. All the while, they will be emitting vast clouds of methane, contributing to changing of climate.

"And there is worse. In the sea adjacent to your capitol lies the island of Beros. It contains a large volcano, like Mt. Grim though far smaller, that has become active in the last three years. The vents and feeder dykes under the volcano have combined. In a major eruption, given the geologic instability of the island, a mass of 500km3 with an estimated mass of 1.5 x 1015 kg—will catastrophically fail in a massive gravitational landslide and enter the Reich Ocean, generating a 'mega-tsunami'. The debris will continue to travel along the ocean floor as a debris flow. My computer modeling indicates that the resulting initial wave may attain a local amplitude in excess of 600 meters and an initial peak-to-peak height that approximates to two kilometers. It will travel at about 720 kilometers per hour, inundating the Belliam coast one hour later, the southern coast of

Grand Roads in about 3.5 hours, and the eastern seaboard near the capitol in about six hours, by which time the initial wave will have subsided into a succession of smaller ones, each about thirty to sixty meters. These may surge to several hundred meters in height and be several kilometers apart while retaining their original speed."

Malporin's face paled. "My God, it could wipe out most of the colony's settlements, the capitol, the spaceport, all the industry. This colony follows the typical pattern; everything radiates out from the spaceport along seacoasts and navigable rivers."

"This too, I believe to be a deliberate act. My analysis of your seismic activity records suggests that someone has been using shaped-charge fusion bombs to alter the dykes and feeders and weaken the seafloor near the volcano. Indeed there seems to be an unprecedented rise in earthquakes, volcanic action and other seismic events that would appear to be melting the polar icecaps."

"How do you know all this?" Kemisa demands.

"Because I discovered the mechanism by which they are reaching the base of these volcanoes," I say. "I destroyed a tunneling machine under Mount Grim. It was being used to create fractures in the rock and redirect the volcanic vents to reawaken the volcano."

There is a long silence after that remark.

"And where is that device now?" Kemisa asks.

"Melted in the planetary mantle by now. After I dispatched the crew, I reprogrammed the machine to bore down into the depths until it was destroyed. It was too dangerous an asset to leave to the enemy to recover."

Kemisa's look tells me that she thinks I am insane. She glances over to Dassa who nods.

"But you didn't see this machine yourself?" she demands of Dassa.

"No, but I saw the signs of its passage and the traces of a large ship that had landed it."

"Why wouldn't you have surfaced it?" Malporin asks. "We could have used it as proof of their attacks."

I cock my head at him. "Proof to offer to whom? The Confederacy has fractured into the Star Alliance and many independent worlds. None of which will have any particular interest in tangling with a force as deadly as this over an illegal colony on a non-aligned world.

"No. Public knowledge of this might well cause them to accelerate their plans especially with the disarray among oxygen-breathers."

"Can this be?" Mal mutters, as if to himself.

"I can only tell you that I interpreted the data from your records, the pattern is there to be seen by someone looking for planet-wrecking. There are many additional forces being used here, but these seem the direst."

"And the native hostilities?" he demands.

"Whether that is serendipitous to the planet wreckers, or part of their plan, I do not know, but to a native species that seems to facing the end *of their world, it would be natural to channel their anger and frustration at the alien newcomers. And if not, the idea would be easily planted."*

"Who is doing this to us and why?" Malporin asked.

"Your world is under attack by one of the most advanced and alien species in the known galaxy, the silicon-based Ribisans."

"What!" Malporin said.

Kemisa looked at Dassa. "Is this true?"

"Yes," Dassa said, her voice distant and cool.

"My best guess this project started two years after opaloids were first exported from Damasia. Someone traded one to a Ribisan; it must have been a raw stone with the rock you called klinker attached to it.

"Their technology, knowledge of heat, and high pressure work exceed any species known. Some scientist among the Ribisans decided to experiment with a combination of heat, pressure and chemicals which created a revolutionary crystalline storage matrix, capable of circuitry on a nanometer basis and storage on multiples of terabytes.

"The level of computer technology that could result from these new crystals could revolutionize cybertechnology in the Confederacy, its effects would ripple through the galactic economy.

"But the Ribisans have other plans for this scarce natural resource and this arises out of their unique biology. Ribisan brains are rather like crystalline computer storage arrays. They have progeny for two purposes, to perpetuate their species and to provide replacement bodies for themselves. They essentially core out a child's brain and have their own brain implanted in the child's body.

Distaste was stamped on the face of each of the biologicals facing me, for in this were the Ribisan's furthest from all other known life. They murdered their children to survive.

"But even the Ribisans cannot forever outrun death. With each transfer the brain becomes less viable until finally they suffer a form of senility and finally expire.

"Until now. These crystals, once treated, have enough storage to keep the personality of a Ribisan intact through the transfer. With these implanted in their brain, they can survive with vastly less of their original brain functioning. It's a reprieve from death, a practical immortality. Let's call this group of Ribisan, the Stuldbrugs."

The three stare at me, evidently I am the only one with an appreciation for classics. "It is a reference from an old book, for people that have lived on beyond their natural time."

Kemisa and Malporin shifted in astonishment and their eyes met.

"But...but why not trade—" Malporin said.

"You imagine these Stuldbrugs would leave their chance at immortality in the hands of others? What price might those others set?" Dassa said.

"Others," I added, "who might also divert the crystals to other uses. As I said, it would revolutionize cybernetic and AI in known space. We

don't know how much klinker is required to make one of these, let's call them X-stones. You said the treated stone was three times heavier than the original. It is unlikely that there would be enough for all the uses people would want them for."

"Yes," he said, a dazed tone in his voice. "Though how such a thing is possible I can't even imagine."

I continued. "The Ribisan social system is built on something a human might call "ethical cowardice" after all, when you live for over a thousand years, you have a lot to protect. They are intensely religious, xenophobic and the only life form of their kind. Even the words I just used, religious, xenophobic, are only analogs for a mind made of silicon with liquid methane running through it. One cannot expect that even basic human concepts would equate to what they really feel.

"Yet one thing we can rely on. Ribisans cling to life with tenacity and these Struldbrugs could only be more so."

"So," Kemisa says, as her tail swishes furiously. "They have decided to make sure that their supply of these X-stones is uninterrupted by making life uncomfortable on Damasia in the hope we will leave?"

I shake my head slowly. "Not uncomfortable. They are seeking to make it impossible for any known oxygen-breathing biological life form to live here without the protection of domes and environmental suits. They are trying to bring about a Permian level extinction event by altering the biosphere to take it out of the Earth class, making it at least temporarily something more like Venus."

Malporin face had a stricken look. Kemisa put her hands to her head and rocked side to side, a gesture I knew from Jaelle to mean more surprise than grief.

"Do you have any other proof of this conspiracy, having disposed of the most compelling evidence, this alien machine?" Kemisa finally says, her arms folded across her chest.

I fix my eye on her. Her doubts are beginning to irritate me. I project another image on the wall and flash up video of the borer working in the tunnel from before I attacked it. Then I add interiors of the machine, including visuals of the dead crew, nothing shows me in the frame, as I was the camera.

"Beyond that," I add, "you have the simple fact of the massive and inexplicable planetary change you are experiencing. There is no natural cause or explanation, yet these things do not simply happen. They require a proximate cause."

Kemisa meets my gaze. "You destroyed the Indigene force. Didn't you?"

"We were discussing the Ribisan threat, though I grant you that I see their tentacles behind the divisions between colonists and natives."

"Why don't you answer her question, Aurelia?" Malporin says his voice grave.

"Because I chose not to," I state.

Another long silence.

"What can we do about these Ribisans?" Malporin says. "With the state of the Confederacy, I'm sure the Navy has other concerns."

"Even if they wanted to," Kemisa adds. "How long would it be before any significant force got here?"

I nod. "We cannot expect outside help in any useful time frame. We must face the threat with the assets here."

"What assets?" Kemisa says dismissively. "There's a clapped out auxiliary warship at the capitol, a few aerospace and atmospheric fighters and maybe a battalion of real troops on the whole planet."

Malporin shakes his head. "Worthless against such an enemy."

"There is evidence," I begin slowly, "of another force present in this system, one which might serve as a counterbalance to the Ribisans."

"Gods of Denlesch," Dassa explodes. "You're not considering the Ederi?"

"The who?" Malporin asks.

I give Dassa a warning look. "The name is rumored to belong to the Pale Ones."

"Pale Ones," Kemisa repeats. "Oh, the Baldies who have been attacking the Confederacy?"

"To my knowledge the attacks have been at Guild targets," I say. "But the news reports indicate that a ship of theirs was sighted in this system."

Malporin nods. "Yes that's why they've been scrambling to put the Chin, that auxiliary warship into service. But why would they come here? There's no significant Guild activity on Damasia since that bunch of Dua were wiped out for claim jumping."

Kemisa nods. "There's a criminal element, but it's local."

"And you would know?" I couldn't help myself.

But she stares back unaffected. "And I would know."

"And I can confirm that," Dassa adds.

"Dassa's family had Guild connections," I say, which is true as far as it goes. "She knows things."

"It's interesting what you both know and seem so thoroughly prepared for." Malporin says dryly. "When do we get to the part where you tell us who you are, and why you came here."

Kemisa nods.

I use a look that used to allow me to get away with not answering things when Wrik would press me on something I was disinclined to discuss.

"I'm not an idiot you know," Mal continues. "You've hit this planet like a one woman assault force leaving the impossible and the unexplained in your wake everywhere you go. If you're a Free Trader, I'm King of the Moroks."

Evidently my cute look is no longer effective. Wrik used to let me get away with anything when I was being cute. Perhaps I am too far out of practice.

"I have more skills than you would expect," I say finally. "But do not overestimate what I can do in this situation. Dassa, Seachange and I are all the assets I can bring to this table. You will just have to accept—"

"No," he says standing. "I'm sorry Aurelia. I like you. Maybe so much that I've let that cloud my judgment. Maybe that would be ok if this involved just me. I might decide to trust you with my life, dumb as that would be on such short acquaintance. But I can't risk the people I represent and a whole world on my feelings."

Now it is my turn to show anger. "Do not crowd me, Malporin Rand. Your world is my problem only so long as I elect to make it so. I am no agent of the Confederacy, or lone crusader for justice."

We stare at each other. He is breathing hard. Kemisa reaches out to touch his hand. "Mal, sit. She holds all the cards here and she's got a plan. She's not spouting gas."

I realize, that to gain their acceptance for my plans, that I must reveal something, even Malporin has come to the end of the rope he is going to allow me.

Finally, I speak again. "I am not now a Confederate agent, but I have been one. You already have enough clues to know that my mutation is not limited to my eyes. I am older, stronger and far deadlier than I appear. I have cyber-war and CBO capabilities that do not exist elsewhere on this world and have used these on the Ederi before to good effect. They have reason to fear me, and I have knowledge of them that no one else does."

"And you?" *Malporin says to Dassa, perhaps seeing her as the easier source to exploit.*

She shrugs. "I am Guild, low-level but still hunted by the Ederi for that reason. While I travel with…Aurelia… I forgo Guild contact, unless she sanctions it. She protects me from the Ederi, and I crew for her."

"So Confed and Guild," *Malporin says, eyes narrowed.*

"Ex-Confed," *I insist,* "more than that I simply will not say."

Kemisa and Malporin exchanged looks, after a second, she nods.

"OK," *he says.* "We need your help and I believe you have been honest with us as far as you went, which, for the record, isn't very damn far. The Indigenes weren't killed by cyberwarfare or chemical or biological ordnance. As near as I can tell they were hit by a steel tornado. What do you propose to do?"

"We propose a deal to the Ederi, some form of access to the stones, in complete secrecy, provided they interdict the Ribisans from their assault on this world."

"You think that the Ederi are a lesser threat than the Ribisans?" *Dassa said, clearly upset.*

"*Logically, yes. While there has been collateral damage from their intrusions and attempts to impede them, the information we have—*"

"*Which is months, hell, most of a year out of date!*" Dassa snaps.

"*—remains,*" I finish, "*that they only attack the Guild.*"

"*Doesn't that give us a negotiation roadblock?*" Kemisa said, her fangs in evidence. "*Given that Dassa is on their hit list?*"

I nod. "*One in a long line of difficulties we will have to surmount.*"

"*How would we even contact the Ederi?*" Dassa grumbles. "*Or do you plan on flying around the system with me tied to the nose of Seachange with a sign saying, "Come and get it?"*"

I give her a glare. "*Do not tempt me. No, in my previous encounter with them I was able to obtain a few characters of their language off their bodies and equipment. I can broadcast these, though if nothing else works, I can just broadcast Dassa's name. That should get their attention.*"

The Dua-Denlenn girl pales and cups a hand over her right breast. Malporin and Kemisa exchanged troubled looks.

"*We will meet them on the moon, and I will strike the best deal I can. Understand that is the limit of what we can achieve, and there is no certainty of what they will do. But for all of this to have a chance of working, it must be kept secret, or you will inherit nothing but a war zone as various powers fight over the carcass of your world.*"

I search the faces before me. Malporin and Kemisa reluctantly nod. I look at Dassa.

"*Since when does my opinion matter?*"

I continue to look steadily at her.

"*Oh, all right,*" she said, "*like we have a choice.*"

After the stunning reveal, Kemisa and I made our way back to her apartment. Once there Kemisa stalked around like a cornered animal. I sat in a chair by the window, my arms wrapped around me.

Kemisa growled. "Your captain seems determined to make sure that neither you nor I profit in any way."

"What do you mean?" I replied, though I had a good idea where this conversation was going.

"Oh, she doubtless knows about our explorations in the capitol. Very little seems to get past your captain, she seems to inhabit every computer system and communication method that there is. If I didn't know better… no…impossible. Anyway, I think she suspects that we were looking into the prospects of setting up a Guild cell here on Damasia."

"Now, not only is she going to forestall that and keep you poor and dependent on her, she proposes to use you as bait in her insane scheme and has the nerve to pose as your friend!"

Kemisa pulled a bottle from her bar and poured a stiff amount into two glasses. Calmer now, she came over and handed me one. "The only reason she even put me in the know, is to use my services among the local criminals, gray traders and Indigenes for her own purposes. She's got Rand so twisted up, that he would dance to any tune she plays. I like him, but he's simple-minded when it comes to a pretty human female. Otherwise I'd have kept him for myself. Hah, wonder what Toyama would make of that?

"No, we are all dancing to Toyama's tune, but it may be time to change the music."

"How?" I asked. It sounded plaintive to my own ears.

"She's working one end of the equation. From what you said, she has history with the Ribisans. That past enmity may be blinding her to the appalling danger of making a deal with a species we've only met in combat. Well, we don't have that history. Ribisans may be bizarre, but they've dealt with both the Guild and the Confederacy for decades. I can't see how it would be easier to deal with the Ederi, totally unknown and dangerous, over the Ribisans. For Goddess' sake, no one but you two has ever even spoken to a live one."

I couldn't quite control the spasm of fear that shot through at the remembrance of that last "conversation" with an Ederi. I stood up and walked over to the window, glass in hand, looking at the spire of *Seachange* in the distance. Oh, if only my ship would blast off for somewhere, anywhere else!

My ship... but was it? The ship was Maauro's. I was occasionally useful supercargo. My attempts at a better alignment were fraught with misunderstandings and setbacks, as one of us misread the other's signals. I think in terms of alignment, of serving a power that protects me and gives me leave to seek advantage under that protection. She, in return, uses the human word, friend, and given what she is, who even knows how close she comes to getting that right? Not that I would even know.

She doesn't have a clue how much it terrifies me when she is weak, or loses herself in memories, lassitude, or these profitless side adventures. Denlesch be, but she even thinks this "friendship" entitles her to me to show me weakness and indecision. How could I possibly rely on her long-term?

I remembered Maauro's coolness and anger, then her gentleness and the occasional bursts of perfect alignment we'd experienced, that I'd hoped to build on. Had I only erected an edifice of sand?

"I don't know what to do," I said finally, as Kemisa walked up behind of me. "I don't want to cross Aurelia, but perhaps we are too different to align properly and this thing she calls friendship, seems ethereal and weak to me."

"Come to bed," Kemisa suggested gently. "Things will be clearer in the morning."

I followed her into the bedroom and undressed. As I slid under the covers, Kemisa took me into her arms. Her fever warm body slid over me, driving my worries and concerns out of my mind, for the moment.

When I awoke in the morning, my face in the valley of Kemisa's breasts, I realized that she was right. With the sun had come certainty that my incomplete alignment with Maauro meant I needed a backup plan, or I could only live on in uncertainty and danger, never knowing when the fragile thing between us would finally break, or in what circumstances. I would set toes in the water Kemisa was beckoning me into. Perhaps I could align better with the Nekoan, who was so much more like the Guild people I had known, though far kinder and more sexual, than an ancient war machine that thought it was human.

Yet, my hearts were troubled, in a way they'd never been before, as I remembered how Maauro had looked at me when we left the cemetery. I sighed and closed my eyes, hoping for some minutes of peace before Kemisa awoke and I had to cross a river over which there might be no return.

CHAPTER TWENTY-NINE

WE TOOK KEMISA'S FLITTER AND HEADED DOWN toward the coast to Biltsang. I'd told Maauro that I wanted some time with Kemisa, and that we were going to head to the beach near the port. Maauro had only nodded, reminding me to make sure that Kemisa kept the terrifying secret she'd been given. I told her it might be a few days. I was surprised by how hard it had been to lie to her and how easily she'd bought the deception.

We flew into what was laughingly called a port. True, it was an ideal harbor with a long isthmus protecting a shallow and broad bay. But there were only about forty or so buildings clustered around a half-dozen wharfs. Biltsang had started as a port, mostly to supply Pilbara and the mines upland, other than a little fishing, there was no other commercial activity. With the developments at Pilbara and Tillet, life was returning to Biltsang as well.

Kemisa had connections here as well. We stopped at general store where Kemisa occasionally rented a room. We dropped our bags and the flyer there, then waited for dark.

"I have a meeting set up," Kemisa had said before we left, "with a Morok named, Trell. He's one of those who will sell anything to anybody. He has contacts at the capitol and here. The seaport makes for an ideal route for smuggling supplies. I'll bet my tail that if the Ribisan's are getting supplies, or spreading weapons among the natives, Trell is involved. He could be our way to open an alternative to Aurelia's plan."

At the time it seemed reasonable. Now that we were walking through the barely lit streets of this primitive port, it seemed much riskier. Still, Kemisa strode through the streets as if she owned them. It didn't take us long to reach the wharf front. Then Kemisa slowed. Her caution spoke volumes to me.

We walk down a dark alley that my Guild training warned me against. Overhead, some seabirds called; it had the feeling of a warning. I kept my hand under my jacket and on the handle of the slug-thrower I wore in place of the usual stunner. This close to the ocean, the air smelled of: salt, dank and rot. Biltsang had been largely abandoned when the highlands came under attack. When the airbridge to the capitol was severed, most of the remaining population boarded a freighter and left. The Constabulary and enough diehards remained to keep the first Indigene raiders at bay, so the port survived. Now that same freighter sat in the bay, its yellow and gray, slab sides reflecting the moonlight. About half the town's lights glimmered, showing the state of the resurrection.

In the warehouse district Kemisa now lead me to, only a few lights fought the darkness, but I thought it was by choice here. Kemisa waved me forward. We approached a door with a blue light above it and a faded sign that said, Trell Imports. Only Kemisa's twisted tail revealed her own tension. A silhouette in a window, lit by the pale reflected light of a computer screen, shifted as we approached. The door under the light opened. A grim-looking human stood there.

"Halt," he growled.

We did.

"What do you want?"

Kemisa nodded. "I have an appointment with Trell."

He looked us over; eyes sliding over me in a way that made me tighten my grip on the pistol.

He grinned. "Your girlfriend is the nervous type. That makes me nervous."

"She's young." Kemisa says. She tapped me on the arm, and I let if fall slowly to my side.

He moved back and I follow Kemisa in. To the right sat a Drisnian. The small humanoid was monitoring screens showing the area around the warehouse. His was the silhouette we'd seen through the window. The warehouse around us was a mix of prefab, stucco and some wood. I could see that it stretched out over the harbor, making it easy to conceal the cargoes unloaded there. Two boats floated inside, one was larger and looked made for cargo, though I thought that anyone who would dare the deep sea in such a small ship was crazy.

Blue and dull-yellow lights didn't so much alleviate the interior darkness, as create pools of light, which we stepped in and out of as we headed for an office on the far side. The human was sure-footed. Kemisa saw well in the dark. Only I had to carefully watch my footing on a floor cluttered with spools of rope, chains and boxes of all sizes, along with less identifiable debris.

We stopped outside the office, which was little more than a shed, built into the warehouse wall.

"Boss," the human called.

"Send them in," the voice was guttural with a thick Morok accent.

We filed in to face a large Morok wearing a work-shirt, seated at a desk lit by the blue lights his kind preferred.

I kept distaste from my face as I looked at him. The face was brutish, even for a Morok—his eyes, which would have been red in better light—were black blisters in a face humans would have called, goblin-like. He was fanged like Kemisa, but these jutted up and, unlike Kemisa's weren't tucked out of sight when she wished them to be. The effect was less charming. Near his left hand was an old-style military laser pistol.

"You look for me," he grunts.

"Yes," Kemisa responds. "But I don't do business like a rug merchant standing in a doorway."

The big Morok's body shook with silent laughter. "Me. Northern Morok, from the great ice caves on homeworld. Eyes no good for bright light." He adjusted a toggle on the light on his desk. More of a yellow light suffused the room. He waved a hand at a chair. Kemisa strode in and dropped into the chair with her usual easy grace.

I stand where I can watch both him and the human outside the door. The human leans against a crate and watches me.

Trell glances at him. "Fenwar, go back to loading. I call you if I need."

Fenwar faded back into the darkness but I kept my attention split between Trell and the door. For all I know, the fade could have been a ruse to get us to let our guard down.

"Kemisa Rasan," Trell says. "I know you. Mostly legit, but small-time operator sometimes."

Kemisa shrugs. "When needed."

"Hear Malporin Rand runs you now."

"We're colleagues."

The eyes slide back to me. "Who she?"

"Guild," Kemisa said.

The one word changed the atmosphere in the room and my status. Now I gazed coolly at him. The glance that came back was wary, and the arm near the gun didn't seem so casual.

He studied me. "Not High Guild."

"No," I said as it would be ridiculous to claim more at my age. "Courier."

"What house?" he coughed out.

"The Baron's if he still lives, otherwise I am a freelance."

He returns his gaze to Kemisa. "What do you do?"

"My friend is young, but the power she works for is old."

"Old, yes, but mostly dead these days," he says.

"Guild plays the long game," I add. "The Pale Ones are a passing plague. Dangerous yes, but the Guild will endure."

"So you say."

"When it does triumph," I say, "the Guild will remember who it owes favors to." I didn't bother to add, and those who it did not. The old threat seemed hollow with merely one Guilder on world.

The Morok didn't seem impressed and just shrugged his shoulders. "You got off world connections, you come to Trell. What you want?"

"Our world is going to hell," Kemisa said.

"Was always Hell," he replies.

Probably was for him, I thought. Moroks generally preferred warm tropical regions of planets, though he claimed to be from a dark and northern part of his world.

"An unbelievable hell," Kemisa repeated, "at least for oxygen-breathing life."

Skilled as Trell was, even he couldn't cover his momentary freeze as the expression, 'oxygen-breathing life.' His left fingers twitched momentarily. I shifted my weight, causing him to look at me. Where his earlier look had been dismissive, he now knew I was Guild. He leaned back in his chair, letting his hand slide away from the laser.

He gave an elaborate yawn, displaying yellow teeth. "Interesting thoughts, but what business do you bring?"

Kemisa took a deep breath. "Someone has been funneling weapons to the Indigenes, hand weapons mostly, but there were some missiles too."

"Bastards," he said.

Kemisa grinned mirthlessly. "Come now, Trell. You've been known to violate the interdiction on weapons to the natives."

Again the great bulk shook in a silent laugh. "I sell them guns to shoot my own ass off with?"

"For enough of a markup, you would. I might too, especially if I had a plan to relocate before things got really bad, or maybe the people supplying the weapons didn't tell their middleman that the world was going to die."

A long silence followed as the Morok thought. I divided my time between the door and the Morok.

"Tell more," he adds, but his voice is subtly changed. We had his interest, or had alarmed him or both.

"Trell, there's only one race that doesn't breathe oxygen in all of known space. I know the Ribisan's are behind you. I know they're the source of the weapons. I know you've been bringing in supplies for their operations. It could only be you. And most of all, I know why they want this planet."

This was the crisis. Trell might have been told to kill anyone who had knowledge of the operation, but his hand stayed very still on the desktop.

"Why?" he asks.

Kemisa shakes her head. "That's knowledge that is too expensive and dangerous to wave about freely."

"So?"

"I want to reach out to whoever is sending armaments to the Indigenes. To tell them that there is a less drastic way of dealing with the situation, one that will allow life and profit for all sides."

"Maybe they no care. Maybe they just prefer you dead."

I was conscious of a bead of sweat making its way down my spine.

"We aren't alone out here, Trell. You know how close I am to Rand. We practically run the southern continent now. There's a starship captain on the scene now, and I don't recommend you, or they, tangle with her.

I don't know how, but she's responsible for the annihilation of the Indigene forces within days of her landing. She seems to have a direct line to Death

"If something happens to Dassa and I … well there's only profit if I'm alive. Killing me will cause everything I've told you about to become public. That starship I mentioned, will be heading straight to the nearest Confed base."

"Who know if it will even be there?"

"Once they know what it that the Ribisan's want, whatever power is occupying that base will come running. It won't matter to the Ribisans if it is Confed or Alliance that attacks."

Kemisa was weaving a whole cloth from fragments of what she'd put together and what served her. It would frighten her to know how accurate her guesses were.

"What is in it for me?" he asked.

"A ten-thousand credit opaloid for conveying the message. Twice that, when I get a reply."

"You have?"

"I get. Don't take me for an idiot, Trell. Dassa will meet your man just outside the Territorial Defense office at 0800. They'll be out of their racks and through with breakfast by then. She'll have the opaloid in a black bag."

Again, a long silence, I didn't believe the Morok was slow. This was intimidation, but it was bouncing off Kemisa's nonchalance. "Fenwar will meet your Guilder."

Kemisa slowly reached into her pocket and pulled out a data crystal. "There's an encrypted message on there." She slid it across to the Morok, who let it lie.

"How they open?"

"The Ribisans will crack it quickly enough," I said.

He grins at me. "But you're sure that I can't, huh?"

I shrugged.

"Fenwar see you out." He pressed a button on my desk. Fenwar showed up within seconds, so much for his loading duties. His face betrayed as little as before.

Kemisa rose slowly. I came off the wall the same way.

"Until 0800," Kemisa said. She turned toward the door. I crabbed out sidewise, watching the Morok until we were safely out of the room. We followed the silent Fenwar out past the moored watercraft, and the Drisnian watching his monitors, until we reached the door. Kemisa slipped through first; I faced Fenwar and backed out. The hard-faced human stared at me all the while.

We couldn't run, but we made the best speed we could to the main street where the streetlights were comforting at least. Once there, Kemisa shuddered from her nose to the tip of her tail. I understood the feeling, though Dua express it differently.

"Back to Asada's shop," Kemisa says. "I'd rather head for Pilbara, but we have to make the opaloid drop."

"Yes. But back to Pilbara after that. We are safer closer to Aurelia."

"But you won't tell me why we're safer there?"

"Wouldn't the reason be obvious?" I said, sighing.

Kemisa gave a bitter laugh. "I suppose so. But if she suspects a thing about this…"

"Then I'm dead, and you're likely a rug for her quarters, and neither of us will have to worry about the Ribisans or the Ederi."

CHAPTER THIRTY

THE OPALOID DROP WENT SMOOTHLY. I MET FENWAR JUST outside the brick and metal barracks of the planetary constabulary. The dozen or so rangers were supposed to protect the port and the open range. During the Indigene risings, the rangers had been restricted to defending Pilbara.

I watched from alongside one of the few sizeable trees near the barracks. Two rangers were working on a flitter, with the engine compartment open. I found their presence equally reassuring and perturbing. I had from infancy been taught to avoid police of any sort.

Fenwar showed up on foot. Biltsang was so small that most people didn't use vehicles in town, unless they were moving cargo or equipment. From his nervous glances at the barracks, he was no more comfortable with the proximity of the law than I was. He waited at the corner of a general store. I thought that location iffy for my security and instead sat at the park bench, under the broadest of the three large trees.

I took a bite of the sandwich that I had brought and unscrewed the cap of my thermos to pour some cold tea. From the vantage of this small hillock, I could see well out to sea. Some small fishing vessels were making their way out past the freighter that sat in the bay. Spray broke over one arm of the natural jetty that embraced this bay. Beyond the breakwater, some large sea animal broached, its black form gone so quickly one was tempted to put it down to imagination.

After a minute, Fenwar walked over and sat at the other end of the bench. He stretched his long legs in front of him and pulled his hat down over his face, joining me in contemplation of the sea.

"Trell says we have a deal. He'll talk, try and set up a meeting."

I nodded and sipped my tea. "How soon?"

"Can't say. Where you staying? We'll get word to you."

I considered. We couldn't plausibly be away from Pilbara long, and Kemisa didn't want to stay in Biltsang now that we were on Trell's radar. "Reach us in Pilbara on Kemisa's com, but assume it will be monitored. Just advise that the cargo that she ordered is in the warehouse, and she has to come and collect it."

Fenwar snorted, "Cloak and dagger."

I shrugged. "It pays to play it safe."

"First you pay to play."

I reached in my pocket and slipped him the stone wrapped in a soft black fabric.

Fenwar pocketed it without looking. There was no need. If the stone was less than billed, there would be no contact made.

"Looks like this meeting of the expendables is over," Fenwar said, rising. "Tell your cute kitty I said hello."

I debated whether to kick him or not but decided just to continue looking out to sea as he walked off. I finished my tea and sandwich, then lingered for a while to keep in character before I set off, careful to dump my trash in a canister. No need to get ticketed for littering.

Five minutes later, and after both doubling back, and checking my trail, I met Kemisa at her flitter. She was pulled over in the parking lot of grocery store, talking to some locals she knew. I waited until she spotted me. A minute later, she'd disposed of her company and drove over on the flitter's ground wheels. I hopped in beside her.

"How did it go?" she asked.

"No issues, but Fenwar seems to have the hots for you."

"Pah! Not with someone else's sex organs."

"I told them to reach us at your home base."

"Yeah, no point staying around here in reach of Trell, in case they didn't like us making contact. It will be hard for them to do anything about us in Pilbara."

I sighed. "Pity. I enjoyed the couple of hours we had at the beach."

Kemisa smiled. "We don't have to go straight back, Kit."

"Yes?"

"There's a little cove about a half-hour away, it's private."

"Great, our suits are dry—"

She leaned over and kissed me. "Kit, we won't be wearing suits."

"Ah." The day was looking up.

The cove and Kemisa were all I could have hoped for. We splashed, played and made love in the dunes, then splashed again to get sand out of places it shouldn't be. There was no food closer then Pilbara, so we rocketed back in the flitter, had dinner at a small place Kemisa knew and headed home, tired from sun and surf.

CHAPTER THIRTY-ONE

THE CHANNEL TO THE EMERGENCY COUNSEL GOES LIVE AT 1.17AM *local time, with an alarm of disaster. I monitor this channel along with every other one of significance since the night of the great battle. The constabulary barrack down at Biltsang is reporting an immense explosion at the dockside, fire and casualties.*

I hear Malporin, likely roused from bed, trying to make sense of the confused reports.

I too am focused, remembering Kemisa and Dassa's recent trip down there. Perhaps I am overly suspicious of the Nekoan, but the coincidence concerns me. I wonder how to insert myself into the situation without making my spying so evident. I am saved by a call from Malporin.

"Hello," I answer.

"Hi, it's Mal. Sorry to wake you."

"I wasn't sleeping, couldn't drop off."

"Listen there's been a explosion down in Biltsang."

"What happened?"

"We don't know. Things are very confused down there. I want to take a look myself, see about getting relief efforts together."

"Feel like company?"

"You've read my mind. One, thing, I think we should collect Kemisa and Dassa, they were down there most recently."

Mal's voice sounds puzzled. "I don't think they learned anything sunbathing … unless you're suggesting…."

"For now, I suggest only that if our sleep gets ruined, theirs should also."

"I'll pick you up at Seachange."

I listen in on the emergency channels in Biltsang while I wait for Mal. It would be odd for me to wait out in the cold and dark so I remain in the ship until I see his GP. Then I walk out. The sky above is nearly starless due to the high dust in the atmosphere and the night is chilly. Damasia will never be a resort spot. Puffs of wind ruffle the cape I am wearing.

Mal pulls up. Despite the late hour, he looks alert and ready, something I like in a male. I slide in and he accelerates off.

I pull out my com. "They may be in bed. We should call ahead."

He nods. "We don't want to walk in on anything naughty."

I give him a mock glare.

Dassa's com does not respond. Neither does Kemisa both go to message.

"Well whether they are asleep or not," I say. "They are likely in bed. Well, no help for it."

"Kit," Kemisa whispered in my ear. "Wake up."

"What," I said muzzily.

"There's someone on the roof. No, more than one," she added, her big, cat-ears up and quivering.

I slid out of bed, grabbing the stunner I wore while off the ship, then my pants and shirt and shoes. Kemisa scrambled out of bed and did the same, then moved opened a drawer built into the bed and drew two belted pistols out. She tossed me one and I was grateful to feel the solidity of a slug-thrower in my hand. I holstered the stunner in favor of the more lethal armament.

Kemisa moved to the window that overlooked the stairs and I peered out of the highlight alongside the door. Kemisa had one way glass there, but I was careful to keep the thicker wall between me and anything outside. Neither of us could see anything. My ears were good, but I couldn't hear anything.

I looked at Kemisa, who padded over to me. "What the hell?"

She shrugged. "Maybe the answer from the Ribisans was no. Bold of them to strike us all the way up here if so."

"Keep an eye out," she said. "I'll call for help. She pulled a com out of her hastily donned jacket. "Damn."

"What?"

"We're in trouble. The signal is jammed; this is serious."

I tried mine, hoping that Maauro's magic would save the day, but mine was as dead as hers.

"Looks like we have to save ourselves," Kemisa said. She cracked the door slightly and sniffed a few times before resealing the door. "Damn it. Too many smells and too recent, I can't tell what's out there."

"What do we do?"

"We wait for the situation to change," she replied. "If they are waiting out there for us and we just run out, we're done for. If they try to break in, using flashbangs, or gas, we have a chance at least."

"And if they chuck a grenade in?"

"Then I'll be glad I did you extra hard last night."

I couldn't suppress the slightly hysterical laugh that burst out of me. "Shhhh," Kemisa said.

We returned to out watch on the outside, dreading the sight of scuttling figures in what little light the street threw.

We drive through the darkened streets, which are nearly deserted. Pilbara rolls up early, save around the Pick and Shovel, doubtless encouraged by the climate change. We head to an old part of town, which is more narrow and chaotic than the rest of the town. We park in the lot closest to Kemisa's apartment, which is in a three-story, wooden building, painted a dun color, with an exterior staircase. The Nekoan's apartment is on the third floor.

We get out of the vehicle. Mal zips his jacket with a muttered curse and an apologetic look at me. I smile in return. The lot is a short walk to

Kemisa's building, around trash containers, parked cars and a skip filled with someone's renovation work. I reach out and suddenly pull Malporin into the shadow of the skip.

"What's going on?" Malporin whispers."

"It seems we aren't the only ones who want to drop in on the love-birds," I say. While my comment contains humor, the situation does not. I detect six beings moving around and over the three story building. Worse yet, a jammer is operating. I cannot reach the pair on their comps. If I slash through the jammer, it will likely alert the stalkers to my presence.

But the worst handicap is Mal's presence. He's unarmed and with him present, I cannot use my full capabilities without revealing my artificial nature.

"I saw two people on the roof," I tell him. "I don't think they are there to replace shingles at this hour."

"I'll call the police," he says, pulling his own comp. He looks down at the comp and swears. "No damn signal."

"They must be using a jammer," I say, upset with myself that I did not consider this earlier when I couldn't reach either of them. "Listen, a jam-mer is only effective for a short distance, or they'd be setting off alarms all over. Take your comp and head toward the town, call for the police as soon as you get out of range."

"And what will you be doing?" he demands.

"Someone has to warn them, and Dassa's crew to me."

"You want me to leave you here with God knows how many cut-throats? Hell, no!"

"Mal—"

"Forget it. You run and get the police. I'll warn them. Kemisa is my friend, remember."

I keep trying to forget that, I think. "Mal, you listen. I'm a pro at this and you aren't. You follow me. Do what I say, when I say it."

He nods after a long searching stare.

We close in, silently in my case and with too much noise in his. But the stalkers are intent on Kemisa's top floor apartment. I pull Malporin deeper into a shadow. "There are six. Two on top of the building, two round back and these two near the front door."

He peers out to my annoyance. "How can you tell?"

I tap the side of my head. "Big eyes, means good night sight."

"What's the plan?"

"I have a special comp. When we get closer I think I can break through the jammer. Kemisa will be armed, right?"

"Count on it, enough for Dassa as well."

"Then we take out the two guards by the front door. I'll alert Dassa to escape down the exterior stairs and bring extra weapons for us."

He nods, his big fists knotting.

I sigh internally, then vow to myself if the fight starts to go badly, and Malporin is endangered, I will have to reveal what I am.

We creep forward. The two ahead of us, by the foot of the stairs, are humans. I focus on the two up on the roof. Both wear headgear and could be anything but Okarans, as they are too small. It occurs to me that they could have IR sensors, so I drop my external temperature to where I will not register, save on the most sensitive of instruments.

The enemy by the foot of the exterior stairs is only twenty meters away. They must have done something to the stairwell light. The only light is from a streetlight fifty meters away.

I pull out my comp and press it to my throat in subvocal mode, though it is mere theater. In an instant, I burst through the jamming and transmit my instructions to Kemisa and Dassa, remotely forcing both their comps on. "Take your weapons and attack down the exterior stairs in ten seconds. We'll take the two at the foot of the stairs, watch the roof and there are two around the back."

Mercifully both respond instantly and do not ask questions.

The jammer is fried. I spoof the various sensors the six are using, scrambling anything other than open sights. They have not yet reacted.

I grab Malporin's shoulder to get him to focus on me. I hold up ten fingers folding one down each second. He nods.

The door above bursts open. Dassa and Kemisa dive out and to either side on the landing. A reflexive shot rings out from the pair ahead of us, but misses.

I lunge forward, driving faster than a biological can move, but nowhere near my top speed. Malporin lunges too, but I leave him behind as I intend. I'll blame it on my mutation later. From my ring finger, my built-in stunner fires; set low enough to make them woozy and slow. I hit the first one, catapulting him into his companion. Both go down in a heap. I go down in a forward roll, and come up with one of their silenced carbines in my hand. The second human tries to rise and bring his weapon to bear on me. I crack the butt of my carbine on the side of his head, then spin and fire two shots at the pair on the roof, while wishing there was some sensor or camera I could invade to find out where the other two are.

My shot misses the first enemy on the roof as the silencer has altered the flight characteristics of the projectile. Armed with this knowledge, I hit the second enemy between the eyes.

Mal arrives just as the first man rises, only to meet Mal's fist driving into his midsection with the big miner's full weight behind it. He bends double and Mal's knee hits him in the face. He flies backward into the staircase, to fall, loose-limbed and unconscious, his weapon spinning into the darkness with a clatter.

All this gives me time to retarget the remaining enemy on the roof. He's popping over the roof edge, his silenced weapon flashing down rounds. Kemisa fired a shot that caused him to flinch. When he pops up again, I take him with another head shot.

Dassa fired a shot to my right. She has spotted an enemy coming around the building from that side. A Morok stumbles around the corner, but my shot is blocked by Malporin, so I must leap to one side. The Morok and I fire at the same instant. Mine takes him in the midsection. He falls, but his return shot bounces off my chest, fragments, and shreds part of my fabric cloak. Damn.

I spin, hoping that Malporin has not seen the strike, but he is on his hands and knees, looking for the weapon that fell from the man he downed. This put him to my left and at the corner of the building, just as the sixth man rounds the corner almost on top of him. Mal is below his weapon and surges upward from the ground, grappling with his enemy and forcing the arms holding the weapon up.

But the enemy is no tyro. With one hand he holds the weapon away from Malporin. The other snatches at wickedly long knife belted at his waist. I lunge forward, and leap over Malporin, swinging the carbine by its barrel like an ax, staving in the skull of my enemy, despite his light helmet. The carbine fractures in my hand from the power of the blow but, no matter, the enemy are all accounted for. There may be a wheelman nearby, but he will not engage and is probably already fleeing.

Kemisa and Dassa clatter down the stairs. The Nekoan is clutching her leg. I scan immediately and am relieved to see that the wound is a graze, the skin only cut by a vertical shot resulting in a cut of 17.89 millimeters over 4.3 centimeters. Mal is huffing from a few blows that landed on him, but is otherwise unhurt. He finally comes up with the pistol he'd been searching for. Dassa is down now and reaches an arm around Kemisa to keep her weight off the cut thigh. The three biologicals are looking in all directions over the barrels of their weapons.

I cannot completely reassure them of the lack of additional enemies without revealing the source of certainty. Aloud I say. "We only saw six, and they're all accounted for."

"Damn," Malporin said. "You see like an owl."

"I think, she's right," Kemisa added. "I only heard and smelled six."

"She's right," Dassa straightens and lowers her weapon.

"Anyone alive to be interrogated?" Mal asks, looking around.

"The one you decked is," I say. "I hit the two on the roof with headshots. I think other three are done for as well. Dassa, check them to make sure."

She eyes me, but goes over to the bodies to make a cursory examination, knowing they are already dead.

I cannot properly treat Kemisa's wound without producing medical supplies that I would have no reason to be carrying tonight. "We've got to get Kemisa to the ER."

"It's not bad," she says, shaking her mane of rough hair. "Your cape's done for. Can I get some strips for binding from it?"

I reach down and pull the long knife from the man whose skull I stove in. I quickly cut some strips from my cape, and gesture at her to sit on the low wall in front of the bushes, then kneel and bind her leg. "This is hardly sanitary."

"I don't believe that infection is my big worry," she replies, wincing as I tie off her leg wound.

Mal grabs his comp out. "Whatever you did with your comp, Aurelia, seems to have done for their jammer."

Kemisa suddenly focuses on me and we are eye to eye.

She knows, I think, returning her steady gaze.

"Mal," I say, "Call the police."

Kemisa looks down at my sadly damaged cloak. "You're fortunate, Captain Toyama," she whispers to me. "From where that bullet rent your cloak, it looks like it should have hit. Instead it seems to have broken up. As usual, you don't even have a scratch."

"God loves me," I reply.

"It must be an interesting relationship," she replies. "Unique even."

I stand and offer her a hand. She hesitates for a second and then takes my hand. I gently help her to her feet.

Mal comes over having completed his call to the local authorities. He touches her arm. "How is it?"

"Ah," she replies with a smile. "It's nothing. I'm just getting slow and old."

"That will be the day," he says with an easy smile.

"What brings you two to my door in the middle of the night?" Kemisa asks.

"There's been an explosion down in Biltsang." Mal say. "A big one, it took out much of the pier side."

Her bat ears go straight up. "What the hell?"

Dassa pauses in her examination of the bodies.

Their reactions tell me that both are surprised by the news. With a human, I might have inferred something from their body language. With these two, I am uncertain.

Kemisa starts to demand details, but Mal raises a hand.

"Aurelia's right. Kemisa, you need to get to the ER."

"I'll take her," Dassa says.

Mal nods, "We'll handle the police."

I watch as Dassa leaves, with Kemisa's arm over her shoulder, taking a lot of the Nekoan's weight. I want to question them both. It's no coincidence that the port which these two visited, and Kemisa's apartments are targets, but the knowing look in Kemisa's eyes gives me pause. Who knows where that conversation would go once it starts? And given Kemisa's wound, pulling Dassa away from her girlfriend would look very odd.

Minutes later, the police pull up in a white land cruiser. We have not moved the bodies, and the man at Mal's feet has not stirred. Three officers get out of the vehicle.

Mal grimaces. "That's three-fourths of Pilbara's police force right there."

The human leader, a tall man with a weather-beaten face comes up to us, trailed by a female Denlenn. One immediately sees the difference between her and Dassa in the eyes, which look human and the extra joints in the arms from how she rests her hand on the butt of her pistol. The third officer is a younger human male, and he heads directly for the bodies with a cool glance at us.

"Hello, Mal," *the leader says.* "You've had some trouble?"

"Six hoods tried to take out Kemisa."

A grin splits the officer's lean face. "Your pretty kitty in trouble again? That cat will be the death of you."

"It's not like that Ev," *Mal says, spreading his hands with a sidewise look at me.* "Well, at least I think it's not."

"Where is she?"

"We sent her to the ER, in the care of my crewperson, Dassa." *I answer, electing to take control of the conversation.*

"Captain Aurelia Toyama," *Mal says,* "this is Evdard Trescott, Constable, Deputy Cherval, and the fellow checking the bodies, is Arnvald Stel."

"I recognize you of course, Captain," *Trescott says, extending a hand that I take and shake briefly.* "We're all very grateful for what you and your ship have done for us. Sorry to have you dragged into a local matter."

Perhaps not so local, I think.

"What happened?" *Trescott asks.*

Mal fills in the details of the night's engagement. The Constable sends his Denlenn deputy to check the roof and the two I headshot there. She returns with confirmation, about the same time an ambulance shows up to collect the unconscious man.

The lead ambulance attendant stops to talk to Trescott. "The live one has a skull fracture and a broken jaw. He won't be talking to anyone soon, probable intracranial bleed and definite concussion. He'll be lucky to remember what species he belongs to."

Truscott grimaces. "Ok, Arnvald. Where's the meat wagon?"

"Coming. We'll have to stack them. Going to be a real pain to get the dead ones off the roof."

Trescott looks at me. "You're quite the lethal little lady. You killed the two on the roof, one of the two down here and the two who came around from the sides."

"Yes," *Mal agrees with a thoughtful, searching stare at me.*

"Dassa hit the Morok," *I reply.* "I finished him off."

"Very good shooting, Captain, especially with unfamiliar weapons, must be those big, pretty eyes."

The constable is no fool, but I blink my big pretty eyes at him. "Human mutation, big eyes for seeing well in the dark, and I am stronger than a human my size."

"I'll say," Trescott replies, hefting the bent carbine I'd stove in the skull of the knifer with. *"You'd better stay on this lady's good side Mal. She's even more dangerous than Kemisa."*

The Denlenn deputy returns. "Ev, I've run scans on all of them, none of them are in any database. They're not local, but I can't find any record of them landing on the planet either."

"What the hell?" Trescott mutters.

I look at Malporin. "I believe we may have discovered some of the mercenaries you've told me about."

Trescott scratches his head. "Well, we are going to need statements—"

"Ev," Mal says raising a hand. *"Captain Toyama and I were on our way down to Biltsang to see what happened down there. We stopped here to get help when this occurred."*

"Mal," Trescott says, *"there's a planetary constabulary barracks down there; they were defending the port during the native troubles. They can handle it."*

Mal gestures at the bodies. "Not if there are off-world mercenaries involved."

Trescott is silent for a few seconds, digesting this. "Well, I don't like it, but you're the head of the emergency council. Check in with me as soon as you get back."

"Ok Ev, I'll do it."

Trescott turns to me. "Wish I'd met you under other circumstances, Captain Toyama.

I nod. "As do I."

We take our leave quickly, heading for Mal's GP.

"We can take the council flitter," Mal says. *"It's back at the council building lot."* Then he wipes a broad hand over his face.

"Are you ok?" I ask.

"Yeah. I don't spend that much time in gunfights though. I've killed Indigenes since the Troubles. But it's not the same as seeing Confeds, especially other humans killed."

"No, it surely isn't."

"And look at you," he said. *"You're not shaken at all. Hell, your hair is barely mussed."*

"I have, I am sorry to say, done this before."

"Often enough to be used to it."

I can only nod.

"You won that fight damn near single-handed; the rest of us might as well have not been there."

"Not true," I say as we walk. "I found the assistance most useful."

We reach the GP and Mal opens the door for me. I give him a reassuring smile. He does not return my smile, but merely slides behind the controls.

We got into Kemisa's GP and I started the engine. She sat on the other side holding her leg with one hand.

She smiled thinly at the evident concern in my face. "Get moving, Kit."

I pulled out. "Don't worry. It's only ten minutes to the hospital."

"We're not going there."

"But your leg!"

"Stings, but nothing worse. Kit, we're in a world of hurt here. Aurelia knows we were in Biltsang. Even if Mal doesn't put it together, she will and come up with us. Hell, I think she already has, but didn't want to start in on us with Mal present. There's something about her she doesn't want him to know. Isn't there?"

I ignored her question. "Where are we going then?"

"Go down this street for three intersections turn right at Tanner's store. "We're heading to Bowman's, he's a handy connection to have just now."

"What are you planning?"

"There are two deadly forces on this planet, Kit. One blew up the port and the other is your boss. Both of them are pissed off at us right now, and I don't know which one scares me more."

I felt a shiver strike through me. She was right.

"You may have some immunity from one of them, but I can't count on that."

"Aurelia wouldn't—"

"What's her real name, Kit?" Kemisa asked quietly.

I closed my mouth.

"That is not a human, mutant or any other Confed species. She just wiped up six professional mercs in seconds, and I don't think it would have taken that long except that she wants to keep up the fiction she's a living being."

"She is a living being," I said dryly. "Don't doubt that anywhere she can hear it."

"You're holding out on me, Kit."

"Dammit, Kemisa, read between the lines. I've been ordered to silence about her. Or do you think I should casually disregard the instructions of someone even you're afraid of?"

She was silent for a few seconds then sighed. "Yeah. Ok. In your place, I would do the same things in the same order.

"Take the next left," she directed.

We sped on, with Kemisa calling directions in between working on her comp. She was doubtless moving money around and making contingency plans. Then she called Bowman, while pointing out the next turn to me..

"Bow, it's me. I got trouble. Open the garage door so we can drive in. Yeah, dammit now. We'll be there in a minute."

We turned on to a street of small shops, some of which showed damage, or abandonment from the Indigene rising. A few of the buildings had second floor residences and Kemisa gestured at one of these. Next to the loading dock, a garage door gaped open. I slid the GP into the dimly lit garage.

Kemisa turned to me. "Kit the neighborhood has grown unhealthy and may get worse."

I heard her implication, but the idea of casting loose of my ship in this hellhole world, with a woman I had only known for weeks seemed mad. Surely, Maauro would understand. I'd just shown initiative in developing an option. It was all her fault anyway! Her weak leadership had left me all these options. Any competent Alpha would have long ago headed me off, or anticipated these moves. If there was fault here, it was hers for being a lousy leader for our pack.

"I'll...I'll drop your car back at your place later. I should get back to the ship."

Kemisa nodded slowly. "No rush, Kit. Keep it for the day. You're apt to be busy."

I nodded, uncertainly. Many things crowded onto my tongue, with the result that nothing came out.

Kemisa leaned forward and kissed me, then slipped out of the car. A door opened, and silhouetted against a light, I saw of Bowman holding a rifle. Kemisa pushed past him, and he closed the door.

I backed out and turned the vehicle around, the garage door came down so quick it almost hit the GP's hood. I dared not be absent when Maauro returned. As I sped for Seachange, I wondered what I could get away with not telling Maauro.

We cover the distance to Biltsang quickly in the high performance flitter we'd picked up at the council building. I use the time to try and understand all that is happening. I am somewhat distracted by the scene between Kemisa and Malporin, which leads me to believe that that their relationship was both closer, and more recent, than he'd led me to believe. I had to wonder about the reason for that. But more pressing is the issue of the attack, and its circumstances.

I spot smoke rising from Biltsang's harbor for several hundred meters before an offshore wind tails it out to sea. A few seconds later, Malporin spots it too.

"Circle the port," I say. Malporin nods. We head out over the sea, in a leftward bank. I stare out of the canopy, using such sensors as I can in

the situation. There are several docks leading out into the shallow bay. The remnant of the largest one shows me the point of explosions. The blast was formidable, damaging some of the buildings on the shore, as well as the docks around it.

"What do you see?" he asks.

"The damage is exactly what I would expect from a submarine-launched torpedo, remotely detonated under the dock," I respond, unable to tell him that with my sensors, I can see the five-meter deep crater gouged into the seabed below the wreckage.

"What was there?" I ask.

"Trell Imports," he responded. "They had the biggest dock, really it was a warehouse and covered boat house."

"Tell me about Trell."

"He's someone I've had my eye on for a while. I suspect him of gun-running to the Indies, but I couldn't prove it."

"So much for a little jaunt to the seaside," I growl. "Has Kemisa had dealings with him?"

He hesitates then says, "Yes, but they were legitimate deals. He moves cargo for a lot of people. Hell, I've used him too. There's not a lot of options in Biltsang."

I consider this. "Let's land."

We finish our circle and come down by an official looking building. It says planetary constabulary and looks like it would house a squad or so of regulars. A small military hovercar, in similar markings to what I saw at the capitol space port, is parked near it. The lot for regular vehicles on the other side is full, and I see officers and civilians milling about. An officer comes out from the building, as we land in front. He waits until the dust settles from the flitter's VTOL engine before walking up. We both hop out of the small machine.

"You're Malporin Rand?" the officer says, offering his hand.

Mal nods.

"I got the message you were coming. I'm Lt. Mayala, in charge of the station."

Mal gestures to me. "This is Captain Aurelia Toyama off the SS Seachange."

The young officer gives me a grin. "Wow. I heard you were a looker, but there never seem to be any decent pictures of you. Not that they would have done you justice."

I raise an eyebrow. "You sound like you would like to take me to into custody."

He gives a chuckle to Mal's evident annoyance, then turns serious. "We're still picking up the pieces down here, Mr. Rand. Between casualties, fire-fighting and evidence gathering we've been up to our eyeballs."

"How bad?"

He shrugs. "*The damage you can see. Right now we have seven confirmed deaths and four missing. Not too many injuries since the explosion occurred in the early morning. Most of the people who were hurt, were injured in fighting the fires. Not much hope regarding the four missing either.*"

"*Damn,*" Malporin swore, "*eleven dead.*"

"*Well,*" Malaya says, after a glance around to make sure no one was near, "*nine of the dead and missing are Trell and his company. They must have been having a meeting. I'm new here, but my sergeant tells me that was most of the local criminal element.*"

"*But not all criminals?*" I ask.

"*No. There was a small fishing smack going out, a local couple. Blast got them and their boat.*"

"*What do you think it was?*" I ask. Malporin gives me a puzzled look. I return a tiny shake of my head to keep him quiet.

"*Word is that Trell was suspected of selling armaments and smuggling other contraband. We figure he brought in something unstable, had all his people in to work on some big deal involving it, when it blew him and his crew to hell.*"

"*Yes,*" I reply, "*a very plausible explanation. I am sure you are correct. I gather there was no warning, nothing unusual or suspicious beforehand?*"

"*Not that we know of. Like I said, it was early hours and we only had two officers on patrol. They were on the landside, watching out for Indies. As the freighter had pulled out the night before, there was no one down dockside. Except Trell and his buddies.*"

"*Thank you.*"

I leave Malporin to speak with the officer, who takes him to the town manager. They will discuss efforts at relief from Pilbara and rebuilding. I walk to the water's edge. To an observer, it will appear as though I have slipped off my shoes and dipped my feet in the water's edge. In fact, I merely generated a skin of material for fake shoes. From my toes, sensors extend and I sample what I can, getting sonar and other scans of the area. When I see Malporin return, I throw my "shoes" back on, push any sand out of the material and am again whole.

"*Do you want to look around more?*" he asks.

"*No. It is clear to me what happened. A submarine was used. It waited until the freighter left the area before firing a torpedo. Whether that was from fear of the freighter's instruments detecting it in these shallows, or some concern about sinking the freighter, I cannot tell. Still, it is convenient that the authorities blame Trell for the explosion. It's true in a way. Trell became a liability or a threat to his Ribisan employers and they eliminated him.*"

"*A Ribisan sub or more mercenaries?*" he asks.

"I suspect the Ribisans themselves. Their expertise at dealing with liquids under pressure would make them excellent submariners. Worse for us though. A mercenary sub would likely be an ad hoc affair, a conversion from something commercial. A high-tech Ribisan vessel will likely be impossible to detect in open ocean by comparison."

He nods. "Let's head back to Pilbara. I promised the town manager I would get an aid convoy together quickly.

"Yes. Let us return. I have questions to put to Kemisa and Dassa."

From the worried look on Malporin's face, I believe he has divined my thought. If what I begin to suspect has happened, I may end up with a new rug for my cabin, made of either a slippery Nekoan, a treacherous Dua, or both.

I found myself pacing the decks of the Seachange, waiting for … something. Some word from Maauro, some development, but the com remained obstinately, even accusingly silent for voice and text. I didn't dare call her. While the ship's AI would route my call, who knew the outer limits of the Ribisan's technology? They were the most advanced species known.

The true reason was simpler, I was afraid to call Maauro, afraid she knew, afraid she would drill through any evasion I could make.

Worse still, there was no word from Kemisa. With her at my side, I might at least find the courage to face Maauro.

Finally, I couldn't stand it any longer. I pulled my com out and called Kemisa. The com chimed one and then flickered with incoming text. "Kit, come to my apartment, check the bed." I looked at it dismayed. It read like a flirtation but the dissociative feeling between my hearts said otherwise. I ran down to the garage and hopped in Kemisa's car as soon as the AI could roll back the hatch.

I floored the car's throttle and made my frantic way back to the scene of last night's ambush. The yellow police tape had already been violated at the door of Kemisa's apartment. I pushed in to check.

"Kemisa," I called, knowing that there would be no return call.

I found a letter resting on the bed we shared. The envelope was large and my name prominently written on it. With a numb feeling I picked it up and opened it. One read handwritten notes so rarely, I had to concentrate to read Kemisa's bold scrawl.

Dear Kit

Sorry it has come to this. I do not share your confidence in Aurelia's forbearance and forgiveness, at least where I am concerned. You see I know who and what she really is. That's quite a power you hooked up with. Frankly I thought Maauro the android was a myth, a tall tale spread by spacers. Now, I know otherwise. Maybe I can trade my sudden flight for the fact that you kept that a secret from me. I've kept this knowledge to myself, not even telling Mal. The one thing I know from the stories about your Maauro is that she carries a grudge, so I am not giving her any reason to pursue me.

I have lived as long as I have, by knowing when to cut my losses and run. Now is that time. The Ribisans have clearly decided to eliminate anyone that can connect them with the world-wrecking. Not that this will help them with Maauro here. Still, if I stay I will get eliminated; my part is too well known.

I hope your choice of staying works out for you. I've booked passage on the Galaxy Express; the ship leaving soonest. I've used every favor I'm owed to get out of Pilbara quietly, by air, so by the time you read this I will be gone. If you change your mind, find Bowman, he can help you get out, but it will cost.

Galaxy Express will stop at the Sala Colony which is where I plan to start over. Find me there, is you want to. I will be glad to see you and we can pick up where we left off. If not, I enjoyed our time together.

Stay alive, Kit. See you out in the galaxy

Kemisa

I drop the letter back on the bed and look at the deserted room, fancying I can still smell her scent. I know she would have left nothing very valuable, but she would also be traveling light and fast. On the sink counter I find an ornate comb that I remember her using on her thick, luxurious hair. I pick it up and wrap it in the letter, wondering why even as I do it.

Kemisa had fled with little concern for me, but would I have done any differently? I'm Dua and self-interest is in my biology. But I still have to beat back the sting of tears. I was torn between two very different alignments in Kemisa and Maauro. Unwilling to commit to either, I'd fallen into the gap between them, like a character in a classic play. Now I had no one.

I checked the time. *Galaxy Express* would lift in an hour. There was no way to reach her even if I could have persuaded Maauro to take me in *Seachange.*

I could call her. The satellite link was working for the moment. But I could not think of a single thing to say that would not be pathetic, and my last shreds of pride would not allow me to be pathetic in Kemisa's eyes.

No, I'd had my first love, or maybe she'd had me. That was a closed book now. I turned my back on the first bed I'd ever made love in, but still took the comb and letter with me.

When I returned to Seachange, Maauro was standing at the top of the gantry. I stood frozen, staring up at her.

"The galley, Dua, and now."

I followed her in and wondered if I would live to step out of her ship again. We stood as far apart as it would allow.

"Biltsang was struck by a sub launched torpedo that destroyed Trell and his operation."

"I see."

"There were eleven lives lost. Two of them seem to have been civilians; there were additional injuries and a great deal of property damage."

Sweat rilled down my back.

"You know something about this," she said, her voice, flat and mechanical.

My breath came fast and shallow. I slowed it, no weapon or evasion could save me now. I had only my wits.

"Yes."

"Your life might depend on what you say next."

"Then I am probably dead. Your plan to deal with the Ederi over the Ribisan's struck me as unwise. We sought to open a separate channel. Kemisa believed Trell was involved. She was right. He was our pipeline to the Ribisans."

"Stupid girl, I know Ribisans. They are untrustworthy, too different for an understanding."

"Don't you see?" I said desperate to pierce her naiveté. "Everyone is untrustworthy. There is no such thing as trust, self-interest is all there is. Find the self-interest and you can build an arrangement that will bear weight."

"And what was your self-interest, Dassa?"

"I feared becoming a bargaining chip between you and the Ederi."

She cocked her head. "I promised I would protect you."

"You seem much more concerned with protecting Nipkin and her world, then me. What would I matter on such a scale anyway?"

Her lips drew tight. "Do not judge me as if I was a Dua. I keep my word."

"You've repeatedly shown me that I am less in your eyes then this child—"

"Who even as we speak, is lifting off this world for Evenfall and a new and safer life," she grated.

Dismay filled me. I hadn't known this. "Well then, she will have Kemisa for company. She finally figured out what you are, and between you and the Ribisans, she's decided to flee Damasia. Which one of you she fears more, is an open question."

"She left you behind."

"Say rather that she did not wait for me. She took the sensible course and fled at best speed. She'll be happy if I catch up."

"You should have done that, rather than face me now."

"It seemed to me that both paths were equally perilous, stay or go."

"What did you think that you still had here? My protection, my good will?"

I looked at the floor.

"Do you!" Maauro raged, and I stepped back. "I gave you my word and you treated it and my friendship as if they were nothing!" Her eyes went black from lid-to-lid. Before I could move she's seized me by arm and throat.

"And so," she growled, her voice metallic and sexless, "you've finally outstripped your grandfather, achieving something that he never dared. You've succeeded at betraying me."

Her hand tightened. *Gods,* I thought, *she's going to crush my throat. Please let this be quick. She's not my kind, she doesn't torture for fun; she just kills.*

I stared transfixed at the white face and black eyes, now skull-like in tunnel of my vision. My breath hissed in my throat, and my arm was growing numb, but I was afraid that if I struggled, she might tear my arm off.

Suddenly, she flung me away from her, to fetch up against the metal cabinets with force enough to stun. I fell to the floor, half-conscious, but aware of a cut on my shoulder, bleeding from striking a metal edge. I gasped air down my abused throat.

"Why?" Maauro demanded, walking over to stand over me. I raised my good arm to ward her off, but she did not strike again. "Why would you do this?"

"You were...so...erratic," I managed. "We'd made our money, but you keep endangering us more and more by staying, by finding greater and more powerful enemies to contest. I wondered if you'd gone mad."

"Or were you just a coward, thinking only of yourself," she spat back, "unwilling to risk yourself for others?"

"Of course," I said, before I could stop myself. "I'm not mad. I might be expended by others. One expects that, but to sacrifice myself for others...?"

She stepped back, a stunned expression on the perfect face. We stood frozen, staring at each other across a gap of incomprehension that widened every second.

Her eyes faded out from black, to be replaced by a troubled green. "Get out of my sight. I'll decide what to do about you later."

I stagger to my feet and move toward the doorway, not running, never running in the presence of a predator. Even as I did, I was aware that something unprecedented had just happened. Decision and action had always been instant for Maauro, at least in my experience of her. Apparently I'd confounded her, but I had no idea what action she'd take when she did decide.

Again, I considered racing for the airlock, but what if it did not open? By fleeing I'd compound my problem with her, and certainly if I removed myself, I'll never be allowed back. She saw my actions as more than a beta testing her leader's strength, as if the dispute was personal. For her it unmade our alignment. I should have realized.

Another thought crowded in. What if I went to the airlock and it did open? With my alignment gone, I'd be alone on a world unfriendly to my kind at best, and now with deadly factions stirred to awareness of my existence. The Ribisans knew of me, and if the Ederi didn't yet, could it be long before they did?

Even Malporin and the settler's graces to me were due mostly to Maauro. Whatever merit I'd gained by fighting for Pilbara and Tillet would not balance with the casualties and damage done in the seaport. Maauro might even point Malporin in my direction. Without Kemisa, I couldn't handle his enmity too.

Schadenteer shudders through me: alone, unaligned and on an alien world without the Guild to appeal to. This was a nightmare. I found myself at the door to my cabin. I entered, then collapsed on my bunk, drawing my knees up and wrapping my arms around them to stop my shivering.

I'm staying, I finally decided. Better to hope for forgiveness and endurable punishment than to chance a hostile world. She's already foregone killing me out of hand. Perhaps I can find some service to her that will redeem this "betrayal."

Still, if it is to be stranding, then better to face that prospect sooner. I clean my cut and awkwardly place wound tab over it. Then I carefully, but quickly, head for the galley. Once there, I have the ship's AI make me a month's worth of emergency rations and a pack for them. The tiny brown boxes will keep starvation at bay if I am to be flung off the ship. I head back to my room and pack my few belonging and such credits and specie as I have gathered, preparing as best as I can for what may come. After that, there is little to do but wait and watch the doorway.

I seethe on the bridge of my ship. That fool. That treacherous, no good Dua! How dare she upset my plan! She's tipped our hand to the Ribisans, and the extent of the disaster is unknowable. They are now aware that we know of their actions, and worse, the identities, if not the capabilities of their enemies. They've eliminated their agents down at the Biltsang, in the process causing fatalities and casualties among civilians. We've parried their first strike against Dassa and Kemisa with no loss, but how will they followup?

I bring all Seachange's sensors on line and prime the communications laser. I segment some of my CPU to be instantly responsive to any incoming aircraft, or missile, and ready both the laser and a blast of my most virulent computer viruses in case anything is detected. I turn the rest of my attention on countermeasures. What can we do now that the enemy is warned?

The answer is immediate. I must accelerate my plans and reach the Ederi before the Ribisan's followup. It may be that they are satisfied with removing the links to them. I am grateful that what media attention there has been in regard to Pilbara and Tillet has been minimal. While I am mentioned, it is unlikely these Ribisans will connect Aurelia Toyama with my identity of Estrella Lostly from over a century ago. Still, if any people remember me, it would be them.

Yet, they will know that Dassa came from Seachange. It's time to relocate.

I run down, leap out the airlock and into the Mule, racing over to Malporin's office. People are running about, reacting to the firefight here and the explosion at Biltsang. I find him in the main office, catch his attention and signal for him to slip away.

He meets me in a coatroom. I start to fill him in.

"Damn," he replies. "Kemisa never went to the infirmary—"

I wave a hand. "Disregard her. She has fled the planet on an outgoing freighter, cutting her losses."

Disappointment flits across his face. "Well, I can't say that doesn't sound like her." His face hardens. "Where is Dassa?"

"Confined to quarters," I say. "By rights I should have her in chains. Those two idiots have traded our advantage of stealth and surprise and gotten a bunch of people killed to boot."

He raises a hand. "I know, but it wasn't what they intended."

"Be damned to their intentions," I reply, stamping my foot. "Kemisa was looking for an advantage and that Dua bitch sold me out to her."

Malporin stares at me in surprise.

I control myself after the outburst. "We are going to have to accelerate the plan. I'm going to lift off from the port. Once in space, I'll broadcast the signal to the Ederi for a meeting on the dark side of the moon."

"I'll come with you," he says standing.

I place a hand against his chest. "You cannot. If this fails and we are destroyed, you're the only person left who knows what is going on and can try to do something about it."

He wants to argue but my logic is inescapable. "Dammit, I don't even know what's to happen. Is that volcano going to blast the island in to the sea today, tomorrow or ten years from now?"

I nod. "I will do an analysis when and as I can, using special equipment I have aboard. We must know more. But first we must buy time and only I can do that for you."

He steps forward and I realize what he is going to do. For the first time since I have been biological, I freeze in indecision. Malporin's arms encircle me and his lips meet mine. I feel youth, passion, and it is strong and compelling, intoxicating even. I do not slap him, but neither do I kiss him back, remaining balanced on a knife edge between past and present. As we separate, it occurs to me that Mal is in love with an edited version of me. He does not know the whole truth.

So, I only look down and leave my hand resting against his chest for a few seconds.

"Come back safe," he manages.

I reach up and touch his cheek. "I will."

Then I turn quickly and head for the door and my vehicle. As I slide behind the wheel, I am looking for something to distract me from the confusion of being alive. Mal has said he needs more information on what is to come. He is correct. I will divert as much of my CPU to the full analysis of the planet-wrecking as I can. Some of the work I have done before is relevant, but this will still be an immense program to run, analyzing almost every aspect of a planetary ecology and with many variables, at a time I must do other complicated things. Well, at least it will limit the amount of time I can spend thinking about Malporin.

As I start out, I begin segmenting my CPU and diverting resources.

CHAPTER THIRTY-TWO

SEACHANGE THUNDERS INTO THE HEAVENS WITH ME AS something between a prisoner and a refugee. Maauro had not restricted my movements, not that she would really need to do so. The ship's omnipresent AI knew where I was every instant, and thus so did she. I did not test the locations where a reaction might be triggered, the bridge, armory or engineering spaces. I spent most of the time in my cabin with short forays to the galley. I knew I should approach Maauro, beg forgiveness, promise anything, but the remembrance of her terrible eyes and the awful power of her hands on me, weakened my resolve every time I started toward her cabin.

My only hope lay in the fact that I was still aboard this ship, thin hope given that we were bound to see the Ederi, but all I had.

Either I have some value to her or not, I finally thought, steeling myself. *It's time to find out.* Before fear could stop me again, I forced myself up the levels to the bridge. I was almost shocked when the hatchway opened. Maauro stood in the center between the two flight seats, staring at the stars ahead. She turned slowly. Her eyes were their usual soft green, but her face was devoid of expression.

"I did not summon you." Her voice matched her face, neutral, betraying nothing.

"No," I replied. "But if I am to be of any use to you, perhaps you can brief me. Unless my role is to merely stand in the open until they incinerate me. A fate you doubtless feel I deserve."

She did not respond for a few seconds then, "We will land in three hours. They cannot have preceded us here, given that I did not set a location for the meeting until four hours ago. The signal degradation on their reply, tells me they were not in lunar orbit. I have not decided what I need you for."

"The only issue unresolved is how badly the Ederi need these x-stones," I said, casting around for something, anything, I could contribute. I had to find some way out of this dungeon, or I was surely doomed.

Maauro shrugs. "The commercial and military uses are obvious, albeit in the future. The problem will be, getting them to realize that this future profit is worth their current intervention."

"Is that in fact the case?" I wonder aloud.

"What are you saying?" she asks, for the first time a hint of animation moves in the perfect, white face.

"What if the Ederi not only need the stones, but need them now? What if their presence here isn't totally by chance?"

"Tell me more," she says. "I am not following your reasoning."

"There is little reason in what I am saying, only intuition. The Ederi tech is superior to Confed, allowing a relatively small fleet to evade and attack, despite the presence of the far larger Confed forces. But this advantage is chiefly in one area, the light curtain. You said yourself that a light curtain of such effectiveness would task even you."

She nodded. "I would have to devote so much of my processing and storage ability as to effectively consume almost all my resources."

"Yet, their general level of technology is not as uniformly advanced as is this light curtain," I said, excitement building in me. Perhaps, as the old saying goes, desperation is the mother of invention.

"True. I had noted the oddity as well, but have no explanation for it."

"Perhaps someone gave them light curtain technology, and they lack the resources to make it themselves, or to design and create the nano-meter processers that ultra computers like you, have. Since they cannot make such processers, they too would need to find the natural material for them!"

She simply stares at me. "Continue. Your use of supposition is fascinating."

"I have been trying to think of anything that I could offer to be of value to you. Non-linear thinking is what I have, and unlike the others, I know enough of the overall picture to make guesses the others could not imagine. The Ederi may have heard a rumor about the stones, or found one. But I am thinking that, instead of a speculation about the some improved future, you are talking about a military supply of the highest present importance. For all we know, the light curtain might well burn out chips of even this order, given how much power must be run through those systems.

"Think of it. You said the light curtain would task you to where you could do little else. Yet, their ships operate. They must have something like these stones to support computers and AI's that, at least in this one area, exceed even your own capabilities."

"And so few things do," she replied. "Yet, why only in one area, the light curtain, why not weapons, sensors, intruder and defense software?"

"*Gods,*" I thought, "*did she just joke with me? Might there be a chance to save myself?*"

Aloud I said. "That is why I wonder if this technology is not originally theirs, but something they found or were given. Now that they know it is possible, perhaps they are trying to find means of expanding the light curtain technology. To do that, they would need their own source of stones, independent of whoever gifted them this technology and aimed them at the Guild."

"Why am I listening to this?" Maauro said, as if to herself. "You've woven this out of spider webs and dreams."

"Fault my scenario," I challenged, doubling down. "The Ederi are here, where they have no reason to be. They were damaged on emergence, and yet they have stayed. Doesn't that indicate a high priority mission? It's not you, it's not me, or opaloids, or wrecking a planet's ecology. What else could it be?"

Maauro shook her head and her glossy black hair shimmered. "There are holes in that which I could pilot *Seachange* through sidewise. Still...."

"It's intuition, I know," I added. "It's all I can offer you."

I barely saw her move, but she was next to me before I could draw a breath. I froze in place. Her face only inches from my own.

"That may be true," she said, in a mild voice, incongruous with the frozen tableau of our bodies, "would that it came in a package I could trust."

No words of mine could reassure her across the gulf of what had failed between us, or calm the flame of her anger. Even if I tried to explain my actions, she was not psychologically constructed to see them as I did. A master of my own species would have relegated my failed attempt to history by now with a painful, even humiliating punishment, or with death, if the attempt had come close to unseating their alpha status, but they would have understood why it had happened. They might even expect it, to keep them sharp.

With Maauro I was frozen in time, caught at the moment of my attempting to seize status. I could apologize, human-fashion, but she knew enough about my people to know that these would be empty words, yet not enough to know how to move forward.

Stupid, I think to myself. *She knows all there is to know about my people from the databases. This isn't a matter of knowing. It's a matter of feeling, and right now her feelings are the human ones of this thing called trust and friendship.*

"Would it help if you beat me?" I asked.

Surprise flits across her face, and she actually steps back. For an instant, I think I see something like embarrassment. Then it is gone. She again stares at me cold-eyed. "You may yet be of some limited use to me. I will grant that this intuition of yours is interesting."

I opt for silence and merely nod.

She looks away. "Your intuition hangs together. If it survives contact with our enemy, it may provide me with the leverage I need to induce them to cooperate with us."

"You need only tell me what you wish me to do."

"For now, return to your cabin. You have given me things to think about. I wish to do so alone."

"Yes, Captain," I say, not daring the intimacy of her true name. I back away from her, not from fear she'll attack, but as a gesture of the respect she clearly feels I have not shown before. One never turns one's back on the truly dangerous...

CHAPTER THIRTY-THREE

LAND SEACHANGE ON DARK SIDE OF THE MOON, BETTER TO CONCEAL
this contact from prying eyes, Ribisan, Damasian or other. A slit valley
suits my purpose, and I drop the ship into this rift. It would force the
enemy into a narrow space above us to make a direct attack, making any
counterattack by me easier. To further safeguard us, I take my armspac
and climb out of the valley out to the surface of the moon. There, I conceal
it on a pivoting carrier I have made. The carrier also has a sensor
specifically to detect occlusions caused by the light curtain. The Ederi
have been told to use a shuttle to land. My armspac is more than sufficient
to destroy the shuttle; it could even do significant damage to a small ship.
Beyond this, we can only rely on the Seachange's amped up laser and the
plague of tailored virus I can release. I am confident of my preparations
and return to the ship.

Hours pass. I am conscious of Dassa huddled in her cabin, amid her
little pile of possessions.

Like a child getting ready to run away from home.

I start. From where did that thought come from?

No, I thought, taking issue with my inner voice for the first time. I
trusted her and she betrayed me. People died at that port. Some were
criminals, some may not have been. I cannot know.

The inner voice is silent, but for the first time I draw a sense of disappointment. We are having a fight.

A signal impinges on my consciousness; I am grateful for the distraction. An Ederi vessel approaches. Its light curtain is up, but my special-
ly-designed sensor acquires a passive sensor lock. I will await their contact, no point in letting them know I can see their ship. The vessel is larger
than Seachange, to call it a mere scoutship is inaccurate, yet it does not
have the look of a warship from what I can make of its silhouette. I think
it more some form of tender of smaller craft. Even as I look, a small vessel
detaches itself, presumably the shuttle, though it is too far to tell by
occlusion.

"Dassa," I voice internally through the ship's speakers. "The Ederi
come. Go to the armory, draw a stunner and slug-thrower, load out with
squash-heads and meet me at the main cargo deck. Our company should
hail us in twenty minutes and thirty-three seconds and land an hour
after that."

My time proves accurate, though the landing is delayed as they make
a pass to inspect us in our foxhole. Communications are text only, but
we set up the details for them to land above the valley and for one Ederi
to make his way down by jetpack to our cargo hatch.

Dassa and I wait silently in the ship until I see the jetbelted figure lift off from the dull-black shuttle and descend into the valley.

"Go to the special cargo hold and listen in from there," I tell Dassa. With an uncertain look at me, she leaves.

The Ederi lands near us and removes his jetbelt, which sits upright on its frame. It slowly walks toward our ship, both hands held up and out. I send down the small exterior elevator, which Dassa and I used on Damasia. The alien hesitates, then boards it and is whisked up to the cargo deck personnel airlock.

The Ederi stands on the other side of the airlock. A sidearm hangs on the outside of its suit. I scan through his suit with 99.431 confidence and detect no other weapon, dangerous tech or explosives. I cycle the airlock and the Ederi steps in. Moments later the inner door opens. My visitor walks in to stare cold-eyed at me, his hand not far from the weapon but the flap is down on it. A fast draw would be impossible. I face him with a laser riding on my hip, though that is for show. At this range, I need nothing not built into me.

Slowly, he removes his helmet, and sniffs the air with the caution of a veteran spacer. His mouth moves, but no sound comes out, he is sub-vocalizing for his translator. "So you are the captain?"

There is none of the pidgin standard the scout crew used in interrogating Dassa. "I am."

"You are the one who destroyed our landing craft on Evenfall?"

"I did."

"Why?"

"You violated the sanctity of my home and attacked a guest under my protection."

"We hunted a Guild criminal, a courier, who carried information of interest."

"No one hunts anything within the walls of my home."

He nods, perhaps a human gesture he has studied. "You are the AI, self-named as Maauro, deadly enemy to the Guild that we too, do battle with."

I cock my head. "I did battle with the Guild when it assailed me, or mine, or otherwise offended me, usually by proximity. Otherwise, they and their doings are of no interest to me."

He stares, at if I have confused him. "The previous team," he finally says, "did not know of your continued existence, or they would never have engaged you. We do not desire your enmity. Your home would have been respected had we but known."

"Which raises the question," I say, "of how you know now. How is it that news of an encounter on Evenfall has reached a scoutship here?"

"Luck cannot be discounted in the affairs of living beings. Yet, it does not do to over rely on it either. Our ship transited through Evenfall and learned the fate of the landing ship from its carrier. An investigation was *launched. One consistency we have noted about the species of your Confederacy, is the willingness to trade information and access, for wealth. Rarely, do we find it difficult to obtain confidential agents.*

"Though you covered your tracks well, your companion was less successful. Contacts of hers yielded the name Travers and a connection to a Comet-class exploring vessel. We did not believe our team succumbed to an elderly widow. With our abilities, which in some respects rival your own, the truth was discovered."

"You have not begun to see the outer limits of my own abilities," I respond.

"You are too logical a being to indulge in over-confidence. Now that we know what you are, we will not be taken so easily again. But let us put this talk of enmity aside. We do not threaten your Confederacy, nor do we threaten you."

"You destroy the Guild with military efficiency," I say, "and with the intelligence assets of having penetrated the innermost counsel's of the Guild."

The alien's bland face gives the impression of smiling. "Something even you, for all your advanced technology, did not succeed in doing for all the impressive destruction you wrought."

I shrug. "Nor did I try. My mission was to deter the Guild, not destroy it."

"Well then, it seems we are formidable parties, well met."

"Well met indeed," I toss back.

"But why do we meet?" the Ederi asks.

"Before we proceed to that discussion, there is the matter of the courier to be dealt with."

"We know her as Dassa Falkayan" he says," she carries a crystal we want."

"She is aligned now only to me. Unless I choose to reject her, she is no longer of the Guild."

"Once Guild, always Guild," the Ederi quoted. "This is their own saying."

"Aphorisms," I grit, "will not be useful."

"We have a mission," the Ederi says, raising its hands in an almost supplicant gesture, "a sacred mission to rid known space of this scourge of intelligent life, this blight on civilization. The Guild stretches back through time, predating most of the civilized societies now in existence. How much has been blighted by this cancer, eating at the heart of all that sapient life tries to build? Ancient as you are, do even you know?"

I shake my head. "My Creators had their criminals, like any other species, but the Guild was unknown to them."

"Blessed Creators then."

"Your mission, how did it arise? What offense did the Guild give a race that none of us even knew existed?"

The hands come up further, but now the gesture is one of warding. "This I cannot and will not speak of, to one who is not of the Ederi."

I consider this for a few seconds. "Relent in this matter to the extent of the girl and her property. It will be to your interest."

"We will judge that for ourselves, but do you not see how our mission is of the highest priority? Do we not act for the good of all species?"

"What I do not see," I answer, "is how one girl's life can delay, or derail, such a mission."

"If a deadly disease is to be extinguished, it must be destroyed in its entirety,"

"Absurd," I scoff. "Even if the present Guild could be destroyed, it will merely reincarnate in some other form, under some other name perhaps. The criminality that is part of biological life is not something you can remedy with ground assaults or orbital attacks. It is innate in its nature."

"This," he said, "may be a matter for angels then. Perhaps we cannot transcend our natures, but for any to have a chance to glimpse the true path, first they must be free of the grip of devils."

I am troubled by his manner. Religious fanatics are the most invulnerable to reason and logic.

I cross my arms and stare at him, waiting.

"Yet," he continues, after a few seconds, "we are not ourselves angels and must work with the tools that are provided. The Great Cause is never to be impeded and goes forward like the coming of the tide. Yet, perhaps it is not necessary that the ocean swallow every part of the beach so quickly."

"Just so," I concur, encouraged by the unexpected display of pragmatism.

"But for the tide to alter," he says, waving one hand, "is no small matter. There must be a compelling reason."

"The reason," I reply, "is my enmity. But beyond that, there might be recompense for the tide's... forbearance."

"Your enmity is not casually courted. We know that Voit-Veru came within a hairsbreadth of having a colony drowned by you. Still, the recompense might need to be substantial."

"Your campaign within the Confederacy has only been possible due to your light curtain. Otherwise, even in the state it is in, you would be brought to battle far more often than you have. No matter how you are organized and even with the advantage that the location of your world, or worlds, is unknown, you cannot match the war-fighting potential of so many species."

He shrugs this time, looking amused, as if he has just copied the gesture from me. "So obvious an analysis of strategy that I need not confirm or deny it."

"One believes," I say, turning and walking slowly to the nearby table. Once there, I open a metal workbox and extract one of the cadaver

crystals I'd removed from the Ribisan Struldbrugs, "that your technology incorporates data crystals that you have only recently obtained. These are of a new and different technology that allows processing at speeds vastly in excess of their predecessors.

"Perhaps even," I continue, "a stone such as this." I casually toss him the refined crystal. He snatches it out of the air as if his life depends on it. His attention on it is so rapt, that he doesn't notice me move next to him. He freezes when he does. I merely smile.

"This crystal is made from a stone, not uncommon on the world below. Perhaps you even know or suspect this already, hence your presence. I do not know the exact processes by which the base material is made into these crystals, but that will be your issue."

He looks at me intently. "I must return to my ship to show this to my engineers. There must be tests run—"

"You are at liberty to do so."

"How is it that you came by this?"

"You will learn more when you return, prepared to deal."

"This then is the recompense you mentioned?"

"It is but it will not be freely given. Another force seeks these rare materials."

He starts to speak, but I wave it off. "Return when you are persuaded of the stone's authenticity and are prepared to come to terms."

"I am only the captain of a small ship."

"Then it may be that you need summon one who can make agreements."

"For whom do you speak?"

"Only myself."

"No government?"

"I do not operate against the Confederacy, if it even still exists in the form I once served it, but neither do I serve it. Now, I serve only myself."

Even across the gulf of species I sense his skepticism. That too might serve if he believes my connection to the Confederate military is still viable. The alien turns to the airlock, which I cause to cycle open as he dons his helmet. I watch him leave; making certain he leaves nothing dangerous behind. He picks up his jetpack and rockets out of the deep crevasse.

I signal Dassa. "You may enter."

The door slides out of the way and she stands there. Her face is calm, set in its usual impassive mode. It's a face used to bad news.

No, I say to myself, do not sympathize. She betrayed me. She is not my friend.

"What did you observe?" I ask, mostly to fill the uncomfortable silence.

"He is intrigued, seeing gain. In his eagerness to confirm the stone's qualities, he confirms that it is a vital military resource. The question becomes, having acquired knowledge of it, does he act to bargain, or to *destroy us and move independently of you. How much does his desire to kill me, outweigh the acquiring of this resource?"*

"You're not that important," I say, and even as I do, I recognize it as childish and spiteful.

"I agree," she replies readily, which makes me feel even worse.

"But we both know that you carry something of greater significance with you. "Yet, I notice that you do not have it on you."

"Your scan is accurate," she says calmly. "I left it on Damasia in a secure location before I returned to the ship."

"Did you give it to Kemisa?"

She cocks her head at me. "Why would I do that?"

"A last loyalty to the Guild?"

Again the puzzled look, we are communicating even less than usual.

"Say rather, a last act of defiance to my fate and my enemies. We Dua have a saying, "give them no pleasure from your pain."

I nod, for lack of anything better. It seems Dassa is already singing her death song and now simply awaits the end.

Why, I thought, am I finding it hard to remain angry with this Guild vixen?

Aloud I say, "There will be time for tea before he returns." I walk past her and perhaps heartened by my indirect invitation, she follows.

"Let us hope that he does not decide to burst us open while we are enjoying our drinks."

I sigh. "I am, as always, at every control and device on this starship. Beyond that, I watch through the sensors and weapons I planted on the heights above us. They will give us sufficient warning for me to launch physical and viral attacks."

"Nice to know."

"But I do not believe that they will react as your Ribisan prospect did. Ribisan's are ethical cowards, valuing self over all other values."

"Sounds eminently sensible to me," she mutters.

I ignore the comment. "These Struldbrugs can only be more so, near the end of their lives and desperate to live. Their psychology is so different. As one once told me, all other species build the future for their offspring to inherit. Ribisan's use their children for spare parts."

"Yet, what do we know of the Ederi?"

"As yet, little. They seek to create a better future, rid of the Guild, which certainly implies their psychology is similar to ours in that respect. Still, is it not odd that the Ederi can be whipped to such a fever pitch by an organization that, however mendacious it is, cannot have struck at them directly."

"Their hatred of us," Dassa says, "is just that, hatred, pure and undiluted. A Dua would recognize it."

I raise an eyebrow as we enter the galley. "Their zeal appears religious in nature." I'd signaled the AI, and my favorite tea was steaming *gently in my usual delicate cup. I could have done the same for Dassa, but chose not to, again childish spite. I am surprised at myself and embarrassed. She makes herself a cup and waits for me to gesture at her to sit, which I do.*

We sit quietly.

Dassa grounds her cup with a clatter. "I must know. It is at least fair for me to know. Will you give me to them?"

I find the temptation to delay my response disgraces me. What would my husband think if he knew of the sewage in my brain just now?

"No. You will remain under my protection for now...nor will I trade you to the Ederi in the future. You and I have not resolved anything, but I think it best we postpone this showdown until the present crisis is resolved. It will either give us time to do so, or if goes badly, render the matter academic."

She nods carefully.

"Nor will I force the crystal from you. I may destroy it, if I judge that the best cause of action. But not knowing what is on it, I dare not allow it to fall into Ederi hands."

Dassa sips her tea, then looks at me. "You could force it out of me. You could have taken the crystal from me at any time, put me under physical or mental distress until I revealed whatever I know."

I finish my tea then stand. "I could have," I say, then place the cup in the sink. It's delicate, and I usually leave the washing up to Dassa. I head back to the airlock level to await a sign from the Ederi, leaving Dassa in the galley.

Four hours later, a signal arrives in text. The message says to expect two.

I alert Dassa. "The Ederi are returning, remain nearby, but in hiding."

"Yes, Captain, out of sight and hopefully out of mind."

"The screen will be on, one way, so you can follow the conversation."

I track the arrival of the Ederi as they drop into the valley on their jetpacks. Both unstrap the devices and advance on the airlock. Again, I scan the advancing figures and again, only sidearms are revealed. This time however I sense a difference in their bodies. The differing internal structure on the newcomer leads me to believe that this is a female. I study her, the build is lighter, and I see that while the head is as bald as her compatriot's, the face is finer-featured.

The airlock cycles, and the Ederi step through into my cargo bay. They stand side-by-side and regard me from their milky white eyes. I stand silent and unmoving, as only a being that needs not breathe can. They remove their helmets.

Finally, the first Ederi speaks as he makes a complicated gesture at the female. "This is Commissioner Luray. She is of the rank to make binding agreements for the Ederi."

"How fortunate," I say, "to have someone of such high rank just transiting our system."

The female crosses her arms. I am unsure if the look she gives me is amusement or anger, but guess the former.

The male attempts to stick with the official line however. "The Commissioner was en route to an outpost of ours, when we were struck by a micrometeorite. This required us to remain in this system."

"No matter," the female adds, she is not subvocalizing but speaks Standard naturally and with an inner system accent in her light voice. "I am here now. The altered stone that you gave us has been tested. It is all that you say it was. You will perhaps forgive us, but the stone remains on our ship."

I will forgive you, I think, because you have just shown me how valuable the stone is to the Ederi, enough for you to risk angering me in negotiations while you are aboard my ship.

"No matter," I say, echoing her in light mockery. "I can get more."

Her head drops a little, as if to help her focus on me. "I am here to listen. You said that we might obtain these stones from you, but that another force seeks them as well."

"Yes. What do you know of Ribisans?"

"Assume we know what a well-informed member of your Confederacy does."

"It is not my Confederacy, and I am not its."

"So you say."

"So I do."

"Yet, you defend this world."

Silence builds as we stare at each other. Finally the Ederi says. "Speak plainly, Maauro the android, what is it you want of the Ederi?"

"My name is Maauro Trigardt," I correct. "What I want, is to stop the Ribisans from destroying the ecosystem of Damasia and from profiting from their depredations.

"The Ribisan's have discovered a great natural treasure on Damasia. Stones, which when treated with certain chemical and physical processes, alter into what I gave you. They can be cut to form nanometer circuits and create computers of such power they can process the entire personality of an adult Ribisan, and thereafter, will replace any failed part of their own mind. For a being made in part of silicon, this is nearly a guarantee of immortality."

"You too have a need for such processing power for the supercomputers that work your light curtains. I do not know from what source you gained your chips before, but clearly such a resource has great military value."

The two Ederi exchange looks.

"So," the male says, "you expect us to strike these Ribisans for you."

"I expect you to do nothing for me or the Damasians. But you have a mission in the Confederacy—their sensors and tactics will only evolve. You will need every resource to keep your ships hidden.

"If you allow the Ribisans to so alter Damasia that oxygen-breathing life-forms cannot live, or work there, to make it a colony of their own, you will lose access to this resource."

"We could buy them from the Ribisans," Luray answered.

"They will not part with these stones of life, not when billions of Ribisans need this. This material cannot exist on a gas giant. And evidently, it takes large stones, which must be crushed and recrystallized at far greater density to save and store a Ribisan personality. The ones I killed held nine of these stones. Vastly more than it would take make many supercomputers. There will never be enough to fill the Ribisan's need." I did not know this for a fact, but it seemed a plausible theory, perhaps Dassa would be proud of me.

"Beyond that," I bored in. "The Ribisan's are hydrogen-breathers, ethical cowards and xenophobes. They're barely cooperated with the other species of the Confederacy, or before that, the species of the Concordiat they were allied with when they were struck by the Evolvers and the Conchirri."

"She speaks the truth there," the male says, "they betrayed both governments—"

"Silence," the female snaps.

Profound shock spreads through me. Never have I been so glad that I must put emotions on my face through conscious effort. How could the Ederi know of the great betrayals, secrets buried deep in the files of Confederate military intelligence for fear that they would start a galaxy-wide war. The Ribisan's had hid the most valuable aspect of their culture and biology from every other species, despite two genocidal wars. Once or twice in a generation, a Ribisan mutant was born with the ability to predict the future, allowing the Ribisan's to master the currents of time in the multiverse. This knowledge allowed them to sidestep the thrusts of the carnivorous, reptilian Conchirri and the mechanical Evolvers. Captain Rainhell had even speculated that the Ribisan's did their best to send the Conchirri in the direction of the Confederacy, where they were destroyed at great cost.

The ability had faded over generations. I, myself, had killed the last Predictor then swore to keep secret that such had existed. The act, aided and abetted by the Predictor himself, stopped a Ribisan civil war, but I was not remembered fondly by them for that.

How had the Ederi penetrated so far into the databases of the Confederacy? What they knew was, if not impossible, staggeringly difficult.

"Your friend is correct," I say. "You will not be able to make deals with them. Neither bribes nor intimidation will work. We tried to reach out to them. They blew up most of a seaport in response.

"With other oxygen-breathers in charge of Damasia, you will be able to buy or trade for the stones, using agents and middle-beings. You might manage even some clandestine mining on your own.

"So you will move against the Ribisans, not for me, or for justice, or for any reason, but that you want the stones."

"The Damasians will sell?"

"They will. The locals are far from the Confederate navy. Unless, of course, you move in on Damasia in a big way. Such an action would cause knowledge of the base stones, which are regarded as worthless on Damasia, to become generally known. Then you would face the Confederate military, or whatever power it is that comes to dominate this space."

"Best then," Luray says," if this knowledge of the stone's uses is restricted."

"The knowledge," I assure, "is not widely held."

"Our mutual interest may require that it remain so."

"I am pleased to know that we have a mutual interest."

She gives me a measuring stare again. "We have been told of you, Maauro, told to watch out for you, to be wary of you, and to avoid conflict with you, so long as you do not oppose our holy mission."

"I care nothing for the Guild."

"You protect one."

I do not answer.

"This life seems have value to you."

"It has enough value that this deal is contingent on your leaving her alone."

She cocks her head. "Do the Damasians make this so?"

I sigh. "Do not make me state the obvious. If the Damasians do not tell the Confederacy, I can do it myself. My condition is not negotiable by you or the Damasians. You must balance your mission against one former Guild, little more than a child, and whatever she carries, against access to a military supply of the first importance. To which, you must add my active enmity. If I return to the Confederate military...."

Luray paces around the cargo bay. The male Ederi seems nervous, with his all white eyes, it is hard to tell where he is looking, but his glance seems to cut back between us. Finally she stops. "What you say makes sense. Very well, we will deal with you, Maauro Trigardt. We will give up our claim on this Dassa and anything she holds. We will do this on the basis that you warrant that she is no longer Guild, and that what she carries does not again make it into the hands of the Guild. More, you will arrange for an onworld contact for us to reliably deal with."

If I was breathing, it would have come out in a whoosh. I nod. "The contact will be Malporin Rand of Pilbara. I will transmit a code to your ship for you to use with him and he will have the same."

"You seem to have thought of all contingencies," Luray says.

"My time with a Dua-Denlenn has been instructive in some ways. She has taught me some interesting things about self-interest and how reliable it is in guaranteeing behavior."

Luray's body shakes, apparently with suppressed humor. "Meeting you was as interesting as I was warned it would be."

"By whom?"

"So Maauro Trigardt, there are some things you do not know. I regret that I will not illuminate your ignorance."

"Then we are done here."

"Yes, we are. I am sure that your path and that of the Ederi will cross again."

The aliens resume their helmets and turn toward the lock. I cycle them out. Success, at least for now.

Within an hour, the alien's launch from the moon, heading for a rendezvous with their ship. I watch them until they are so far away they no longer occlude the stars and can pose no threat. Then it is time to launch for Damasia for what I am now determined will be the last time.

I open the hatch, to find Dassa standing there. She has unbelted her two holstered weapons and stands there, offering them to me. I push them aside. These ritual displays of submission are meaningless to me. The weapons could not harm me in any event.

"When we land," I say. "Go get your crystal and return here. Fail to do so and I must hunt you."

"I will do as you say," she says, head bowed.

I exit the ship, reacquire my armspac and return. More by force of habit than anything else, I return to the bridge to find Dassa sitting quietly there. Seachange shudders under my feet. I'd instructed the AI to take off as soon as I was aboard. At such a low orbital velocity, I did not feel the need to be seated.

We fly back to Damasia in silence, each with our thoughts to occupy us. The AI does not need my intervention to land us in Pilbara in the rare clear weather. As soon as we are down, Dassa unstraps and we head planetside, not waiting for a gantry, or anything else. The exterior elevator deploys and we ride it down. There is a stiff wind blowing, but neither of us touches the other.

I set foot on soil of Damasia. Soil which has borne so much trouble for me, just as the subroutine monitoring the massive program analyzing the cumulative effects of the Ribisan ecological assault signals that the program has run its course. Awareness of the result floods my consciousness.

"Oh, God, no," is driven out of me.

Dassa turns to me, fear shooting into her face. "What is it? Are you sick?"

At another time I might have been charmed by her reaction, seeing me as a lifeform akin to her, but I am sick, sick at heart.

"You almost staggered," Dassa says, a note of accusation in her tone.

"I have received, or perhaps it is more that I have realized, some bad news," I reply.

She visibly braces herself.

"It does not directly affect either of us."

A pent up breath escapes her. "What is it?"

I slowly shake my head. "This is terrible news, but it must be given to another first. Retrieve your crystal, return here. Await me outside the ship." I wave and hail a passing conveyor. Dassa heads for the where the rental vehicles are. I ride the conveyor to where I had parked Mal's GP, which he'd loaned me. My Mule, along with everything else is sealed aboard Seachange.

I drive to the council center in disquiet and despair. Once there, I park and, letting nothing of my inner state show on my face, I head in. A quick inquiry tells me Mal is in his upstairs office waiting. I take the stairs up and open the door.

He rises to greet me. "You're back. Thank God. How did it go?" I am relieved that he only provides me with a quick hug.

"The Ederi will do as we asked. You will be there contact on this world." From inside my coverall I pull a standard data crystal. "This contains all that is known of them and the codes and frequencies for reaching them."

"Excellent," he says, taking the crystal in his big hands. His smile fades as he looks at my downcast face. "Aurelia?"

"Mal," I add. "Please sit down. There is more."

I pull him along with me to one of the sturdy chairs. He drops into it and I kneel next to him.

"Let's hear it," he says. "All of it now and get it over with."

"I had time to finish the program analyzing what has been done to Damasia by the Ribisans. I'm sorry, Malporin. There is no way to stop the burning of every coal field on this world, or of the polar cap's melting. The volume of methane and volcanic gases pouring into this atmosphere, along with the destruction of plant life both here and in the seas, will make this planet untenable save under domes."

He looked as if I had struck him. "Then the natives…"

"—are doomed, unless you move them into domes as well. The damage can be contained with planetary engineering, perhaps reversed in the next century, but the Damasia you knew, is already destroyed.

"The colony, the tsunami?"

"If the Ederi stop the Ribisans from using tunneling nuclear charges to trigger a catastrophic collapse of Beros Island, we can buy a march of

decades to relocate the colony. Perhaps with targeted nukes you could trigger a smaller collapse and relieve pressure, but it will always be a sword hanging over the colony."

"The bastards, the mother-raping, filthy bastards," Malporin began, his big hands knotting. "God rain hell on them. Filthy sons of bitches."

I'd learned in my marriage to break up such angers. Moved by such an impulse, I reach over and take both his big hands in mine. They shake with grief and anger. I have just pronounced a death sentence on all he knows.

"I'm sorry," I finish.

"What do I do?" he whispers, and I know it is to himself. "How do I fight this?"

I can only look at the floor.

"How…how soon?" he finally asks.

"That I can't be certain of, much will depend on how much further damage can be avoided. But the cascade is started; the effects will be undeniable in a decade, with luck, perhaps bearable for twenty or thirty years. No longer than that though."

I see a glimmer of hope in his eyes and it stabs me. I want to cry.

"That's time, maybe time enough," he says.

I am silent, but do not release his hands.

"I am going to stay and fight for my world," he finally says. "Will you stay and fight with me?"

I bend my head lower, God, I would rather be battling my greatest enemy then here at this moment.

"I guess," he says, when I do not speak, "that was a no."

"I'm sorry," I whisper back. Finally, I find the courage to raise my head again and look at the young human with his earnest, rugged, yet handsome face.

"I know there is something here," he insists. "If you will give it a chance—"

I gently put a hand to the cheek I'd earlier touched when we left, fighting temptation.

"I must tell you some impossible things," I say, dropping my hand. "First, you must promise not to repeat what I tell you. Do not ask me for explanations I cannot give you. Take this as a measure of what I feel that I do so. Agreed?"

He stares at me, but finally nods.

"I am so much older than I appear to be. No, do not speak, I am not through. I have been married and lost my husband through natural causes."

"I'm sorry," he blurted out.

"Thank you. The pain of that separation is not recent, but is undimmed. I am not ready for what you are offering me. I may never be. In many ways I am more…peculiar than you can imagine. I am grateful

for your feelings. In no way am I taking it lightly. But I am also terribly frightened."

"I would never hurt you!"

Gently, I again lift my hand to his face, but this time only to lay a finger across his lips. "I did not say that I feared you would. Indeed I have no such concern. It is not you that frightens me, as much as the possibilities that come with you. It may not make sense to you, but I have enjoyed the bitter and the sweet of this before. The sweet is the stuff of dreams. Ah, but the bitter, the taste of that is terrible beyond words and still in my mouth.

"If what I said is not clear to you and because of your youth I can explain it no better, then I can only be sorry, but my answer must be, no."

He stares down at the ground, grim and hurt. I longed to take him in my arms, but fear giving in even a little will cause my emotional dam to burst.

"I would wait..." he whispers.

"Listen to me. I have already lived a long time. No, you promised not to ask me for explanations, merely accept what I say. I may live for a very long time to come, but I cannot say I will walk this road again. It's not fair for me to ask you to wait, worse it would be selfish, bordering on criminal, the waste of what you are, a good man, something rarer than you know. Find the person you are meant for— make her happy, but let me go. Don't even hold me in your dreams. I would not see your life so blighted."

"I guess I have no choice," he says. "When will you leave?"

"Now, Mal, now. It will be the easier for us both."

"May I kiss you goodbye?"

Oh, I am so afraid of this, but I find myself nodding. He takes me in his arms as I steel my resolve. But his kiss is warm, it beckons, it promises, but I resist. I take refuge in my synthetic nature, trying as best I can to distance myself from the woman I was. If I let myself fall into this kiss, I will stay.

He steps back and his voice is shaky as he says, "Goodbye Aurelia, despite what you asked, I can never forget you."

For a brief moment of madness, I am tempted to give him my real name, but the moment passes. "Farewell, Malporin, I promise that I will never forget you either. I wish you joy."

I stand and spin on my heels. I will not run to my ship like a teenager. I move with dignity and deliberation, at least I hope so.

CHAPTER THIRTY-FOUR

AS I PULL AWAY FROM MAL'S BUILDING, I CONTEMPLATE THE FUTURE *and the closed path of Malporin's offer. He would have waited for me. I have no doubt of it. But Malporin will grow, change and age. I will not age, and I am not sure that I will change much more. I have perhaps completed most of that journey already. I have freed myself from my origin as a mere weapon, to sentience, independence, and finally, love. I've even metamorphosed into a biological life form. Now, I am again the android. In many ways it is a relief to be armored, powerful, and with the mind of quantum computer. But is it not my first step backwards? I have been this before.*

I am thinking too much, I know, but Malporin stirred so much in me that I thought gone, or at least dormant. With an effort, I dismiss it all. I am a spacer in the truest sense, designed for and at home in the vacuum. Even if I had been a human, or Dua-Denlenn, I would be leaving people behind in time and space. It will take us four months of travel to reach our next destination from where we are. But for the galaxy and Malporin, two and half years will pass before I set foot there. By then, I will be a distant memory to a young man who may have fallen in love in the interim.

It is better this way.

When I arrive at the ship, I face my other problem. There, at the base of the ship's elevator, sitting next to her travel cases with her possessions and I know from the AI, a thirty-day supply of food, is Dassa. We must have this out. Now. One way or the other.

Even as I walk up to her, I cannot quite quell the anger I feel, which has its origins in my time as human woman. Am I right to feel so, with such an alien being? Or is it, dare I admit it to myself, that for the first time since I resumed my life as an AI, that my feelings have been hurt, feelings that have not returned to the distant coolness of my original synthetic mindset? I am no longer M-7 and it seems now that I have lived as a human, I am no longer even the original Maauro, whose emotions were usually so measured.

Dammit, I'm mad. She betrayed me. I thought we were becoming friends. She hurt my feelings and she's not even really sorry! Worse, she really doesn't believe she did anything wrong.

I stop before Dassa, with the ship towering over us both. The Dua-Denlenn girl rises and returns my stare. I cannot read desperation in her all blue eyes, but I feel it is there. Good.

"So, you are angry with me, and you hate me," Dassa says. "I understand that I must buy my way back into your grace."

"Your kind is good at selling things," I reply, "often things they do not own. But you have nothing of value to me, and you are nothing of value to me."

"I have the crystal. Why you did not simply take it from me, I do not know. I do not understand you at all, but it seems that you will not use force on me in this regard. Very well." She reaches down the front of her pants to where I know she keeps the pair of data crystals. She produces the larger one; it glints in the light like an emerald.

"I will give you this crystal and with it the story, such little as I know it, of the greatest Guild project in its long history."

"What care I for the Guild, or their doings?"

"You are enmeshed in the war of the Guild and the Ederi so long as you travel known space. Neither will soon forget you. Beyond that are their effects on the galaxy at large. Things are falling apart. How long and how badly are yet to be answered. You may find secrets on this crystal that will allow you to master the many tides of the seachange around you," she finishes.

The crystal will have the highest level encryption that Confed and Guild science are capable of but in time I might break this. I have done such before. It seems a small enough price to pay for the knowledge, and I must confess it has piqued my curiosity since she showed up.

"Very well, I can tolerate you until I find some place—"

Dassa shakes her head definitively. "You do not understand, or choose not to remember. I don't know which or why. But in doing this I become what my grandfather was, traitor the Guild. There is a word in the language you have adopted, it is the equivalent for what grandfather and I am— apostates.

"While you can take this from me, and I can do nothing about it, I do not trade it for mere passage. If I give it and all I know to you, then I am finally aligned to you. We are using words that do not mean the same thing to each other, and even if you used the ones from my language, you lack the biology to know what lies beneath the words. Whether you like the concepts or not, they are how my kind is hard-wired. If I am aligned to you, I will stay so while you remain strong, you in turn make a place for me and do not leave me as prey to others. Where you go, you make that place for me. I am in your service—"

"Service? When did I ask for that? You were supposed to be my friend after all I did for you," I yelled, frightening myself with my sudden loss of control.

"I can't be!" Dassa wails. "I can't. I don't know what that means. It's just a sound. I know it means something to you. I try to come close, but it is too difficult. I'm not a human; I can't get it right."

"Damn it. I'm not a human either, but—"

"Yes, you are," she screams.

This checks my growing anger.

"You are," she insists, tears streaking her face. "Whatever and who-ever made you, whatever you once were, now, you're just a human in a machine body.

"I'm Dua. I can't become a human for you."

The wind buffets us as I look at Dassa, hugging herself and shaking. My anger fades. Have I, supercomputer, fifty-thousand-years old, with at least four incarnations as M-7, Maauro the android, Maauro the woman, and now whatever I am— made the most basic mistake of all? I'd wanted Dassa to be the friend, the companion and confidante lacking from my existence. I'd wanted her in ways I had never considered with the older, sophisticated Dusko.

I'd tried for more and we'd failed. I'd seen her as treacherous and unfaithful. She'd seen me as weak, an alpha losing her grip and endan-gering the pack.

It hit me then. Dassa had behaved this way before, back on Evenfall when she tried to kill the local thugs sitting on our car. I'd laughed at their pretensions, but Dassa saw this as weakness, a failure that her biol-ogy and psychology made her try to fill. It had struck me as odd then how relieved she'd been when I harshly asserted my authority, removing her need to make choices.

When she perceives me as weak, it terrifies her, I realize, disordering her world and triggering her instincts to try and save the pack.

The wind blows as we face each other. She continues to stare at me, fear and anxiety on her face.

Fear and anxiety, maybe it is the closest analogue she has to be being sorry.

Wrik, what should I do?

And again I feel him, a precious touch, the impossible moment of communication. "Take a chance," comes to me, though in what way I cannot tell.

"I ought to leave you behind," I say suddenly. "Or I ought to beat you senseless for betraying my trust."

She is silent, but her hand is clenched around her precious crystal, her shoulders hunch and I realize that she is preparing herself to be beaten, as doubtless her Guild instructors and too many others have beaten this child. Unbidden, my memory casts up the scans of her many broken bones.

"I will accept your declared alignment to me," I say, finally.

A small gasp escapes Dassa.

I put my hand out for the crystal.

"Swear it," Dassa says, now she is visibly shaking.

"What oath can bind an android and a Dua-Denlenn?" I demand.

"Swear it on that which I know you value above all else. Swear it on your husband's name and I will relinquish all claims to the crystal and any alignment but yours."

"While I stay strong," I murmur.

"When will you ever weaken?" Dassa whispers. "It is so little risk for you."

I sigh. Wrik what have you gotten me into? Aloud, I say. "In my husband's name, I swear to accept your alignment with me, to protect you and never to leave you as prey for others."

Dassa places the crystal in my hand. Then suddenly she turns and sits on the ramp. She wraps her arms around her knees.

"Are you crying because you have given up all that you had?" I ask softly. "Or because you now have a place with me?"

"Both," she manages, "or neither. I don't understand what I am feeling. All my life I wanted to be part of something that could not throw me out."

I reach down, take her arm and slowly, but firmly pull her upright. Her body is stiff with fear and confusion until I pull her against me. After a few moments, she relaxes slowly, carefully, even putting her chin down on my shoulder.

"This has been a hard world for us," I say. "There's been pain, confusion, mistake after mistake and now perhaps a little wisdom."

"I don't feel any smarter," she whispers.

"As we go forward from this place," I say, making my voice firm, but keeping my embrace gentle, "I will try to understand that you are Dua, but you must understand one thing above all else, betray my confidence again and we are ended, nor will I guarantee your life in the event of another incident like this one."

I feel her chin on my shoulder as she nods, easy in my arms despite a threat that would have made a human, or most others tense. With Dassa, it is the opposite. I'm exerting my dominance as her alpha, putting choices out of her reach and only allowing her the option of pleasing me. Her universe is now properly ordered. She will be...happy, in whatever fashion Dua are happy.

"No threat to paddle my bottom?" she asks.

Amazing! She is joking with me, very nearly flirting. The reversal from her emotional desolation of only moments ago is dizzying. I release her and step back. "No. I am beginning to think you are looking forward to it."

"What now?" she asks, wiping her face.

"I still want to find the answer to the mystery of the Creator's disappearance," I say. "We are far from Enshar, and there's much trading to do in our future if we ever want to get there."

Dassa glares at Pilbara and the mountains beyond. "I will not miss this place."

"Don't be so severe," I said. "You found a lover here, perhaps not the best one, but your first. I found a friend and a man who wanted to care for me. We did some good here. How much only the future will tell."

CHAPTER THIRTY-FOUR

"Fifty millennia and yet you remain an optimist," Dassa says, with a small, weary smile. *"How?"*

"I told you when we started out," I reply, as I take the girl's hand in mine and we turn toward Seachange. *"I have faith."*

THE END

ABOUT THE AUTHOR

EDWARD MCKEOWN is a writer and editor specializing in science fiction and fantasy with occasional forays into literary and nonfiction. Ed escaped from NY, but his old hometown supplies much of the background to his humorous "Lair of the Lesbian Love Goddess" shorts, as his new hometown in Charlotte, North Carolina does for his "Knight Templar" fantasy series. He enjoys a wide variety of interests from ballroom dance to the martial arts. He has also edited six Sha'Daa anthologies of wry tales of the apocalypse and a wide variety of short stories. Find him on Facebook and at edwardmckeown.weebly.com.

Ed is best known for his Robert Fenaday/Shasti Rainhell series of SF novels, set on the Privateer Sidhe, issued by Hellfire Publications.

MORE BOOKS BY EDWARD MCKEOWN

FROM

AN IMPRINT OF COPPER DOG PUBLISHING, LLC

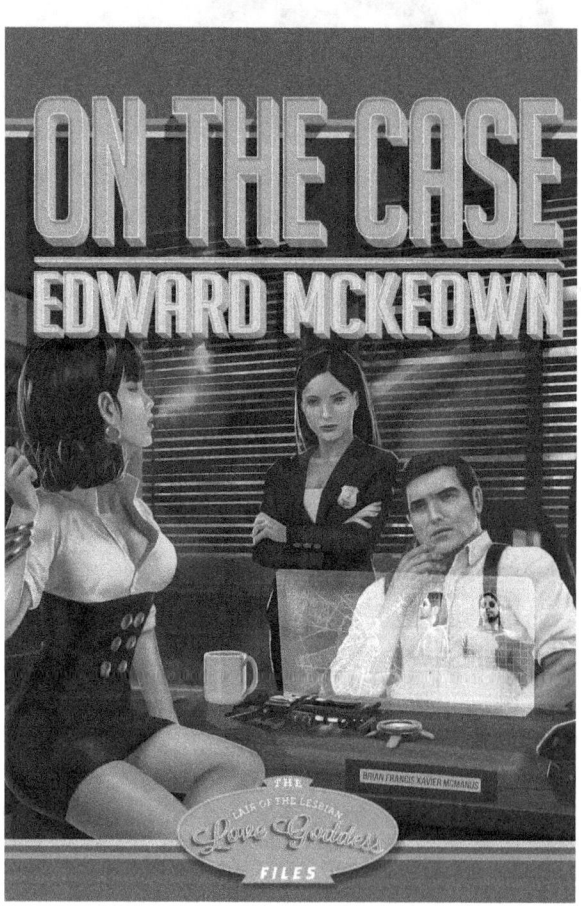

MORE BOOKS BY EDWARD MCKEOWN

FROM AD ASTRA BOOKS

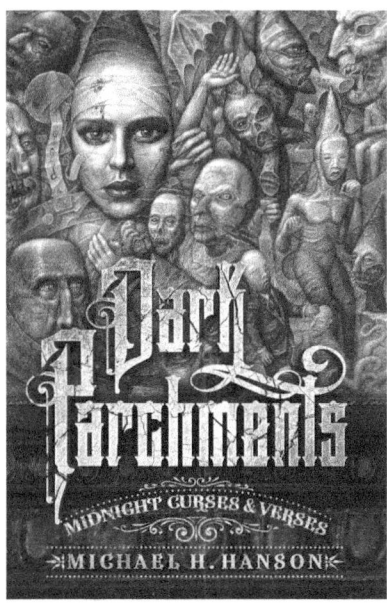

CHAPTER 1

I ATTACK THE ENEMY BASE IN THE COMPANY OF TWO OLDER M4 COMBAT *androids. We are launched from a Daggerwing assault-ship and shed our mobility capsules as we land on the asteroid. The Infestation claim the base is a lifeboat station but Intel says it is equipped with heavy weapons and sensors.*

The weapons are there. A disrupter battery fires on us; another lashes out at the Daggerwing and the ships beyond. As we race across the surface of the iron asteroid, a disrupter hits the lead M4. It staggers and slows. Other weapons switch fire to the slowing android. It is destroyed.

I am an M7, the newest combat android, a prototype, faster and better armored. I duck into a crater and return fire from my armspac. Explosions bloom and the disrupter battery is wiped out. The remaining M4 and I crash through the base airlock. Infestor drone soldiers are inside, clad in vacuum suits. They open fire. There is no room to dodge, so we trade fire from our onboard weapons and armspacs. The Infestors' small-arms have little effect on the M4 and none on me. We destroy them and race through the rest of the facility, killing Infestors as we encounter them. I head for the command center. M4 will attack the long-range disruptors firing on our ships.

Explosion. The corridor I occupy shatters, killing those Infestors I have not already dispatched. A mine, or perhaps my weapon, has set off a secondary explosion. I pause for self-repair. I am made of hyper-alloyed metals, ceramics and polymers. My outer casing has ablative layers and sections made to absorb blast damage. I exchange damaged exterior parts for interior and extrude new material to replace vaporized sections. Fortunately, I have taken no core damage. I waste no time on the aesthetics that make me look like a member of my creator's race. I carry enough spare material inside to regenerate two legs and an arm so I can get my armspac and reengage the enemy. I am much smaller now, having used up my spare material.

M4 reaches the disrupter battery, sited atop an arsenal. The bulk of the Infestor forces are arrayed around it. We confer for a millisecond. The battery is firing at our ships in the asteroid belt. I am already damaged, as is M4, and additional resistance is possible at the command post. By ourselves we may fail to take the station and suppress its weapons.

We agree on a plan of action and M4 self-destructs, detonating its plasma generator. The blast destroys the disrupter battery and its supporting forces.

I continue my attack alone and resistance crumbles. M4 may have killed the unit queen with its explosion. I neutralize the command post and mop up the base. In the process, I take seven prisoners. These I drag to a lower level and interrogate. Little useful intel is gained from these low-level creatures. After the last Infestor expires, I cleanse myself of their fragments. Then I delete the memories of the actual interrogation while saving the intel. This procedure is technically against my programming, but the longer I operate, the more latitude I discover in my behavioral routines. I do not know why I feel the need to do this, save that of late I have found the process of interrogation disturbing. I was created to destroy the Infestation and have done so for the seven years of my existence, yet I find more reasons to delete such information as time passes. I function more efficiently without these memories.

I reach the surface of the asteroid and step out under the stars, triggering my recall signal. No answer. I repeat it several times, then extend my sensor net to maximum and pick up a cloud of ionized gas. M4 did not destroy the disruptors fast enough. The Daggerwing, along with the support and repair staff who care for me, are gone.

I detect flashes of nuclear fire beyond my ship's remains. Ambush. The base may have been bait in a trap. Our forces are destroyed or driven off.

Since I do not face imminent capture, I delay self-destruct and continue repairs. I am dismayed by my level of damage even though my exterior chassis is mostly restored. Much of the damage can only be repaired at home base, which now I doubt I shall ever see again.

I consider my course of action. If the system has fallen to the Infestation, they will likely return to this asteroid. I should lie in wait to ambush any rescue party.

I turn my scanners to the sky for a last long look at the stars, which now are my only companions, before turning to walk into the silent base. I switch to minimum power settings. My wait may be long.

CHAPTER 2

I HUNG AROUND IN BARS A LOT. NOT THAT I'M A DRUNK. I went through a short spell of drinking after I was cashiered from the service for cowardice. But the bottle is slow suicide and I'm too young and interested in living for that.

No, I hung out in bars because that's where a human can find work on Kandalor's Vanceport. The Spacewitch is one of the places expeditions launch from. Not the big government expeditions from the Confederacy or the Combines, which wouldn't use somebody like me, but the shoestring expeditions from universities or organizations short on cash. I can fly interstellar. Not everyone can handle the hyperspace visualization. I can also fly atmo, which a lot of starjockeys can't.

So I staked out a small table in the back, away from the long bar with its brass and dark wood where the bad and dangerous hang out. My table sat under a hanging of red-fringed velvet, keeping me in comforting shadow. Square-D, the owner, knew me and would send over people looking for my type of skills. Square-D didn't care about me one way or another, but pilots brought trade to the Spacewitch and, he got a cut.

Luck was with me. Square-D was talking to a tall, dark-skinned woman in green fatigues. He nodded in my direction and she turned toward me. She was tall, with a pretty, symmetrical face and an overripe figure that strained the fatigues. I guessed her to be older than me, perhaps in her late twenties or early thirties. Her vest hung open and I saw a holster under it. She strode to my table.

"Wrik Trigardt?" The voice matched the body, round and pleasant.

I'd left my real name in the past, with my honor. "Just Wrik." I neither stood nor extended my hand; manners belonged to another time and place.

She slid into the booth and rested her breasts on the table as she leaned forward on her elbows. I got my eyes back up to her dark brown ones in time to catch the flash of white teeth against her dark skin. OK, she'd caught me looking, one for her.

"I hear you're a good pilot both on Kandalor and nearspace."

"Farspace too," I said. "I have an interstellar rating."

"Nearspace will meet my needs," she said. "You look kinda young to me."

I shrugged. "I've been flying since my early teens, military training as well. As they say: 'It's not the years, it's the light years.'"

I studied her. She had a slight accent I couldn't place. Something about her said Old Colonies or even Home World. "What needs are those, Miss…?"

"Name's Candace Deveraux, out from Earth. Call me Candy and I'll shoot you in the knee. I'm looking for a private ship and pilot to take my colleagues to a certain riftoid."

"Treasure hunters."

She raised an eyebrow at me. "Prospectors and salvagers. You have a problem with that?"

I raised a hand. "No offense. I make a living hauling people around Kandalor and the near-rift looking for Old Empire relics and tech. Sometimes they even find stuff."

"But for every one who finds something, a thousand go broke," she quoted, leaning back. "True enough. Before we go much further, I'd like to know a little more about you. I gave you my name and world…"

"My name, you know. I'm out of a Confed colony world, former military pilot."

Her look said she knew this already. "Some people say you're out of Retief, a separatist colony. So why are you—?"

"Talking to a darkskin?" I finished for her.

She nodded. "Boers and Trekkers colonized Retief to get away from any contact with blacks. You regard us as inferior."

"I don't regard you as anything," I said, "assuming I was in fact born there. I take people as they are."

"Yet you fought in the Uprising?"

"As I said, you're assuming I was there. From what I heard, the Confederacy came in and told them to admit darkskins to Retief. Then they backed it up with force. Retief didn't last long after the Confederacy got serious.

"If that's enough 'get acquainted' for you," I said, and then, after sipping my drink, added, "I charge two hundred credits a day with fifty more if I go into vacuum. You pay for port fees and fuel. I get a hundred-credit advance now to reserve my time. You doubtless pulled my flight sheet at the port."

"Doubtless," she said, smiling. "I set the schedules and you learn where and when we fly when I decide."

"Deal." I tried to conceal my relief and surprise. She'd accepted my opening rates.

"Give me a number where I can reach you. You'll get twelve hours warning. Tell anybody where we are going and I'll shoot you in the other knee."

I passed my card to her and she inserted it into a portacomp. A few keypunches gave her my number and me one hundred credits.

She slid my card back to me. "You gonna buy me a drink with any of those credits, spaceman?"

"Uh, sure."

She laughed. "Just kidding. Next time come up with the idea on your own." She managed a nice sashay for a big woman as she walked away. I was tempted to whistle but afraid she might take target practice on my knees.

I finished my drink and slipped out the back of the Spacewitch after leaving a healthy tip with Square-D. Distracted a little by my good luck, I failed to do my customary check of the alley before I started down. I caught the heavy, earthy smell just before a thick, furred arm fastened over my throat and arm.

"So, Wrik, what are we up to?" I turned slowly in Truf's iron grip—there was no point in struggling with the bear-like Okaran—to face Dusko, the tall, Dua-Denlenn who ran a third of Vanceport's underworld. The Dua-Denlenn looked like a woodland elf gone to seed, with pale skin and blue pupilless eyes.

"Dusko," I nodded slowly. "I was just coming to see you."

"Of course, human," Dusko said, looking me over as if I were edible. "You owe me fifty credits."

Sweat trickled down my back. "I have it here."

"How fortunate for you, though perhaps disappointing to Truf here."

The Okaran whiffed a breath in my ear. "There will be other opportunities."

"My cardcomp's in my inside pocket," I said.

"Let him go, Truf. This youngling's too prudent to be dangerous."

I pulled out the cardcomp and handed it to Dusko, who ran his own card- comp over it and made the transfer.

"Who was the offworlder you were talking to?" Dusko asked. "Any-thing I would be interested in?"

"A rift-haul for a prospector. She's cautious. No up front info from her."

"So no way to set her up," Dusko shrugged. "Doesn't sound worth my effort. You will let me know if there's a chance for mutual profit off her."

"I did last time," I said.

"True," Dusko said. "Their personal effects brought a nice sum. If it eases your conscience, they turned out to be druggers."

I tried not to remember the traders I'd led into Dusko's ambush. But it was either them or my ship and the ship was all I had.

"Good doing business with you," Dusko said. "As Truf said, there will be other opportunities. See you around, human." The languid Dua-Den-lenn stepped back into the darkness, followed by his hulking guard. I leaned back against the wall, feeling the night air sift through my shirt and fighting the chill. Dusko was right. I was prudent. I had a knife in my boot and a slug-thrower in my back belt, but I wouldn't try an Okaran with the small caliber weapon at such close range. Throwing down on any of the established Guild was insane, anyway.

I decided to sleep in my ship, an old *Dauntless* class scout I'd named *Sinner*, a leftover from the Conchirri Wars long ago. Before heading out, I arranged for the port recorder to forward any message from Candace Deveraux to *Sinner*.

I hopped a native transport, which was the cheapest transport available. The open cart, towed by two oxen-like animals, was an odd contrast to ground cars or flitters but it was emblematic of Kandalor, which combined poverty and wealth as well as high and low tech. It had been a forgotten world until a Confed expedition stumbled across it and the races of the Old Concordiat. A few native Kandalorians, muffled in their robes, glanced at me with their bulbous black eyes but otherwise ignored me. I returned the favor and tried to breathe shallowly, the smell of the natives competed with that of the draft animals.

Sinner sat at the spaceport's edge under a metal overhang I'd rented to keep off the worst of the weather. She was about thirty meters long, a bulky ovoid with short stubby wings and lots of interior volume. I'd painted her anti-corrosive chrome yellow. Unlike military craft, we civvies want to be seen. I keyed in the secure code and locked myself in, letting my breath go in a rush. On Kandalor you live like a rabbit or a wolf. Maybe I'd have an extra big helping of carrots tonight.

One week later, I was doing some scut-work on a small Indie-freighter when my comp buzzed. I took off my gauntlets and sealed the engine port before answering. "Hello."

"It's Candace. Time to go prospecting. How soon can you launch?"

"I'm in good shape for a Rift run this side of the 38th in four hours. If we are going out farther, I'll need to add wing tanks."

"We aren't going farther. I've got the flight plan on file with the Port Authority. They'll download to you just ahead of launch."

"Cautious, aren't you?"

"Wouldn't want any problems with local interests."

I swallowed. "There won't be."

"Good, I'd hate to shoot such a pretty boy, at least until I was through with him." She laughed and clicked off.

Candace showed up at the *Sinner* early, as I expected. She liked to set the pace. Two men accompanied her. One was tall, with dark, suspicious eyes and a hooked nose over a beard, unusual in someone who expected to use a space helmet. The other was a dark-skinned like Candace, but whipcord thin and balding, with the look of a spacer.

"My associates," Candace said, gesturing to hook-nose. "Harung." She pointed at the other. "Maku Treska." Both nodded.

"We've got a cargo sled coming. My boys will do the loading," she said.

"Long as I check it after," I said.

Treska looked at me. "The kid doesn't trust us to load. I was flying when you were waiting to be delivered."

Candace looked at him with annoyance. "Quiet, Treska. I don't want to fly with anyone dumb enough not to check his own ship's load."

Treska grumbled but headed for *Sinner*'s capacious cargo bay. Harung gave me an unfriendly stare and followed.

I looked at her. "No weapons on my ship. Hope you left your knee-shooter in the port lockup. Explosive decompression can ruin your whole day."

Candace grinned at me. "Gonna pat me down, Wrik? I've got a lot of area to cover, many dangerous curves to hide things."

Her smile and manner had probably bent men to her wishes all her life. "Sounds like fun, but I don't think I want to pat down your buddies, though, so we'll use a scanner."

She gave a look of mock disappointment. I could feel my blood stirring. Human women were rare on Kandalor, and I had little to offer one. Truth was I didn't have much experience there, either. Candace's mocking smile told me that she suspected it.

Stick to business, I thought, *you're out of your depth with her.*

I checked the load and scanned my passenger for weapons. We boarded *Sinner* and settled in. Candace rode in the second seat on the flight deck. Her companions strapped in the far less comfortable cargo compartment, grumbling loudly enough to be heard. Candace smiled and shrugged.

Sinner kicked free of Kandalor's surface and started a slow ascent. Kandalor stretched out forever below us, seducing the eye and the imagination. Empires had come and gone on this world while humans lived in caves and waved stone axes.

"Beautiful," Candace said, looking out at the mountain and huge forests beyond the spaceport area. In the distance lay the ruins of one of the many lost civilizations. Haze made the wildly tilting towers appear blue.

"Yep," I said. "You've got spaceports and primitive tribes all on the same world, an archeologist's treasure trove."

"Here and in space," Candace said absently. "Those empires extended out for hundreds of light years. Lots of good stuff out there."

"Going to tell me what we're looking for?" I asked.

"Just drive the taxi, Honey."

"Yes, Ma'am."

Candace talked as we boosted toward the Rift, using my ion engine for a slow, steady thrust. I found myself liking her. I didn't want to; friends are an expensive luxury for a Rifter. I set the autopilot and we turned in early. I had trouble falling asleep, thinking of Candace's lush body in the bunk above me, wondering what it would be like.

We came up on the Rift in the next watch, not that there was anything to see. Even in as thick an asteroid belt as the Rift, it would be unusual for any two objects to be in visual range.

We set course for a large riftoid well in from the edge. One of a million such rocks unvisited by anyone since the planet blew to hell. Gradually the riftoid grew from a tiny point of light to a gray, pitted, roughly spherical rock about 2000 kilometers in diameter. Scanners showed it to be almost pure nickel-iron. A huge impact crater marred part of it.

"That's the one," Harung said. Everyone was crammed into my cockpit, staring hungrily at the pitted gray surface. "Just as I remember it."

"Probably part of the old world's core," Treska grunted. "That would account for all the metal. It'll give it a bit more gravity than you usually get in a rock this size."

We drifted down to the surface. Treska was right; gravity was strong enough that I didn't need to fix anchors. I did it anyway, space rewards the cautious.

"Suit up, everyone," Candace ordered.

I looked at her. "I'm just driving the taxi."

"Don't be like that, Honey. Now that we're here, don't you want to see what we came for?"

"Depends."

"What do we need him for?" Harung demanded.

I sighed. "She doesn't want to leave me behind in the ship so I can hold you up when you come back with whatever treasure you came for." I looked at Candace. "Ever get tired of working with people who aren't as smart as you?"

"No," she replied. "I only like smart men in bed."

Harung glared at me.

We suited up and walked out onto the surface of the riftoid. Treska unlimbered a large mining scanner. Evidently he got a fix on something, as he began moving in quick little hops, kicking up dust. Candace and Harung followed, lugging their equipment. I thought about waiting where I was, then decided it might be safer to stick with the herd. Five minutes later, we found ourselves in a small crater, looking at an oddly-shaped hatchway of yellow metal nearly three meters across.

"What the hell is it?" I asked, excitement getting the better of me. Dust indicated that the hatch hadn't been opened in a long, long time. The design didn't look like anything I'd ever seen.

"Maybe an Old Empire asteroid station," Treska said absently.

I looked around. "Over 50,000 years old."

"Or more," Treska said. "I spotted it when I was here with a freighter that came out of hyper too close to the Rift and had to dump delta-V to avoid a collision. I kept the readings on my scanner to myself. Those Combine bastards wouldn't have given me a percentage of any find."

"Why don't you tell him your life story?" Harung growled as he placed heavy jacks around the hatch.

Candace used a laser drill to place a monofilament probe through what looked like an inspection port. "As you suspected, Treska," she said, "hard vacuum on the other side. Start the jacks."

The power jacks took five minutes to crack the airlock. We used pry bars until we could squeeze through in space suits. A few more minutes on the inner door and we were shining our torches inside.

The interior of the station was familiar looking; form follows function. We saw a rack of odd-shaped spacesuits hung on the bulkheads. Whatever wore them had been much bigger than a human, multi-legged, with a large skull or a need for a lot of headroom. Boxes and tanks lay all over the floor. The metal of the floor worked with our magnetic boots.

"This is a military station," I said.

Candace looked at me. "Why's that?"

"A lot of compartmentation, thick hatches to deal with explosive decompression. Though I'm surprised a military station wouldn't have been dug deeper, for blast protection."

"Maybe it was converted from something?" Harung said.

"Who knows?" Treska shrugged.

Candace nodded. We played our flashlights around the gray and white metal halls, looking at unfamiliar inscriptions and dead light panels.

"It kind of reminds me of the old lifeboat stations they have in Sol's system from before the advent of hyperdrive." Candace said.

"We might find an Old Empire ship," Harung exclaimed.

We started down the sloping corridor and came to a partially opened doorway.

"Christ, look at that." Treska pointed.

At our feet lay a large pile of shredded fabric covered with white dust. Nearby lay boots, though not for any human foot, and a thing that could have either been a power rifle or some sort of heavy tool.

Candace bent down. "Crew. Must have died here in the doorway. Wonder what tore up the uniform?" Cautiously, she pushed open the doorway and looked in, a prybar in one hand and flashlight in the other.

Harung brayed a laugh. "Looking for something? That corpse has been there for fifty millennia in vacuum. The fibers degraded and fell apart. We'll bag what's left for the scientists. They'll pay plenty for material from the corpse of an unknown species."

"Look, a ship!" Candace exclaimed. Her light illuminated a small vessel beyond. It looked like it was made of some translucent, half-melted, dark-green glass. Yet it was recognizably a spacecraft.

"If you're right about this being a lifestation," I said, "there's your lifeboat."

Harung pushed past Candace and me with Treska on his heels. The smaller man accidentally kicked an alien boot. It spun silently away into the darkness beyond our lights. I shuddered.

Candace knelt by the fragments of fabric and the metal implement. "A weapon?"

"Maybe," I said. "It has that look, but I don't see any sights."

"Well, any charge it had must have gone before the pyramids were built."

The space beyond was wide and flat, big enough for several small craft. A hatchway that must have once opened outward formed the roof of the hangar; for all that we had seen no sign of the hatch on the surface. Harung and Treska clambered all over the small ship, peering into it with lights.

"Wrik," Candace called from the far side. I went over. She was standing over a pile of white dusty fabric and more boots, buckles and webbing. The fabric was shredded like the first one.

"What the hell?" I said.

"There's a passage up ahead. If this is like a Terran lifestation, it will lead to the medical and crew quarters."

"After you," I said.

She frowned at me. "You're a bring-up-the-rear kind of guy, aren't you, Wrik?"

"You weren't hiring at Hero's Hall."

We left the others to explore the ship. Our magnetic boots raised a thin film of dust, to hang and fall slowly in the low gravity. Colors here were more vibrant than in the more utilitarian areas. The combinations hurt my eyes.

We reached the crew quarters. Debris covered the area. All manner of odd-looking furniture lay scattered and broken.

"Decompression?" Candace asked.

I shrugged.

IF YOU ENJOYED THIS EXCERPT, LOOK FOR THE MAAURO CHRONICLES, BOOK 1, MY OUTCAST STATE AVAILABLE ON AMAZON.COM AND COPPERDOGPUBLISHING.COM.

Copper Dog Publishing LLC

OUR IMPRINTS:

MoonDream PRESS

RACKET RIVER PRESS

Pumpkin Hill Press

To find out more about our imprints
and our upcoming releases, visit our website:
www.CopperDogPublishing.com
or our Facebook page:
www.facebook.com/copperdogpublishing